Eddie Stone pointe  ole section." He kicked a͞ flat headstone surfaced wit the death date of JULY 1987. "This used to be where we buried unclaimed bodies after two weeks. These days it doesn't happen much with all the DNA crap."

He stepped toward the fence, then cleared off another area. Five gray markers appeared, all said UNKNOWN and JANUARY 1995. "These are the five homicide victims Director Marconi told you about."

Those deaths came into focus like a cold slap. "Why couldn't you identify them?" I asked.

"No heads, hands, or feet."

"Excuse me?"

"Whoever did this kept the skulls, hands, and feet. With no teeth and no fingerprints, we had nothing else sophisticated enough to help us."

"No guesses even? A missing person's report?"

"Nope. We found a connection, though."

"To what?"

"To each other, it seemed. The victims were male, all wore brown leather jackets, and the damnedest thing—a piece of Orehnjaca was stuck in the breast pocket of each victim."

"Oren Jaka? I've never heard that word."

He grinned. "I hadn't either. It's a Serbian bread dessert. A nut roll or something."

"These murders sound more like mob hits."

"Bingo. We've thought similarly over the years but couldn't connect it to local gangs." A blast of north wind shuffled the leaves, covering the headstones again. "I don't think it's only a local issue, and neither does the director.

Peculiar Activities

by

Mark Edward Jones

Henry Ike Pierce, Book 1

Peculiar Activities

Cover Art by *Tina Lynn Stout*

The Wild Rose Press, Inc.
PO Box 708
Adams Basin, NY 14410-0708
Visit us at www.thewildrosepress.com

Publishing History
First Edition, 2021
Trade Paperback ISBN 978-1-5092-3817-0
Digital ISBN 978-1-5092-3818-7

Henry Ike Pierce, Book 1
Published in the United States of America

Dedication

For Ms. Peggy Price. My wonderful high school
English teacher.

To Jackie, my love and my life.

MEJ BOOKS, LLC

EDMOND, OK 73034

"False face must hide what the false heart doth know."

~ William Shakespeare, *Macbeth*

Chapter One

It was a nice leather jacket—regrettably, its owner had lost his head. Cold case murders were my new responsibility, or so they told me. Even so, my third day as a detective found me at a park, standing next to not-so-cold body parts scattered along a creek's muddy bank. I took pictures, examined the area for evidence, and hurried back to my office, confident our coroner could pick up the pieces.

My office mate chattered all afternoon, insisting I learn of the various methods available to dismember a body. Five o'clock came, finally, and I headed out for a beer, finding one at Manny's Bar, the latest place to see or be seen in downtown Alexandria. The bar huddled in a row of renovated colonial buildings hosting restaurants, taverns, and whatnot shops. A purple neon *Manny's* sign flickered above a massive picture window, revealing booths and tables packed with customers sipping their happy-hour drinks.

I ventured inside and found two unclaimed barstools, their lime-green covers splitting from years of sliding, bouncing rear ends. Picking up a damp, tattered beer list, I climbed on a stool just as someone jostled me when taking the other. It seemed my new boss had decided to join me.

Angela Marconi dropped her oversized black purse

into a cluster of peanut shells tossed on the brick floor. "Hey, Detective Pierce. Your first case today, right?" She beamed a huge smile at the bartender.

"Yeah…didn't you assign it?"

"Right, right. It'll be a tough one." She rested her elbows on the bar, straightened a pile of napkins, then glanced at me. "So…I got more blowback today about your hire."

I pushed the beer list toward her. "Is the commissioner having second thoughts again? Are you?"

There it was. Some people would call it a sardonic smile—a smirk would be more accurate, something legendary in the department. "No, no…no second thoughts from me. Commissioner Bates worries about the age thing—our youngest detective and all that."

"I can handle it…and how did you know I came here?"

She winked. "Lucky guess. Let's get a beer."

The bartender stood nearby, drying three mugs, the same three since we seated ourselves. He noticed me watching and turned away to stop a dripping brass tap, one of many attached along the dark paneled wall.

"One beer is my limit," I said. "Lieutenant Stone told me to come in early tomorrow and start my paperwork."

Marconi tapped her feet on the barstool's middle rung. "I'm buying this round, so it doesn't count. What do you like?" She waved at the mug-drying beer slinger. "Hey, get us a Sam Adams Irish Red."

I shrugged. "Guess I'll take a Sam Adams, then."

"I know that guy," she said, followed by another quick wave. "Hey, Manny."

The bartender peered over his rimless reading glasses, then stepped toward the row of beer taps. "Angela Marconi?" he called out. "My Angie Doll. I thought it was you." He handed us frosty mugs filled more with foam than beer, then patted her left hand. "You look the same. How long has it been since Jack died?"

"Twenty-five years...and, no, I do *not* look the same." Marconi leaned over and grabbed her purse, digging through it while I chugged half my beer. I had no deep yearning to be a part of this grand reunion, but curiosity got the better of me. "So? Who's Jack?"

Both her hands had disappeared inside a ragged pocket on the outside of the purse. She stopped digging and sighed. "Jack Marconi is my late husband. He started just like you, Henry—a patrolman, then a detective."

Manny's eyes widened.

"It wasn't too long before he...and Manny here...joined the agency around the time we married."

"I'm sorry," I said.

She yanked on the purse's jammed zipper.

"I mean, I'm sorry your husband died, not that you married."

Manny slapped the damp dishtowel over his shoulder. "Government work. Very secretive." He stood below a dusty bison's head attached above the bar's dark shelving, its face showing a remarkable resemblance to its owner.

"Crap, I can't find his picture." Marconi dropped her purse back on the floor. "Yeah, he was doing something for the government."

Manny wiped his forehead with the towel. "Jack

got too nosy for his own good."

"Nosy? God, Manny, that's an odd way to put it. He did his damn job." She glanced at her left hand where a ring might have been, the tips of her fingers a pale yellow from a smoking habit she swore she had quit.

"No matter, Angie Doll, it's terrific seeing you again. I'm sure Jack would be proud of you becoming the division's first female director."

"Yeah? You've kept up?"

"Word gets around. Anyway, I've owned this place for a while. I'm surprised you haven't come to see me."

"I've heard of it, but doesn't every town have a Manny's Bar? It's supposed to be the newest spot for the young crowd, right?"

"Seems so," he said. "They migrate from one place to the next. I'll take their money as long as it lasts."

She sipped her beer, then dabbed her mouth with a dry napkin. "I've wondered what happened to you over the years. You vanished like a ghost after Jack died."

"I'm no ghost."

"Right," she said, showing half a smile, "but since Detective Pierce here has found your bar, I won't have to be a stranger."

I pitched a handful of empty peanut shells on the floor, one landing on Marconi's purse. I doubted she would appreciate my advice. "My detective training would suggest the best way to find a person is to start with his or her name. It's called *Manny's* Bar."

Marconi ignored my comment and gave a sideways glimpse at my feet. "Is there something on your shoes?"

I glanced at the barstool's bottom rung—sure enough, my new black loafers had more than lost their

4

shine. "Yeah…I barfed."

"You threw up?" She smirked again. "Your crime scene wasn't pleasant from what the coroner told me."

"I've never seen a human body cut up like beef," I said. "What about you?"

Manny grinned and turned away. Was he laughing at me or the murder?

I dipped my napkin into a water glass, leaned over, and tried to rub off whatever had dried hard to my shoes.

Marconi eyed the door, then turned back toward me. "You'll get used to such things…unfortunately." She smoothed her blonde and gray bangs into place, so uneven it appeared she had cut them herself, then mumbled something about the time.

"I'm sorry, what?" I asked.

"Here's something I remember from *my* detective training. Unless our victim today hacked himself into pieces, this murder is much like killings we investigated in the nineties. All those happened in Alexandria before …" She grabbed her purse again and guzzled the last of her beer.

"Before what?"

Foam dripped from her top lip. "Several more murders occurred in Prague."

"Prague? The murderer moved to Europe?"

Her face reddened. "Come to my office first thing tomorrow, Detective Pierce. You've gotten involved in something we're all going to regret." She pitched a twenty and another smile to Manny, then slid off the barstool. "Good to see you, buddy. Great business you have here." Her smile flipped to a frown as she shoved through the crowd.

Reluctant to continue a conversation, I stared while Manny took her glass and pitched her wet napkin in the trash.

He stood straight, then tilted his head. "Something else, Detective?"

I hesitated but said, "I'm a little confused by her story."

His eyes offered nothing but a vacant gaze. He placed his palms on the slippery copper bar, his fingers splayed in the wetness, and he leaned toward me, close enough I could see his longest mustache hairs twitch with his breath.

"She did not tell you everything. Her husband's death was no accident. Someone murdered and dismembered him in Prague after he tracked a killer he believed had crossed the Atlantic. His murder became another of the unsolved deaths. He thought he was on to something…something big." Manny shoved an index finger on my chest and sneered. "Pay attention, new Detective. Angie Marconi knows her business. Learn from her if you dare…and watch your smartass mouth." He scowled, then turned back to the sinks, filled again with unwashed mugs.

Burned popcorn kernels and brown peanut skins filled the bottom of the wicker basket in front of me. I rotated on the barstool, surprised by the score of standing customers huddled in clusters, many staring at the vacant seat next to me. A young woman burst through the door, glanced around the room, then hurried toward me, bouncing onto the empty barstool while the other patrons dithered. A breeze of flowery perfume swirled around her, reminding me of a fragrance my grandmother might wear.

Nika Campbell introduced herself and initiated typical small talk, trying to talk louder than the noise of many voices and clanging glasses. The charming two-story building had been both horse stables and a warehouse in its past, its brick walls generating echoes from dozens of conversations. She bought me a second beer, this time served by a younger male bartender while Manny washed and dried the never-ending stacks of mugs and glasses.

Nika wore an expensive-looking blue dress, and a BMW emblem dangled from her designer purse—no wedding ring, but a classy watch hung loosely around her left wrist. She worked for the State Department, not unusual in Alexandria, where hundreds of men and women worked for the government or other influencers. A petite brunette with big brown eyes, she gave a slight giggle at the end of every sentence.

"Okay, Henry Pierce, I've gone on and on about me. Your turn for the where and what."

"The what? Oh…well, I grew up near Blacksburg. After I graduated, I moved closer to the district and worked as a patrolman at Mount Vernon. Now I'm a detective here in Alexandria."

"How exciting." She giggled, then munched on the cherry from her whiskey sour. "I bet it's fascinating work. Say, I have a neighbor who needs a detective. Could I have your card?"

I opened my wallet and offered one of my new business cards. "I work for the city's homicide division."

"You couldn't help my neighbor?"

"Only if it's connected to a crime investigated by the city police. I'm restricted to those cases."

She dropped my card into her purse. "What's the 'I' for?" she asked.

"What?"

"It's noisy in here, isn't it?" She patted my arm, then left her cold hand on mine. "I said, what's the 'I' for?"

"I?"

"Your name. The business card says, Henry I. Pierce."

I raised an eyebrow. "It's the initial for my middle name."

Her shoulders slumped. "No kidding? What's your middle name? Gawd."

"Ike."

"'I' is for Ike?"

"Yes, my grandmother liked Eisenhower."

"Who?"

"Eisenhower. The general. President Eisenhower, for God's sake."

She rolled her eyes. "So, where does Ike come from?"

"His nickname was Ike, and my family still calls me that."

"Your name is Henry Ike Pierce?" She giggled again and grabbed my hand between hers. "Don't be so sensitive. My middle initial is 'I' for Irina—it's why I asked. My father was Slovenian...Slovakian...one of those."

"But when you introduced yourself, you said your last name is Campbell."

"My mother chose it. She was a Kovać, a Keurig...crap, I can't remember that either, but she changed it after my father left. She called him an *izdajalec*…a traitor."

"A traitor?"

"That's all I know." She looked away and sipped her drink, now mostly melted ice.

The day had been exhausting, and my early evening now included murders in Prague and giggling Slovenians. "Nika, I'm scheduled to see my boss first thing in the morning to review a case. It's been nice to meet you."

She gave an exaggerated wink. "Okay, Mister Detective, go solve a crime. The city needs your help from what I've read. Here's my number." Dating someone new wasn't something I wanted while starting a new job, but I took her business card anyway.

"Have a good evening," I said, trying to hurry toward the door.

Manny hovered near the entrance, wiping a table while watching me wade through the sea of people. He grinned and opened the frosty door. "My, my, Henry Ike Pierce. It seems you have stepped into several piles of it today."

"Yeah, thanks for the…great evening." The door smacked my right heel on the way out.

I ducked under the dripping canvas of a low-hanging, lime-green awning and stepped onto the wet sidewalk, lit only by strings of lights clipped to the trees lining Duke Street. Parked next to the front door, a somber man sat behind the steering wheel of a white BMW 7 Series. He stared as I struggled to slide between its bumper and a Mercedes parked ahead of him. I jaywalked across the slick cobblestone street and used both hands to clear my Toyota's slushy windshield.

The door at Manny's opened again. Nika's smile gone and her phone smashed against an ear, she slid into the back seat of the BMW. The sullen driver maneuvered out of the tight parking spot, the engine growled, and the car slipped away through a shroud of snow.

Chapter Two

"Detective Pierce? Director Marconi is off the phone."

Kate Skelton, a gorgeous redhead, had married in the spring and was well into her first pregnancy. As Angela Marconi's administrative assistant, she sat behind a gray office divider with one section open to monitor incoming visitors. Turning away from a dirty window overlooking a packed parking lot, I thought of Ms. Moneypenny announcing me to the MI6 director— Kate seemed to think otherwise.

"Thanks, Kate, I haven't been to this office before. I interviewed in the conference room a few weeks ago."

"Cool."

"Now's your chance, Henry," Angie Marconi yelled from her office, interrupting my thoughts of a shaken, not stirred, martini. "Come right in."

I strolled by Kate and a whiff of her perfume, joined right away with a heavy smell of cigarettes from the director's suite. Marconi, like her office, appeared forlorn this morning. An old desktop computer sat high on the credenza, its broken CD drawer stuck open collecting dust. She had more files strewn about her desk than were inside the open drawers of the gray, steel file cabinets lining the wall.

"You look a little rough, Henry. How late did you stay at the bar?"

"Longer than planned." I followed her pointing

finger to a maroon corduroy chair. "I had an odd conversation with a young woman," I said after sitting.

"Ah, the singles scene. What was odd?"

I didn't want to start the morning this way, but she asked. "She had expensive jewelry and clothes and an import with maybe a security guard or chauffeur sitting in it. But she's, apparently, a lower-level employee at the State Department. It seems her parents are from southeast Europe."

"Europe again, huh? Look, Henry, if you want to succeed in the dating scene, you must turn off the detective's brain and loosen up a bit. Otherwise, you'll find clues instead of a girlfriend."

"I suppose, but she's not my type, so I don't see it going anywhere."

"Too bad. A young man in D.C. has much to choose from. The bar wasn't bad, though. What did you think of Manny?"

"Manny? He's a little rough," I said, trying not to criticize her friend. "You said he and your late husband served together?"

"In a manner." Marconi stared past me toward the file cabinets. "Manny didn't last long in that job, but he stayed in Alexandria permanently around the time Jack and I married." She leaned over and swiped a cobweb crisscrossed between the leaves of a plastic plant sitting alongside her desk. "Jack and I had an awful argument before he died. We were married about a year, together much less." She looked back toward me and sighed. "Look, our conversation may seem idle chit-chat, but the crime you came across yesterday—it wasn't happenstance I assigned it to you. The other new guy isn't a fit."

"Tim? I appreciate that, but you mentioned I would concentrate on cold cases when you interviewed me. Plus, according to Manny, I'm wet behind the ears and a smartass."

"Cold cases always come second, and, yeah, it sounds like Manny, although it's true." Her quick smile struck like a dagger. "You could be the best of our younger detectives, but don't let it go to your head. Your old boss had confidence in your abilities, but he told me you could be a slow decision-maker."

"I'm not sure what he—"

"Never mind for now. More experience will help." Marconi stood, stepped to her fogged window, and traced '5 + 1' in the moisture clinging to the glass, a small crack in the pane showing on the lower right. "Look, I need a fresh mind on this, which is another reason I hired you. But cold cases can frustrate the best, and people lose interest. Unfortunately, that means the long-dead victims are forgotten, too. We need somebody not associated with the old investigation of what might be related murders from over two decades ago—someone with energy. My late husband found himself in the same position. Fresh into the world of detective work before he jumped into a job with a federal agency. It was right in the middle of investigating five murders that occurred in Alexandria and Huntington. We found all five bodies at two parks."

"And yesterday's body we found at Angel Park...but wait. You said your husband worked for the government or something?"

She turned away from the window, leaned on the edge of her desk, and folded her hands. "Yes, yes, we'll get to that. So, you can see how I would assume this new case is connected even though it's been so many years?"

"Sure, I would've assumed the same thing. Director—"

"No. Here in my office, it's Angie. But don't forget it's always Director or Ms. Marconi in public."

"Certainly." This wouldn't be easy. She didn't look like an Angie, just a Marconi. "Manny volunteered something about your husband."

"Oh? Not surprising. Manfred Jurić never bites his tongue."

"Jurić? What nationality is that?"

"Croatian. Why?"

"He doesn't have much of an accent."

"No, he doesn't. During the early part of the Yugoslav breakup, Manny came here after a gang murdered his wife near Zagreb." Marconi sat, put her coffee cup on the desk, almost missing the tarnished, turtle-shaped coaster. She stretched her neck, then laced her fingers together to support her chin. "What did he say about Jack?"

"He mentioned your husband's death again, someone murdered him, and his body had the same, uh, characteristics as these other cases. He said Mr. Marconi had tracked someone to Prague."

"Yeah, yeah, the Prague part. Jack may or may not have been on to something in Europe. And, yes, he died in the same way as the other victims, except for the leather …" She stared into her lap.

"I'm sorry, ma'am, I'm getting lost in all this. I don't understand how a cop from Virginia joined a federal agency, investigated local murders, and then someone killed him in Prague. Everything I've come across since yesterday afternoon starts down a dark alley that ends up in Europe."

She broke open a fresh pack of nicotine gum, selected a piece, then shoved it in her mouth. "I've been telling you in general about these murders. There are many other moving parts."

"I hope I can help."

"As I said, more later." She propped her head on her left hand, her hazel-blue eyes almost obscured by her puffy eyelids. "With the death of Jack all those years ago… well, caution should be our guide. These old cases had a centrifugal force throwing facts and people in all directions. We'll start with the new murder at Angel Park. It should be a standard investigation but might relate to the old murders—perhaps it's a copycat killing. I don't know. We need to consider both."

"Okay. I'll go back to the park today and continue my inquiry."

"You're not the lead. You'll be *part* of the investigation." She yelled toward the office lobby. "Hey, Kate. How about a fresh pot of coffee? And get Detective Pierce some wipes. His shoes are still dirty."

Sure enough, I had forgotten about the mess on my shoes I never cleaned thoroughly at the bar.

"You don't want dirty shoes on your first case."

"Yes, ma'am." I stood and crept toward the door.

Marconi leaned forward and whispered. "Lose the tie, Henry. You stick out around here."

****

I wandered to the breakroom, reflecting on our discussion.

A deep voice bellowed behind me. "Hey, Pierce. Did the boss bust you down to a meter maid?" Richard

Forman was supposedly the precinct's funny man, although I found him more annoying than amusing. "I heard you were in her office forever."

"No, I'm still a—"

"Dicktective? Ha-ha." He slapped me on the back as I poured my coffee. I grabbed a paper towel, wiped up the spill, and then burrowed through the cabinet for anything to soften the bitterness of the black liquid in my cup. I found packets of a crunchy cream substitute sitting behind the coffee cups.

"Which decade was the cream bought, Dick?"

"It's the humidity. I guess you survived your meeting?"

"All good, Dick. We discussed my case she assigned me yesterday. It's a murder…a messy one, too."

"'The Case of the Dismembered Corpse.' You need any help with it since you're the new guy and all?"

"Not sure. I'm going back to Angel Park today and look around."

"I bet you won't find anything."

"Why?"

"If it's related to those murders from twenty-something years ago, everything will be a dead end. Sounds like a fun case, though."

"Fun?"

"Hey, Sergeant Forman," a voice shouted from the hall. Eddie Stone stopped at the doorway. He was Marconi's number one assistant and long-time detective lieutenant in the division. "Quit worrying about the new guy's case. I've got robberies over by the King Street metro station near the Masonic Memorial, and you're up."

"Yes, sir." Forman left without another word. I heard he was a decent detective but too compulsive, and the periphery details of cases would distract him. One of our academy instructors quoted Confucius and told us, 'Person who chases two rabbits will catch neither.'

"Good morning, Detective Pierce." Stone stood barely over five and a half feet tall, the top of this head coming an inch above my shoulders. A turquoise and gold Jacksonville Jaguars stocking cap covered his bald head.

"Good morning, Lieutenant Stone. I'm finishing up my coffee."

"Bring it with you. We're headed to Ivy Hill Cemetery."

"But Director Marconi told me to go back to Angel Park."

"I've talked to the director. We'll go there, too. I want you to see something at Ivy Hill first. You're with me this morning."

Our office sat a few miles from either park or thirty minutes in Alexandria traffic. Stone's old Ford cruiser smelled like greasy French fries, likely from the eight or ten empty bags of fast food scattered about the vehicle, several crushed under my feet. I thought lowering the window an inch or so, but the dreary November day wouldn't allow it. The back seat looked like storage for a horde of old music cassettes with cases on the floor, tapes in the seat.

We sped through the cemetery's west gate, swishing through piles of dead leaves cluttered at the entrance. Other random mounds swirled and shifted to wherever the last gust of November wind dumped them. Stone clenched his jaw, then wiped his mouth with a sleeve. "Dammit, I wish they would keep this cemetery neater. Some years are like this, where the leaves drop all at once and cover the smaller grave markers." The brakes squealed, and we jerked to a stop. "My wife's is over there. The tall white one."

I glanced to my right. "I'm sorry, I didn't …"

"No need to be sorry, Pierce. She had cancer. Trust me, it's easier to let loved ones go than watch them suffer. Six years next month, two days before Christmas. It doesn't seem possible. And I'll always regret she's buried here—she never wanted to move from Florida." He sat, staring toward his wife's grave. "We have a son in New Jersey. We live close enough she could visit him a few times."

"Oh? Is this what you wanted to show me?"

"No, no, follow me." Stone turned off the engine, pulled on his cap, and pushed his door open against a sharp gust of wind. I followed, kicking my way through drifts of brown and orange foliage.

He stopped and pointed to our left. "There."

I saw nothing but leaves and trash smashed against a deformed wire-mesh fence near the east exit.

"This whole section." He kicked away the leaves, and a flat headstone surfaced with the name of Unknown and the death date of July 1987.

"This used to be where we buried unclaimed bodies after two weeks. These days it doesn't happen much with all the DNA crap. Come over here." He stepped toward the fence, then cleared off another area. Five gray markers appeared, all said Unknown and January 1995. "These are the five homicide victims Director Marconi told you about."

Those deaths came into focus like a cold slap. "Why couldn't you identify them?" I asked.

"No heads, hands, or feet."

"Excuse me?"

"Whoever did this kept the skulls, hands, and feet, or disposed of them somewhere. With no teeth and no fingerprints, we had nothing else sophisticated enough to help us."

"No guesses even? A missing person's report and such?"

"Nope. No persons reported missing. We found a connection, though."

"To what?"

"To each other, it seemed. The victims were male, all wore brown leather jackets, and the damnedest thing—a piece of Orehnjaca was stuck in the breast pocket of each victim."

"Oren Jaka? I've never heard that word."

He grinned. "I hadn't either. It's a Serbian bread dessert. A nut roll or something."

"Wait a minute. These murders sound more like mob hits than a serial killer."

"Bingo. We've thought similarly over the years but couldn't connect it to local gangs." He hesitated as a blast of north wind shuffled the leaves, covering the headstones again. "I don't think it's only a local issue, and neither does the director. Let's get back to the car. My balls are freezing."

I didn't hesitate. Standing in the cold took its toll on my body parts, too. We wrestled the doors open and slid into the car seat. Stone let the swirling wind slam his car door.

I glanced at him, then back toward his wife's

headstone. "These deaths seem coordinated. How close did they occur? The markers only say January."

"Yeah. The Jones Point murders happened on January tenth of ninety-five. We found the three bodies the next day, and two days later, we found the other two at Mount Eagle Park."

"It still sounds like a hit job. But a Serbian mob in D.C.? It almost sounds silly, Lieutenant Stone."

"Call me Eddie. Here in the car, at least." He opened the center console and pulled out a baggy of white-powdered donuts. He offered me one, tasted his coffee, then emptied his cup out the car door. "Damn, I hate cold coffee. Let's get another. But, yeah, the story sounds a little crazy." The engine groaned to a start. The heater fan whined, sucking in cold air and spewing it straight on our feet. He sped through the entrance and pressed in a cassette. *Freddie's Dead* blasted out the speakers. "I love Curtis Mayfield."

I shouted over blaring music. "Some cases go cold as soon as they happen."

"Right. Again, that's why Angie welcomed another view of the old crimes after the new homicide happened. Fresh eyes and ears. That's you." He ran a stoplight. "Oops."

I spewed an exhale, adrenaline surging through me after a near collision. "Have we tried to disinter the bodies? Surely, we could gather DNA—"

"Nah. Nothing worked." He turned into a gravel parking lot. "We tried again ten years ago. They denied us."

"But why?" Silence. "Why was it—"

"I heard you, Pierce. I wish I could answer that. Federal judges interfered."

"Federal?

He nodded and leaned on the brakes. "Yep. The coverup becomes the priority, not the facts." The car bumped the curb in an empty spot between a white Mercedes and a black Chevy SUV. "Hmm. Kastrati's Koffee and Bakery. The name of this place has changed. I guess he has two shops now."

I strode inside, hoping for a public bathroom as all my morning coffee had caught up with me. A man behind the counter with a thick black mustache motioned his head toward the rear exit. By the time I returned, we both had steaming cups of black coffee and giant cinnamon rolls. "Lieutenant Stone, I appreciate this, but I had my breakfast. I'm not that hungry."

"Call me Eddie, and don't thank me. I told Rijad you would pay." He chuckled and pointed at me. "And what kind of breakfasts do you eat? It doesn't look like it's enough."

"Yogurt and juice."

"Yogurt? Blah…that's hospital food."

Scraping sounds drifted from the back while the cook cleaned his stove, the smell of rancid grease more potent than old coffee. A yellowed countertop ran the length of five tables, and the ancient coffee maker had several stained pots waiting for washing. Two booming voices in the kitchen sounded like an argument, but I couldn't understand their language.

I took a bite of the roll, then mumbled. "What's Kastrati? Italian?"

"Bosnian," a deep voice said. The man behind the counter with the huge mustache had approached us from behind. His hairy arms seemed as big as my waist.

"Sorry. I thought it was—"

"Not Italian." He crossed his arms and glared.

"Okay…only curious." I handed him ten dollars. He yanked a handful of change from his apron, several coins falling to the floor—an unusual gold one rolled under our table. I bent over to help, but he snatched it back, banging his head under the tabletop.

"Lucky charm," he said after standing. He rubbed the crown of his head, then handed me two quarters. "My home city is Bihać, near the Slovenian border. I left after fighting Serbs for months and months—a never-ending bloody mess. My parents and brother died, but my sister and I made it to Virginia in 1995. Legally." His eyelids narrowed. "Anything else you want to know?"

I took a slow sip of coffee and returned a stare. "Not for now."

He glanced at my colleague, back toward me, and sneered. "Eddie said you're the new guy."

"You two have met?" My question prompted a laugh from both men.

"Yeah, I know Rijad. I hadn't realized he had opened this place."

"Two places, Eddie. We have another near the Masonic Memorial."

"We are investigating robberies there from last night," I said.

Eddie frowned and tapped my shoulder. "Whoa, Pierce. We don't have to tell our business to everyone." Noted. A stupid thing to say in public.

"Eddie and friends will handle it." Kastrati put a hand on my shoulder. "Be careful, new detective." He strolled back toward the counter, hands on his hips, his eyes fixed downward on the black-and-white checkered linoleum floor.

Eddie sighed and checked his watch. "Finish up. We need to get to Angel Park and look at your crime scene. The coroner and director are meeting us there at eleven o'clock."

****

I said little on the way to Angel Park. Eddie offered nothing more, turning up the music even louder. I had learned a ton of information, and they had scheduled us to meet with Director Marconi and the man I had crossed yesterday at the crime scene. Coroner David Wulz was no shrinking violet and offered me no information the previous day while gathering body parts. He said even less after I vomited on my shoes.

"You met Dr. Wulz yesterday, I suppose?" Eddie asked. The car's brakes squealed again when we stopped at the park entrance.

"Briefly. He treated me like the new guy and ignored me."

"Yeah, Wulz can be an asshole, trust me. Angie likes him, though. He does his job and goes home, but I don't think he has other work friends except for Dick Forman. I think Dick and his wife feel sorry for David."

"What do you think, Eddie? In the last eighteen hours, I've met a Croat bartender, a Bosnian baker, the dingbat daughter of a rich Slovenian, and found out about Serbian nut rolls stuck in dead guys' pockets."

His jaw muscles twitched for a moment. "Didn't you know they called this area Little Belgrade?"

"How would I know that? The worst crime I used to see was an occasional D.U.I. tourist." I knew the detective job would offer a significant change, and I had looked forward to it but never dreamed Alexandria could be this different.

He scratched his stubbly face and wrinkled his brow. "It makes things interesting, doesn't it? Most of those folks keep to their own and try to leave the Yugoslav ugliness behind, but we have occasional problems."

"The dismembered bodies? Did ethnic issues drive those murders?"

He scanned again for Marconi, then fished in the glove box for another white donut. "My intuition always told me this related to old score-settling from the Bosnian and other wars, but we got nowhere with that angle. Nobody wanted to pursue it—I still don't know why."

I had nothing else to offer and stared at the metallic angels placed on each side of the west gate greeting visitors into the park. The icons appeared to be copper but without the natural patina. Someone had propped the gate against the bushes lining the entrance. Visible indentations showed in two places where a vehicle had rammed it.

A brown Dodge passed us, heading straight into the park, with Marconi in the passenger seat, throwing a glance toward us. "Finally," he said. "Twenty minutes late. The coroner probably held her up." He revved the engine and popped the Ford into gear, snapping my head against the headrest.

Coroner Wulz slid to a stop, avoiding the swollen creek, and Eddie slammed on the brakes just before rear-ending the Dodge. Marconi scooted out the Dodge's passenger seat and wandered closer to the stream, pulling her overcoat tight around her. "God, the wind hurts—I forgot how close the high school was."

I motioned toward the creek's muddy banks. "Down a little farther," I said. Wulz stopped at the water's edge, and I couldn't bite my tongue. "I saw tire tracks here yesterday. It looks like your car has obliterated them."

Wulz ignored me while picking leaves from his plaid trousers. A few reminded me of poison oak, but I kept quiet. "Why didn't you take impressions of those yesterday? An experienced detective—"

"I followed our protocols. The casts are at the station, but I hoped to review with the director."

Marconi raised her left hand slightly to end the argument. "It's fine, Henry." Earlier, I hadn't noticed the wedding ring on her finger.

"It's an obvious body dump," I said. "The tracks stopped where the Dodge stopped. The torso laid near where the water starts today. There wasn't much blood, right?"

I pulled up the pictures on my phone and handed it to Marconi.

"The water is definitely up from yesterday," Wulz said. "About a foot." Wulz seemed distracted, yanking on a branch scratching at his car. He drifted away from us, following the bank on our right.

"Were the hands or feet missing?" Marconi called out.

Wulz turned back, muttering under his breath.

"This body seems a little different than what I remember from the old killings. David?"

Wulz's wanderings had caked his tattered sneakers with fresh mud, although they weren't much worse than usual from what I had seen. He appeared to make a science of messiness. "All these leaves have caused the stream to dam up," he said.

"David, quit roaming around and listen to me. We have an active crime scene, and I would appreciate not having things even more disturbed."

He crossed his arms and gave back a frown.

"Let's try again, coroner. I see from Detective Pierce's pictures that the arms are not attached, and the hands are missing. Did you recover the victim's head? What about the feet?"

"No head or feet either, Angie…like the old murders."

She shifted her weight, leaning harder against the Ford, and snapped a bubble in her nicotine gum. "What about a mask?"

Wulz squinted. "A mask? No…no mask. Why?"

"Never mind." She sighed and glanced at Eddie. "This might offer an opportunity."

"Or another road to nowhere," Eddie said. He joined Marconi, leaning on the black hood of his Ford. Only a shadow of the city's seal could be seen, and the hood's partial lettering displayed *Call 9-1-*.

"Seems like we're scatter shooting," I said. My three associates' conversation reminded me of my earlier talk with Marconi—scattered details, but no overall point.

Wulz snorted. "We know what we're talking about, Pierce. You need to keep up."

Marconi smoothed her bangs. "Tell me what you're thinking, Henry."

"When I arrived yesterday, two policemen had taped off the area, and the coroner and the lab team had arrived. A few other bystanders stood around, mostly nosy joggers. I stepped down the bank and noticed the body parts. I knew of the decapitation since I didn't see the head, but since I hadn't known of the prior murders, I didn't pay much attention to the other limbs."

"The treatment of the appendages isn't exact to the old murders," Marconi said.

"Sounds so," I replied. Another jogger pushed a baby carriage along the path. "If this is a copycat murder, this minor difference might show they missed something from the original crimes. The perps were in a hurry, I'd guess. I took these pictures yesterday before Coroner Wulz arrived. The tire tracks—"

"Tire tracks don't always work for real, Pierce," Eddie said. "They always find the guy on TV, but it's not that easy."

"Okay, but I didn't want to regret not doing it. Anyway, the body was male and had a brown jacket on," I said. "I didn't check his pockets. I left it up to—"

"David?" Marconi asked.

He appeared to be daydreaming. "Pockets? No. I told you I found no identification."

Eddie came to attention from his slump. "David, pay attention. Did you check all the pockets? Was there a breast pocket on the jacket?"

"Yes." I held up my phone like the Statue of Liberty holding her torch.

Wulz rolled his eyes. "The pocket had two small zippers, maybe two inches long. One was real and the other for show—a decoration, I guess. I had my gloves on and got only two fingers in it. I pulled out crumbs of something."

"Hell," Eddie said.

Marconi aimed her right index finger. "David, I

want you to go back to the lab and tell me what was in that pocket."

Wulz ticked off his points with both index fingers. "Angie, I told you several times the body had no I.D. We will have preliminary DNA results in ten workdays."

"At least DNA is an option this time," I said. "If we can figure out who the victim was, it would put us ahead of the old murders."

Eddie clenched his jaws. "Coroner, you need to speed this up. We need to know as much as possible, as soon as possible."

"Before we're not allowed to know?" Marconi asked. "David, you have until five p.m. today to give me more info."

"Okay, but I'm not sure what the crumbs have to do with anything, especially this. It seems like a waste."

"Do what I asked. We need to discuss the timeliness of your test results." Marconi turned away and opened the left back door of the Ford. "Gentlemen?" She pushed aside a handful of cassette tapes and slid into the back seat, then Eddie and I got in the car. Before he turned the key, I grabbed his hand.

Eddie glared and pulled his hand away. "Don't do that."

Noted. "Director. Another thing. Did you notice Wulz cleaning off his pants when he came back from the creek?"

Marconi stared out the window. "David is always a mess. He's terrific with the technical part of his job, but you have to take the rest of it."

"He cleaned off leaves and a few pine needles."

Her eyes darted toward me. "So?"

"Do you see any pine trees here?"

Her blank, tired eyes sparked to life. She slapped Eddie on both shoulders. "Eddie, be a dear and run down there. See if you can find any more pine needles."

A loud exhale, and he buttoned up his jacket again. "So, they killed this person somewhere with pines around, then dumped the body here?"

"The needles came from somewhere," she said.

Eddie cursed the stiff wind and slammed his door, returning shortly with a few needles. He opened the glove box, pulled out an empty baggy, and shoved the needles into it. "Here you go, then." He started the car, switched to a Marvin Gaye cassette, and we headed to the gate. "What do you do with those? Anyone might have come along here with pine needles stuck to them. Joggers maybe…or an animal."

"You know, pines surround the whole area near the Masonic Memorial," I said.

"And that's where the robberies occurred last night," Marconi said.

"Hang on," Eddie said. "We've found random pine crap, and you all are tying together a bunch of different speculations. Talk about scatter shooting."

Marconi shook his headrest. "Eddie, come on. We can't ignore anything. Is there something particular between species to let us narrow down the area we're talking about?"

"Your assumptions aren't facts. Pines are all over Virginia," Eddie said. "It might be another goose chase for nothing."

Marconi drifted out of our conversation, hanging on to the armrest as we nearly doubled the speed limit. We pulled into the police station, and Eddie turned off the engine.

"Eddie, listen," Marconi said. "Why does it take so long to process DNA samples and return the analysis? We need to move fast."

"If they do it right, it will take a couple of weeks for a full analysis, but maybe less for something preliminary…according to David."

"Your girlfriend in the lab. Get her to help."

"I told you she's not my girlfriend."

"Come on, Eddie, isn't it time? I know Doris likes you."

"Whatever. What's your point?"

"Talk to her, Eddie. See if she can speed things up. Take her out on a date and make passionate love to her."

Eddie puffed up.

"Try to move this thing along."

He opened his door, stood in the wind, then leaned over, sticking his head in far enough to see Marconi wearing a giant smile. "I'll talk to her." He slammed the door and hurried up the front steps. A woman smiled and stopped to talk, but he waved her off.

"Do you torture him often?" I asked.

"He needs to get out more—he's been moping around for years."

I should have known better but said, "I noticed you're wearing your wedding ring today."

Her face reddened while she pulled herself out of the back seat. "Okay, a zinger for you. After seeing Manny last night, I thought a lot about Jack and put the ring on. Now I can't get it off. I'm not the same size I used to be." We hustled up the cracked cement steps. "Meet me at my office at four o'clock. I'm getting everyone together. And don't be late."

****

No one sat up front when I strolled into the suite. Sure enough, I was almost five minutes late. I opened the door and peered into Marconi's office. "Detective Pierce, get in here." She held a tissue to her nose. Eddie sat on the maroon couch between stacks of paper. "I wondered if you were joining us."

"Sorry, ma'am, it's unusual for me to be late. I've been researching information about pine species."

She glanced at Eddie and then toward me. "Detective Pierce, I appreciate your abilities and your jumping into this case, but we have a problem. Eddie and I reviewed what we found today, and I hear you came across Mr. Kastrati in his place of business?"

"The coffee shop owner?" The man's big mustache came to mind while I sat uninvited in her corduroy chair. "I got the feeling he wasn't too fond of me, at least first impression."

"Pierce, I shouldn't have taken you in there. It's my fault and—"

"Never mind, Eddie, what's done is done."

My face grew hot. "Is there a problem?"

"Lieutenant Stone told me you all went for coffee, but this was not a good situation."

Eddie's frown combined with a twitch under his left eye. He crossed his arms and offered nothing else.

"I'm confused," I said.

"Please listen. Kastrati is on our watch list. There have been several burglaries in the areas around his coffee shops. Detective Sergeant Forman investigated another today."

"Yes, ma'am, I ran into Forman this morning

and—"

"Let me finish. You mentioned something aloud in a public place about the burglaries and our investigation into those."

"In front of Kastrati?"

"Yes, in front of Kastrati. We think he or his associates are involved in several illegalities in the area, and there have been other incidents, too. Now he knows we're investigating, and their activities will likely cease, at least until his bunch feels safe again."

"Sorry, ma'am."

"Director, I should have grabbed coffee for us and gotten out."

"Yes, that would have been best, Lieutenant." She turned back toward me. "You must watch your mouth while in public and around other people. I hope you didn't say much to the girl you met at the bar."

"The State Department woman?" I closed my eyes. "No, ma'am. She knows I'm a detective, but that's about it. She has my business card in case she wanted to call."

"Come on. You need to think with the right head in those situations." She blushed at her faux pas. "Our robbery investigation has taken a hit, and they know we're watching—I hope this doesn't get to the papers. They'll link it to the 1990s murders, and off they go."

"Wouldn't he have guessed we would investigate the burglaries?" I had to say something, but her scowl told me otherwise.

"You act wise beyond your thirty years, Detective Pierce, but possibly I've assumed too much? Tell me the truth. Are you sure you can handle it?"

"I'll do better."

"Are you listening?"

"Sorry, I'm not sure what else to say."

Eddie nodded toward me. "Director, let him hang with me for a while. He needs a little stain on his shiny exterior."

"Okay, guys, we've had a major setback here. Let's cool our jets for a few days." She gulped her tea and wiped her chin after a dribble. "Detective Pierce, a few days in the basement will do you good."

"What basement?"

"Our records are there back to the late forties. I want you to find everything from the cold cases in the nineties we've mentioned and start a file on our latest murder. Ask my assistant for the location. Scan for any information concerning robberies in the area. Secrets are abundant in Little Belgrade." She propped her head on a hand.

"Yes, ma'am. I have expertise in data analytics. I can create a database of information for—"

"Fine, fine, that's great." Marconi stood, and I assumed she wanted me to leave. "Whatever works. And one more thing."

"What's that?"

"Whatever you find…don't tell the whole damn world."

Chapter Three

I thought it wise to stay late on Friday, working in the five thousand square feet of file cabinets and miscellaneous junk stored in the basement underneath our offices. I couldn't have imagined a verbal reprimand would come my way the first week of a new job—still, a dumb mistake. I had exposed our investigation to the man or men that should have been the last to know. Anyhow, I would have ended up here, giving me access to the cold case archives my colleagues had talked about all week.

The basement's one desk looked like surplus from a World War II military base, and the metal file cabinets lining the walls from floor to ceiling had to be near that age. The case files I needed were up top, and I had to climb a splintering wooden ladder to retrieve the heavy cardboard boxes. By late afternoon, I'd discovered the correct files, an aching back, and twenty-five years of dust.

A grubby computer sat in the middle of the desk on top of scores of empty manila folders, its fan grinding and whining when I turned it on. No one remembered the password, so I had to work with the know-it-all computer whiz that everyone had bragged about, but most suggested I should avoid. Subtlety and a clean mouth were not his best attributes. He found me on the ladder's top rung.

"God. This place still smells like piss."

I backed down the ladder. "They told me a sewer backed up last year. Those cabinets in the corner are rusty from it."

"Rusty? That's the reason we call it Piss Junction. What the hell did you do to get shoved down here?"

"I need to research an old case. Why else?"

"You're Pierce, right?"

"Yes. Henry Pierce. And you?"

"I figured everyone knew me." He tilted his head. "Brian Rowe. I'm the glue that holds this place together."

Typical. He satisfied every stereotype of a techie—too many calories and not enough sunlight. I fought back an eye roll. "You may be the glue, but I'm the one stuck here with this computer that uses the small floppy drives."

"I wouldn't call them 'floppy' since they're in hard plastic, but you're correct. This old thing was my best friend for years, and I kept it precisely because it read these old-style disks. Let me try my old password." He pulled off his glasses and leaned his head closer to the screen.

Sure enough, the dusty desktop groaned even louder as it booted up. "My, my," I said. "Sounds like the old girl will make it."

"Girl, my ass. Its name is Jeff."

"You named a computer Jeff?"

"Yes. I always have names for them. Look at the network servers sometime. Mickey, Pluto, Donald, and—"

"Jeff?"

"I named it after my parakeet."

"Does Jeff feel like working today?" There went

35

my right eyebrow.

"Hey, asshole, if you want my help, you can stand there and be quiet, or I can leave."

"All I need is a password for a few days. You can change it back later."

He glanced at me and then typed away. "Hang on."

"Is there a spreadsheet or database program on it?" I asked. He didn't respond. I refused to be part of his pettiness and went about my business, moving the ladder away from Piss Junction, as he called it. I should make a sign for the area and call it Brian's Junction. Same difference.

"Pierce, come here." I strolled back, wanting to end this. "Your new password is 'brianisagenius.' One word."

"Nice. Do your business cards say that, too?"

He glared, pushed his glasses back on his face, and hurried up the stained cement steps.

"Will this Windows 2000 machine grind any data?" I asked.

He stopped on the top step but didn't turn around. "Don't know, don't care. If you don't like it, BYOD, if you know what that is."

"Bring my own device," I yelled back. "My phone has more power than this. Maybe Siri and Jeff can go on a date, if you know what that is." The metal door slammed behind him, and I flipped the orange switch, shutting off the computer. The old paper documents would have to do.

****

The phone rang early on Saturday morning, waking me into a hangover. Not the worst I'd experienced, but one brought on while sitting in front of my television after my dinner of cottage cheese and turkey lunch meat. I'd made excellent progress on a six-pack of a dark Canadian beer. The checkout lady had suggested a just-arrived Czech beer, but the sound spewing from my mouth had told her otherwise. I had had enough of eastern Europe this past week.

"Ike? Honey, did I wake you up?"

My mother. I had to get my head together. "Hi, Mom."

"I hadn't heard from you all week. I figured my new detective son was in trouble."

"We talked on Sunday night."

"Oh? It seems longer. How did your first week go? How are you doing with a female boss? Did you make any friends?"

"My boss is okay. No new friends. I'm investigating a new case and haven't had time to get out much."

"Show some confidence, Ike. Enjoy your new situation. It's Saturday, though. Get out of your apartment tonight. I hear young women are everywhere."

"Yeah,…half the town is female."

She was silent for a moment, then said, "I saw Isabel yesterday, honey, and she asked about you."

Isabel…my old girlfriend, who had married last year. "How is she? Have any kids yet?" My head pounded—some of my mother's conversations took an hour.

"She's not married now. And no kids."

"I'm not interested, Mom. You remember how Isabel treated me before we broke up."

"But you're thirty now, and—"

"This is the same thing we talked about last Sunday. How's Granny?"

"Ike, I'm not sure what's going on. She's had terrible gas since Tuesday. I'm thinking of taking her to the clinic this weekend and see if they can figure it out."

Gas? "Mom, it's always good to hear from you, but I need to eat breakfast and get to work. My boss let me bring files home instead of sifting through them at work."

"Don't work too hard, honey. Your father worked himself to death."

"I miss him, too. Give Granny my love."

"Do you want me to call you when we find out about her gas?"

"No, no, that's fine. I'll call you next weekend. Love you."

"Love you, too, Ike. Please be careful."

Such a sweet woman. Loneliness enveloped her after losing my dad almost two years ago. Our relatives wanted me to move home, but to what? Life in the coal mines? I had my career started and had no intention of moving back. A few more bites of yogurt and some juice, and I dove into the mess I brought home from the work basement.

I took a break well past one o'clock. The files were a mess, a few more organized than others, but trying to make sense would be an ordeal—then another buzz from the coffee table. "Damn phone," I said aloud. The number calling wasn't familiar, and I hesitated to answer. "Hello? This is Ike, I mean Henry."

A giggle on the other end. "Can't you remember your name, Detective Pierce?" That laugh—the woman from the bar.

"Nika? What's going on?"

"It's Saturday."

"Yep, it's Saturday. I brought work home. What are you doing?"

"I'm looking for a date tonight. I guess I'm too spontaneous, but I wanted to call you. Are you up for some fun?"

I wanted to say no but remembered my mother's comments about the old girlfriend lurking in my hometown. "Sure. Getting away this evening would be nice. Have anything in mind?"

She laughed again. "Before or after dinner?"

Was I ready for this? "Okay, dinner it is. Where and when can I pick you up?"

"Let me. I live over in Falls Church, and I'll be in your direction later this afternoon. Let me pick you up at six o'clock. There's a great Italian place in Arlington near the memorials."

"All sounds good." A relief, as I didn't have time to clean my Corolla. "But if you're driving, I'll buy dinner."

"Who is calling who? Everything is on me tonight."

"We'll see. You need to let me do something."

"I bet we can think of *something*." She giggled again. "I'll see you in five hours."

A dial tone.

Back to the folders, and then the phone again. I think I had fewer interruptions at work. "Good afternoon, boss," I said in my cheeriest voice.

"Hey, Henry. I tried to call a few minutes ago, but I got your voice mail. How's it going? Are you finding much?"

"I was on the phone with…never mind. It's been challenging. There were so many people involved, and they all differed on how they organized their thoughts and papers. Your late husband seemed to be the only one with linear thinking. I also found Eddie Stone's materials and another coroner named Wulz?"

"Sammy. Samuel Wulz is, or was, David's father. He died in a car accident near Fredericksburg, right in the middle of the investigation. Gosh, I had forgotten how crazy things had gotten. We lost Sammy and then my late husband. Another detective named Johnson up and quit…she moved to Atlanta." I heard her blow out her cheeks. "And then someone took the ex-director's notes."

"How did you…have you gone through everything already?"

"Henry, I've been through that stuff a million times. But it's been years. At some point, all the former director's notes disappeared. If you were a conspiracy theorist …"

"I'm not," I said. "Most conspiracies are a lack of knowledge. We conjecture to fill in the blanks."

"Maybe so—please be careful with the information you find in those boxes. I'm uncomfortable with you taking those from storage."

"I know. I've been careful and marked all the individual pieces to match their original folders. Now I'm trying to collate by subject."

"I hope we aren't wasting your time, Henry. I'm out of gas and worn out on this entire affair."

"Understood," I said.

She sounded worn out, and some days appeared it.

"And another thing," Marconi said. "Tag anything you see about a mask."

"You said something about a mask the other day."

"Yeah…they described it as a leather balaclava with an odd mechanical mouthpiece."

"Balaclava?"

"Yeah. A cover for the head except for the eyes— it's kind of a mask, anyway. The authorities found a leather one at the site of my late-husband's body, placed where Jack's…where Jack's head should have been."

"I'm sorry, Angie," I said. "Were there similar masks…balaclavas, found near the bodies at our parks?"

She sighed. "Nope, which might be a reason these weren't the same killers. God, Henry, these cold cases can drive you mad. Anyway, the new murder at Angel Park comes first." Another sigh. "So…what are you doing this evening? I hope you aren't sitting around your apartment. That's what Eddie and I do."

"You remember the ditzy young woman from the bar I told you about?"

"Yes."

"She called me."

"I see." Silence for a moment. "Yes, you must get out and do things while you can."

"She's different, though, and a little pushy. She's picking me up and wants to pay for it all."

"Right, then. I'll be interested in how it goes. By the way, we need a written report of what you find for Monday morning."

"Oh? I'll do what I can."

"We'll talk again but have it ready for ten o'clock

when we meet with Commissioner Bates. I'll be in touch." Another dial tone.

The police commissioner? He wasn't a fan of my hiring, and my stomach knotted. I grabbed another pile of notes and papers, sifting and sorting, organizing and filing, wishing I hadn't agreed to the evening out.

****

Six o'clock straight up. A gentle tapping hurried me to open the door. It was Nika in a blue dress, the shortest I'd ever seen, and a plunging neckline hard to ignore. I must have been staring as she pushed her way into my apartment.

"Henry Ike Pierce, don't you look great? This place is…a convenient location for work? We had to circle the block a few times before parking."

"We?"

"My driver, Charlie,…a friend of the family."

"I saw him the other night, I think." A little rich girl has taken an interest in me? "You look fantastic, Nika—like you stepped out of a fashion magazine. But aren't you cold? Do they call that a micro-dress?"

She giggled again. "Yes, I'm cold, but I wanted you to see." She whirled in a tight circle.

"It's great." How could she not be freezing her ass off? "Shall we go?"

****

Nika asked me something as we sat at a table in the Ristorante Paradiso. Two whiskey shots in the car had clouded my head.

"What did you say?" I cupped my hand over my ear, trying to hear. Our table sat on the lower floor near the aquarium, its bubbling pump adding to the noise. A potent smell of garlic overwhelmed Nika's sweet perfume.

"Charlie, our driver, isn't he great? He's like an uncle." Although several people waited at the front, the maître d' had shown us straight to our table when the owner noticed Nika. This was as puzzling as anything else this week. The restaurant's lower level had a more intimate ambiance than the upper floor. They had covered the tables in red-and-white checked tablecloths, and gentle accordion and violin music flowed through small speakers. The area must have been a well-used space—the yellowed floor linoleum showed scores of dents from moving tables and chairs over the years.

"Charlie doesn't say much. Can I ask you a question?" I asked after pulling off my glasses to clean them.

She grabbed my hands and stared at me. "Watch out now. Those big brown eyes are glowing without your glasses hiding them. So, yes, I'll tell you anything."

"How does a State Department employee have a driver and afford to eat in places like this?" The waiter poured us a glass of wine, his wide eyes giving a glance down Nika's dress.

She leaned close to my face. "It's family money." Her breath hit me like another shot of whiskey. A peck on the cheek and she grinned. "You don't mind, do you?"

"The kiss or the money?"

"Either." She giggled, then took a sip of her wine.

"It's not my business, Nika—I was only curious about the driver and all. You look like a movie star ready for the red carpet. You must have a hundred boyfriends waiting in line."

"Maybe, but I wanted to go with you tonight." She winked, bit into a piece of bread, and rubbed my leg with her foot. "So, Mister Detective, you've gotten information from me, and now it's your turn."

"What would you like to know?"

"Come on, Henry. Where are you from? Why are you in Alexandria? You don't sound like you're from here. You mentioned Blacksburg the other night…siblings, etcetera."

"Okay. My parents' farm is near Rocky Gap, northwest of Blacksburg. My dad served in the army for twenty years and then managed our farm and tried part-time coal mining before he died. My mom was a substitute teacher. She miscarried several times, so I don't have any siblings."

"Only one Henry Ike Pierce?"

"Guess so. I attended Virginia Tech—I was never far from home. I graduated with a criminology degree and earned an MBA in computational modeling and data analytics. I was the first one in my family to graduate from college, much less from graduate school. My father passed two years ago. Heart attack, they said, although he had no previous heart issues, and it broke my mother's heart, too. My grandmother lives with her now, and they're the ones who call me Ike. They both get their pensions, and I help if they need anything."

"Aren't you the sweet one? My degree is in Journalism from American University. I would like to get my MBA and possibly be a senator someday. My mother doesn't have to worry about money, at least. My dad took off but left a trust for her…for us."

"What did your dad do?" My question surprised her, judging by her widening eyelids. She wiped her mouth with the white cloth napkin, leaving red lipstick smeared across it.

"Let's talk about something else, Henry, Ike, whatever." Her mood had flipped. The waiter took our salad bowls and sat in front of us two plates of steaming spaghetti and golfball-sized meatballs. "I hope you like this. I ordered it before we came."

"Sure. I love spaghetti. I'm sorry I asked about your dad."

"Never mind," she said and held up her hand. "Not a pleasant subject. Try the spaghetti. We have strawberry cheesecake coming soon." Her smile returned as I took my first bite. "Tell me about your week."

"I met you on Wednesday, only three days ago, and I've been working on my first case. It's a tough one. I spent yesterday digging around in the basement and today trying to sort through what I found."

"Sounds fascinating. Wasn't there something in the news about a murder in a park?"

"Yeah, that's the one."

"Gosh, the paper said someone dismembered the body. Do you have any leads? You think it links this to those murders, whenever that was, a million years ago? There have been all *kinds* of stories over the years about those."

"The body was in several parts, yes. That's all I can say, okay?"

"Right." Her lips offered a smile, but a glare came from her eyes. "Sorry, it's the wanna-be journalist in me wanting answers." She furrowed her forehead as if mulling a problem. "Back to those similar murders many years ago…what do you know about those deaths?"

I placed my fork down, feeling like it was quiz time again. "Yes, I read about those, too—not sure if it's related or not. I'll leave it up to others to decide."

"I doubt it's related. A coincidence," she said while glancing at her watch. "My boss says I'm too curious sometimes."

"What do you do at the State Department?" My turn for questions. Most girls on a first date wouldn't be so interested in murder.

"It's boring," she mumbled. She took another sip of wine and rested her chin on her hands. "Yeah, your case will definitely be interesting and a learning experience. Tell me more at some point." She signaled to the waiter, and he brought us the cheesecake. "I'm stuffed," she said right away, pushing the plate toward me after a tiny bite. "Let's get cartons for this to go. You can have mine."

Things wrapped up remarkably fast. We grabbed our dessert, I helped her with her coat, and we made our way to the front door. "Hey, Nika, they never brought the ticket."

"Oh...I come here a lot. The owners have my credit card number, so it's taken care of."

Odd, bizarre, I couldn't think of another word. Nika leaned against the opposite car door during our trip to my apartment, not next to me as she had earlier. Poor girl must have had enough of my country-boy manners and stories. Bored. Used to money, flash, and fun, I bored her talking about work and dead bodies.

"We're here, Mr. Pierce," Charlie said in his growling voice, breaking the long silence.

"Okay. Thank you, Nika. That was a wonderful

meal, as was the company."

"You're welcome. I had fun." She leaned over and kissed me on my left cheek. "Hope to see you around," she said and then whispered, "please be careful."

Charlie opened my door, never watching me get out, and slammed it shut, almost catching my jacket. Gliding around the car, he nodded toward Nika, then dropped into the driver's seat. The car pulled away while I watched from the curb, holding two servings of strawberry cheesecake.

Chapter Four

A new brown stain showed itself on the stairwell carpet of the third flight of stairs leading to my apartment. I didn't want to guess its origin. Rounding the last corner, I heard a female voice, talking on the phone, I presumed, as I couldn't hear the other party. A familiar voice, too. I peered around the corner, and sure enough, my boss stood outside my door.

Marconi tapped the screen and dropped the phone in her purse. "How about that? It's not even nine o'clock, and you're already home. Say, the red lipstick on your cheek is cute."

I jerked my left hand to my face trying to wipe away Nika's lipstick. "Director…Angie? Why are you here and standing in the hall? You found my apartment?"

"We need to talk."

"That's never a good way to start." I pushed the leftovers to her while I searched for my keys. The second lock always stubborn, it finally turned, and I pushed the door open. "We barely touched the cheesecake." I turned on the lights in the kitchen, grabbed two forks, and we sat on the couch working on the leftover dessert. "Go ahead and enjoy it. The spaghetti filled me up."

"You must tell Ms. Campbell thanks for the treat. It's delicious," Marconi said. She wiped her mouth with a paper towel and gave me her smirk.

"Wait a minute. How did you know her name?"

"Didn't you tell me the other day?"

"No, and how did you know when I'd be back? You could have been standing in the hall for hours."

"I *am* a detective. I'll fill you in, but we need coffee."

"There's no decaf."

"Even better and make a big pot. Eddie will join us in a few minutes. I'll save him part of the cheesecake."

"Please, if there's more to tell me—"

"When Eddie gets here." She waved me off.

Three heavy knocks on the door interrupted us.

I opened it, then gave a slight bow. "Nice timing, and welcome, Detective Lieutenant Stone. Our Saturday night party is complete."

Eddie patted my shoulder. "Nothing better than sitting around talking about dead people. What else are three single people going to do on a Saturday night in the D.C. area?"

"I'll start the coffee. There's half a piece of cheesecake my seemingly well-known girlfriend wouldn't eat."

Eddie slipped off his Jaguars stocking cap. "Thank you, sir. Angie, what's up? Your call…your voice sounded strained. I came as soon as I could."

"I'm sorry for the surprise, guys. Get comfortable—I have quite a story to tell. I trust you both, and Eddie, you already know parts of this."

"Go for it," I said, still standing by the closed door. I needed as much information as I could get, but I didn't want these two hanging around in my apartment all night.

"Show me what you've found. I may need those

notes to jolt my memory," Marconi said.

No one had ever accused me of disorganization. I handed over her late-husband's documents from one file piled on the coffee table.

"This is a long, convoluted tale." She made a face. "God, what's that smell?"

I threw my bag against the wall, then sat on the arm of the couch. "I joined a gym."

"Wash your stuff now and then. Good lord. Anyway…here goes." She sipped her coffee and drew a breath. "Jack Marconi worked for the National Security Agency when he died."

"The NSA?" Eddie asked. "Interesting. He only told me about a federal agency." She didn't respond. "I wondered why he quit his new detective job. It hadn't even been a year."

Almost begging, I said, "Did you skip something already?"

Marconi wiped cheesecake from the corners of her mouth. "Okay, here's a chronology. Jack worked as a cop for around five years before they promoted him to detective. Good thing he got the detective gig, too, as he didn't care for his old patrol boss. He and I met at the same bar Manny owns now. I thought about it the other night but said nothing. I don't remember what the name of the bar was, but it looked the same. That ugly green …" She took another sip of coffee, then sighed. "We dated for a year, and then he received the detective position offer a few days after he proposed to me." She stole another bite of cheesecake from Eddie. "It couldn't have been more than a week after our engagement when the murders in the park happened."

"The dismemberments?"

She frowned. "Well, yeah…the ones we've been talking about. Jack got nowhere with those. Soon, he told me about this guy named Manny, who claimed to be an informant. He had attached himself to the ex-Yugoslav communities and offered information on the recent immigrants, or so Jack said. He told me it surprised him that Manny, as a Croat, would want to live in the middle of the Bosnian and Serb communities."

"Refugees came here?" I asked.

Eddie groaned and shook his head. "Boy, this was over twenty-five years ago. Were you even in kindergarten?"

"Yes, but remember, Eddie, the refugees that came," Marconi said. Her comment drew a blank stare. "Eddie, come on. You remember a few Serbs claimed themselves to be government big shots who had tired of the killing and their brutal *Generals* as they called them."

"I remember a little Angie, but I was a desk-bound cop then. A robbery suspect about shot my calf off, Pierce." He pulled up his left pant leg, revealing a dent like a melon baller had taken a chunk out of the calf muscle. "How do you know all this, Angie? Jack spilled the beans?"

"Jack told me a bit," she said. "I worked as an assistant to the director then, Henry. My boss didn't offer much, but Jack mentioned things to me."

"Okay. What happened next?" I asked.

Eddie poured another cup for himself.

"Jack thought Manny was great. Manny's information about the murders at least helped them narrow down to who the killers were not. They learned

51

enough that Jack and his boss thought the investigation needed to move beyond the city limits."

I got up again to slide open a window. The thermostat in my apartment hung next to the enormous picture window overlooking the street. Attached to the wall in the coldest part of my apartment, it triggered the antiquated heater to run too often. "So, you're talking about the NSA now?"

"Right," Marconi said. She licked her fork. "Our boss, a guy named Laraby, had been NSA for two decades before taking over as director here in Alexandria. He and Jack made several appointments with Laraby's old acquaintances and passed along information concerning the murders. The NSA acted interested, but those folks soon left Laraby and Jack behind and used Manny as a direct contact for their own purposes. Jack became enamored with the entire business and soon hit up Director Laraby to reference an application to be an NSA agent. We married in November 1995, then Jack resigned from his city job in January 1996.

"You're talking a year after the murders occurred?" I asked.

"Right. A federal district court had stymied the homicide division the whole previous spring and summer."

"I still don't get why a district court got involved," I said.

Marconi scraped her fork across her plate one last time. "You know as much as I do. Jack trained with NSA for only a short time before he announced one day he was off to Prague for his first assignment, partnered with this guy named Manny."

"It all happened fast," Eddie said. "I remember you missing work off and on."

"Yes...I was pregnant."

"What? I had no idea, sister. What happened?"

"I only shared the news with my parents and Jack, and he wasn't happy about it at all. He never even told his parents about the pregnancy or that I miscarried in my first trimester. He and Manny left on their trip, and he never said much when he got back."

I had yet to figure out why everyone thought Jack Marconi was such a great guy. I changed the subject. "Your chronology is helping me. I'm sorry if it's hard to talk about."

"Yeah, let's present a timeline to the commissioner on Monday. That might help—he'll need a reminder." She leaned hard against the couch's arm, her right hand dangling the fork around when she made a point. "So, after a second trip, Jack comes back and tells me Manny up and quit."

"Wait, I remember this part," Eddie said. He stood, moved to the picture window, a few snowflakes blowing against it. "He told me a guy that joined up with him said he had had enough. It was Manny?"

"Yeah, had to be. Jack grew suspicious of the whole affair. He said Manny acted funny on his last trip to Prague, whatever that meant. I tried to get Jack to quit, too—I wanted him to come back to the police force."

I stood and stretched my back. "These dots are even less connected than before we started. We have a recent murder in a park, and our cold case murders may relate to it. There are competing nationalities here that escaped wars in southeast Europe and might be responsible for these troubles. Now you've told me your husband went from a detective job to an NSA agent, and his Croat friend acted as an informant and owns a local bar. And somehow, all this may intertwine with Prague murders from the nineties? What the hell?"

Marconi crossed her arms. "You sound confused."

I blew out my cheeks. "I may have made the wrong choice in taking this job. This is the most convoluted mess I've ever—"

"Sit. There's more," she said.

"I hope so." I plopped so hard a dust bunny shot out from under the couch toward the TV.

"This is only the first layer. How about more coffee?" she asked.

So far, the facts came at me like moths fluttering around a bulb.

She combed through her bangs with her fingers. "Jack disappeared on his fourth trip to Prague in April 1996. I was unclear what he was investigating and had no way of knowing if it related to any detective work he did with the city. It devastated Director Laraby, knowing he had helped Jack get his NSA job and thinking I blamed him. I didn't, but Laraby never seemed the same. He took early retirement the next year. We had an interim director before the biggest dumbass took over. Luckily, I had moved away, and I worked in Norfolk for a few years. In 2014, they asked me to come back as director, and I've been here ever since."

I flipped to a new page on my notepad. "Please tell me the circumstances of Jack's death. I don't want you to have to relive it, but it would help me understand."

"Okay. Laraby came in on a Monday morning,

called me into his office, and asked me when I had last talked to Jack. I said it had been over a week. That's when he told me the NSA had lost track of him until that Sunday night—the local authorities had found his body in Stromovka Park, and his body…wasn't complete."

Eddie shot me a glare.

"How did they decide the body—?"

"The torso still had his identification in a pants pocket. The same ritual, though, plus the mask I told you about that the killer had left." She shook her head and sighed. "Jack had some terrible faults, but I loved him. Why couldn't he have let it go?"

Eddie leaned against the back of the couch and put his hand on her shoulder. "Because he was a great cop, that's why. Jack talked to me a lot when he worked for us. I'm sure he loved you very much. He did his duty."

"And that got him killed."

"All we can do is keep plugging away like we've been doing all these years," Eddie said. "And now, we've got the Wonder Kid to help us."

"I need to ask a few more questions to clarify things if you're up to it," I said. Marconi shook her head, and Eddie stepped to the window, his back to us.

He pulled the drapes closed. "Before we continue, a black Chevy SUV has been sitting in the empty lot. The windows have a bit of tint, but I can make out two occupants. I think the engine is running."

"Shit." Marconi hopped to her feet, crept to the window, and pulled the drape aside enough to see the vehicle.

"Might be a drug deal or something," I said.

"What kind of neighborhood is this?" Eddie asked.

A door slammed, and an argument spilled into the hall next to my door. "See?"

"Keep an eye out," Marconi said. "Turn off the lamp. Let's move into the kitchen."

I cleared off the breakfast table while Eddie stood in the shadows watching our watchers.

"Call Dick Forman, Eddie. Have him drive by and get a plate number," Marconi said.

"Will do. I can only see a part of it from here."

My colleagues had put me in a spot. Now unknown people knew where I lived, and none of this had helped with the Angel Park murder.

"Okay, we have the events lined up," I said. "This presentation we're putting together will help me understand things. But there are so many—"

"Pieces missing? What do you suggest?" Marconi asked.

"I'm trying to comprehend how this latest murder might connect to the old murders and how your husband died in Prague while investigating those cases."

"Right. The other murders in Prague were similar…according to Jack. No hands, head, etcetera."

"Thank you. What I would like to do is show a timeline and overlay these crimes. I talked to David Wulz before I left yesterday. He actually helped me carry the case boxes to my car, and he said the breast pocket of our latest victim had crumbs of something in it. The creek rose, soaking the torso, and he couldn't define what was in the pocket other than a piece of a baked good."

She fidgeted and smoothed out her tight sweater. "It seems a connection, doesn't it?"

"It's looking like it," Eddie said. "Hey, the SUV took off. I never noticed Forman drive by."

"Interesting. Forman's usually prompt," she said, "except for writing up his reports."

"When it drove off, I noticed the plates started with a 'D' and ended in three-three-six."

"District tags? Okay. Anything will help. Call Dick if you want or talk to him on Monday and see if he can narrow it down."

"I'll try him."

"Would you be willing to listen to a little conjecture on my part?" I asked.

Marconi chewed away on a piece of her gum. She threw up her hands. "That's why you're here. You know, you remind me of Jack. That guy had it together. Please conjecture away."

Eddie snooped through my cabinet until he found two bottles of liquor. "Hang on. I'm sitting for this part." He poured Irish cream into his coffee and stirred with the dirty fork's handle. He sat on the arm of the couch and grinned. "Now…go ahead."

"Okay. I think we can relate the old murders to the current, but I don't think it's committed by the same person. Maybe a copycat or a new generation—I don't know. It's likely connected to ethnic issues, or someone has used it as an excuse to reignite old grievances. The time I've had for research has yielded no similar murders, at least on the east coast. I discovered stories of two beheadings in San Diego in 2007, but the police determined those killings were Mexican gangs fighting over territory."

Eddie put his phone back in his pocket. "No answer from Forman."

"Are the murders linkable to other criminal activity going on?" I asked.

"The robberies?" Eddie asked. "Yeah, it's probably linked to the Kastratis at least. That's not new."

"That's where I'm headed—the Kastrati Koffee and *Bakery* shops. When we had our cinnamon rolls the other day, I noticed several kinds of pastries when I came back from the bathroom. One of Kastrati's employees pulled out a tray of unsold rolls labeled Navrtka—those have nuts. From what I found out, it's a Bosnian version of Orehnjaca."

"Crap." Marconi spat her gum in a napkin.

"And something else. The torso in Angel Park, according to Coroner Wulz, had a tattoo on its lower back that said *Uradi sve što je Potrebno.*"

Eddie frowned. "What?"

"Serbian. It means 'Do Whatever is Needed.'"

"Interesting. Can we differentiate between those two pastries?" Marconi asked.

"I doubt it," I said. "Say, Eddie, who decided the pockets from the old cases had Orehnjaca in them?" I asked. "Who would know that and where the information comes from?"

"Not sure—a story got passed around. It might be in your paperwork there somewhere."

"There isn't a lot of difference between the two pastries, although sometimes the Bosnian recipe will have dried fruit as an ingredient and cooks longer— that's according to a recipe on the internet, so it must be true." I imitated one of her smirks.

Marconi's lips tightened together into a slight frown. "Eddie, why didn't Wulz advise me about his report? Shouldn't I be aware?"

Eddie shrugged.

"Wulz told me yesterday in the parking lot on the way to my car," I said. "He mentioned he would have a report for you Monday morning."

"He'd better. Eddie, can you remind me to call David first thing? He needs to work again on his procedures."

"Sure, Angie. I doubt David meant anything by it."

Marconi ignored him. "Okay, we think there's a good chance old hatred is still lurking, but what are the motivations? How do the robberies fit into all this, or do they? If this Angel Park victim was a Serb, maybe the ones in 1995 were Serbs, too?"

"It's possible," Eddie said. "The robberies around the Masonic memorial occurred near the Serbian community, if that means anything. There's an old, busted strip mall in the middle of the neighborhood."

"Has Forman filed his report yet after his investigation?" I asked.

"I haven't seen it." Marconi glared at Eddie. "We need to press on this—hard. I want Wulz in my office at eight a.m. and Dick Forman at eight-thirty. You need to be there for both."

Eddie clenched his jaws and sighed. "We'll be there. But Pierce, why would a robbery turn into an ethnic murder? I can't close that circle."

"The robberies occurred at pawnshops, the closest one near the burger joint you like," I said.

"Pawnshops," Marconi repeated. "They could have been looking for anything."

"Guns?" Eddie asked.

"Possibly," I answered. "We need motivations and how it ties together. I have another question."

Marconi covered her mouth to hide a yawn. "One more, Henry. I'm exhausted." I offered no sympathy. She showed up late to get this started.

I pushed away my coffee cup. "Who is Nika Campbell? How did you know her name and that I came back early after my meal?"

She stood as Eddie's phone rang. "Answer that, Eddie. Henry, you won't believe it. We have layers of crap on top of crap. My advice, for now, is don't go on any more dates with Ms. Campbell."

Eddie held his phone away from his mouth. "Angie."

"I hadn't intended to. But, again, how do you know Nika Campbell?" I asked.

Eddie shouted. "Angie, listen."

"What?"

"Someone phoned in a call about an unmarked brown Chevy parked and idling in the library parking lot." I heard chatter through his phone from the other end of the conversation.

"What do you mean, unmarked?"

"It's Dick Forman's car, Angie."

She grabbed her coat and purse. "Come on, guys. It's starting again."

****

The brown Chevrolet sat alone in the parking lot near the orange-bricked library's front entrance, its colonnaded portico reminding me of Jefferson's home at Monticello. The parking lot's bright white lights cast a glow on a copse of leafless birch trees surrounding the lot. Yellow police tape wrapped around and between three poles.

Two patrol cars and an EMT unit sat nearby, their

flashing red and blue lights reflecting against the library's windows. A policeman waved at Eddie and directed us to park next to the ambulance. The Ford's brakes squealed as we rolled to a stop.

Marconi threw open her door. "Update, guys." She ducked under the tape, then marched closer to the Chevy.

Eddie and I hurried to follow, the bitter night wind whipping around us. Wes stopped a few feet from the driver's door with its shattered window. "That's Dick's car for sure," Eddie said. "Who's the primary here?"

The female officer nodded toward Eddie and me, then addressed our boss. "I'm Officer Krista Jimenez. This is Officer Stewart and Officer Miller. I was on routine patrol when I noticed this Chevrolet with its lights on, but I couldn't see anyone in the driver's seat. I drove into the lot and investigated. The driver's window had been shattered inward, a body slumped to the right into the passenger seat. I called for backup and an ambulance."

Jimenez hesitated, waiting for a reaction. Marconi said nothing while Eddie fidgeted with his holster. "I found a significant blood pool from an obvious wound to the victim's head. I leaned in and checked for a pulse in his arm. The EMT unit arrived and confirmed he was deceased."

Marconi cupped a hand over her mouth and shut her eyes. She grabbed Eddie's right arm and pulled him toward her. "Come on." They approached the car with me following. Marconi peered through the smashed window. "Oh, God…his family."

Eddie stepped back, leaning against a light pole while Marconi pulled her phone–I glanced into the car.

Dick had fallen to his right, blood covering the seats with spatter spread across the passenger window.

"What the hell, Eddie?" I asked. "He was supposed to be driving by my apartment."

Eddie wiped his face. "Yeah…this isn't a random shooting."

"How do you know?"

"I've done this for almost forty years, my friend. That's how I know."

Marconi grabbed Eddie's shoulder, clutching her phone in a fist in her other hand. "I called Commissioner Bates. He'll follow protocol and contact Dick's wife for body I.D. God, Eddie, you never can tell in this line of work."

"Something's not right with this," he said.

She swiped at her bangs, then sighed. "Yeah…why was Dick parked at the library at eleven o'clock?"

Chapter Five

The following two days became a fog of plans, discussions, comings and goings, back and forth to police headquarters. Saturday night had turned into Sunday morning while the department came together to investigate Dick Forman's death. Coroner Wulz refused to autopsy one of his co-workers, so Marconi located a coroner from Arlington to take over his duties. Dog tired by the time I returned to my apartment late Sunday evening, I flopped on the couch and fell asleep. One hell of a first week.

The alarm went off too soon Monday morning. Marconi had told us not to come to work until noon—they had canceled her meeting with Commissioner Bates. A welcome respite, as I wanted to gather my notes from Saturday night and get organized before returning the boxes of evidence to the work basement. I had collected a wealth of information, but the cold cases, and even my Angel Park investigation, would become a lower priority.

I'd grabbed a ham and cheddar cheese sandwich at the deli near my office when my phone rang. "Pierce? Could you come on in instead of waiting until noon?" Eddie asked. Exhaustion seemed to strain his voice.

"Almost there. I'm finishing up my sandwich from Walt's."

"You're at Walt's? Man, I would do anything for some food. I can imagine the smell. Please bring me corned beef on rye with lots of their spicy mustard. I'll pay you double what it costs. And chips and the same thing for the director. She just walked in and said she's starving, too."

Although only a hundred feet from our offices' front door, I pivoted and headed back to the deli. I doubted either of them had slept in two days. After dropping off their lunches at the reception desk, I took the evidence boxes to the basement, then returned to Marconi's suite.

Kate sat in her usual spot. She offered no verbal response when I appeared but motioned with her head to go into the office.

"Henry, come in. I'm starving." Marconi leaned against the edge of her desk, still in the same clothes from Saturday night. "Hey, Kate, take half my sandwich."

Kate peered in, scratching her protruding belly. "Yes, ma'am. I didn't realize it was close to noon."

Eddie grabbed his sandwich, then sat next to a massive man in civilian clothes, bald, and wearing a gray Manchu mustache. "Thanks, Pierce. My first thing to eat since the cheesecake."

"Detective Pierce, I would like you to meet Archer Sullivan. He works undercover for us," Marconi said. She spat her Nicorette into the trash and stuffed her mouth full of nacho cheese chips.

Archer stood and offered a trembling right hand, "Call me Archie. Eddie and Angie have filled me in." He took a step toward the door.

"Good to meet you, Archie. It's been an eventful week."

"Archie helped take care of Dick Forman's

arrangements," Marconi said. "It's devastated Harriett, as you'd expect. She's flying both her kids home as soon as she can."

"It's terrible," I said.

Archie strode over to a file cabinet and slammed a drawer shut. "Dick was a good man. Why did they do it?"

Eddie wiped his mouth of mustard clinging to his lips. "They? Who are you talking about?"

Archie didn't reply.

Marconi ignored them. "So, Henry, the SUV had parked by your apartment and then disappeared before Dick drove by. Since he was out and wide awake, his phone showed he had messaged Archie to go with him to get a snack. Archie had worked on a drug bust in north Alexandria, and they decided to meet at the library. Archie said he was on the way when he heard the report. The shooter marched up and shot him straight through the glass, shattering the window and killing Dick. He never drew his gun."

"Are there any ballistics reports yet?" I asked.

"It's a .357," Eddie offered.

Marconi took a deep breath. "The Arlington coroner mentioned the bullet went all the way through his head. It lodged in the passenger door."

"Dick found several guns had disappeared during the pawnshop robberies," I said.

"Right. I meant to look at that report," she said.

"Yes, ma'am. I called on my way in and talked to ballistics. Dick's partially written report noted the pawnshop had three guns stolen—two .44s and a .357."

Archie wiped the sweat off his head. Both hands trembled. "Maybe someone watched him when he went out there to investigate last week. What day again?"

Eddie seemed perplexed. "I can't even…Wednesday, Thursday?"

"Yes, yes," Marconi said. "Everything is running together. Archie, I want you back out there. Tell Tim to take over the north side drug investigation, tell him those are my orders, and no piddling around. Good God, I can't imagine a simple call to track down the SUV caused all this."

Eddie would pound me for this later.

"Listen, I called this morning first thing," I said. "Those bits of a license plate number Eddie saw—"

"I planned to do that."

"Sorry, Eddie. There's a woman at the District's DMV."

"A girl again." Eddie rolled his eyes.

"It's not that. But using the letters and numbers, we have variations of up to two hundred sixty vehicles. None matched the SUV across the street from my apartment."

"Stolen plates?" Marconi asked.

"Possibly."

"Okay. Is there more?" Marconi asked. She clasped her hands around the back of her neck.

"Yes. One variation showed a license plate registered to a Farid Kastrati. It's a plate for a Hummer."

"That has to be a relative," Marconi said.

"It wasn't a Hummer out there across the street—it was a Chevrolet SUV," Eddie said. "I don't understand. Rijad Kastrati might be a little crooked, but I never suspected his bunch capable of murder."

"I don't think it's him," Marconi said. "His family,

though …"

"Hang on," I said. "We need to prove it's more than a coincidence. The perps may act dumb or say someone stole the plate. The good news is, we have the tire track analysis complete. Those tracks are common to a pickup or SUV."

"There's a lot of those around," Eddie said.

"True," Marconi said while picking bread out of her teeth. "Archie, put a watch on the Kastratis. Keep an eye out for a black SUV at both of their bakery locations. Eddie, you and Henry go to the main coffee shop at eight-thirty sharp tomorrow morning. I'll meet you there, and we'll find out about those plates. And I need that damned DNA analysis on the Angel Park body. I know it's preliminary, but something…anything. No one is any more affected by Dick's death than the rest of us, and I need Wulz to get on with it."

"Yes, ma'am," Eddie said.

"Forman's funeral services are Wednesday at two o'clock. It would be nice to make an arrest before then." She slapped her desk, then asked, "And Detective Pierce?"

"Yes?"

"You see what loose lips may cause?" she asked.

"My comment at the coffee shop about the robbery?"

"Yes. If Kastrati wasn't alerted—"

"Dick might be alive?" I hadn't considered it. My verbal slip in front of Kastrati may have set off this whole chain reaction that led to Forman's murder. "God, I wouldn't have—"

"I'm not accusing you, Henry, but I'm saying this

is an excellent example of why we keep our mouths shut."

"Yes, ma'am."

"I'll see you all in the morning at eight-thirty sharp."

Eddie took me aside on my way out the door. "A bad first week, son," he said.

Something else bothered me, though, but the police station was the last place to talk.

****

The four funerals I remembered attending had been days full of sunshine. A coincidence, maybe, or perhaps not. Even my dad's burial on a January day two years earlier was beneath a brilliant sun in the frigid wind. Another wintry day, but one so bright, we all needed sunglasses standing near the casket. My first funeral for a police officer was harder than I would have guessed, especially for someone I had known a few days. The uniforms of a hundred police officers from Alexandria and surrounding communities attended the service for one of our own.

Our visit to Rijad Kastrati's bakery had been fruitless. He mentioned Farid, his brother, but this Farid died in Bosnia in 1996. The only other Farid he admitted to knowing was a great uncle, still alive in a village on the border of Bosnia and Montenegro.

The evening after the funeral, I sat on my couch munching from a can of Pringles. A call from Eddie.

"Pierce? We need to talk."

"Go ahead."

"I have concerns about an issue from Dick's murder, but I want you to keep this between us. Our ducks have to be in a row before we let Angie in."

Who is this 'we' he's referring to? I wanted to keep my nose clean after last week. "What are you thinking?"

"How did someone find out Dick would be at the library?"

I hesitated but asked, "Eddie, how well do you know Archie Sullivan?"

"Bingo. We are thinking the same, young man. And to answer your question, hardly at all. Angie brought him into the department five years ago for undercover work. She heard good things about him when she worked down at Norfolk. Archie and his partners busted two drug cartels that shipped into Norfolk for distribution to the naval base. He made a name for himself, and she put him on the same duty here. He's always mobile and seems to avoid headquarters as much as possible. Archie's had no major busts for a while, so I'm not sure what he's doing. I talked to Angie once about him, and she blew it off. She didn't act interested in my questions, and figured drug issues are more of a district problem than an Alexandria one. Archie keeps plugging away, doing whatever he's doing."

"Sullivan is the only one Forman would've told about the library, right?"

"Right. The SUV had disappeared the other night before Dick drove by, so I don't see how anyone other than Archie would have known. The library has no cameras in the parking lot."

"And another thing I noticed—"

"Yeah?" A long sigh came through the phone's speaker, then silence except for a clock ticking.

"Sullivan stayed quiet when we discussed that

license plate. He stayed involved in our conversation about the guns until the plate number came up, then he folded his arms and stood there like a lump after I mentioned it."

"Pierce…we got us a crooked cop."

"I thought so but hesitated to say anything after my screwup last week."

"Don't let that stop you. Yes, you need to be aware of…anyway, back to Archie. I've seen him carry a .357 sometimes, not always. He didn't carry one the other day."

"Is there any way we could get ballistics to match the bullet that killed Forman?"

"We have to be a thousand percent sure about this. Getting access to Archie's gun will cause a commotion." Eddie sighed again. "Oh, this makes my heart ache. One of our own people sneaking up and assassinating someone, supposedly his friend."

"Yeah. Is this tangled with the Angel Park murder? I'm jumping ahead here, but what if this involves Archie Sullivan? Maybe Dick found out something?"

Another sigh. "God, I hope it's only Archie. Once that virus is around, it can infect a bunch of people."

"Can you back me up if I work on something for the director?"

"Sure. What're you up to?"

"I took our I.T. guy Wonder Woman comics, and now he likes me better."

Eddie sputtered. "Lord, no telling what Rowe does with those magazines."

"No comment, but I can access our online records from my apartment. I'm set up, and I can work from here this weekend. Will Angie be up to meeting with us on Monday? I have several avenues I need to pursue, including the Kastratis' finances."

"I'm all for it, Pierce. You call me back Sunday night, though, and give me a heads up about what you've found. Angie is a good boss, but we want to stay on her best side. She let you off easy last week. She can be a handful if you cross her."

"Got it." I didn't want another black mark this soon.

"And Pierce?"

"Yes, sir."

"Can I call you something besides Henry? My high school principal had that name, and all he ever did was beat my butt."

"My family calls me Ike, my middle name. But few other people outside my family—"

"Great. Thank you, Ike, for all your hard work."

"Sure. We'll talk soon."

****

"Commissioner Bates, this is Henry Pierce." Marconi had gotten her meeting with the commissioner eight days after they canceled the last one because of Forman's assassination. "He's one of the new detectives we've talked about and is working the Angel Park case for us."

"We met briefly last month, right, Detective Pierce? Director Marconi and I have discussed your hire a few times. Eddie Stone has been a great help over the years, and I've known the coroner almost as long. Too bad he's not here…anyone?"

"I haven't heard from him," Marconi answered after glancing at Eddie.

Eddie didn't look up and straightened the end of

his tie, a teal one, no doubt with a Jaguars football logo at the bottom.

I tried offering my right hand, the one holding my coffee mug. "Uh…yes, my brief time here has been eventful," I said.

Bates glanced at my cup. "Yes, it has. We want to stay busy, but what a mess." He had a mass of gray hair in a pompadour style, reminding me of a preacher my grandmother watched on Sunday mornings. "All right, let's get started. I have a noon lunch with an assistant city manager. They want to know how and why we got one of our own men killed, and they want to know today."

"Commissioner, I've asked Detective Pierce to offer a summation of Dick Forman's death and investigation," Marconi said. "And if time allows, the Angel Park murder needs review."

"Great. Detective Pierce, let's see what you've got."

My palms sweaty and my throat dry, I picked up a bottle, gulped my water, and then handed out summary sheets of information I had printed. The dirty, white plastic blinds on the windows remained open, so anyone walking by could see us.

My voice shook. "I appreciate the opportunity to review this information and offer ideas about these murders." I grabbed my coffee cup and swallowed a mouthful, burning my tongue and throat. Sputtering a bit, I said, "The coroner working this case believes Sergeant Forman died between ten and eleven p.m. on Saturday night last week. Lieutenant Stone received a call at eleven-fifteen that one of our unmarked cars was idling in the library's parking lot. The EMT squad pronounced Forman dead before we arrived. We returned to the police station by midnight to begin our investigation."

Bates followed along. "Who is the *we* you're talking about?"

"Lieutenant Stone and Director Marconi came to my apartment to review the Angel Park murder, and possibly, the related cold cases, when we received the phone call."

"Fun Saturday night, huh? Director, I'd guessed you'd want to dust off those 1995 murders. It came back to me when I thought about the Angel Park body. But let's not get sidetracked. Detective Pierce, let's stay with the Forman murder, and then we will discuss Angel Park. It's easy to get lost in the weeds on all this."

"It certainly is." I glanced at Marconi's expressionless face. "Dick had investigated a pawnshop robbery near the Masonic Memorial. It involved guns—two .45s, a .357, and we found out, an antique shotgun. The cash register remained locked, and they didn't jimmy it."

"Who owns this pawnshop?"

"Aleksandar Stanich."

Bates rubbed his forehead. "Hell."

"He's the patriarch of a Serbian family that's been in this country since late 1999 after the NATO bombing of Belgrade. They own three other pawnshops in Arlington and one in Fredericksburg. The businesses have done well over the years."

"Yeah, yeah, Stanich is familiar."

"Right. Stanich claimed the missing shotgun as an heirloom from the second world war. He said he told

Dick Forman his father fought with the Chetnik guerrillas against the Nazis and then against Tito's communists, and his father acted as a close aide to Draža Mihailović, the movement's leader."

Bates continued to listen carefully without distraction from his vibrating phone. "I didn't know all that history, but no matter, Stanich is a jackass. Any evidence collected? Fingerprints...cameras on the premises?"

"The cameras are fake," I said. "Mr. Stanich did not want to incur the expense. Sergeant Forman had found two sets of fingerprints, limited though since the perpetrators appeared to have tried to wipe the place down. One set we've identified as Bekić Čazim, a brother-in-law of Rijad Kastrati."

Bates emitted a groan worthy of a toothache. "Hell. The Kastratis involvement doesn't shock me as far as the robberies go, but murder?"

"Our thoughts, too, Commissioner," Eddie said. "That family always seems to be on the periphery of many illegalities. We finally tracked down Čazim as the Chevy SUV owner, black like the one we noticed outside Detective Pierce's apartment. It had stolen plates, or someone had switched them. They had it registered in the name of a long-dead brother of Rijad Kastrati. That's why Dick was out that night, looking for the SUV parked outside Detective Pierce's apartment."

"Okay. Let's bring Čazim in for questioning."

"Yes, sir," Marconi said.

"Detective Pierce, does the second set of prints belong to another Kastrati associate?"

"No, sir."

"Who then?"

Marconi interrupted. "It's Archie Sullivan."

"What?" Bates squinted at her as if looking at the sun.

"I know—it's unbelievable."

"Shit. A dirty cop. God, wait until the newspapers get hold of this."

"I have more," I said.

"More?"

"The ballistics on the bullet that killed Dick Forman track it back to a gun stolen from Stanich's pawn shop."

"Holy hell," Bates mumbled.

Marconi rubbed her forehead. "Archie was the only one Dick Foreman had contacted, supposedly meeting him at the library for a late snack, and we concluded he had to be the shooter. Who else, unless random?"

"Random? No way...but a cop killing a cop. I would never have believed it." Bates grabbed his phone and called his assistant. "Pam? Cancel my lunch with Wallace. Get me an emergency meeting with the mayor, city manager, and our idiot public information officer. Tell them it concerns Dick Forman's murder. We've had a breakthrough." He pitched his phone back on the conference table and rubbed his eyes. "I've been in law enforcement for over thirty years and never had to deal with this. It makes me sick to my stomach."

"Uh, sir, there's more." I cringed.

He stared at the ceiling. "Give it to me."

"Our analysis of the tire tracks at the Angel Park murder show it is likely from an SUV or similar vehicle. And one more thing," I mumbled.

"Go on."

"We found pine needles at Angel Park, but that section of the park has no pine trees. The needles came from Pitch Pine trees, which are the same species growing behind the strip mall with the pawnshop."

Bates rubbed his forehead again and stared at his phone. "Fine…that's likely where they did it. God, I hate this for Dick's family. But we might as well move on to the Angel Park murder. My assistant changed my other meeting to three o'clock this afternoon, and now I have a little time."

I took a deep breath and continued. "We believe Čazim is a person of interest in the Angel Park murder, or at least it's planning. We can't be certain one way or another whether Sullivan wasn't also a participant—"

"Oh, no."

"—whether Sullivan wasn't also a participant or even the Kastrati clan—"

Eddie waved a hand. "Sir, I've been concerned about Rijad Kastrati for a long time. His bunch runs the Bosnian community like a poor man's Mafioso. But I'm surprised by the way this has turned. Again, I wouldn't have guessed Rijad's bunch would get into murder."

Marconi rubbed her hands together. "I don't think it's him, at least directly."

Bates nodded. "I get it. You've investigated or watched over his gang for many years, and it's natural to think you 'know' someone. But I must tell you this reminds me of a case I had in Baltimore many years ago. We tracked Irish Mob thugs, but it turned out they were much more sophisticated than we thought, reaching into the worst neighborhoods in the city. We finally arrested a dozen and charged them with fifteen murders."

"Yes, sir…something seems off, though," Eddie said.

"Let's see where the rest of this may lead. We have much more," Marconi said.

Bates put up his right hand. "Okay, okay. I see on this summary sheet you labeled Angel Park info about Serbs, Bosnians, a tattoo, and so on. Let's breeze through these bullet points and wrap this up. I want Čazim and Sullivan under arrest before I have my meeting today."

"I would discourage that, sir," I said. "Not about Sullivan, but if we arrest Čazim too soon, we may cut off any opportunity to pull in others."

"How so?"

"Let's announce Archie Sullivan's arrest. He must be the one who pulled the trigger on Dick Forman. Leave Čazim out there sweating and see what else we can find," I said.

"Pierce, I'm a little hesitant to leave a murderer out in public," Bates mentioned.

"This may track back to the 1995 murders," Marconi said.

"The dismemberment murders?" Bates cocked his head to the right. "Come on, director," Bates said, his voice growing louder. "We worked on those cases over two decades ago. Do we just *want* it to be related?"

Marconi's face reddened. "Commissioner, I believe from the evidence our team is putting together that Dick Forman's death is a sideshow to something much bigger. It could lead to not only solving the Angel Park murder but the 1995 murders, too. It may even lead us back to the Prague killings my late husband investigated."

Bates sat back in his chair and hurled a sigh. "Angie, you've got to stop the Captain Ahab routine. Moby Dick, in this case, is a myth. This has gone on for how long?" Bates glanced at the table, then back toward her. "Nevertheless, I'll keep the faith. But Angie?"

She wiped her eyes and sighed. "Yes?"

"Call someone and get Sullivan in the tank."

"Already on it. I've been getting messages. Archie was on an assignment this morning, or that's what we thought. We found him leaving Kastrati's new coffee shop at nine-fifteen, then tracked him to an Arlington neighborhood where we arrested him. He's cooling his heels."

"Arlington? Message your contact and tell them to keep him isolated. I don't want this getting out yet."

"Will do."

"Now, Pierce," Bates showed a smile so tight I thought his face would shatter, "tell me what else."

"Čazim is a brother-in-law to Kastrati…and he is a former son-in-law of Stanich's."

Bates stroked his gray pompadour like a cat grooming itself.

"He married Stanich's youngest daughter, they separated in 2018, and the divorce became final in early 2019. No children and definitely not amicable," I said.

"We think the Angel Park victim is Serbian, and he was tied to Stanich?"

"The victim had a tattoo in Serbian. I can trace the specific phrase in the tattoo to paramilitary squads during the Bosnian War. However, this victim appears too young to connect directly to the war. Stanich told me about his three daughters—one became estranged after marrying 'outside his community' as he called it. He said he had no sons but admitted to having three nephews he's supported since his brother died. We should get DNA samples."

"Yes, yes, please arrange it. The lieutenant's girlfriend works in our lab, right, Eddie?"

"She's not my girlfriend."

He winked at Eddie. "So, how do we get a DNA test without causing a crap storm?"

"We'll come up with something," Marconi said.

I continued. "Sir, I believe Čazim or an associate killed one of the Stanich family or associates and then tried to make it seem a serial killer had returned from the nineties. But the current killer missed something. They had not treated the body at Angel Park exactly the same—someone detached the legs this time…and the nut rolls in the pockets."

"Excuse me?"

"The 1995 murder victims had Orehnjaca in their breast pockets. I found Sam Wulz's notes."

"That's great," Eddie said. "After all this time, I wondered if it was only a story."

"I wondered myself, but the older Dr. Wulz mentioned in his report that he had identified it as a Serbian nut roll by the ingredients," I said.

Bates shouted. "Good God, I remember now, but what does it have to do with this?" Even in the chilly room, sweat formed on his reddened forehead.

"Our latest murder also had a nut roll stuffed in the victim's pocket, but with further analysis, we've found this roll had raisins and dried apricot pieces as ingredients."

Bates leaned back in his chair and clasped his

hands behind his head. "I don't feel like trading recipes. What are you telling us?"

"This version of the nut roll is Bosnian and called Navrtka. It's on sale at Kastrati's shops."

"Got it. Okay, more good evidence, but still circumstantial. Why again do you want to wait for Čazim's arrest?"

"Commissioner, Detective Pierce found a few old tax records," Eddie said. "I examined those, and they're from around the time of Čazim's marriage into the Stanich family. Rijad Kastrati and Aleksandar Stanich had a short-lived partnership in the strip shopping center, Stanich Plaza, that housed the pawnshop and offered a storefront for one of Kastrati's bakeries. That's how Rijad got to know Bekić Čazim. When Čazim divorced, the shopping center partnership dissolved, and there has been even more bad blood since then."

"So Kastrati is likely involved in all this whether or not he pulled the trigger?"

"On the periphery, at least, it looks that way," Marconi said.

Bates turned back to me. "Detective Pierce, you mentioned the cold case murders. What's the connection to this?"

"That's a little more tenuous." Weak, unsubstantiated, shaky—I wasn't sure which synonym to use. "Those bodies might be Bosnian, local Serbs could have killed them, and the calling card was the nut roll. I would recommend disinterring—"

"We've already tried that." Veins throbbed on Bates' temples. "Angie, didn't you give him the background on this? You should have."

"I did, but we had no evidence back then, substantiated or unsubstantiated, to offer the judge. This incident might help," she said.

Eddie shook his head. "It's worth a try."

"Okay, let's stay hot on this," Bates said. "The nut roll thing is a start…I guess…but it's not enough for evidence—"

"The feds stepped in," Eddie volunteered.

"Oh, right, the federal judges. Director?" Bates asked.

"The latest murder may justify a disinterment if we can relate it close enough to the Angel Park investigation. It would make it harder to turn down," Marconi said.

"True." Bates spun his telephone on the table. "You all are doing an impressive job of pulling all this together. We're about to bring Forman's killer to justice, and we're on the right track with everything else. Let's meet this Friday morning. Keep a watch on Čazim and anyone else we need to haul in on the Angel Park murder. We may open old wounds in these communities, so any conflicts will fall back on us."

"Sir, I have two comments to make under the heading 'Other Items.'"

Bates wasn't listening. His assistant entered without knocking, leaned over, and whispered.

Marconi, waiting on a response, opened her hands toward the ceiling. "Well?"

The assistant stood straight, then walked away. Bates had grown pale as the conference room wall. "Archie Sullivan is dead. He grabbed a deputy's gun and killed himself."

Chapter Six

I gazed out the window on Saturday morning—a fresh dusting of snow blanketed my car. My apartment was chilly again, but, no matter, my urge for coffee drove me into the kitchen after bumping up the thermostat. Sitting on my couch in my underwear and house shoes was not the best way to get warm while waiting on the coffeemaker. I dug under cushions hunting for the TV remote, then grabbed my maroon Hokies blanket off the floor.

Our local news ran hot with the murder and suicide of local cops. I flipped stations a few times and stopped on national news. Migration from North Africa to southeast Europe was the topic, and an older man with a bushy-gray mustache stood for an interview in front of the Truman Building. His cheeks rosy red from the cold, he tried several times to cut the reporter short. Right behind him stood two aides, both young women with heavy coats and earmuffs. The blonde's teeth chattered, but the brunette...those big, brown eyes. Nika Campbell. She didn't seem to suffer from the cold, and I pictured her again in the short dress she wore on our date. The coffee machine beeped, and I distracted myself with a good dose of Irish cream.

A hot shower, then I thought again of Nika. But why? Her personality flip-flop, dumping me off early on our date, and the constant giggle. Then, Angie Marconi's curiosity about her—how did she know her name before I mentioned it? And Marconi waiting for me at my apartment when I returned, then warning me to stay away from Nika? My detective's brain jumped into overdrive, but I needed groceries instead of worrying about Nika.

****

A typical return to my apartment—me struggling to hold grocery bags, keys, and phone while trying to get through the door. My mother chattered on about Christmas and how she missed me at Thanksgiving.

"Okay, Mom. I promise I'll try to be there. Christmas is on a Saturday, so I'll ask for Friday off. But I'm the new guy, and my request will be at the bottom of the pile. If that doesn't work, I'll drive down Christmas morning."

"Wait…I have a great idea, Ike. Granny and I can come up there on Christmas Eve and stay for the weekend."

"Okay, but remember I told you my apartment is tiny." I would give up my bed and couch—time to shop for a blow-up mattress.

"We have to see you. We want to see your new car, too."

"It's a 2015 model, Mom. It's only new to me."

"Anything is better than the heap you used to drive around."

"Okay, I'll talk to you soon. I need to put away my groceries."

"I hope you're eating lots of protein—watch the sugar. Wear protection if you go on any dates. Okay? Love you. Bye-bye."

I made a sandwich and warmed up the coffee. Finishing my grout-scrubbing project came next. Dark grout held the countertop's tiny red tiles, but my cleaning had changed it to a light gray. My mid-seventies apartment had had few updates. Beige linoleum covered the floors of the kitchen, living room, and bathroom. The tan carpet in the bedroom looked newer, but I feared sitting on it with so many darker hues scattered in spots. It would need a good shampooing before Christmas.

No matter its faults, I would improve this place. Anything would be better than my old apartment, much nicer, but it came with a lazy roommate and girlfriend, who never seemed to leave. I had too many nights listening to their headboard banging against the wall, coupled with sounds reminding me of my parents' farm.

Gobbling my sandwich and tortilla chips, I focused on Nika. If I contemplated the park murders at all, it would remind me of her questions and make me much more curious. I hesitated a few times but couldn't resist. I pulled out her business card and dialed, as jittery as the first time I called a girl in high school.

"Hello? Nika?" A few seconds of silence.

"Is this Henry, or Ike, or whatever?"

"Yes. You can call me either."

"What are you doing?"

"Not much. I saw you on TV this morning."

"Yeah, the reporter ambushed us with her TV camera. I looked terrible."

"No, no, you looked great."

"Thanks," she said. "So, the news from Alexandria revolves around crooked cops—"

"Thanks, I'm doing well. Yes, there was one bad cop."

"It seems out of control."

"It's not out of control. We've identified …" She's a sly one. "Things are settling down."

"What makes you think so?"

"I didn't call to talk about work. I thought since you bought dinner last Saturday, it could be my turn this weekend."

"Geez, Ike, you call a girl kind of late, don't you?"

"You called me later than this a week ago."

"True." There it was—a partial snicker. "But I hadn't planned to go out in this weather."

"I see."

"You sound awfully disappointed, so what if I come over and we can talk? I love Chinese. Order something out, and I'll show up around six o'clock again," she said.

"Great. I can pick you up, and we can get food on the way."

"No, Charlie will drop me off. You don't have to drive in this mess."

I offered no arguments and got back to cleaning my kitchen. With any luck, Charlie wouldn't sit outside in the BMW and wait.

****

I rolled over to my left, waking with a rough hangover after sharing two bottles of wine. A pitch-dark apartment this Sunday morning—the clock said seven-thirty, but a dark, dreary sky peeked through the curtains. Movement next to me, and my foggy memory cleared. Nika never left. Why had I let this happen? I had the food delivered, and she brought the wine, lots of conversation, and later, sex. I had grabbed my headboard, nervous the neighbors might hear. A faint groan came from under the covers.

"Oh, God, my head is exploding. Where do you keep the aspirin?"

"Cabinet, bottom shelf, left of the kitchen sink."

Nika rolled out of bed without covering herself. The nosy woman across the street would be shocked to see a naked body walking through the kitchen. She shuffled back and squirmed in next to me. "Ready for another round?"

"Look, Nika, I didn't intend on this happening. I only wanted to see you again."

"You saw me for sure. God, your apartment is so cold."

"I can turn the thermostat up again. Wait, where are my clothes?"

"Your pants and shirt are in the living room, and your maroon briefs in the kitchen for some reason."

"How about breakfast?"

She groaned. "Okay. Scrambled eggs and toast? And put your clothes on. I wouldn't want you to freeze…there."

"As you said, it's cold in here."

I dressed in the kitchen and started breakfast. Nika came strolling in and sat at the table wearing my V-Tech sweatshirt she must have dug from one of my drawers. "I hope Charlie didn't wait too long last night.

She smiled. "I told him to go on home. He's coming by soon."

I tried to hide a smile. "I feel like this is planned."

"As always." She returned a grin. "And I enjoyed talking about your time on the farm. We should do this again…a date, I mean."

"Sounds great. Here's your toast. I have apricot or

peach jam, and the eggs are ready."

"Do you have a big week coming up, Ike? With the turmoil, it must keep you busy with a lot of stress?"

"Stress isn't too bad, but I could see how years of it would wear you down."

"It's fascinating. I would have chosen a different career if I had it to do again."

"Doesn't the State Department job have interesting days?" She had offered no information last night. I handed her a plate of eggs and peeled back the aluminum cover from my strawberry yogurt. "When we've talked before, I understood you to be a lower-level employee there. Yesterday, you were on TV with the Secretary of State. *The* Secretary of State."

"Happenstance. I attend meetings concerned with immigration issues in Europe and accompanied the SoS. It's one thing I've found interesting."

"And the blonde with you?"

She rolled her eyes, then salted her eggs. "That's Bensi Jonsson—originally from Sweden and came here as a kid. SoS is fascinated with her. No doubt he's doing her but trying to keep it quiet. There's talk about them all over the Truman building."

"You're Slovenian."

She rolled her eyes again. "It's not the same."

"You attend meetings on immigration. Is that all?"

Her smile vanished, and she wiped her mouth.

"All routine stuff. I read a lot for the assistant SoS-Eastern Europe and write follow-up briefs as needed."

"At least it's a subject near the area your parents are from."

"Yeah…I'm tired of talking about that, Ike. Do you think these Alexandria murders are driven by old ethnic hatreds?"

I hesitated, then said, "Maybe. That's one aspect we're considering."

"And a cop killing a cop? It all sounds like a mess. Little Belgrade seems like it's coming to a boiling point."

"That's speculation. We don't know why the undercover policeman was bad, and the papers say the Angel Park murder is revenge. It might be true, maybe not."

"You know more than you're telling me, Ike. I figured you can trust me by now."

"It's not a matter of trust. It's not my place to discuss details of an on-going case."

"I guess I'm too curious."

"Why are you so interested?"

Nika put down her cup of coffee, took a deep breath, and escaped to the bedroom, leaving most of her food on the plate. I could hear her voice, I presumed on her phone and not talking to herself, then she shut the door to the bathroom. It seemed forever, but she emerged and grabbed her coat. "Charlie is here."

I glanced out the window, and, sure enough, he had parked across the street in the same spot where the black SUV lurked a few nights ago. "He's a little early."

"Yeah. Thanks again for a great evening, Ike. And breakfast, and everything else. You're a nice guy. Let's get together again sometime." She leaned in with another peck on the cheek.

"Yeah, sounds good." Talk about hot and cold. She had no medium settings.

"Talk to you later." She escorted herself into the

poorly lit hallway and slammed the door.

I jumped in the shower, figuring enough was enough. A phone call to Marconi later would clear this up.

****

I fell back asleep after a shower and woke in the early afternoon. My headache cured, I made a tuna sandwich and turned on the second half of the Jacksonville game since Eddie would talk about it Monday morning. Time to call my boss.

"Henry? This is unexpected. I had hoped you would wind down this weekend."

"I've tried to. But something happened, and I need help."

"What?" she asked.

"Nika Campbell is what and who."

"Did you happen across her again?"

"Yeah, you might say that. We had an unexpected date."

"Now, Henry, I suggested you stay away, but that's your business."

"Yes, it is."

"You don't sound good."

"I need you to tell me what you know about her. Everything," I said.

Silence, except for a dog barking.

"Henry—"

"Now, to reassure you, I offered no information about our murder investigations, even though she became overly inquisitive this morning."

"This morning? She spent the night?"

Good job. I gave it away.

"Yes, she did."

"I worried about that. She's very attractive."

This was like talking to my mother. "Sorry, but once again, I'm asking you what this is about. You seemed aware of her already. You said her name before I mentioned it, and you've admitted you know what she looks like. Tell me what's going on."

"Ease up there, Detective Pierce. I'm still the head of your department."

"Understood, but I feel like there's much more I need to know."

"Fine. You asked."

Eddie told me to stay away from our boss's wrong side, but I had had enough secrecy.

"Henry, I believe Nika is an agent."

"An agent? What kind? For the State Department?"

"I can't narrow it down more. A femme fatale, if you will."

"How did you figure this out? Does the City of Alexandria have spies at State?"

"Stifle the sarcasm. I've been around for a long time, and my contacts run deep. Ms. Campbell's job is legitimate, but there's a suspicion she's working for others."

"How do they know?" I asked.

"She's had a lot of leeway and is getting sloppy...making mistakes from what I've been told."

"What is she after, and how does this relate to me? I'm not following."

"Those are good questions. Ms. Campbell has contacts in the district, and higher-ups have suspicions she's feeding information to players outside the country. And as far as *you* go? You're an assignment, Henry, not a love interest. Sorry, but that's what I think."

Not a surprise. "But why is she so interested in local crimes?"

"This is another layer of this story. Neither my contacts nor I have figured out the links yet. Somehow, Ms. Campbell's actions intertwine with the issues we are having in Alexandria. She got herself assigned to the Secretary of State. A perfect spot for her and what she's doing."

"Which is what?"

"Henry, I think she's connected to someone in Homeland Security and/or someone else in the intelligence community, and not in a good way."

"What's the bad way?"

"This will sound nutty, but I think there's a protection racket in one or more agencies."

"Protecting who, and what?" I asked.

"We know there were war criminals on all sides during the Yugoslav breakup: Bosnian Muslims, Bosnian Serbs, Serbians, Croats, and others. Srebrenica had to be the worst atrocity—almost ten thousand Bosnian Muslims were slaughtered. They jailed a few war criminals in the late nineties, but others escaped. A few came to the U.S. with the knowledge of our government."

I sat back on my couch. "No way."

"Yep…but remember the times. That's always important for context. The Berlin Wall had fallen, the Soviet Union had dissolved, the first Gulf War, the first attacks on the World Trade Center, etcetera. It was no holiday from history, and our government tried to gain intelligence from whatever sources we could find."

"Are you telling me we helped war criminals

escape to this country because of the information they had?"

"That's what I've been told. But it's not the first time—it happened after World War II. The worst of the bunch is a Serb, Miomir Kurić, a big shot in the old Serbian government. He never turned up and is presumed hiding in Europe. God, I hope we aren't protecting him, too."

"I remember this part, and I'm aware of Kurić and his associates—the worst players in Europe since the 1940s."

"Right."

"And disturbances between these local groups attract attention from these interested parties, so they keep a lid on anything embarrassing going public."

"That's what I'm guessing," she said.

"And is that why the courts got involved back then? Someone got to a judge?"

"Likely…and Eddie knows this, too. I've tried to get the commissioner interested, but he either didn't believe me or didn't want to deal with it. He calls me Captain Ahab."

"I noticed. And I'm guessing you know all this because someone is feeding you information."

"Good guess."

"I'm surprised the Secretary of State hasn't shut all this down," I said.

"That guy? Nah. He's more interested in young women than doing his job. But that's like most of those guys. It's catching up with him according to gossip, but that's how Nika Campbell got his attention."

"Okay. Sounds like Nika's feeding information from the State Department to her actual bosses, plus anything she can get from me?"

"And probably others. But go slow—don't cut her off all at once. It might spook the spooks if you know what I mean."

"This is incredible. There really are conspiracies," I said.

"Appears that way, doesn't it? The key to a real conspiracy, though, is that it's small. Too many parts and someone, somewhere, will talk. To tell you the truth, though, I don't give a damn about all that. All I want to do is solve these murders."

"And the murders in Prague?"

"Yeah, but that's a much harder nut to crack," she said.

"No doubt. First things first, though. I think we get with Eddie tomorrow and figure out a way to push the first domino."

She cleared her throat. "We're on the same page if you mean Kastrati's brother-in-law, the Čazim fellow."

"Yes. It's time to pull the scab off this and see what happens."

Chapter Seven

Eddie Stone brought Bekić Čazim in for questioning, and the discussions stalled right away as I had feared. Bates and Marconi took turns interrogating him and then tried teaming together. Marconi told us Čazim had stayed mute, answered only with glaring eyes, relying on his attorney to speak. Today was Eddie's turn, and he wanted me as his guest.

Čazim had made himself at home in the interrogation room. A small man, shorter than Eddie, with dark hair pulled into a tight ponytail above his collar. A mid-century, orange vinyl loveseat appeared to be his favorite perch, leaving his attorney to sit at the rectangular metal table with an interrogator. Eddie marched into the room with his cup of coffee and a yellow notepad. Instead of sitting opposite the attorney at the table, he lowered himself next to Čazim and smiled. I chose a spot standing by the hissing radiator as it struggled to heat the cozy room.

"Good morning, Mr. Čazim and Mr. Attorney. I'm Assistant Director and Detective Lieutenant Edward Stone. This is Detective Henry Pierce. I'm sorry, sir, I don't know your name since I wasn't with Director Marconi when she talked with you."

The attorney sat with his arms crossed and sneered. "I am Milosh Sahiti, Mr. Čazim's attorney." He made a show of looking at his jeweled-encrusted watch, its glass face throwing a reflection in my eyes. "After all this time you've held my client, you have only thirty-five minutes left before we can walk since you have made no charges. Is there an underlying prejudice against my client because of his culture?"

Eddie returned his sneer. "Thank you, Mr. Sahiti, I did not forget the time, so I'll be brief, and we can move forward." Eddie turned away from the attorney. "Mr. Čazim, we are charging you with the kidnapping and murder of Luka Jankovich." Eddie removed a pocket-sized card from his shirt, extended his arm, focused for a moment, and then read him his Miranda Rights. "Mr. Čazim, do you understand your rights as I have read them?" More silence. "Detective Pierce, please note I read the defendant his Miranda Rights, and he refuses to acknowledge those."

"Yes, sir." I hadn't seen this side of Eddie—smooth, professional, and a little scary. Eddie stood, opened the door, and waved a uniformed police officer inside, who pulled Čazim to his feet and cuffed him. His mouth remained shut while she made him sit again.

"Thank you, Officer," Eddie said. He chose to remain standing. "Please wait outside."

Sahiti pounded the table. "You have no evidence."

Eddie ignored the attorney, continuing his stare at Čazim. "We have evidence, Mr. Čazim, that you and an associate kidnapped Luka Jankovich from a parking lot at Stanich Plaza on the evening of November tenth. We believe you murdered him behind the strip mall and dismembered his body at Angel Park. The tire tracks from your vehicle pair with those found at the crime scene—we found paint on the busted cemetery gate we matched to your vehicle."

"Impossible. You are trying to frame my client—"

Eddie continued. "I'm sure you knew the late Mr. Jankovich. It's hard not to know when an ex-spouse remarries."

Čazim glared at his attorney.

"Copying disposal methods of bodies from crimes many years ago may have seemed like a good idea," Eddie said. "However, we have expanded our procedures over the years and can identify bodies no matter their condition. Now, do you have anything to say?"

"Mr. Čazim and I must have a few minutes to talk," Sahiti said.

Eddie nodded and motioned me into the hall next to three occupied offices.

"You knocked them back a bit," I said. "I'm not sure what they expected. Could he have been oblivious we were on his trail, especially after we identified Archie Sullivan as a perp?"

"Arrogance and someone's money are keeping him secure. Remember, I haven't said we know who his accomplice was. And that's where it'll get sticky because they'll point toward the accomplice as the murderer and try to make Čazim his accessory. Archie is dead and can't defend himself."

"Will they try to work a deal? You haven't told them—"

"A deal? Angie and Bates may not be up for it. The guy's a killer. An agreement wouldn't be for much except substituting a life sentence instead of the death penalty. But we need to keep the Stanich family in mind. It's Stanich's son-in-law that's dead and the ex-son-in-law we're accusing of murder."

"Čazim may know more about Stanich's activities

than we give him credit."

"Like what?" he asked.

"We've speculated this is a family feud with an ex-husband taking out his anger on the present husband. An act of passion, spite, or whatever."

"Yep, that's our theory," he said.

"And I don't doubt it's likely a love triangle gone bad. But remember, Čazim gets around. A part of Stanich's family as an in-law for a few years, then divorced, and now he's a brother-in-law to Rijad Kastrati. He may shed light on both families."

"I don't know. Čazim is a murderer. I don't like to make deals with murderers."

"I'm only saying that if he gets shoved into a prison somewhere, he may take a lot of information with him." An officer strolled near us, headed to the water fountain, nodded at us, and filled a plastic bottle.

Eddie grabbed me by the elbow and pushed me a few steps toward the emergency exit. "All of that may be out of our hands," he said.

"You remember I tried to examine Kastrati's finances before the commissioner told me to cool it?"

"Yeah. Why was that?"

"I don't know. More intrigue. Anyway, before that, I also took my nosing around to include Stanich's operations."

"Go on."

"The Staniches' income is way off their expenses."

"Ike, listen, I can't get sidetracked with Stanich right now. We need to nail this case before it gets away from us." Eddie glanced at his watch. "I'm giving them five more minutes to talk, and then I'm walking in." He looked up at me and tilted his head. "And what do you mean their income doesn't match their expenses? Everyone wants more income and fewer expenses. It's a business—it's called making a profit. Nothing unusual."

"No, it's the other way around. Their expenses are more than income. I think the pawn shops are a way to launder money for something I haven't figured out. I found payouts for items for the shops and their subsequent sales, and other miscellaneous payments— large, round dollar ones."

"It sounds suspicious, but one thing at a time, man."

The overworked copier sitting next to us gaped open with a repairman coming and going to his truck. "Eddie, listen to me," I whispered. "I've found evidence that Archie Sullivan received two big payments from Stanich."

"Payment for what?" he said, not whispering.

"Who knows? I doubt Archie pawned something on two occasions for a nice, round ten thousand dollars."

Eddie clenched his jaws, then shouted. "What?" A man got up from his desk and peered out into the hall.

"You okay, Lieutenant Stone?"

"Yeah, yeah, go back to work, Jerry. So, Ike, you're telling me Archie got payoffs and somehow got involved in the murder of Stanich's new son-in-law? I don't get it."

"Eddie, don't you see? Čazim might turn if we play our cards right. We could find out much more about both families if he cooperated."

"I get it, I get it." Eddie sighed and motioned with his head. "For now, let's break this up and get on with it." He didn't knock, sauntered back into the interrogation room, and sat next to Čazim. Officer Miller followed us inside.

Sahiti stood. "Detective, we need more time to finish. My client has the privilege to speak with his attorney alone."

"It's been almost fifteen minutes. You two can talk later. That's your privilege." Eddie motioned to Miller, who pulled Čazim up, then out the door.

"Mr. Sahiti, we will hold your client until tomorrow morning when you may discuss bail with the attending judge. Do you understand?" I asked.

Sahiti held up a hand. "So be it, Detective Pierce. It will be short, and we will bail out. I promise you."

"That's the judge's choice," Eddie said. "Now, good day. Detective Pierce, would you show Mr. Sahiti to the exit?"

"No need. I'm familiar with this building."

Eddie grinned, watching Sahiti storm out of the room. "There you go, Ike. That's how you do it. Man, I'm starving. I missed my white donuts today, and that always pisses me off. Let's grab Angie and get some lunch."

****

Most of the lunch crowd gone, the three of us slid into the corner booth at Manny's. Marconi ordered an onion burger, and Eddie ordered the grilled cheese sandwich someone had recommended. He groaned when I ordered a chicken wrap and fruit salad.

"Ike, how do you not starve all the time?"

Marconi rolled her eyes. "Ike? Why do you keep calling him Ike?"

"It's my middle name."

Eddie winked at me. "I don't like the name Henry from way back."

"Are you saying Eddie gets special treatment and I don't?"

"Okay, okay, but I would like to keep it in our little circle here. It's only my family that calls me Ike and…a few others."

"Girlfriends?" Eddie chuckled.

"I refuse to answer. My Miranda Rights and all."

Marconi snorted. "You should call them your Nika Rights. But I'll stick with Henry—too confusing for me to change now."

"Ah, great joy from the corner today." Manny stood at attention, holding pitchers of tea and water. "Beautiful December day, even if a little cold."

"Yes, it's great," Marconi said. "The owner himself is filling our drinks?"

"Worthless help—a daily tragedy or another keeps at least one of them from work. Such is life in the restaurant business. But what is so funny? I need a laugh."

"Detective Pierce here gets teased about his love life."

"Ah yes, the new detective with dirty shoes," Manny said. He made a show of checking under the table. "I'm surprised you haven't run him off yet, Angie Doll."

Marconi opened a packet of pink sweetener—half of it burst on the table. "Dammit. What? Yes, yes, Pierce is sticking with us." She forced a smirk.

"By the way, Mister New Detective, the young woman you talked to a few weeks ago showed up last night with another fellow."

"Is that so?"

"Our new co-worker here seems to keep a few lady friends," Eddie said.

"A little tidbit, Angie Doll. The young man with her?" Manny asked.

"Yeah?"

"Not too bright. He had left his name badge on until I mentioned it. Eric, something—it started with a 'B.' Homeland Security. Short kid with long blond hair."

My face flushed when I heard his workplace mentioned.

"She seems well-liked, doesn't she?" Marconi said.

I slapped the table with both hands. "It's good you're interested in your customers. Oh, look, here comes our food."

Manny glared at me. "This is Patricia, one of our new servers. She will do great for you. See you, Angie Doll. Gentlemen."

Eddie took a massive bite of his grilled cheese and mumbled. "I'm not a fan, Angie. Why do you think so much of him?"

"A connection to the past, I guess. After Jack's mother died last year, Manny is the only person around here that knew Jack. But yeah, he can set off alarms."

"Manny's too nosy," I said. "The first time I came here, it was after you left, he had someone else serve us, but he stayed close, keeping his ears perked."

"Anyway," Eddie said. "Čazim is in custody, and we agree his damn lawyer is a peacock."

Marconi dipped another fry in ketchup. "Give me your thoughts about all this, both of you. Commissioner Bates will want an update."

I glanced at Eddie.

"Let me talk first," he said, "but I want Ike to jump in."

"Go for it."

"The evidence we've gathered allows for a conviction of some sort for Mr. Čazim, but once we connect him to Archie Sullivan, his attorney will place blame on Archie—a crooked cop influenced his unfortunate client."

Marconi closed her eyes. "The bullet came from the gun stolen from Stanich's pawn shop, and we found it in Čazim's SUV."

"Right, but it could be an 'I didn't know the gun was there' type of thing."

"The gun was under the driver's seat," she said.

"Archie may have planted it there. Circumstantial …"

"Eddie, dammit, this should be an open and shut case. If we are already poking holes in our own theories, the D.A. may back away from a murder charge and only try to convict him as an accomplice. We've got him on being there, right?"

"Čazim has no alibi other than from two family members: his wife and Rijad Kastrati's cousin. They refused to say yes or no," I said.

"Kastrati, Kastrati," she said. "So, who is this victim? The dead guy hardly gets a mention."

Eddie chewed another hunk of the sandwich, then swallowed. "Your turn, Ike."

I guzzled my tea and cleared my throat. "Luka Jankovich is, or was, a second-generation Serb, the first Jankovich born here. He's ten years younger than the Stanich daughter—Čazim's ex-wife. His story is a little refreshing, though."

"Why?" Marconi asked. She motioned to our waitress for a water refill.

"He's clean, apparently. He graduated with honors from Penn, worked as an engineer, and lived in Philadelphia for two years before moving back here and meeting the Stanich woman. That's about it. Then the affair happened, and Čazim was on his way to divorce court. Stanich pushed the 'Bosnian' out while welcoming a Serb into the family."

"That's interesting, but if Jankovich was clean, why did he have a tattoo on his back that's associated with Serbian gangs?"

"I'm not—"

"Never mind. That's a complication I don't want to deal with right now." Marconi closed her eyes and leaned against the booth's green cushion. "We may need Commissioner Bates to talk to the D.A. about toning down the charge if there's a hint a conviction might go bad. The D.A. is running for mayor, and I'm sure he'll want a deal rather than risk losing a public case. So, who is this Čazim? Where'd he come from?"

"By fate, circumstances, or whatever, a Bosnian Muslim somehow married his way into a Serbian Orthodox family. Čazim became part of their operations until his wife found someone else. After the divorce, he found his way back to the Bosnian community and married into the Kastrati family—but old passions die hard. It appears he could not forgive his ex-wife, and he took away something that would hurt her the most…her new husband."

The server returned and placed their desserts in the wrong spot.

Marconi returned my look with blank eyes, taking a bite of her cherry ice cream after she and Eddie switched plates. "What else?"

"Had I mentioned that the Staniches and Kastratis appeared to have had a brief co-ownership of the little shopping plaza."

"The strip mall with the pawnshop?"

"Right," I said.

"Yeah, and even with so much animosity between the two families," Marconi said.

"Yep. I'm guessing Čazim, in his vindictive little mind, wanted to steal one of Stanich's guns at the shop and use it as the murder weapon. Somehow, he got Sullivan to help with the break-in and then the murder. Sullivan wiped almost all evidence from the crime scene, except for a few prints we found on the refrigerator in the office," I said.

"They were hungry? What idiots," Marconi said.

"Čazim must have known the cameras were fake, so they didn't need to worry about that. They broke in, and Jankovich either happened by or they found him there."

"Was he the original target?"

"Not sure, but Čazim and Sullivan didn't pass up the opportunity. That's why Jankovich's Nissan sat in the parking lot the next morning."

Eddie nodded. "They must have taken Jankovich around back and murdered him."

"Seems likely," Marconi said.

"And Dick Forman came by the next day to begin his investigation," Eddie said. "I don't think he knew of Jankovich's disappearance or made an association to the robbery."

Manny had strolled by our booth several times, flipping a gold coin in the air, looking bored after the noon rush. I waited a moment until he passed.

"Dick found the prints. Unfortunately, he may have said too much to his supposed friend, Archie Sullivan, who turned around and killed him since Dick represented a direct threat."

"Yeah, it had to be something straightforward from Dick to make Archie react as he did," Marconi said. "Archie figured he would get fingered, and everything he had been doing with either family would go public."

"But, Angie," Eddie said, "his killing a cop wouldn't make this go away."

"I can't explain Archie's thought process. If you look for logic within the thoughts of a murderer …" Her attention drifted away while she stared at her left hand. "So, what have we found about Čazim's background? Where did he come from? What motivates all this? My interrogations yielded nothing with the horse's ass lawyer sitting there."

"Čazim's entire time here has been one of bouncing between families and jobs," I said. "He was ten when he immigrated, then lived with his aunt and uncle in Oxen Hill—they are both deceased now—he has no other relatives locally. Čazim is a high school dropout but received his G.E.D. and tried several jobs. He showed up in a 2010 Arlington police report charged for stealing gas and got probation. Subsequently, he was arrested three other times for shoplifting in Alexandria from 2011 to 2014. Čazim met Ms. Stanich around this time, and they started dating. They married in late 2015. I've found nothing about how he linked up with Archie Sullivan."

"Tell me how the attorney gets paid. How can we find out?"

"It's probably a friend of the family," Eddie said.

"It has to be Kastrati money," I said.

"That would make sense. Guys, this is fantastic work, but how do we proceed? We need something definitive. Čazim and Attorney Jackass know we have him as, at least, an accomplice. But unless Čazim wakes up one morning with a conscience, or we find unambiguous evidence he's the one who pulled the trigger, then Archie Campbell takes the hit. Archie's a dead, dirty cop, and no one will care."

"More drinks here?" Manny held the tea pitcher. I hadn't paid attention as he approached the table. "You spoke of Rijad Kastrati? If murder is an issue, I would guess it involves him. Never trust him…he's not what he seems."

"Thanks, Manny. We'll be leaving soon," Marconi responded, ignoring his comment. "Solving cases and saving lives again."

I kicked Eddie under the table. "Yes, Mr. Jurić, we have a case we cannot lose. The Angel Park murder has been solved, and we are celebrating."

Marconi gave me a look that usually would make my hair curl. "Detective Pierce gets a little ahead of himself."

Manny scowled at me. "I would like to hear sometime. Your work is always on my mind."

Eddie tried to encourage his departure. "Thanks, we are about to wrap up."

Marconi half-smiled. "Bring me the tab, old friend." Manny ambled away, offering no reply. "Detective, I've told you once already to mind your mouth—"

Eddie waved his hands. "It's okay, Angie, we got this."

"Fill me in before I put you both in the basement."

I hesitated and took a breath first. "Angie, we should trust no one. Many webs are woven through this community."

"Look, Manny is like a hornet's nest—you don't want to poke it." She straightened herself in the booth as he approached with our ticket, and we stood. "Gentlemen, we've hogged this space too long. Let's get back to work. Hey, Manny, if I don't see you soon, have a great Christmas and New Year." She passed him forty dollars, then motioned us out the booth.

Manny watched us push through the doors. With no inflection in his voice, he responded, "Season's greetings to you, Angie Doll."

****

Čazim stayed in jail, our evidence too overwhelming for the judge to grant bail. In the meantime, I worked at night and the following weekend on sprucing up my apartment for my Christmas guests. My mother determined she would haul my grandmother to Alexandria for the holidays. I bought a blow-up mattress to sleep on, leaving my bed and couch for my folks.

They arrived after noon on Christmas Eve and somehow found their way to police headquarters. A commotion came from the hall, and I glanced around my office door to see Angie Marconi leading the way with my family in tow.

"Ike, baby, I see you," my grandmother said, waving.

I threw away the trash scattered around the floor and straightened my desk, grateful my office mate had left for the day.

"Hi, Ike, we found you," my mom shouted, dropping her thin windbreaker on my desk.

"Hi, baby." My grandmother still gave the best hugs after all these years. Her gray curls bounced against my face.

"You said you were meeting me at my apartment later?" I asked.

"We woke up early and couldn't wait to see you. I figured out my navigation on the phone you gave me, and it brought us straight here."

"Almost," my grandmother said. "We were about to cross a bridge into Maryland when that dang Sarie woman tried to get us to drive into the river."

"No matter. We made it."

"I guess you've met my boss, informally. Angie Marconi, this is my mother, Susan Pierce, and my grandmother, Rita Faye Henshaw."

"And it's not Mrs. Henshaw. Call me Rita Faye," my grandmother said.

"Ike, your boss is so attractive," my mother said. "Us middle-aged girls can keep it together, can't we, Angie?"

A smile covered Marconi's face. "I guess so. Though it takes longer, right?"

Eddie hurried down the hall, obviously unable to resist joining us. "And who are these lovely ladies?"

"Detective Lieutenant Eddie Stone, this is my mother, Susan Pierce, and my grandmother, Rita Faye Henshaw."

"Pleased to meet you, ladies." Eddie shook their

hands gently. "I've enjoyed working with your son or grandson."

"Lieutenant Stone, I love your head," my grandmother said. "My dear late-husband's head shown slick as ice."

"Geez, look at the time," I said. "Are y'all thirsty? I have water here, but I bought diet drinks for the apartment."

"No, Ike, we want to get your key and wait for you there. I bought groceries and wanted to make you spaghetti tonight. And your Granny made bread, and we can garlic it up."

My mom's spaghetti—my stomach rumbled. "Sounds good. Here's the key, and I cleaned already."

"We've seen how you clean, dear. We'll give it a once over and get it spic and span before you get there. Angie, Eddie, it's been good to meet you all. What are y'all doing for Christmas?"

"Neither one of us have family close, so we usually go to our favorite Chinese place and have lunch together," Marconi answered.

"Chinese? What kind of Christmas meal is that?" my grandmother asked.

"Now you two come over to Ike's tomorrow at noon. I'm cooking a huge ham, and I'll make fresh green beans we canned from our garden, mashed potatoes, and Momma will bake her rolls," my mother said.

"I don't know, Susan, it seems like an—"

My mother shook her head. "No arguments."

Eddie offered no hesitation, rubbing his hands together. "Mrs. Pierce, that sounds like a meal my late wife would cook. I don't think you could keep me away."

"Looks like we'll be there," Marconi said.

"Wonderful. Ike, you get back to work now. Do something good for the city and earn your salary. Let's go, Momma." They marched back down the hall and left us standing there with my two bosses grinning ear to ear.

****

"Hey, Eddie. Merry Christmas," I said after opening the door. I took his long wool coat and spread it across the back of my couch next to Marconi's black leather jacket.

"Thank you, Ike, and Merry Christmas to you."

My mother stood with her hands on her hips. "Now, Lieutenant Stone, you'll need to put away the Jaguars stocking cap. If it were the Steelers, I wouldn't mind."

"I go for college ball," my grandmother said. She had brought her mother's gravy boat and set it gently on my crowded table. We crammed around the four chairs that came with the table, along with a metal fold-up seat at one corner. "I love Ike's Virginia Tech stuff. He could have played basketball, you know."

"Come on, Granny, you know it would have been at the community college in Wytheville. I wasn't good enough for division one. Take a seat at the table, Eddie. Angie's in the restroom. She brought wine and chocolate chip cookies."

"And it's a wonderful wine, too." My mother's goofy smile meant she was a little tipsy from her second glass. She placed the hot rolls in a basket and brought them and a tub of margarine to the table. "Can you believe Christmas is already here, and soon it will be a new year?"

My grandmother shook her head. "2022. Growing up, if someone had said something about the twenty-first century, we all would have thought we'd be living on Mars by now."

Marconi appeared and grabbed her glass off the end table. "This is great. The smell of baked bread makes me happy. Wonderful memories go with it."

"Thank you, I've used that recipe since my mother gave it to me as a teenager, so around twenty years ago," my grandmother said. She snickered.

"Ike, turn on your phone and find some music. I'm saying the food is ready. At home, I would have a big fire going, and Andy Williams' Christmas songs would play."

"Would the toaster oven work?"

"Ha-ha, Mr. Funny Man. Come on, everybody."

Eddie hurried to help my grandmother with her chair, and we all sat.

"Lieutenant Stone, would you mind giving thanks?"

Eddie obliged, then my mother passed the mashed potatoes first.

A tear streamed down her cheek. "We had so much fun with your dad, didn't we, Ike? He used to remind me of the old saying that sometimes a memory can't help but form a tear and run down your face." She rubbed away the wetness.

Marconi sighed. "Susan, I want to tell you I feel the same way about my parents and my late husband. This time of the year can be joyful and sorrowful at the same time."

"Ike told me about his death and that it happened

far away. I'm so sorry. What was he like?" my mother asked.

"Quiet. Tall, brown eyes, and lots of dark hair…like Henry. Anyway, let me tell you how much we appreciate having your son work for us, right, Eddie?"

Eddie had disengaged from our conversation and worked on another piece of warm bread. "What's that? Sorry… thinking about the bread my wife used to make—always lots of butter."

"I said, you've enjoyed working with Henry, right?"

"Sure, he's making an outstanding detective. Glad we got him," Eddie said.

"Thanks," I said. "It's been an interesting few weeks."

"Ike has been good at everything he's done." My mom patted me on my shoulder. "He has a hard time understanding how good he can be—it tends to hold him back. He went to school a little too long, but I'm glad he finally got his masters."

"I got two degrees in six years, Mom. Plus, I worked part time."

"Susan, I hate to bring work into our conversation, but I thought it would be good to let Henry know something that's happening at the office. Right, Eddie?"

Eddie wiped his mouth. "You bet, Angie. Can I tell him?"

"No. Henry, I've spoken with Commissioner Bates, and Eddie has concurred. We are promoting you to Dick Forman's old position. You're moving up to sergeant. Two salary steps, actually."

"Really? Commissioner Bates is okay with this? I'm stunned."

A great smile covered Eddie's face. "Don't be surprised, buddy. You've pushed this whole Jankovich murder investigation along. You act like you've done this for years."

Marconi agreed. "The main negative is that the city is cutting us back two other vacant positions."

"Two detectives? That will be quite an extra load."

"Yes, it is. That's why I got you a raise."

"Are we going to get rid of someone? And what will the other detectives think about me as a thirty-year-old sergeant?"

"Tim Walton is already leaving," Marconi said.

"Tim? After seven weeks? He doesn't strike me as the type to jump ship. Did something happen?"

"He said he got a better offer down in Charlotte."

"He's from there," Eddie said, "and don't worry about your colleagues. They can come talk to me if they have a problem."

My grandmother grew ashen. "Wait a minute, Ike. Isn't the Forman fellow the one that died? There might be bad juju with his position."

Marconi choked, almost spitting out a piece of bread. "I can assure you, bad juju won't be a problem."

I leaned over to hold her hand. "It's okay, Granny. I'll be careful."

We veered away from work talk, and my mother took over the conversation. I don't think she took a breath for ten minutes. Still, I welcomed all the stories about my dad, Sergeant Henry Oliver Pierce, assigned to a special forces group in 1983 and participated in the Grenada invasion. A Cuban unit shot down his helicopter, and he and another ranger were the only survivors on board. Like my mother, memories of my dad ran down my cheeks.

Chapter Eight

Stewing in jail for a few days encouraged inmates to rethink their situations. Apparently, Bekić Čazim was no different. First thing on our return Friday morning, Marconi hurried to the interrogation room after a message from Čazim's attorney. I paced through the halls, waiting for information. The news of my promotion spread, and, along with congratulations, I received a few grunts of acknowledgment. Not everyone appreciated the new guy moving up the ladder so soon. I refreshed my coffee and hurried back to my office.

Marconi's assistant, Kate, stood at the door waiting for me, scratching her growing baby bump. "Good morning, *sergeant*. I'm here to change out your keys."

"Locks changing?"

"Nope. Director Marconi said she wanted you in Dick's old office—the one between her and Lieutenant Stone."

"Really?"

"It *is* the sergeant's office."

This was ideal. The office had a terrific view of the park across the street. Forman's compulsiveness left his office always organized and clean. "Did she say when this would change?"

"We are switching keys now, so you need to get your stuff moved before we lock up this evening."

"Great, I can do that. This office I share with Tim

is tight, but I assumed since he resigned, I would move his desk out for more space."

"Cool," she responded, uninterested again in my jabbering. "Let's switch keys, and you can get started. The director is in her office catching up on phone calls, and Lieutenant Stone should be back in a few minutes. I'm sure they'll want to talk to you."

****

The location of my new office made me hard to avoid. Kate offered nothing more, shrugging when I stuck my head into the suite three different times that afternoon. I gave up and began unpacking. Crawling up onto my credenza to find the best spots for my diplomas, I right away dropped the hammer behind the desk. "Crap."

"Potty mouth." Eddie had crept from behind and then handed me the hammer. "I don't think Judy in Risk Management would want you crawling over everything. How about a ladder?"

"You should have seen me in the basement. I'm like Spiderman."

"Your Spidey Sense didn't tell you I stood behind you, did it? You've been busy here. Looks good."

"Thanks. I appreciate moving in here. I guess Dick had it painted not too long ago, and this desk and credenza look in good shape."

"Yeah, he always wanted something new—very obsessive. His wife told me she always had to find him a project, or he'd try to reorganize all her stuff."

"So, where were you all day?"

"Did you miss me?"

"I thought you and Angie met with Čazim and his attorney."

"*Attorneys*, now. And an FYI, Angie left a few minutes ago for Louisville for her grandma's arrangements. Mrs. Cistello was a day short of ninety-eight years old. Angie will be back by Friday. Since Angie's parents have passed, there wasn't anyone else to take care of things."

"Nice long life, huh? And what did you say? Two attorneys?"

"Yep."

"Pro bono?"

Eddie smiled. "Doubtful, considering all the bling on both people."

"Who's the other attorney?"

"Mr. Sahiti's wife. She never told her first name other than Missus."

"The preening and pretentious find one another, don't they?"

Eddie snickered. "Always. Our idea of letting Čazim sit in jail for a few days during Christmas break seems to have worked. He has a voice after all, but his lawyers are keeping him within their guardrails."

"What have you found out?"

"Yeah, I thought you would want to know. Guess what?" He gave me a slight punch on my shoulder. "You're with me all night."

"Yeah? How many bars are we hitting?"

"Not a bad idea, but this will be more fun. Strap on your holster."

"Sounds serious." Maybe my grandmother was right about bad juju.

"Angie talked to the D.A., he went to the new city judge, and we have us a search warrant signed, sealed, and delivered."

"For what?"

"We are surveilling Stanich Plaza tonight and may enter and search as needed."

"Search for what?"

"Maybe nothing. Čazim claims the Staniches are in the middle of a heroin network, and drug interdiction is all Judge Wilson would consider."

"But heroin?"

"Yeah, an old drug making a comeback if it ever left. Čazim claims those old storefronts that appear unused are holding drugs, money, and whatever else."

"Can we trust this, Eddie? What if Čazim's attorneys are in the middle of this intrigue? What if we get out there and everything's clean?"

"That's possible, but we were explicit with them. If Čazim's lying to us, any deals are off. That's why we need to do this tonight. It wouldn't be smart to wait."

"Did Archie Sullivan come up?"

"Yep, as we predicted. Archie's the bad guy, and poor little Čazim kept showing up at the wrong places at the wrong times. I think most of his story is crap, but we'll see."

"Is Čazim is trying to get back at the Staniches?"

"Probably." Eddie fidgeted with his holster's strap.

"But Eddie, consider Archie for a second. How undercover do you think he was?"

"What do you mean?"

"Archie could have discovered a drug side of the Stanich operations and blackmailed the Staniches, or they sucked him in, then he became part of it. Like I told you, I found two deposits of ten thousand each in Archie's bank statements for October and November this year."

"We've several things we need to come back to. Angie and I argued all afternoon about this. I told her this stuff is way beyond why we started this investigation. Luka Jankovich is the victim, and we're investigating his family based on what his killer told us. It all seems backward. And we've got Archie Sullivan with his double-dealing and the Kastratis and how they fit. It's the same old stuff, and we keep circling in a whirlpool and getting nowhere."

"What's next?"

"It's after five o'clock. Time to go to work."

****

We parked ourselves at Eddie's favorite burger joint, right across the street from Stanich Plaza. His police cruiser would have been too noticeable, so we took my dirty Toyota. He ate two cheeseburgers with their special sauce, then piddled around with his new phone. Finally, we were ready.

From our side of the street, the pawnshop looked dark other than backroom lights. The parking lot was empty except for a Dodge pickup with two flat tires sitting near the culvert running along the lot's back side. The near-abandoned strip of stores sat alone on the corner of the lot with a deep creek running along the back—lights from the nearby Masonic Memorial shown like beacons into the night sky.

"Let's drive behind that busted-ass pickup and see if we can park," Eddie said. "That way, your car is hidden from the street. I hope you brought gloves and a heavier coat. We may be outside for a while."

"This coat is fine, but as usual, I've left my gloves at my apartment. My mother says I need to put a string around—"

"Doesn't matter. I could never draw a gun with gloves anyway," he said.

My gut knotted, and it must have shown on my face.

"But don't get tight, Ike. We need to keep our wits."

The street behind the shops ended a few feet over the culvert. I took a deep breath, edging my car into the brush on the creek's north bank with a sharp drop to the water thirty feet below us. "Best I can do without drowning us. Come on. I'll follow your lead," I said.

Eddie slipped on scattered chunks of asphalt as he pulled himself out of my car.

"You okay?"

"Yeah, but you almost had to fish me out." We fought through the pine tree branches hanging over the embankment.

"This creek merges with the one at Angel Park—it meanders all over the city."

"I didn't know. It's a lot deeper here," I said.

Eddie stopped on the fractured asphalt path behind the shops. "Look at that rocky hangover near the culvert," he said. "One more flood, and the entire place is going down. I don't get why they wouldn't want cameras back here. It's wide open for burglaries."

"No cameras, no evidence."

"The truth, my friend. Hey, it looks like we have five back entrances to those shops before turning at the right angle. That's the pawnshop. We'll check those first and see if they're locked. Nothing wrong with cops checking locks on doors, is there? The neighborhood has had a few burglaries, right?"

"You are exactly right, Lieutenant Stone. We are

doing our duty." Halfway down the path, one light shone from high on a pole leaning twenty degrees toward the creek. "What if they're all locked? Does the search warrant allow us to break into a building?"

"Yes, sir, if we have probable cause."

I yanked on the first door's padlock. "The lock on this one doesn't look like anyone has touched it in years. It's all rust."

"Let's check the others. Oh, crap."

"What happened?"

"My ankle. This path is really crumbled …"

"Be careful. I'm glad you didn't wear your stocking hat. The overhead light is barely enough to see, and I'm following the shiny spot on your head. It's like a beacon."

"Ha-ha, smartass. Yeah, this second lock is rusted up, too. Keep going." His limp less noticeable, we continued creeping along the narrowing alleyway. The creek's water rushed below, but the darkness hid the bottom of the ravine.

"You're right, Eddie. These folks will have problems if we get another big rain. The area next to the pawnshop is about to disintegrate."

"That would be a favor to the community. Damn, this place is nasty. The parking lot has more holes than a hunk of Swiss cheese, and the signs are all busted." He yanked on another lock. "Same here. These doors haven't been opened in forever. One more to go."

"Then what?"

"We go around front."

I grabbed Eddie's arm. "Wait a second."

"What?"

"Shh. I heard voices."

"Are you sure?" He followed me into the darkness under the pine trees. The gray metal door creaked open—the same door we were about to check. "That could have been awkward," he whispered. Two men emerged—each wore a black hoodie and carried a red backpack. "Hold your breath."

No problem. I couldn't breathe, anyway, and my heart pounded like a bass drum. Eddie pulled his gun from its holster, and I did likewise with mine. The two men strolled down the path disappearing around the corner, and we both stepped back into the light.

"I couldn't understand what they said."

"Me neither over his sneezing. Didn't someone tell us Stanich has nephews?" Eddie asked.

"Yes," I answered, "three nephews. Did you notice, though?"

"What?"

"They let the door slam. I didn't see them lock it."

"Good. Now's our chance."

"What if they come back?"

"We have our warrant, Ike. We have an accusation of drugs and money laundering, which gives us probable cause to search the place, plus a murder occurred here. You poke around inside, and I'll stand by the door for a minute. Use the light on your phone. We want nothing to show on the side facing the street."

"Got it," I said.

Eddie watched for visitors while I turned the doorknob.

"Not locked, but rusty," I said.

"Try again."

I twisted harder and felt a slight turn, enough to open. The hinges creaked to wake the dead. "Sorry."

Eddie pushed around me and stuck his head into the darkness. "I'll use my brand new phone's light. It's brighter than my last one."

"You've told me it's brand new three times tonight. Is your girlfriend going to call or something?"

"Hey, I paid more for this phone than I did my first car…and she's not my girlfriend." He disappeared through the entrance, and I followed. Rows of cardboard boxes lined against the outside windows, blocking the parking lot's view. "Doing okay?" he called. "Nothing over here but an oily smell…it reeks of diesel or something."

"Must be a leak somewhere. I hear dripping, like a bad faucet," I said. A car muffler growled, and I stared over a stack of heavy cardboard boxes—a black SUV's headlights glowed. "That's crazy, Eddie."

"What?"

"Those backpack guys may have been eating at your burger joint, too. They're leaving in a black Suburban. It noticed it at the hamburger joint when we left," I said.

"I didn't pay any attention. I wonder if they saw us?"

"Eddie?"

"What?"

"These boxes screen the street view and make a corridor up and down these buildings."

"The important question is, what's in them?"

I pulled one off the stack and fumbled around, trying to rip the tape off. "I've got to get more light, Eddie."

"Just a minute." The fluorescent ceiling lights came alive. Eddie cursed, and we were in the dark again. Another try, and one row of lights shone above us. "There. Sons of bitches."

A few steps farther into the first room and a tiny, light-oak desk sat in the corner under a 1995 Yorkie dog calendar. One drawer was empty, and someone had stuffed the other with a chaos of papers. I grabbed what I could and jammed them in my coat pocket.

Eddie stirred near the exit.

I returned to the row of cardboard and pulled the top box from the closest stack. The tape already ripped open, there was nothing inside but wadded *Alexandria Banner* newspapers. I pulled the second in the stack, this box much heavier. "Eddie, come over here."

He trudged over and followed my pointing finger. "What the hell? Looks like a rainbow."

"Euro banknotes. Various denominations. The yellow ones are two hundred, green is one hundred, and the purple ones are five hundred," I said.

"Get another box." I ripped a third one open, and the contents were the same. "What would they be doing with Euros?" he asked. "Wait. Look at this purple one…the E.U. flag on the upper left."

"What about it?"

"It's smeared or something—the stars are blurry. I bet it's counterfeit. Start taking pictures. I'll look around more." He disappeared into the hallway on the right—I ventured left.

I took several photos of the boxes, opened and unopened, and included a background in the images to identify our location. Light fading and the smell of fuel growing oppressive, I came to the last room and found two massive machines, something that looked like old-style newspaper printers. Strewn around the floor, ink-stained plates of different denominations lay in an odd pattern. I grabbed one expecting heavy metal. Instead, it was a discolored gray plastic, weighing only a few ounces and shedding yellow ink over my hands. Hurrying back through the hall, I found Eddie sitting on a stool surrounded by yellow backpacks.

"I found the printing presses in the back." I wiped my yellowed hands on a stack of dirty rags. "Only two of them and not sophisticated. Why would any of these phony European banknotes be of value in Virginia?"

"Don't know." He threw a yellow backpack at me. "Open it."

I unzipped the bag halfway when the zipper stuck. I yanked again, and the contents exploded over the room. "Look at that. Packs of hundred Euro banknotes."

"Yeah, look at that," Eddie said. He clenched his jaws, then kicked at the bills I'd scattered. "Good job, Ike. Pick that up and put it back as you found it. About half of these bags are full. There must be millions in counterfeit notes here."

"Why risk having all this stashed?" I asked. "Then they leave the door unlocked. They stuck it in backpacks and then moved it somewhere? But remember, they had red backpacks."

"There aren't any other red ones. Take more pictures of the fake money for now. Get a few serial numbers, too."

"Do we take examples of this with us?" I asked.

"Hell, no."

"Why not?"

"Are you a Treasury agent? I'm not. We've identified this, and now we call in Treasury. That will take care of the Staniches. After that, we finish up the Jankovich murder."

My shoulders dropped, and I frowned.

"Come on, Ike. We aren't equipped for something like this. It's huge. We have to let the proper agencies take over."

"I know that, but outside agencies haven't been helpful in those cold cases, have they? And what's that noise? I keep hearing it."

"What noise?"

"A clicking sound."

Eddie opened his mouth, his eyes widening. He grabbed me by the coat sleeve and yanked me toward the door. "Go, go!" We stumbled outside toward the pines, and he shoved me to the ground between tree trunks.

A concussion of sound and heat drove my face into the dirt and blew Eddie forward onto his knees and hands. He rolled once close to the precipice down to the creek. Two secondary explosions followed, leaving us choking from the smell of burning paper and plastic.

My ears screamed like a train whistle. I rolled over to see the entire Stanich structure in flames. "I think I'm dying."

Eddie gasped. "Dying wouldn't hurt this bad."

"What happened?"

"A setup."

"What?"

"That clicking sound…they rigged it to blow—an explosive device and propellants to help it burn." He struggled back to his feet, leaned on the tree trunk, and brushed off his clothes. "That's what the smell was. Shit, I should have been paying attention."

"It's the lawyer, Sahiti. He tipped them off, didn't he?"

"Somebody did, and there were no drugs like Čazim claimed. They're running a counterfeiting ring, a huge one." Sirens screamed in the distance. "Come on, Ike. Let's get back to your car. It sounds like our friends in the fire department are coming." He groped around in his coat and pants pockets, searching for his phone.

"Here. Your brand new phone didn't melt. I pulled it out of the dirt. I'll send you the pics later."

"Uh, okay." Eddie's chest heaved in the chilly night air. "What am I supposed to do with them? Do we take your phone down to the drug store to print them?"

"What? No, I'll email them, and you can forward on."

"You'll have to show me how."

"When you talk to Angie, tell her I'll forward them and copy everyone else."

"Even better." He fingered the back of his neck and gasped a deep breath.

"Let me see. Yeah, your neck and the back of your head blistered. It doesn't look terrible in this light, but we need to get you looked at."

"I'll make it, but it's really tender. Let's get back to your car."

Eddie dragged his foot a bit as we made our way along the rim of the cliff. The fire on the north side was burning itself out. "The first explosive, I would bet."

"That's logical. It's where the printers sat," I said.

"We were damn lucky. The clicking sound— dammit, I should have paid attention. And the smell …"

"Not your fault," I said. "How would you know?"

"Didn't you have explosives training?" Eddie leaned against the hood of my car. I unlocked the doors, and we both slumped into the Toyota's deep bucket seats. The engine sputtered in the cold but came alive. "God, my neck is killing me. I need to find my wife's old salve."

"You may need more than that—you can't let it get infected. What do we do now?"

"We raise hell with the attorney," Eddie said. "I'm tired of this crap with Čazim. We need to get on with it. Čazim killed Jankovich, and he got Archie to hack up the body. Archie may have suggested that particular disposal method since those old stories have circulated for years. Čazim isn't old enough to have known about that, much less anything of the little pastry identifier they left in the pocket."

"That's premeditation, Eddie. They weren't carrying around a Bosnian pastry roll by accident. Čazim knew what the end game would be. He wanted to set up a smokescreen, after the fact, using Archie's knowledge about the old murders."

"Could be. Drive over there near the entrance. I know those guys." We roamed through the potholed parking lot, covered with shattered glass and building remains. I stopped near a police car, and Eddie put down his window. "Hey, Jerry, got any details?"

The older cop frowned, glanced at me, then back to Eddie. "Looks like a big fire."

Eddie glanced at me and then back to the cop. "Yep. You reached that conclusion by yourself?"

"Yeah. What's the matter? You look like hell, Eddie. You guys smell like oil or something."

Eddie opened his mouth and glanced at me again.

"Rough evening. Do you need any help?"

"Let me see what's going on first, and I'll let you know. You any good at fire investigations?"

"A little out of my area." The cop strolled away.

Eddie rolled up his window, then winced as he leaned his head back against his seat. "Angie won't be happy."

Chapter Nine

The burning pine trees ignited like brilliant torches on the creek's east bank. We watched the firefighters work to bring the blaze under control. "Let's stay in the car for a minute," Eddie said.

We pulled into the burger joint's parking lot, and I killed the engine.

"Jerry and his guys can handle the police side of this. Let's see who else shows up."

"Fine, but do you think they knew?" I asked.

"They, he, she—someone knew."

"Eddie, that's millions in fake Euros that burned. Too bad we didn't keep—"

"We've got a good fire investigation team. I bet they'll find enough scraps."

"Why would they destroy their own property?"

"Emergency planning on their part, I guess," Eddie said while rubbing his ankle again. "Great…it's swelling."

"I'm going inside to get ice for you." His phone rang as I shut the door. I brought back a cup full of ice to hold on to his blistered neck. Sliding back into the seat, a picture of Marconi shown on his telephone screen.

"Angie, I've got you on speaker with Ike."

"Henry, I got a call from Commissioner Bates. Eddie caught me up."

"Good. We found a lot," I said.

"Before or after the fire?"

Eddie touched the paper cup of ice to his neck and gritted his teeth. He looked like someone had beaten him in a fight. "Listen to me, Angie. Ike and I found scores of boxes and backpacks full of Euro banknotes. We're sure all counterfeit."

"Euros? What—"

"Hang on. I tried to explain this a minute ago. We avoided contact with two individuals leaving the premises. They left a door unlocked, which must have been on purpose, and we went about our business. Ike got some pictures and mentioned he heard an odd noise, too. We heard a timer, Angie. It sounded like the one we used in explosives training. The entire shopping center is gone. It's almost burnt out already."

"And with it, all the evidence," Marconi said.

"There will be something we can find. And in case you wondered," Eddie said, rubbing his ankle again, "Ike and I are okay."

Marconi offered nothing, so I said, "I have almost forty pictures I took from inside the building. And I have a pocket full of papers, receipts, or something I found shoved in a desk drawer."

"Okay, I guess," Marconi said. "Has the old man showed himself?"

"You mean Stanich? What does he look like?" Eddie asked. "Several people are standing here close. One older guy has a blanket over his shoulders with several women around."

"He always wears a green ball cap with his logo on it, and he carries a yappy dog," Marconi said.

"I can see a baseball cap," I said. "Yeah, that's him, Eddie. He wore a cap when I interviewed him about the robbery. The dog's name is Draža."

"I don't care about the damn dog—"

Marconi interrupted. "My grandmother's funeral is tomorrow afternoon, guys, and not much I can do from here. Eddie, be a snoop and see what you can find out and call me on Friday morning. I'm flying back around noon. I'll run by the office before you all go home. And Henry?"

"Yes."

"Email me those pictures ASAP. Copy the commissioner and the fire chief. I want to see what you have."

"I'll review the other evidence tonight, too."

"Good. And guys?"

"Yes?"

"Don't cause more problems. Are we good?"

"Angie, we didn't—" Eddie sighed with her hang-up. "Okay. Let's see what we can find out."

Eddie struggled from his seat, and I waited as he came around the car. We took a few steps toward the group. A man in a uniform shook the older man's hand. I stayed in the background, letting Eddie insert himself into the conversation.

Eddie offered tissues from his pocket to one woman wiping her eyes, then shook hands with the man in the uniform. He was one of a few men working for the city short enough to talk to Eddie eye-to-eye. "Harley, your guys took control of this well. What's going on?"

"We're trying to suppress the last bits of it, Eddie. It's a total loss. We'll have the fire investigators out here tomorrow morning."

"I'll talk to Jerry about leaving the men out here to

guard the place," Eddie said, which caused an immediate eruption from the old man.

"When fire out, everyone go home." Stanich appeared near eighty years old. The bags under his eyes so heavy, they cast shadows on his cheeks. His curly, silver hair flopped under his cap onto his wrinkled forehead. A gold upper incisor flashed in the dark whenever a bit of light caught it.

"Mr. Stanich, this is Eddie Stone, assistant director of the detective division for the City of Alexandria."

"I am Stanich. And what does Detective Lieutenant Stone say about this?"

"Mr. Stanich, when the fire is out, we'll leave the personnel here until our investigation is complete," Eddie said. "This is only a fire investigation, but we believe it to be arson. If so, it is a criminal case."

"No, no. I do not want that." Stanich shook his head. "We will start over."

"Mr. Stanich, we must insist. Arson cases are criminal—"

"No. You leave property to me."

"This is out of your control, Stanich. An explosion and a fire occurred, and we'll investigate as we see fit."

"No, I am familiar with police here, and they will steal what they find." Eddie clenched his jaws and fists.

I stepped in.

"Mr. Stanich? Sir, do you remember me? Henry Pierce. I came to talk to you after the robbery when someone stole your guns."

"Yes, yes, I remember you, and I don't have my guns back."

"No, sir. We believe someone used one of those guns to kill Luka Jankovich, and it remains evidence.

We haven't found the other weapons."

"Ah, poor Luka," Stanich said. He gazed at the night sky. "It is Bekić Čazim. He is the devil." He pointed at one woman nearby. "That is my daughter, Amina. She is, was, married to Luka. You must do justice for him."

I wanted to remind him that Amina also married Bekić Čazim—she brought him into the family.

Eddie wiped his face. "Stanich, we are doing our best to bring justice for Luka. We have a fire—"

Stanich shook his head and whacked the ground with a cane. "No. I am a contributor to this community, Detective Lieutenant. I'm sure investigation will be short and have a satisfactory ending."

Eddie ignored the comment and glanced at me. "It would be helpful if we could get a list of items lost in the fire."

"I have no listing."

"What?"

Stanich answered much louder. "I said, no listing."

"You don't have an inventory? How do you insure it? Wouldn't they want a—"

"I have no insurance. I pay for everything." Stanich wiped his brow.

"Father, calm down," another woman said. She appeared older than Amina. "Detective Stone, this isn't getting anywhere. Let's deal with this today, and tomorrow we'll talk to anyone that needs information."

"Thank you, Mirna." Stanich offered his hand to Eddie, who shook it instinctively, triggering a growl from the dog. "So, Detective Lieutenant, you do what you must, and I will do same. Agreed?"

Eddie stood for several seconds, then scowled.

"Mr. Stanich, we'll find how this occurred. I can promise that."

Stanich offered nothing else, then motioned his daughters to follow him. They crossed the street to get a closer view.

"What a son of a bitch," Eddie muttered. "Harley, we have a special interest in this case."

"Yeah? We can tell you fast if it's deliberate."

"Hello, Chief Daniels," I said. "I'm Henry Pierce. Director Marconi has instructed me to email you pictures of the building before the fire. We heard an explosion just before the fire and suspect it involves Stanich's family somehow."

"Good to meet you. I'll get with Angie and Eddie when the investigation is complete."

Eddie nodded toward my car. "Come on, Ike. Let's go home."

"How did he know your rank?" I asked.

"Say what?"

"Harley introduced you as assistant director. Stanich called you Detective Lieutenant...several times."

"He's right, Eddie. I never mentioned your rank," Harley said.

Eddie wrinkled his brow. "Stanich knows me? Interesting. Angie said she's out-of-pocket tomorrow. Ike, we need to get on Commissioner Bate's schedule. I want him aware of Stanich's attitude and what we found before the place blew. Another discussion with Čazim and his attorneys seems prudent."

****

An early call, six a.m. Almost seven hours of sleep this time. "Ike? I just hung up with Angie. Her temper has cooled, and I got her up to speed. She's good with us talking to Commissioner Bates if we keep her updated. Ike?"

"I'm here, I'm here. I'm trying to wake up."

"We need to be at work by seven-thirty. Bates is an early riser, and I want to catch him before he gets pulled away into other things. Harley will be there, too."

"Okay, see you." My bed was nice and warm, but I had to get moving. No breakfast today. I showered, dressed, and grabbed the pile of pictures off the coffee table.

****

Bates' office smelled of pine when we arrived. The Christmas wreath sat in the trash, dead needles forming a trail from the door. He motioned us to sit at the table in the corner, then ignored us for several minutes while typing away on his keyboard.

He removed his reading glasses. "Men, I've mixed feelings this morning. I had hoped to coast this week between Christmas and New Year's. But that's why we get paid the big bucks, right?"

Harley didn't respond, and Eddie only nodded. As head of the fire department, Harley Daniels was Bates' peer and didn't have to take his gruffness. With Marconi absent, Eddie and I wouldn't have that choice.

Bates tapped a pen on the table. "Now...Detectives Stone and Pierce, we received a search warrant to investigate Aleksandr Stanich's pawn shop and associated structures. Later, you two began a search, and a fire destroyed the entire strip mall down to the ground. I would appreciate more details."

Eddie nodded. "Yes, sir. We executed the warrant

at seven-thirty p.m. and became suspicious of two men leaving from the back of the shops. The men carried backpacks, and we avoided contact. They had left a door unlocked, so we entered and started our search."

"And your findings?"

"We uncovered a substantial stock of counterfeit cash—Euro banknotes. We found cardboard boxes full of fake money, and most of it not good fakes. They batched them in bundles with straps that looked like the ones used at local banks."

"Euros? That's interesting. Did you keep samples?"

"No, sir," Eddie replied. He threw me a glance.

"Anyone can say pure speculation."

"Yes, sir. After looking around for a few minutes, Sergeant Pierce and I heard an odd noise I believed to be an old-style timer. We escaped just as the explosion occurred. I smelled an odd odor when we entered. I should have recognized it."

"What did the backpacks contain?"

"Fake money," I said, "just like in the boxes. We counted thirty or so bags that appeared full."

"Commissioner," Eddie said, "from the backpack we opened, I estimated one hundred thousand Euros—there could have been millions in fake bills."

Bates glanced at his watch. "And what about you, Harley?"

"The explosion ejected various remnants around the parking lot, into the street, and residue in a parking lot across the street. But …"

"But what?"

"The central explosion covered an area larger than a handful of plain C-4 would have done, Jimmy—

military-grade considering the debris radius."

"We're lucky it didn't vaporize you two. What about any pieces of the Euros?"

"Very few fragments," Harley said. "All the boxes burned, but we may find something. I hadn't known of the backpacks, but glancing through the rubble last night, I found scattered bits of yellow cloth. We'll take a second look."

"The printing machines were old," I said. "The banknotes are like the originals released in 2002—none the newer Europa variety."

"Europa variety? I'm not aware of currency updates. You're supposed to have pictures?" Bates asked.

"Yes, I emailed you, but here are the hard copies." I passed copies of the pictures to everyone and gave them a moment. "Those should serve as documentation of what we found."

"Not necessarily," Harley said. "Stanich could say he used it as a storage area for empty boxes and other crap."

"The last photo," I said, "shows a reflection. If you look closely, you can see the Stanich name on the window in the background. In other pictures, serial numbers are visible on the money we found. I'm not sure if that will be of benefit."

"Excellent idea, Pierce," Bates said, "but the evidence will be tenuous. Stanich had a plan in case we sniffed out their operations. They would burn it the hell down. He and his legal team will insist there's no evidence and stir up problems with the city council. I know he's ingratiated himself with the mayor somehow."

"Sir, two more items." My comments forced a smile from Bates.

"Sergeant, there always seems to be another item from you."

"Yes, sir. Please see photo number six. Bottom of the box toward the left. See the words?"

"Looks like an address. Praha? Where's that?"

"Prague."

"And?"

"Shipping labels," I said.

"You're saying someone mails fake banknotes to the Czech Republic? For what purpose? I can't believe we would be so lax anymore."

"Or it's a repurposed box from something else," Eddie offered. "Director Marconi—"

Bates held up a hand. "Wait, Eddie. Say nothing to her about Prague, or she'll be off on another goose chase."

I waited for a second, but Eddie didn't respond. "Okay, and I promise this is the last item." I pushed the papers toward Bates I'd gathered at the shop. "I've reviewed these."

He rifled through them and stared back at me. "Names, addresses, and dollar amounts. Not sure what it means."

"One more here," I said. "Look at this."

"Holy crap. An entire page says 'A. Sullivan' over and over."

"The two I highlighted?"

"Ten thousand dollars? One in October and one in November."

"Those match two entries I found on bank statements we found in his apartment."

"Fantastic. That will help to tie the Stanich operations to a crooked cop. But wait, what are these? This page is different—several are different."

"I think some are payouts, and a few are collections. For what, I can't be sure. Also, notice the top two examples show the Stanich Pawn Shop stationary—those are more likely legitimate transactions. The last column has an occasional entry with a product like 'Gun,' 'Jewelry,' and such. The format for credits and debits is the same on all the pages."

"A mixture of legal and illegal stuff," Eddie said.

"You should be able to knock this one out of the park, Jimmy," Harley said.

Bates didn't respond, crossed his arms, and stared at the documents. "Stanich, or his men, set it up. Someone tipped them about our warrant. If so, we can charge them with attempted murder."

"Tipped off? Definitely," I said. "The only other people who knew were the judge and the people in his office. Otherwise, it would have to be Čazim's attorneys."

Bates rubbed his eyes.

"They thought something was up," Eddie said. "I find it hard to believe this attorney would help Stanich, though, if his client killed Stanich's son-in-law, the Jankovich fellow. This fire complicates things."

Bates agreed, then pointed toward me. "Pierce, go through those records and find anything common between the names, addresses, amounts, etcetera. That might yield something, too."

"Yes, sir."

"Harley, I appreciate your attendance on brief

notice, and anything you can give us is great…but the faster, the better. We can't linger."

"Got it, Jimmy. I'll be in touch."

"I don't want to run you off, but I have a different case I need to discuss with these men," Bates said.

"Okay, you don't have to tell me twice," Harley said. He poured another cup of coffee into his oversized mug and sauntered out the door.

"Geez, he's a likable guy, but slooooowww. I hope we get something this week," Bates said. "Eddie, what's up with the back of your neck? That's a big bandage."

"Got a little burned last night."

"You don't want it infected, so don't be stubborn."

"Me?"

"Yes, you. And tell the workers comp folks, or they'll be after my ass." He glanced at his watch. "Now, gentlemen, I think we are well on our way to blowing up the Stanich bunch, I guess blowing up isn't the best thing to say, but it still leaves the Jankovich murder. Tell me more."

"Commissioner, you remember we encouraged Čazim to cooperate for consideration of a deal," Eddie said.

"Yeah, but that's over. Čazim double-crossed us, or his attorney did, and you two almost died."

"Besides saving his own skin, there may be other motivations," I said.

Bates shut his eyes. "Like what?"

"We can't forget the Kastrati angle," Eddie reminded us. "With Stanich out of the way—"

"Kastrati's bunch can take over his territory," Bates said. "*If* that's what this is about. Hell, for all we know, Kastrati set the device and is trying to blame Stanich and get rid of you two simultaneously. Look, we found another prostitute overdosed near downtown, and I've got to get moving. Here's the deal, guys. Get with Director Marconi when she returns tomorrow, and you all produce a plan. We'll hope to get answers from Harley by Monday at the latest. And I'll post officers out there at Stanich's place to watch over those embers."

"He'll raise hell," Eddie said, "as he did with me."

"That's too bad. An explosion engulfed his business and almost incinerated two cops. I may go out there myself and talk to him. Make him sweat. It does a soul good." Bates chuckled, then glanced over his glasses again. "Let me know if you find something noteworthy from those records, Sergeant Pierce."

"Yes, sir."

Eddie and I exited and headed to my office.

"I have a question for you, Eddie. These documents. They're for this year through November." We leaned over my credenza after I spread out the pages to find the one I needed. My stomach growled.

"We need to get you breakfast. Okay, so what am I looking at here?"

"This. One transaction a month all year."

"Right, and all say three thousand dollars with an address in Atlanta."

"Check the name," I said.

"S. Johnson?"

"A few weeks ago, Angie mentioned a detective named Johnson moved to Atlanta right after Sam Wulz died in the car wreck."

"Sylvia? No way, Ike. This can't be the same

woman that worked here. It would mean she's taking payments from Stanich?"

"Yeah…that's exactly what it means. But why?"

"Makes no sense to me. Before Sam Wulz died in the car wreck, he and Sylvia were an item while he was still married. She quit within a week after his funeral."

"Devastated and wanted to start over?"

"I thought, but maybe not? I figured it was because Sylvia thought Sam's son might take over his spot, and David hated her. He knew about the affair but never told his mother before she died," Eddie said.

"Could Sylvia have taken part in Sam Wulz's death?" I asked.

"Beats me. I thought Sylvia a kind soul, but I can't seem to judge people anymore."

Chapter Ten

New Year's had passed. I needed a restful weekend. My annoying neighbors had moved, taking with them their loud grunge music and constant arguments. A brief phone call came on Saturday morning from my flu-stricken mother. An odd text message from Nika buzzed in the afternoon asking about a party. She called me Eric, so I guessed she had intended it for her latest admirer. I asked how she was doing, but no response. All for the better, anyway. It would be nice to have a girlfriend, but not one deep into whatever swamp she waded.

Around and around, the evidence spun. We had made excellent progress on the Jankovich murder but were no closer to resolving the old Alexandria murders or Jack Marconi's death. The box at Stanich's place bothered me. Was the Prague address a coincidence? Why would the old Serb be stashing fake money to mail to Prague?

Linda Alvarez—a name I had been trying to remember. We had classes together in graduate school. She had been a fantastic student specializing in forensic imaging. I had her email and hoped she might identify the blurry address in my photo. I pulled the plastic container from under my bed, dusty still from my mother's attic, and found several college folders full of papers I had written. Somewhere in this mess, a contact list floated with all my college acquaintances' information. My phone vibrated again—I pushed up from the floor and sat on my bed.

"Henry? You want the good news or the bad news?"

"You don't sound good, boss."

"I'm rattled, but the good news is Sylvia Johnson-O'Brien is flying in on Wednesday if the airports are clear from the snow. She's bringing an attorney, but not her husband. I'm not sure what's up."

"That sounds promising. What's the bad news?"

Marconi's voice cracked. "It's started again. Already."

"What's started?"

"Interference."

"Interference?"

"Yeah, like before. I guess Stanich raised hell over the weekend, and the mayor made Harley pull his team from the shopping center remains."

"What jurisdiction does the mayor have over this?"

"Harley is furious, but he always backs down. He said the mayor wants to review any findings before making them public. We hadn't intended to make it public, so I'm not sure what he meant."

"What's Stanich got on Mayor Lewanski?" I asked. "I didn't find his name on the payee list, but I only grabbed part of it in my rush. It's alphabetical, and the last page ends in the Ks."

"I wonder the same thing. It wouldn't have surprised me to see his name. Find any other names of interest? I still haven't reviewed those."

"When you do, look at the last page, fourth from the bottom. M. Kovać, and big money, too. I found ten payments of at least a hundred thousand dollars."

"Yeah, I've got it here. I see it. Someone we should know?"

"Maybe. It's the only one on here without an address, but the bigger thing is I've heard that last name before."

"You know the name Kovać?"

"Yes, from Nika Campbell."

"Nika? Henry, you didn't go out with her again, did you?"

"No, no…the first time I met her at Manny's. She told me her dad had run off and left her and her mother. She said her mom called her dad a traitor, and they changed their name, she said from Kovać to Campbell."

"And?"

"She claimed her dad was Slovenian or Slovakian. She acted like a ditz and couldn't recall."

"Henry, I think Kovać is common in that part of Europe. There's even an NBA player with that name. But your little friend keeps popping up, doesn't she?"

"It seems so."

"Could you ask her out again?"

"I thought you wanted me to stay away?"

"Yeah, yeah. It might backfire, but if you go out with Nika again and drill her about…I guess 'drill her' isn't the best phrasing." She snickered.

"Yeah…no more drilling."

"She might disclose more about her family."

"I pushed her about it another time, Angie, and she shut me down. She admits her father wasn't a good man, but he had money."

"Let's not forget this. I'll only say if the opportunity arises, and you see her again, delve a little more into her family issues."

"We'll let things happen as they're supposed to. Are we off track on why you called? You mentioned interference?" I asked.

"Right. Mayor Lewanski."

"He can't suppress an investigation, can he? You said the D.A. is running against him in the March election. Suppose the D.A. would like to know about that interference? He could make it a campaign issue—and why would Harley be so easy?"

"Harley's always been a survivor. Bates wants us to go back out there and examine everything ourselves, despite the pressure from the mayor's office. Bag up anything we can put our hands on and bring it back to the lab."

****

The roads reopened early Monday morning after the bright sunshine changed the snow to dirty slush. Eddie planned to pick up Sylvia Johnson-O'Brien and her attorney at the airport and bring them in for questioning. Marconi stayed at the police station. They left it up to me to investigate the remnants of Stanich Plaza.

My arrival was timely. I drove Eddie's cruiser into the parking lot, hoping I would be alone. Far from it. Several parked cars sat in the slush, including a beige Lincoln encircled by three men in dark suits, all deep into a conversation with Aleksandr Stanich. Three other men in leather jackets swept the snow from the cement pads. I sent a text message to Marconi and bounded from the car.

I approached the leather-clad men and flashed my badge. "This area is under investigation by the Alexandria police department."

The three men stopped sweeping—one waved at Stanich.

I glanced at their faces, hoping I would recognize a face from the night Eddie and I visited, but none seemed familiar.

Stanich and his guests stepped closer. His facial expression did not change. "Ah, young Mr. Detective. And what can I do for you?"

A few feet away, Mayor Lewanski and his assistants took their measure of me.

"Sir, we have not completed our investigation of the fire that destroyed your businesses. I need these men to stop their cleanup."

"Investigation over—the fire people gone."

"I work in the police department, Mr. Stanich, not the fire department."

A voice boomed. "And who are you?" The mayor stood behind me in the dirty snow with his hands in his pockets. I offered my hand, but he did not reciprocate.

"Good morning. I'm Detective Sergeant Henry Pierce. Commissioner Bates and Director Marconi ordered me to review the situation here this morning after last week's fire."

"A quick review, Sergeant. The fire examination is complete, and Harley Daniels has withdrawn his investigators."

Lewanski's two smug underlings, both about my age, stood motionless behind the sneering mayor.

"The length of my review depends on what I find."

"Did an illegal search cause this?" he asked.

"The City of Alexandria did not cause this fire," I said.

"We are confident a fire ignited from a chemical

spill, Sergeant Pierce. No retardants or suppressants were available to hinder the fire's spread. Mr. Stanich would like to move on from this incident and rebuild his business."

"Thank you, but I wasn't aware the mayor's office rendered judgment on completing a fire or criminal investigation. Are those Chief Daniel's conclusions?"

"Criminal? Those buildings were ancient, sergeant. Time to let it go."

"Sir, my superiors believe otherwise. Chief Daniels confirmed the fire began after an explosion, then the fire spread rapidly after someone had spread an accelerant. That would make this arson. He mentioned no chemicals of any kind."

"Sergeant, there will be no arguments. This investigation is complete, and I would appreciate your vacating the premises."

"Sir, if there's an issue, I would suggest you talk to Commissioner Bates. I intend to complete my assignment, and you do not have direct authority over me to tell me otherwise."

"By God, I do have the authority, and I demand you leave these premises."

"I can call for backup, and we'll vacate everyone else from this location, starting with the Staniches."

"I'll have your job, boy."

"It's the law, sir. This is a crime scene, and everyone here is interfering with a criminal investigation."

Another Ford cruiser slid to a halt behind the Lincoln—the cavalry. Bates and Marconi hurried toward us, kicking through the slush. "Arthur, what in the devil are you doing here?" Bates asked.

"The man I wanted to see. Your sergeant here seems to believe I have no power over him when I give him a direct order."

Bates took off his blue stocking cap, glared first at Stanich and then Lewanski. "You have no power over an on-going investigation, Arthur. You can scare Harley away, but you won't scare me. Detective Sergeant Pierce is doing as asked. All of you need to leave."

"Careful, Jimmy."

"I have nothing to be careful about. Leave now, or I promise I'll haul you away. I'm sure the newspaper would like that story."

"This isn't over." Lewanski nodded toward his assistants, and they hustled back to the Lincoln.

Bates turned back toward Stanich. "I want to find out if any evidence is left in the snow, Stanich. I hope your men—"

"Nephews. These are my nephews. And why do you harass me so?" The three nephews stood a few feet away. Two smoked while the other sniffed and wiped his nose.

"Don't you want to know how the place burned?" Marconi asked.

"An accident. Arthur say so himself."

"Mayor Lewanski doesn't decide the beginning or end of a fire investigation," Bates said. "And, again, Mr. Stanich, if someone destroys or has destroyed any evidence, we will have a real problem."

"Evidence? Blah. What evidence?" He shifted his dog from one arm to the other.

Marconi popped her gum. "Mr. Stanich, we found evidence of counterfeit foreign money. The fire commissioner informed us that a military-type explosive started this, and a timer was used to ignite the blaze. Don't you think that's interesting?"

The old man's reaction was unforgettable. He handed his dog to one nephew and raised his cane toward Marconi. "Listen, all you. In Serbia, police mistreated me—it will not happen here."

Bates stepped closer, looming over the snarling old man. "Stanich, I won't allow you to threaten my officers or me. You all are hiding something, and we'll find out what it is. Now, you four can either leave, or I'll place you under arrest for interfering in a police investigation and stick you in the back of those police cars. Do we have an understanding?"

"So be it, commissioner. I will not give pleasure to you for arresting me. It is like the old country now." He waved at his nephews, and they sauntered over to their black SUV parked near the husk of the pawnshop.

"Thank you, Pierce. Angie, you two get to work. It seems they've swept off this one pad but search through that pile of slush over there."

"Okay. Let's go, Henry."

"I'll post a few officers here around the clock until you're satisfied. I wanted to do that to begin with before Harley discouraged it," Bates said.

"Sir?" I hoped he would listen.

"Yes?"

"The one nephew. He sneezed a lot."

Bates squinted at me. "I didn't bring any cold medicine."

"Uh, no, sir. I heard it the other night, too."

"You heard someone sneeze the other night? Dammit, what are you talking about? Angie, help me."

"Henry, get to the point, for God's sake," she said.

I took a deep breath. "When Lieutenant Stone and I were here the other night, we saw two men leaving with red backpacks. I didn't recognize any faces, hoods hid them, but I swear one sneezed the same as that one nephew did today."

"Well…interesting, but I couldn't make an arrest based on a sneeze."

"Good observation, though," Marconi said. "We've poked a bear, Jimmy. We need to hang on tight."

"Agreed."

****

The arsonists of Stanich Plaza had been more than efficient—we found nothing substantial. The mayor's office grew quiet as we headed toward the weekend. My colleagues offered nothing new concerning Čazim, Kastrati, or Sylvia Johnson-O'Brien. At a loss for activity, I shaped an idea I feared they wouldn't welcome—time to pull Nika Campbell back into orbit.

Chapter Eleven

"Beautiful country, Ike. Thanks for asking me. I should get outside the Beltway more often."

"It's great, isn't it? It reminds me of home." Nika and I drove west, and despite her coolness a few nights earlier, I had talked her into going to Luray to visit the caverns. Monday, Martin Luther King Day, and we had time enough to make the hundred-mile trip and be back by evening. "What's the farthest west you've been?" I asked my pretty passenger.

"Well…on vacations, I've been to Chicago twice, Las Vegas, San Diego, and my mother took me to Maui several times. She still goes to Hawaii three or four times a year. I'm not sure what all she does there and why she keeps going back. I get bored sitting on a beach. Mostly, I stay east—Boston to Miami and everywhere else up and down the coast. What about you? Have you traveled much?"

Funny, the more times we talked, the less she giggled as she did that first night at Manny's. The ditzy woman character had vanished.

"Finances were always tight growing up. After retiring from the army, my dad worked constantly, and my mother quit her part-time teaching job after her miscarriages. We drove up to Luray a few times and went to Little Rock once to visit relatives. I haven't been farther north than the District. Hey, look at that— what a view of the valley. There's a lot of snow through here. I've seen it stay until early April."

"Yep. I'm glad your little car can make it."

"My *little* car won't have any trouble."

She blew a sigh through her teeth. "It surprised me to hear from you, Ike."

"Busy, I guess."

"Right, me too. How are those murder cases going?"

I wanted to see her reaction. "They're about wrapped up, thank goodness."

"What? The story in the paper said the investigation had come to a dead end."

"Fake news, huh?"

"Whatever."

"We had a corrupt cop that killed himself, and his accomplice is in custody for the Angel Park murder. We're done with it." I peeked at her from the corner of my eye.

She stared out her window. "I thought it related to those murders from the 1990s. Weren't you investigating those?"

"Off and on. The current one is basically a copycat murder. A crime of passion, I guess. Nothing else. Those from the nineties might as well stay buried forever. Say, there's a convenience store up yonder. I need coffee and a snack. What about you?"

She sighed again and picked at her fingernails. "Okay, I'll get a cup."

After buying gas, I ran inside for a bathroom break and coffee. Nika hadn't returned to the car. Wandering back into the store, I found her in a corner under a blinking fluorescent light talking away on her phone. An old pot of overcooked nacho cheese masked the smell of her perfume. I made sure she saw me, then she covered her mouth for a moment as if I could read lips and, at last, ended the call. "Are you ready?"

"Yes, I finished talking to my mother."

"Good. Let's go."

She shuffled back to the car as if headed to a root canal and stayed quiet for a minute, giving her bottom lip a rough chewing. "I'm glad I'm not home today."

I punched the accelerator and jumped into the middle lane. "That's an unusual way to say you're having a good time. I'm glad I'm not home, either."

"It is so much …"

"So much, what?"

"Nothing. Life is hard sometimes, isn't it?"

"Yes, it is. Sometimes it's nice, though. Are you having issues with your mother?"

"My mother? Why?"

"You were talking to your mother in the store, and when you got back in the car, you looked like you'd lost your best friend."

"I wasn't talking to my mother."

"That's what you told me."

"Oh, right, sorry. A friend. Only a friend. My mother is having issues."

"Is she okay?"

"Sure, why wouldn't she be?"

"Lord, never mind. So, how is work going, and why do you keep looking behind us? I haven't missed the exit."

Her furrowed brow seemed stuck. If she wanted to be a spy, she needed more training. "Um, I'm watching the scenery. I love the hills with snow on them."

I tried again. "How is your job going?"

155

"Fine, why? You ask about my job a lot."

"See, Nika, you asked about my job, and now I'm doing the same. We're having a conversation."

"It's fine. Great. Same as always."

Thoughts of leaving her in the caverns crossed my mind. She smiled again.

"Tell me about the fire at that strip mall."

I hadn't mentioned a word of the fire. "It was hot."

"How informative. That's all? No investigation? Mr. Stanich has friends—"

"I hadn't realized how close you keep up with the Alexandria fire department. How do you know about Stanich and his shopping center? I didn't mention it."

"I'm an excellent observer, Ike. It's part of my job."

"I thought your job concerned southeast Europe, not southeast Alexandria?"

"Come on, Ike."

"Who is Eric?"

Her big black eyes almost popped from her head. "Eric? Wow…that's a little stalkerish."

"Trust me, I'm not stalking you. You messaged me two weekends ago about a party and called me Eric."

"Oops about the message." Another forced smile.

"Remember the nosy bartender at Manny's?"

"Not really."

"He remembered you. The bartender is also the owner. Not too long ago, he volunteered that an Eric came with you to his bar and had forgotten to take off his Homeland Security I.D."

"Ike, you're creeping me out. It's not your business—"

"Who you go out with isn't my business, that's

true, but I'm an excellent observer, too. If you want to trade work secrets, you go first."

She chewed on her lip again. "Eric and I are friends, okay? I've only seen him a few times."

"Whatever. I don't care about your relationships, but I want to know where you're coming from. Why it is when you're with me, you're so curious about the latest news from the Alexandria police and now, fire departments."

"Why are you hostile?" She wiped away an invisible tear.

"Here's what we'll do. We have nearly fifteen minutes until we get to the caverns. I'll tell you a few things, and you do the same…and we'll tell the truth." I had a feeling Eric was one of Nika's contacts Marconi mentioned a few weeks ago, or he could be just another schlub like me.

Smugness engulfed her face. "Okay, but you make it sound sinister. Relax."

"I'm relaxed, but I don't want to play any more games."

"Good. Go for it," she said.

I had practiced. "The fire at Stanich's was intentional. We think he had a drug ring and burned everything, including the drugs, before we could investigate."

Nika's eyes grew again. "Oh?"

So far, so good. I wanted her to believe we were moving down the wrong path. "We think Stanich has contacts in Europe and moves the drugs back and forth, but we aren't sure how to pursue that aspect. We may push the investigation up a level—let the FBI or DEA know what's going on."

"Nah."

"What? Human trafficking?"

"Doubtful." She shook her head like a teacher talking to a student.

"Stanich didn't offer much…could be the nephews instead of his daughters."

No reaction from her.

"That's our current conjecture. So?" I asked.

"So?"

"It's your turn."

"Right. Eric keeps me up to date about activities in Europe."

Generic and obvious. "Like what?"

"Oh, miscellaneous stuff. Homeland Security monitors potential terrorists, so we make sure we don't have undesirables coming over from the refugee groups."

"I wonder if I could talk to Eric sometime?"

"I doubt he would talk much business with you."

"Only you then?" I winked.

"Whatever. Hey, the cavern's entrance."

I almost shouted. "Thankfully. All these stories are making me tired. Let's hurry and get our tickets and head underground."

"Sure. Let me run to the restroom." The car door flew open before I killed the engine. "I'll call my mother, too. Not doing well." The door slammed.

I opened my door and shouted. "You said she was fine."

No response as she marched toward the stone-veneer building, a few yards away from the visitor center. I bought the tickets, then headed back to the restrooms, waiting five minutes, then ten. Leaning against the building near the women's side, I quizzed several people about a young, dark-haired woman in a purple overcoat. I even convinced an older woman to check the stalls for me. Nika had vanished.

Chapter Twelve

Someone called from my left. "Young man? Young man, stop…I need to talk."

I had pushed my way through the tourists, searching for Nika near the cavern's entrance. She had been antsy and distracted the entire trip.

"Young man?" I feared my push to the front of the line was about to get me yanked by security, but the same older woman who had searched the bathroom approached me from my left.

"Yes, ma'am. Thank you again for helping."

"Wait. You nearly gave this old woman a heart attack." She wheezed and leaned against a rock wall leading to the cave's entrance. "You try running that far when you're seventy-eight years old. Lord Jesus."

"What can I do for you? I'm still looking for the young woman I told you about."

She gulped the chilly air. "I know you are. I saw her."

"Where?"

"It wasn't two minutes after we talked. They were a good fifty yards north of the restroom, and your lady friend talked to two men in the parking lot. One, a big older guy, and the other one's around your age—he had a piece of a tattoo showing on the front of his neck. They stood near a new white sedan. It was one of those German cars. The big guy standing next to the car watched over them while they argued. I pretended to walk by…but I listened in."

"Thank you, ma'am. You're kind for telling me."

"You two make a cute couple and—"

"We're not a couple. You said you heard something?"

"Yes, and she has quite a salty mouth. You should talk to her. It's ugly on a pretty girl."

"Yes, yes, I'll mention it. What did you hear?"

She leaned closer. "I quote as I don't use this language, 'the bastard didn't tell me much, and it sounds like they're headed down the wrong track.' Then they argued about why he was there."

"Anything else, Ms.?"

"It's *Mrs*. Hockaday, but you can call me Judy."

Several tourists strolled near us. I touched her arm and motioned to move toward a jumble of rocks several feet away from the crowd.

"Oh, these rocks are cold. Okay, then the blond kid told the woman to head back to the city now instead of after."

"After what?"

"No idea, dear. The girl said no and trotted down the stairs toward this entrance. He talked on his phone for a minute, then both men followed her. That's when I came tearing through the crowd to check if you were here. I think they walked into the caverns."

"My name's Henry. I appreciate your search for me."

"Sugar, I know a love triangle when I see one." She leaned toward me again and whispered, "You're much better looking than the other man. He's shorter than her, and his blond hair flew everywhere. And that big guy …" She shook her head.

"Did you ever hear his name?"

"No, they never mentioned it."

"Thank you again. I think I'll use my ticket to check if they're in there. Do you need one?"

"Oh my, no, I've already gone on a tour, and my family is ready to leave. I need to find them. Good luck, young man." She hugged me, strolled back toward the stairs, and then waited a moment to get her breath.

I shifted back into line, and ten minutes later, I stood inside with a group ready for the tour. No need, though. I'd been here so many times with my parents, I could guide the group myself. The Queen's Throne, Pointer Rock, Lipstick Alley, all cavern room names I memorized and loved as a kid. If I stayed toward the back of the crowd, I would slip away at our first stop.

A cool, damp cavern welcomed us with a musty smell, as always, but much warmer than outside. I shed my coat, leaving me covered with my white hoodie. The mineralized water dropping from overhead had given everything a glaze in the artificial lights. We stayed far too long at the rocks known as the Queen's Throne. The guide went on and on, saying things I didn't remember from visits when my dad brought me here. We turned into another mammoth room, where I tried to avoid the dripping stalactites. God, this guide was an idiot, and I couldn't stand it.

"Hey, Cody? Many years ago, the guides told us that Confederates used this room to store supplies and gunpowder during the Civil War. The room to hide whiskey during Prohibition comes after Lipstick Alley."

"My supervisor knows everything about these caverns."

"Your supervisor needs to check," I said.

"It's probably an age thing," he said. "You've gotten things mixed up after so many years."

I wanted to smack this smug little turd.

The group moseyed toward Lipstick Alley. I took a few steps in their direction and then stopped. Cody quickened his pace, and the group ambled through the narrowing trail into the next great room. He turned off the lights behind him, and the caverns went black. If Nika and friends toured ahead of us, it wouldn't be long before they passed me going the other way.

I jabbed on my phone's light, found a dry spot near the Alley entrance, dropped my coat on a boulder, and leaned against a jumble of broken stones. Despite Cody's contrary thoughts of my memory, I recalled my dad's story about Confederates using this room. I missed him—my real-life rock to lean on.

Standing motionless chilled me, and I pulled up my hood. Voices grew closer now, female and male, and becoming louder. I turned off my light, wondering if Nika's two friends had followed her. Outlines of people emerged at the narrow entrance, each using their cell phone as a flashlight.

"So…where is he?" a male voice demanded. "That last group was a bunch of smelly tourists, and this is the last room."

"I told you I didn't know if he came down here for sure," a female responded—Nika, with the unmistakable Ice Queen tone of her voice.

"Come on, then. I think the exit is this way."

"Need a tour guide?" I asked. My question echoed through the pink and black pillars hanging above our heads.

"Ike?" Two lights hit me, then movement to my left.

I stepped forward, holding my hand up as a shield to the lights. "I see you made a quick friend, Nika." Still too dark to see distinct facial features, I made out a stout, short male outline. "Eric? Is that your name? We would have invited you if I knew you liked caves."

They eased toward me a few steps.

"There you are, Ike. I wondered what happened to you," Nika said.

"The last thing I remember, you had to pee. I got the tickets, and you never came out. I figured you had fallen into the sewer system—it looks like I'm correct." My eyes had adjusted, and I saw a few facial features.

Her friend messed with his bangs sticking out from under his jacket's hood. "Detective Pierce. I'm Eric Berkshire, the one you've been asking about." He had a slight accent.

"It's *Sergeant* Pierce. Yes, your name has come up before. Nika mentioned you once, and even a local bartender knows your name. How's your job at Homeland Security?"

"Cut the crap, Pierce. We know all about you."

"What brings you to Luray Caverns other than playing spy with Ms. Campbell?"

"A warning."

"Go on."

"You and your colleagues are trifling with something you cannot grasp," he said.

"I bet we could."

He slipped closer toward me.

"You and your department's investigations need to end."

"I'm not sure why you're worried," I said. "According to Mata Hari here, we're all bastards."

Nika's eyes shot daggers.

"See, Nika, I have my spies, too."

She put a hand on Eric's shoulder. "Eric? How did he—"

"Never mind."

"What do you want, then, Eric? We have ethnic murders going on, a murdered cop, a crooked undercover cop offing himself, laundered money. You want the whole Alexandria police department to sit around with our thumbs up our asses?"

"If the thumb fits."

"Okay, I'll go back tomorrow morning and tell everyone that Eric, the Homeland Security guy, wants us to drop everything because he says so."

"No need. Your bosses don't concern me."

"Again, what do you want?" The light on his phone vanished. An outline slipped toward Nika.

"Ike, you need to worry about yourself," Nika said. The light on her phone went out, too.

Footsteps nearby. Was Nika leaving?

Eric laughed loudly, echoes bouncing around us. "Your colleagues are fools and keep tilting at those same old windmills."

"Like Don Quixote?"

Air exploded from my lungs as if squeezed by a vise. Someone had grabbed me from behind in a crushing lock from two massive muscular arms. A light flashed back on. Eric pulled off his hood and grinned at me a few inches from my face. "Charlie is strong, don't you think?"

"Charlie?" I shivered from a snicker of warm

breath down the back of my neck.

Eric straightened his back. "You like Don Quixote, Pierce? Remember, the Duke said, 'Let us say I dislike stupidity. Especially when it masquerades as virtue.' You and your friends' virtue hide a ton of stupidity."

A grunt from behind me, then a sudden blow to the crown of my head jolted a memory. An errant pitch during a baseball game hit me above my right ear. My knees hit the ground, and I tasted dirt. My mother screamed near the dugout as darkness enveloped me.

****

"Ike? Ike, wake up." My mother's voice. "Baseball game?"

"Mom? What happened? The pitcher beaned me. Where's Dad?"

"Momma, come in here," she shouted to my grandmother. "Baseball, Ike? What are you talking about?"

"I saw the pitch. Dad said to hit the ball with my bat instead of my head."

My grandmother's voice to my left. "Susan, he's out of his mind."

"No, he's not. Ike, someone hit you on the head with a rock. That baseball game was fifteen years ago."

"What?" I tried to sit up, but she pushed me back to the mattress. "Oh…worst headache—"

"You aren't getting up yet. Doc is coming by tomorrow. I think you can move around normally after that."

"Where's Clicker? Has he caught any more squirrels?"

"Ike…we put Clicker down last year. Don't you remember?" My mother wiped her eyes.

"Right, right. How did I get home?"

"Do you remember the cave? The authorities thought a rock fell on you."

"No. It was—"

"Listen. They figured out it wasn't an accident."

"Eric something. Nika and her chauffeur."

"You should have stayed away from that no-good bimbo," she said.

"Bimbo," my grandmother said. "I'll say she's a little bitch."

My mother's chin quivered. "Momma."

"How did I get here? The caverns are closer to Alexandria than here."

"You were in the hospital for forty-one days in Luray. We didn't know if you would ever come out of it." Tears dripped onto her cheeks. "They wanted to kill you, honey."

"I told you bad juju, boy," my grandmother reminded me.

"You've been here three days, Ike. Today is March third. Your friends in the police department brought you down."

"Six weeks? That was quite a knockout," I said, at last understanding I laid in my old bedroom. My mother had left it much the same, my supercar photos on one wall opposite my diplomas and other school memorabilia. She had hung pictures of my dad in place of posters of girls in bikinis that had once covered the maroon wall leading into the hallway. "What's going on? I need to talk to my bosses. Where's my phone?"

"It's a hot mess. Not to worry now, though. Angie and Eddie are coming tomorrow."

"Where's my car?"

"Outside in the driveway."

"All right. I'm ready to eat."

"Good. You've gotten even skinnier than before, if that's possible. They took out your IVs and catheter last night and took you off the medicine that kept you asleep."

"How about your pancakes and sausage tomorrow? Eddie likes pancakes and sausage."

"Aren't you the one to think of your colleagues? You've fallen in with a good bunch of folks. It has worried them sick. But Angie—"

"Angie what?"

"She's not happy you took off as you did with that girl."

"I had an idea…I can't remember what it was. I hope I don't get fired."

"You getting fired isn't an issue." My mother hesitated, turned away, and stopped at the doorway. "So…get some rest, and tomorrow most of this will clear up for you."

Maybe my head injury was worse than she admitted. If I could only talk to Eddie.

****

The clock chimed seven times. No doubt my mother would object, but I made my way down the dark hall to the bathroom by myself. I could still find my way in the dark after all these years. The bathroom smelled of facial night cream, and my old Batman nightlight gave enough light to see. I had forgotten about irritation from the catheter's removal—the sudden burning sensation made me yelp.

"Ike? What is it?" My mother's hearing was as good as ever.

"I'm fine…in the bathroom…headed back to bed."

"I wish you had rung your bell so I could help you."

"All good, Mom."

Now my grandmother was awake. "Susan? What's all the yelling about?"

"Ike had to pee, and he did it by himself."

"How nice. Ike, you need any help?"

"No. I'm going back to bed. Thank you." Coming home could be too comfortable.

I propped myself up in bed and turned on my school lamp, the one I had colored the base with a navy-blue magic marker in the fifth grade. Most of my artwork had rubbed off, but the brass-plated stand had kept its dark patina. I had no headache for now, and despite my growling stomach, I hoped my mother would go back to sleep for a while longer.

My phone. My mother had left it on the headboard next to my Porsche model car. Something had to have been in the news about the goings-on in Alexandria. My social media had been quiet, so I surfed around newspaper sites. There it was—my picture from work on the second page of the January twentieth edition of the *Alexandria Banner*.

Detective Hospitalized after Accident in Luray. 'Late Monday evening, an accidental rock collapse hospitalized Detective Sergeant Henry Pierce in Luray Caverns. Police Commissioner James Bates said his department was investigating in cooperation with local authorities. Falling rocks collapsed on the detective when he wandered off from a tour group. Sergeant Pierce will stay at the local hospital in Luray as the injuries were severe.'

That's one way to make the news. I searched my name in several more issues, but nothing else showed itself. The folks at the *Banner* published no follow-up stories, at least any having my name included. A headline four weeks later grabbed my attention: Detectives Suspended. "Mom? Get up." I stumbled down the hall toward her room.

"What? What's wrong now?" She hurried out of her bedroom in her bathrobe, and my grandmother peered around her door.

"I found an article from Alexandria. It said they suspended Angie and Eddie ten days ago."

"Settle down. Your headache will come back. That's one reason they're coming. They want to update you."

"The article claims insubordination. Mayor Lewanski is the only one quoted—nothing from Commissioner Bates."

"I told you it's a mess, Ike." She rubbed her eyes and fussed with her hair. "Momma, let's get breakfast going. Eddie told me the other day they would leave early and be here before nine o'clock."

Granny appeared in the doorway. "Let's cook up those spicy links I bought the other day. Hey, Ike, I cut out the picture of you from the newspaper and put it in your old scrapbook."

"Thanks, Granny."

"Anything for you, honey." She rubbed my arm. "Why don't you take a shower and get ready for your friends? Your mom and I will take care of everything." A welcome suggestion, and I soon stood in the warm, soothing water. The image in the mirror made me shudder. I had to have lost twenty pounds. My grandmother was right about Nika.

Chapter Thirteen

A din of voices flowed from the living room into the hall while I shaved. More nicks than usual on my throat, but not too tricky—someone had kept me shaven. I pulled out my mother's butterfly-shaped compact mirror to view the wound near the crown of my head. The hair was growing back—the stitch marks still visible, but the scalp was healing nicely.

"Ike?" My mother hammered on the door. "Are you done? Angie and Eddie are here."

"Be right there." I hurried to my bedroom, the same time my mother picked to show my co-workers around the house.

"Ike…you'll freeze in your underwear. Put your clothes on. Goodness."

"Sorry, I'm trying to get back to my room," I said. Both my bosses gave me giant smiles. "Hi, folks. Be right there."

"Good to see you," Marconi said. She snickered, causing my mother to laugh.

"Honey, don't be embarrassed. You're skinny as a rail and not much to see."

"Thanks," I said and slammed my door. I put on gym pants and selected one from a score of my college sweatshirts, then joined everyone at the table. "I never realized how much I would miss that mug of yours, Eddie."

"And me, too, Ike. Jesus, this scared us." He

opened his cloth napkin and dropped it in his lap.

Marconi showed her fake stern look. "To get this out of the way, don't go out on your own again. *Chiaro?*"

"What?"

"Clear? Are we clear?"

"Yes, ma'am, but we talked about this beforehand."

"I thought you would keep it local, Henry, not wander off halfway across the state."

"What's this?" my mother asked. She dropped her fork on the platter of scrambled eggs. "Angie, you knew about this?"

"Only a piece, Susan. All we discussed was his meeting up with this girl and trying to get more information."

My mother stared at her lap, resisting the urge to start an argument.

"Ike, you can't do that stuff," my grandmother said. "You're all we got."

"I know."

"Come on, ladies, let the poor boy recover," Eddie said. "I'm starving. Angie wouldn't stop anywhere." He gave thanks, then my mother offered him a plate before everyone else.

"We have regular sausage, these are the hotlinks Momma bought, and the eggs are straight from the coop. Coffee, biscuits. We have strawberry and apricot jam Momma made last fall. She's won awards at the fair, you know."

Eddie drew a deep breath. "Ladies, it doesn't get better than this. It reminds me of growing up in southern Georgia. My daddy cooked better breakfasts than my mother, but she sure could make the pies."

I couldn't stand it any longer. "Look, you all need to tell me what's happening. The paper said the city suspended you."

Eddie nodded toward our boss, then took in a mouthful of biscuit.

Marconi wiped her mouth. "We have a lot to tell you, but much of it is business I don't want to talk about in front of your family. In fairness, I don't mind telling everyone here that, yes, they suspended us for forty-five days, with pay. The mayor instigated it. And, Henry, you're officially on medical leave with no end date."

"Mom, is my injury worse than you told me?"

"No, honey, Doc will be here later, and—"

"Wait a minute, folks." Marconi waved her hands. "We worked a deal with Commissioner Bates. He's on board with everything. We'll vanish for several weeks, and the official story is you're injured far worse than reported and need more time for physical and emotional therapy. You can't return to work until after that."

"Uh, okay. Why?" I asked.

"Flexibility," Eddie answered. "We're appearing to pull way back on our investigation and staying low for now. In the meantime, we have other plans." He smiled. "Plus, we get to stay here for a few days."

Marconi nodded. "And most of those plans we'll keep to ourselves."

"I like intrigue," my grandmother said. She leaned forward and rested her chin on her hands.

"Never mind," my mom said. "This is police business. Right, Angie?"

"To be safe, Susan, I would rather you two not

know everything. I can tell you Nika Campbell has disappeared. Even my connection at the NSA has lost contact with her. The chauffeur vanished, too. Her friend, Eric, is missing, and Henry?"

"Yeah?"

"Those aren't their names. His name is Erik, with a K. The last name is Baracnik, not Berkshire. He's Czech…from Prague, to be exact."

"Prague again? I thought I heard an accent," I said.

"And Charlie, the chauffeur?" she asked.

"Yeah?"

"His actual name is Chasna Kovačić. He's Serb," Marconi said.

Eddie spoke with a mouthful of biscuit. "These conspiracies people think you dream up are more than real—"

"I'm not that good of a fantasist," Marconi said.

"Tell him about Čazim," Eddie said.

"Right. Čazim confessed to the Jankovich murder."

"Awesome," I said.

"After misleading us on the Stanich Plaza angle, we pursued the death penalty. He gave in but insisted Archie Sullivan dismembered the body," Marconi began. "Supposedly, Archie had the idea to tie it back to the cold case murders to confuse us, as we had guessed."

My mother contemplated something and raised her hand.

"You can speak, Susan…it's your house."

"I know—I didn't want to interrupt. You know, Angie, I'm not always the smartest person in the room, but in his own stupid way, Čazim opened Pandora's Box."

"How so?"

"If they had killed the guy without cutting him up, there never would have been another look at those old murders again. As it is, their choices reopened those cases and caused a domino effect."

Eddie slow-clapped several times. "Excellent. No wonder Ike is so good at this detective stuff."

"You're right," Marconi said. "Their stupidity blew the lid off this from over two decades ago. Now the whole intrigue is back front and center and rolling again."

"We have one other thing we can mention in front of you all," Eddie said. "Ike, they charged Sylvia Johnson-O'Brien with obstruction of justice for not being forthcoming about those payments found on Stanich's stationery. She's held in Alexandria. I guess her marriage is on the rocks after her husband found out. She's terrified."

Marconi smirked. "Yeah, she deserves it, though. "She was terrible to everyone back then."

"Oh?" I answered, my head pounding like a bass drum. "What of Sam Wulz's accident? Any movement there?"

"No, nothing at all. That part is a dead end," Eddie said.

"I can tell by Ike's face he has a headache," my mother said. She dropped her napkin on the table and gave us her stern face. "Ike, finish those eggs and go back to bed. Granny and I will clean this up, and we'll get y'all unpacked. Eddie, I'm afraid tonight you must sleep on the extra mattress in Ike's room. We've scrubbed the floors. Is that okay with you?"

"Sure, Susan. I don't mind roughing it with

Wonder Boy over here…if he can handle it."

A knock on the door stopped the conversation and jolted the faces of my family. My mother hurried to the door and peeked gently through the curtains. "Shoot, it's only Doc Akers. We expected him later this morning. He probably wants breakfast."

"Your doctor makes house calls?" Marconi asked.

My grandmother showed a sly grin. "For us. It's Reggie, my brother."

****

Doc Akers, my great uncle, cleared me to resume all activities. The headaches came and went during the day, but he told us not to worry. Snow had dusted the ground again, with more on the way, so I took Marconi and Eddie around the farm in my Dad's battered, white Chevy pickup. It sputtered in the cold a little more than usual, groaning like an old bull, and the tailgate wouldn't stay latched, but it still had enough life to do its job.

I stopped at a gnarled oak, its biggest branch showing pieces of a rope swing I made in the sixth grade. "My friends and I used to take turns swinging on this giant oak. But later, it became the Time's Up tree. This is where my dad would take me when I had pushed my luck too far. He had a lot of patience, but when he had had enough of whatever I did, he'd say, 'Time's up.' We would come to this tree, and I learned to shut my mouth."

Eddie slapped his knee and grinned. "At least you knew what would happen. At my house, it came as a surprise from my mother or daddy."

Marconi grimaced. "Both my parents taught high school. They had plenty of rulers around the house.

And the nuns, too. I think that's why I have arthritis in my knuckles."

I parked the pickup on a steep downgrade overlooking a creek. We sat for a minute listening to the heater's fan churn. "All right, what are we doing? Are we at a dead end? Are we stopped stone cold again like twenty-five years ago?"

"Comparable," Marconi said. "I know outside the department, and some people within, think I'm an obsessive loon. But I'm not the one that's stopped these investigations when they warm up a bit. This is another example."

"You mean Stanich?"

"Yeah, Stanich. He's cleared the old shops and is ready to rebuild. Harley has given us nothing of use from the remnants. Stanich claims he used the printers for mailers, invoices, and other business stuff."

"The printing plates were hard plastic, remember? There wouldn't be much left of them after the fire," I said.

Eddie dusted off the pickup's splitting, fake-leather dash. "I've never seen a mailer from them. But it seems like things are more positive this time. Commissioner Bates has been great. He's fed as much information as he dares to the D.A., and those little tidbits are leaking out into the mayoral campaign. Our dear mayor is in trouble. If he loses the election, Stanich can come back on our radar without protection from the mayor's office."

"Yeah, I can't figure it," Marconi said. "I can't find any actual connection on how he and Stanich got so close. Eddie found out something, right?"

"Do what?" he asked.

"Are we boring you?"

"No, Angie…thinking about my parents. I would love to go back to a farm like theirs."

"Tell Henry about the Stanich nephews."

"What about them?"

"Eddie. The three nephews—"

"Oh, right…the three nephews are around forty-five to fifty years old. They're Stanich's sister's kids, for sure. Not a good trio, as far as I can tell. We believe they were part of the *Die Teufel's Engels* gang during the wars, the Serbian movement with a German name."

"Yeah, I remember this part," I said. "The leather jackets and those tattoos."

"Tell him the last part," Marconi said.

"The calling cards?"

"Yeah?"

"We have information that many victims found in Bosnia back then had an Orehnjaca stuck somewhere on their bodies, usually the breast pocket if the victims had one."

Marconi pulled the mirror toward her to check for any lipstick on her teeth. "We were going after them for the 1995 murders. A few days after they hospitalized you, we also reminded Mr. Stanich and Mayor Lewanski of our doubt about the fire."

"Yeah, and by Friday, the city suspended us. I thought Bates would have a heart attack, but Angie and I produced a plan over a weekend. It settled him down."

"What's the plan?" I asked.

"Not yet. We're heading back," Marconi said. "I can see the veins pumping in your temples. I promised your mom to bring you back in thirty minutes, and we'll do so. You'll get the rest of our story tonight or tomorrow."

The throbbing pain in my temples halted my objection. I put the truck in gear, searching for reverse with a loud grind, and we eased back onto the dirt road to the house.

"And something else."

"What?" I asked.

"This won't upset either of you, but I heard from Manny the other day. A weird conversation. He surprised me and called on my work phone. He's selling his bar."

"Why?" Eddie said.

"He's not happy with his environment or something like that. It sounds like he's moving back to Croatia. It wasn't clear why he'd leave a booming business. He's found a buyer, it seems. Someone from outside Alexandria."

I parked the pickup and found my mother waiting at the front door in her heavy jacket and house shoes. This was like coming home after curfew. "Ike, it's about time. Your head will explode if you don't listen to me."

****

Dark clouds burst with ice pellets before noon the next day, and snowflakes the size of dimes swirled in the wind. We built a great fire in the red-bricked fireplace, its mantle blackened underneath from smoke stains, then we nodded off to naps after sandwiches and peach cobbler.

I woke to female voices laughing on the other side of the house. Eddie still slept, his neck cranked hard to the right. "Mom? What's so funny?" I called out.

"Come back here to my crafts room."

My parents had intended the fourth bedroom for another child that never came. My mother remodeled it several times over the years, the last combining all her materials and two sewing machines to make it a craft room. She had her mess, but at least she collected it in one place.

I peered around the door jamb and saw Angie Marconi sewing away on a white piece of cloth no bigger than a handkerchief. "Director, you're a seamstress, too?"

"I'm not. I've learned everything in the last forty-five minutes."

"You're doing great, Angie," my grandmother assured her. She patted her on the shoulder and giggled. "One of these days, you'll make a great housewife. We could teach you to cook, too."

"Sounds tempting, Rita Faye. Better than chasing criminals, it would seem. I gave it everything all these years and wound up getting suspended. But I can already cook. My father was Italian, and I've got a million recipes."

"As fascinating as this is, I'll go check on Eddie," I said. "I'll see if he's awake by now."

"You do that, Henry. Tell him he's sleeping his life away while I'm having a blast back here with your folks."

"Eddie had a full stomach," my grandmother said. "Peach cobbler and a hot toddy always knocked out your grandpa, too."

"Wait a minute, Ike," my mother said. She handed me my white hoodie as a tear dripped down her cheek. "I fixed it. Those people ripped the hood when they beat you."

My grandmother sighed. "I scrubbed and scrubbed to get blood out—used Ajax even."

"I'm up, I'm up," Eddie called out. "Did you say my name?"

"They're bragging about you, Eddie," I yelled back. "Staying awake and protecting us." Shouting across the house hurt my head, so I wandered back into the living room. The outline of Eddie's silhouette showed through the front window. I glanced out the door. "You okay?"

He tilted his head back and forth. "My neck. I must have slept funny."

"Yeah, you didn't look comfortable. Aren't you freezing?"

"Trying to wake up."

"I've got to shut this door. Come back in."

"Okay, but is there a place we can talk? Out of range from the others, I mean?"

"I guess so. How about my dad's old shop? It's hooked up to the propane tank, and we can fire up the heater."

"Perfect. Let me get coffee, and I'll help you start it." We grabbed our mugs, then kicked through the snow and ice drifts forming between the chicken coop and the shop.

I found my key hidden in the seam of one of the old logs holding up each corner. My dad said this was the original homestead of the first settlers but said he couldn't prove it. No matter, I didn't need proof. If my dad said it, that was good enough for me.

The shop had changed little since my dad died, and the heater came to life right away. He had a place to store his tools, work on farm equipment, with a smaller area set aside for woodworking. Our initials on his knotty workbench still showed, despite all the dust. I sat and pointed toward Eddie.

"What do you think, Eddie? Have a seat over there."

He eased down onto a stool near one of the workbenches. "I'm jealous again. I could retire to a place like this, no problem. Leave all the police business behind...wow. Watch out."

"It's a mouse. We need to put traps out here. Are you scared?"

"It *startled* me."

"Sure it did, and right, a good place to retire. My parents made many plans, too. But then my dad died a few days after his fifty-seventh birthday."

"Life has its own plans, Ike, whether or not we like them. I'll be sixty this year, and I have many more years behind me than I do in front. We need to enjoy this ride as much as we can because it can stop at any time."

"The truth." I sighed. "Eddie...am I on the right track?"

"Right track? Like what?"

"Police work. I cruised around several years looking for troublemaking tourists, but my first assignment as a detective turns into this nightmare."

"Listen, we've told you why your application stood out to us. Angie knew your old boss, and you came highly recommended, no matter what those tourists at Mt. Vernon thought." He offered a sly smile. "Look, this case you're on has defeated everyone that's touched it. It's ugly, man, it's ugly, and it has nothing to do with you. It's back, like a cancer."

"The Erik guy."

"Who?"

"One of the guys that attacked me in the cave."

"What about him?" He gave me a sidelong glance and slurped his coffee. I don't know how the man ever slept with so much caffeine pumping through his veins.

"He said something…something about people using virtue to cover up for stupidity. Are we the stupid ones, Eddie?"

"Nah, we ain't stupid. Partially blind is a better way to put it."

"How so?"

"We can't see a complete truth, can't see the forest for the trees if you will. We get a piece of something, but we can never tie it all together. You've had that experience now."

"No doubt. I thought Angie was a lunatic when she first talked about a conspiracy. She's reminded me of Inspector Javert chasing Jean Valjean. He couldn't let it go either. But don't you think the government is too incompetent to hide something, and why this crap? Why would anyone care about squabbling old enemies from a place halfway around the world?"

Eddie shrugged. "I'm not aware of the Val Jean case, but I've given up on trying to understand the whys. And it can't be the entire government. They couldn't keep a secret if they had to."

"Benjamin Franklin said three people can keep a secret if two of them are dead."

"Yeah, that's usually the case. This deal, though…I don't know. Something happened, and someone, or several someones, has spent a lot of energy over the years covering up for it. No, Angie isn't loony, but she is tenacious. She'll find out someday…for her and for Jack. And another thing."

"Yeah?"

"Don't fight life, man. Let it be your friend, not your adversary. I've had a hard time remembering that myself."

"Hey. You guys in here?" A sweep of frosty air engulfed us, then the door slammed. "So dark out there."

"Hey, Little Miss Seamstress, did you learn how to sew?" Eddie asked.

"I did learn a lot. Rita Faye is something."

"She's special," I said.

"Gosh, this is great in here. Hey, Eddie, an old player over here…lots of cassettes."

"Yeah?" He stood, then leaned over the table, stirring through the pile of plastic cases. A cloud of dust billowed up around his face. He fanned his face of dust, then sat again.

"You ought to dig through those," I said. "Since the player doesn't work, I bet my mom would let you have a few tapes. I don't mess with them since I download my music."

Eddie rolled his eyes. "Sure you do. I'll ask Susan later."

"Well, guys, I don't want to interrupt the dirty talk and centerfolds," Marconi said after sitting in an old lawn chair.

"Us?" I asked.

"It's been a long day already, Angie," Eddie said.

"Susan and Rita Faye are planning dinner, but we have a few minutes."

"My dad and I had many great talks out here—one

thing I miss the most about him."

Marconi studied me for a moment and took a deep breath. "So, Henry, we're going to Europe."

Eddie slapped his knees. "Whew. I'm glad you brought it up, Angie. I've been about to bust."

"Europe? Why?"

She shrugged. "We've got time off. Why not?"

I glanced up at the gray rafters filled with cobwebs and the mud sacks of a hundred dirt daubers. "Come clean. Y'all are up to something."

Marconi crossed her arms and leaned back in her chair. "Henry, you're one sick young man. Your wound is causing all kinds of havoc with your physical and mental functionality."

"What? No, I'm getting around fine."

"No, you're not. Eddie and I, and others, have arranged for a specialist. It's the only way."

"What the hell?" I asked. Eddie grinned like the Cheshire Cat.

Laughter burst through the rafters. "Relax, Henry," Marconi shouted. "God, I thought you could take a joke."

"What's so funny?"

"You're our alibi. We're using you as an excuse," Eddie said.

"An excuse for what?"

Marconi threw her arms open. "Going to Europe. We've booked flights for Wednesday next week to Vienna, ostensibly to get you treatment for a head injury. They have specialists there practicing new experimental methods. I hope they aren't painful."

"I don't need experiments. And why Vienna?"

"Ike, listen. It's a story, man, our cover story,"

Eddie said. "Vienna is only our starting point."

"I forgot already. Maybe I do need treatment."

"Specialists are there, Henry, but you have no actual doctor's appointment. Okay? My friend at the NSA knows of a neurologist's name we can use as cover. We'll get you a fake appointment to make things look right."

"That seems...strange," I said and threw a glance at Eddie.

"Who is this guy at NSA that keeps helping you all these years?" Eddie asked. "Jack's old friend? Aren't you afraid he'll get in trouble if someone finds out, as in losing his job, if not going to prison?"

"Not a guy, a woman, and she wasn't Jack's friend. She's actually a sister."

"Jack's sister?" he asked.

"No. My half-sister."

"What?"

"I didn't know about her until college. My dad finally told me. We're not best buds or anything, but we help each other as needed."

"But, again, wouldn't everyone over there know if she's helping you?" Eddie asked. He squinted with disbelief. "Wouldn't the NSA make a connection and lock her out cold from everything at the agency?"

"Doubtful. We have a mysterious way to communicate."

"Can you tell us?" I asked. "We can keep the secret."

"I guess so. We use a pen and paper, put it in an envelope, stamp it, and mail it. It's called a letter. My sister says they're so knee-deep in electronic surveillance they've forgotten the basics."

"My God," Eddie said. "Unbelievable."

"What is Vienna's attraction?" I asked.

"Eddie, you tell him."

"Ike, you're supposed to be the super-smart one. Guess what's a three-hour bus ride from Vienna?"

"Salzburg? I'd love to hear y'all sing *My Favorite Things*."

"God, you can be so dense," she said.

"Try harder, Ike. What's to the north of Austria, and what's its biggest city?" he asked.

My head hurt again. "The Czech Republic and—"

"Prague," they both shouted.

"It's all set, Henry. We'll get to Prague, one way or another."

"But again, why Vienna? And once we're there, what do we do? Walk around the street asking about cold-case murders?" I asked.

"Quite a hit to the head, wasn't it?" Marconi asked.

"Then go slow and explain, please."

"Can I say something first?" Eddie asked.

"Please do," she answered.

"I got to ask, and I mean this with all respect, Angie, but aren't we getting in over our heads?"

"Eddie, we've talked about this—"

"I know, I know, but with Ike's injury, I'm not sure we're good to go. I'm only trying to be frank here. We are city detectives, not CIA or something. This is big stuff."

Marconi stood, popped her gum, and gazed toward the door. Ice pellets pecked away at the shop's two windows. The heater gave the only other noise, hissing as it did when fuel ran low. "Eddie, please have faith in me."

"I do, but …"

"It seems a little problematic," I said.

She stepped close to the heater and rubbed her hands together. "I feel wonderful about our plans, guys. I've been working with someone, and I'll reveal a name after we get there."

Eddie sighed. "Yeah, Ike, and another of your old girlfriends read the newspapers."

"Who?" He couldn't mean Nika. Not after the cave.

"Linda Alvarez. She said you sent her a picture with an address on it. She read about your injury and forwarded the information to Angie."

"Am I in trouble again?"

"Since I'm suspended, there's not much I can do now, is there?"

"Yeah, I guess not. What did she say?"

"Ms. Alvarez's forensic efforts confirmed an address. She's great. We could use her in our department," Marconi said.

"The shipping label on the box?" I asked. What incredible luck, and I wouldn't mind crossing paths with Linda again.

"I can't pronounce it, Henry. Here." She pulled a crinkled piece of paper from her coat pocket and handed it to me.

"Sochařská 1Bn4, Apt. D, Bubeneč, Praha, Czechia."

"We Googled it up," Eddie said. "It's an apartment building."

"Really?"

"There's more," he said.

Marconi's chin quivered. She turned away, then

covered her mouth.

Eddie rubbed his hands together. "The address is a block from Stromovka Park—the place where they discovered Jack Marconi's body."

Chapter Fourteen

Marconi used my dad's workshop as an office while we prepared for Vienna. I insisted my family knew something of our plans. Otherwise, their worries about my head injury would be endless. We offered enough information to smooth their concerns, but my grandmother couldn't help repeating 'bad juju.'

Eddie drove us to Charlotte in his old Taurus and left it at a junkyard for safekeeping, or so he hoped. Our cell phones remained in the trunk after Marconi had bought us prepaid burner phones in Raleigh. The junkyard's owner was a distant cousin of Eddie's late wife. The cousin parked it north in the fields of forgotten scrap, we all piled in his old van, and he took us the rest of the way to the Charlotte airport.

The direct flight from Charlotte to Vienna lasted ten hours, with me hunched into an economy-sized seat—my partners shared a two-seat row across the aisle. I found myself in the middle section next to a family of three, including a child with a terrible cold. I couldn't ride on the wing, though, and my earbuds offered me peace for several hours. In the meantime, Marconi and Eddie slept across the aisle from me.

I awoke from a jolt as the plane landed.

"About time, Ike. We didn't think you would sleep the whole way," Eddie said.

"Uh, right, Mr. I Never Snore. I fell asleep an hour ago after hours of resting my chin on my knees. I've had my challenges over here." We taxied to the gate, and I stood at once to grab my bag from the overhead compartment. "Eddie, you may have to carry me off. My legs are numb."

"Quit whining," Marconi said. "Our rooms are a few blocks from here, then we can eat."

We survived a lengthy line at customs, grabbed our bags, and found ourselves on a busy sidewalk waiting for a bus outside the terminal.

"If I had my actual phone," I complained, "I could use the app that translates spoken and written words. Instead, I've got this flip phone that works like a prop from Star Trek."

"I told you guys why I wanted these phones," Marconi said. "We're off the grid here."

"It will be harder to find one another, too, if we get separated."

Eddie clenched, then unclenched his jaw." Come on, Ike. We'll be at the hotel soon, have an Austrian beer and some food, and settle in for the night."

Busses passed by for thirty minutes, none stopping at the spot where we stood. Marconi paced and mumbled under her breath when another bus appeared. She grabbed her bags. "This is it. Elizabeth Street." We crowded our way on, holding our bags and standing in the aisle. She had misread the sign, and thirty minutes later, we stood outside the airport again. "Henry, one word out of you, and I'll send you for brain surgery as soon as we can find that doctor."

"Fine, fine, but look. The sign on the bus said, *Wege*. It means avenue, not street."

"You're such a fun travel buddy."

"Let him do it, Angie, or we'll be here forever,"

Eddie said.

I spotted two young women and hoped my German would pass. "*Bitte, wo ist der Bus zur Elisabethstraße?*"

"*Hier.*" One smiled. "*Fünf Minuten.*"

"*Danke.*" I glanced back at my partners. "Five minutes." My colleagues didn't appreciate my help and remained quiet until the end of our bus ride. "See, Elizabeth Street, not Elizabeth Avenue."

Marconi gritted her teeth. "Henry, I'm not sure whether to thank you or wring your skinny, smug neck. Now get us checked in, and let's unpack. I'm starving, cranky, and I want the biggest glass of wine someone will pour me."

Our unpleasant dispositions soon melted away after a quick dump of our luggage, then a plate-sized schnitzel, followed by a warm apple strudel with vanilla ice cream. Marconi downed two large glasses of white wine, while Eddie and I downed two silver tankards of dark beer, trading dirty looks over the waitresses' outfits.

"Okay, *gentlemen*, and I use the term loosely, once you're through leering at the women, finish up, and let's head back if you two will help me walk straight."

We strolled back to our building two blocks away, and Marconi plopped herself into the hotel lobby lounge seat, staring outside at the traffic. "Let me sit here a minute, guys."

"No, let's go," I said. "The elevator's not busy." We pulled her up, and all of us staggered through the doors. I glanced in its mirrors and chuckled at the three worn-out travelers.

"Finally," Marconi said. "Guys, I don't want to hear from either of you until the sun comes up. *Ci vediamo domattina, amici miei.*"

"What?"

"You aren't the only one that knows another language, Henry. I said I would see you in the morning." She slammed her door.

"My, my. I've never seen Angie that lit," Eddie said. He opened our door, surveyed the room, then plopped on the bed.

I dropped my bag and backpack. "Eddie, can I please have the bed tonight? I've slept like an hour since Monday morning."

"Okay, but it's mine tomorrow night. *Buenas noches.*"

****

All night I flopped around on the lumpy mattress, waiting for sunup. I had dozed off again and woke to Eddie fumbling in the bathroom, knocking something over, and God knows what else. I waited as long as possible, got up, and banged on the hollow, white-paneled door. "Come on, man, I'm about to die out here."

"What? You're awake?"

"Yeah, I need in there." Two flushes, and Eddie cracked the door open.

"Ike, it's the weirdest thing. I had to…I had to push it off the little ceramic shelf inside the toilet."

"Welcome to Europe. I hope you used the brush."

"What? Hell, yes, I used the damned brush. What else? I had an outdoor potty until fourth grade—it was easier than this."

"Okay, okay, get over your trauma and let me in."

I heard Eddie shuffle around the bedroom—a knock, then a door slam. He tapped on the bathroom door. "Come on. Angie said fun time is over."

"This is a fun time?"

"We'll be down near the lobby in the breakfast area. The tables are outside, so bring your coat."

I dressed and hurried downstairs. My colleagues sipped on steaming coffee and gorged on various pastries, eggs, and local sausages. The heaters scattered around the patio did their jobs well. Our table sat near a line of cars parked next to the meters lining the street—a pleasant way to begin the day.

"Good morning, bosses. I hope I wasn't too cranky yesterday?"

Marconi didn't return my smile. "You learn a lot about people when you travel. But we were worn out. Have a seat. The coffee is delicious, the bagels are fresh and warm, and these poached eggs are perfect."

"But I have to tell you something, Ike," Eddie said in a whisper. He leaned toward me. "No yogurt."

"Okay, I can make it," I whispered back, which reminded me, I had ignored my apartment for weeks. I didn't want to think of the milk, yogurt, and chicken in my refrigerator, much less the trash sitting under the sink. "What's first on our itinerary, Angie?"

Marconi glanced around and near shouted, "Your appointment with Dr. Müller is at nine a.m. sharp, Henry. We need to leave here in twenty minutes."

"Why are you shouting? And who's Dr. Müller?"

"The neurologist, Henry. For your injury, remember?" She scowled at me like an angry mother. "Don't worry. Your memory will get better as time goes by."

I rubbed my forehead. "Yes, I forgot again. The injury and all."

Eddie's sat, mouth open, while he dabbed his lips with a black-and-white checkered napkin. He leaned forward and whispered again. "You two are crazy. You both need a doctor."

Marconi responded with her own whisper. "Eddie, I don't know who may be listening."

Eddie and I glanced at each other. I couldn't figure out whether she sounded normal from one day to the next or if she wanted to chase UFOs.

"You're scaring me, Angie," Eddie said.

"Sorry, I'm not sure what to think. I'm afraid I'll blow this."

"We're good, we're good. Now, tell me again, what's next?" he asked.

She heaved an enormous sigh. "Guys, you must get this right. We'll go through the motions of taking Henry to the doctor for his pretend exam. I've shown you the map where a coffee shop sits a mile from here—it's across from a Dr. Müller's office in the same building. He's the real neurologist my contact told me about. We'll walk into the building, so if someone is watching us, it will look like we're going to the doctor. You'll receive information. We can stay in the coffee shop for a while and leave after your 'doctor's appointment' is over."

"Information? And then?" I asked.

"Nothing."

"What?"

"We have three days to act like tourists, and then Monday night comes."

"The Ides of March," I said.

Marconi rubbed her temples. "Hadn't thought of it."

Eddie clenched his jaws and winced as if in pain. "We'll stab someone over and over like Caesar? What the hell are we talking about?"

Her neck splotched pink and red. "Eddie, we've talked about this over and over."

"No, Angie, you've talked about this over and over inside your head. Ike and I get bits and pieces of plans that change every day. It's like playing football with a one-man huddle."

She slurped her last bit of coffee, gritted her teeth, then sighed. "I'm aware it's in bits and pieces. That's the way I meant it. Look, guys, my contact told me there's serious crap going on. If we get separated, I don't want you two to know too much. Monday night is our 'go' night for Prague. We each will take a bus—they leave forty-five minutes apart—beginning at six-thirty p.m. Two apartments are waiting for us in Prague across from the park. We have them until next Wednesday morning. Are we clear?"

"Why are we riding separately?" I asked.

"Security reasons."

"And who's paying for this?" Eddie asked. "Hell, it has to cost a fortune."

"Don't worry about it," Marconi said. "Who's paying for it? You'll know soon."

"Is all of this deception needed?" he asked.

"Maybe not, but we can't be too certain."

****

"Are we getting close?" I asked.

The sun beamed down, and I carried my heavy overcoat. Marconi marched along as if in a parade while Eddie's short legs pushed as hard as they could. The streets shared space with several rail lines buried in

197

new cement running parallel to the avenues. Here and there, alleys and ginnels lead down darker paths behind Vienna's bright boulevards. Red and gray streetcars passed us, all with plenty of empty seats.

"Angie, can't we jump on one of those?" Eddie asked.

We halted on a corner. Marconi whirled in a circle, studying the street signs. "No. Hang tight. I told you earlier we had only a mile to go. What does that say?" she asked.

"Doctor Karl Renner Ring goes north and south. This street is turning into Burgring. Anything sound familiar?"

"Yes, yes. Burgring. Another block on the right. Near a McDonald's."

"McDonald's?"

"Right. Eddie, you back there?"

"Way back. If I have a heart attack, will you slow down?"

"Seriously," I said. "We passed the Parliament building and a few Roman ruins. Can't we enjoy something for a few minutes?"

"We will later, guys, but we must keep our schedule. Getting there on time is important."

"Okay, but sitting in a coffee shop for two hours doesn't strike me as the perfect deception." Eddie gasped for air. "Angie, I'm sorry, but I feel like a blind guy at a magic show. You keep telling us what is going on, but we never see."

"You should trust me, Eddie."

Eddie choked out words between heaving breaths. "I do, but I want to see the goal here."

"Look, I don't have time to compose you a damned

mission statement. Now, go with the flow for a little longer."

What else could we say? We're five thousand miles from home with a woman who acted progressively unstable as the hours passed. For months, all I'd heard was Prague, Prague, Prague, and now we meandered through Vienna's streets looking for a coffee shop.

"There." She pointed over my head.

Sure enough, to the left of a trolley stop, a three-story brownstone building faced the north, an apothecary sign hanging with the name of Doktor Emmerich Müller. Several people hopped off a trolley and headed next door to a bakery storefront with a sizable open patio. Customers strolled here and there looking for tables, sipping on various drinks, and eating fruit-covered crepes.

Eddie bent over halfway, trying to breathe, his legs supporting his arms. "Right. It looks exactly like the Google Earth picture you showed me, Angie."

"Yes, it does."

Marconi gave me one of her smirks. "Time for the doctor, Sergeant Pierce."

"A shrink would be better."

We stepped off the sidewalk into the building's main hall with entrances into the doctor's office on the left and the bakery and coffee shop to the right.

The corridor ended with an exit sign leading to the toilet. We found a corner table inside and ordered a cup of coffee.

"Remarkable, Angie. The server interpreted your order as far as I could tell," I said.

"Thanks. I practiced with my German dictionary

this morning after I woke up early."

"Although you asked her for *Sachen*, or stuff, in your coffee instead of *Zucker*, or sugar."

"Oh?"

"Does it taste funny?" Eddie asked.

"It's sweet, that's what matters." She glanced at her watch. "Henry, better get yourself together and go to the doctor's office."

"And what?"

"Act like you're waiting for someone. Stay a few minutes."

"I need to find the restroom first. Does anyone have change? I can't pee without paying."

Eddie handed over a fistful of coins of various sizes. "Don't forget to flush."

Sure enough, the stalls required money. An exit sign blinked off and on over an orange, dented metal door next to the sink. Now, time to make a fool of myself. I slunk back to the doctor's office door, unusual in this old medieval-era building, with the bottom half frosted glass and the top transparent. Two men stood at the check-in desk. One, a tall man with a beard, dressed casually and could have a successful career as a bar bouncer—the other man was a head shorter and dressed in a dark-blue suit. His looks gave me the hint of a smarmy Gestapo agent in an old war movie.

The two turned toward the door and spotted me. The small man's odd gaze spooked me like deer during hunting season. Whether from intuition or stupidity, I darted back down the hall into the restroom with my new acquaintances following.

I hit the exit door and darted into a dark alley, frightening a feral cat off the lid of a metal garbage can.

What a cliché place to die. I jogged toward the street-side walkway opposite the building's entrance. Out in the open, I heard English spoken and tried to blend into a sizable British tour group. We strolled toward an enormous plaza surrounded by three massive structures.

"We are entering the Maria-Theresien-Platz," the tour leader shouted.

I eased to the right of the group, closer to three other tall men. My followers from the doctor's office appeared through the exit door, turned right, and scurried away from us. I pulled my phone—no signal again. My dear boss had tried so hard to keep us hidden. A nonfunctioning telephone would serve that purpose. Nothing more to do but hang with my group and take a museum tour.

We shuffled onto the marble floors, past the front entrance, where a tour guide waited. "Welcome to the Naturhistorisches Museum, or Natural History Museum, one of Vienna's greatest achievements in collecting and preserving the Hapsburgs' collections of over thirty million objects. My name is Alejandro. I grew up in Spain, in case you are wondering about my accent." He smiled and stepped up to the second step of the white marble staircase. The mahogany banisters gleamed in the intermittent sunlight passing through stained-glass windows to our right.

"Please follow me up the grand staircase," Alejandro called out, walking sideways up the stairs while we followed. "This building opened in 1889. Emperor Franz Joseph picked the white marble for this building from a quarry near Vienna. Later, in what became a foreboding series of events, the Emperor's only son, Rudolf, killed himself, along with his lover, near the time of the museum's opening. The Emperor never visited here again. His son's death broke his heart."

Ah, sweet, a haunted museum to hide from the neurologist's office staff while my colleagues drank coffee. We topped the stairs and headed to the right through a hallway covered in artwork. Alejandro chattered away in a room of ancient Egyptian artifacts holding two mummies and their assorted burial items.

What kind of plan had Maroni hatched? I didn't even have an actual doctor's appointment. I should trust her, but this seemed stupid.

"Please follow me into the Roman room. These antiquities are unmatched."

We stepped into a room filled with carved stone heads perched on marble pedestals protected by spherical glass covers, each a supposed likeness of a Roman Emperor. Tiny, rotating blue spotlights rained down on each bust, giving an illusion of movement. Goosebumps prickled my arms as I thought of our victims' missing heads. Alejandro droned on about the statues when my phone vibrated. Stepping into the hallway, I pushed buttons until it responded. "Hello? Hello? Henry Pierce here." I couldn't hear anything but background noise at first.

"Henry? What happened?" Marconi asked.

"What? Say again."

"Where are you?"

"You sent me into an ambush."

"Excuse me? I went to the restroom a minute ago and didn't see you in the doctor's office. You went there a half-hour ago."

"I would have called, but this phone—"

"Stop. Tell me what's going on."

"Hang on." The tour group had moved on, and I snuck back into the room of Roman heads, much darker with spotlights doused. "Angie, two men waited in the doctor's office when I approached. One pointed and yelled something at me before I opened the door."

"I wonder who the other one was?"

"What?"

"Never mind. So, you left?"

"With all this intrigue, why would I trust anybody? I ran out into the alley and stumbled into a tour group. We are at the National History Museum." A windowsill with black satin curtains pooled across made a temporary seat.

"What are you doing there?"

"Besides learning about dead Roman emperors? I'm hiding."

"Come back to the coffee shop. Something's gone haywire."

"No kidding? Look, Angie, I'm not getting hit over the head again. When I feel safe, I'll find you. Stay there or go back to the hotel. I'll call in a few minutes if I can find a signal."

And mumbling of voices in the background, and then Eddie. "Hey, Ike, stay safe. Come back soon."

"I will, Eddie, but I think we've been—"

"*Spricht du Deutsch*?" A demanding voice, its deep tone remindful of someone.

"*Nicht gut.*" I folded my phone and dropped it in my coat pocket. "Where are you, I mean, *Wo bist du*?"

"Good try, Detective Pierce," a much higher-toned voice responded, sounding like a fake Russian accent. "I recommend you keep your seat while we talk." I leaned against the window opposite my only escape route back through the Egyptian room into the hallway. "We are Stadtpolizei Detektivs Bader and Kruger."

"If you know my name, why did you speak German? What do you want?"

"When someone runs from us, we follow. Why did you run?"

How could I not see the outlines of these two? I sensed movement every so often unless these darkened Emperors' heads had come alive. "Why wouldn't I run? Two men standing in a doctor's office thousands of miles from my home—one pointed at me and yells something. Since my accident a few weeks ago, I get a little paranoid."

"No reason for paranoia. We have questions and a message for all of you."

"Okay, shoot...I mean...ask away." My shaky voice didn't offer the sound of a brave detective. With no gun and a low functioning cell phone, I couldn't provide much resistance against the look-alike Gestapo agent and a hairy bar bouncer.

"Why are you here?"

"The museum? I'm viewing the exhibits."

"He can't help being stupid," the deep voice said.

"Kruger, I will speak. You know what I mean, Sergeant Pierce. Tell us more."

"I had a head injury in a cave accident in Virginia a few weeks ago. My friends found me a neurologist here to see if he can help."

"You act more than functional to us."

"I appreciate that, but my employer wants me to get checked out," I said.

"Come now. Detektiv Kruger and I are not

simpletons. We know why Angie Marconi is here. A fine detective, but she throws all aside for her obsession."

"I'm not sure what—"

"An obsession about murders from late in the last century she hopes she can solve now."

"Don't underestimate her."

"We do not underestimate her persistence…only her judgment."

"In what way?" I asked.

"Her husband died in Prague."

"Yes."

"And she never found the killer."

"Right."

"Her husband had an affair," Bader said. "He fell for a woman on one of his trips for his government. He may have used the excuse of tracking a killer to Prague, but it was a new feminine voice killing his marriage. Your boss could have been late to detect it."

True, an affair might be a reason to keep coming back to Europe. No one else had offered anything other plausible reason. "Did his lover kill him?" I asked.

"Uncertain."

"And what about the other bodies dumped in Alexandria?"

"Other reasons," the man named Kruger answered.

Bader interrupted. "You see, Detective Pierce, you have nothing to pursue. Go home. Tell Angie Marconi to let it rest. If not, she may not like what she finds."

"That's not your business—"

"Oh, it is our business. Remember this warning and pass it on to your friends. Those killings are peripheral noises to matters that need not involve you. Your boss only serves as a means to an end for some people."

Silhouettes drifted toward the doorway, then stopped.

"Go home, Henry Pierce. Take your friends. Live your life and let go. Your boss has never learned to do that." Hurried footsteps, then silence.

****

I escaped the museum and finally found a phone signal. The wind howled between the buildings—ten minutes later, my colleagues joined me outside, and I told them of the men's message.

Marconi pulled off her earmuffs. "Yes, I knew about the affairs—two actually," she answered with her smirk. "One before I miscarried and one after. I found out Jack went back to Prague for a so-called *mission,* which meant he wanted to be with his lover."

"The goalposts keep changing, don't they?" I asked. My patience gone, I contemplated a flight change and return to Virginia—maybe I should go back to Rocky Gap and take care of the farm. "Remember the tree my dad used to take me to? Well, time's up."

Eddie sat hard on a bench next to us, near the entrance of a massive government building sitting opposite the museum.

Marconi swiped her face. "What can I say, guys? Should I brag about something like that?"

"Angie, this kills your credibility." Eddie leaned his stocking-covered head back against cold cement blocks.

"My credibility? Eddie, how long have we worked together?"

"Years and years. And your story was always the same. You were heartbroken and wanted to find Jack's killer, plus the killer of those men at our parks. Is any of that true?"

Marconi fumed and bit on a fresh piece of gum. Her chin quivered. "Yes, it's true. Are you going to let two strangers' stories blow this up?"

"Strangers?" I asked. "They know more about you than we do."

Tears rolled down her cheeks. "I've let you down, guys. I agree. If you can't trust me, we have big problems."

"And what's the deal with the doctor story, and you telling me only one man should be there?" I asked. "I've almost gotten killed once, and you've also inflicted this scheme on my family. Will they be safe?"

"Hold on, Henry, I didn't have—"

"Look, this has turned onto a path I can't go. I'll have my resignation to you next week. My apartment lease is up at the end of April, and I'm going home."

"Ike, ease up," Eddie barked.

"And how much do you know, Eddie?"

Eddie clenched his jaws, stood abruptly, and came toward me. "Listen, young man, you made your point, now shut up, or I'll flatten your skinny ass."

Marconi ran her hands through her hair. "Please. I promise we're close."

"Close to what?" Eddie asked.

I didn't care and buttoned up my jacket, ready to find a ride to the hotel.

"What are we supposed to think?" he added.

"I should have told about Jack's inclinations. Our marriage was brief—we had fun at first...but...he wasn't a good husband, okay?"

Eddie pulled his stocking cap down over his ears.

"That's one way to put it. Angie, I never heard him say a word about another woman. I thought the world of that guy. I can't believe it...but a wife would know."

People strolled by, pondering our commotion. I pulled my scarf tighter around my neck. "Right...Jack was a jackass with a wandering eye. Sorry, but that's what I make of him. Who were those two men in the museum?"

A policeman walked up from behind and tapped me on the shoulder. "*Bitte, kann ich helfen?*"

"*Nein, kein Probleme.*"

He tipped his hat and strolled away.

"He asked if he could help," I said.

"Yeah, I guessed that one," Marconi said. "Come on, let me go freshen up, and we'll have lunch somewhere."

"No, thank you," I said. "You can freshen up, but I'm headed to the hotel."

"Come on, Ike," he said. "Take a minute—"

"I need downtime." Walking away, I soon found a trolley and headed to the hotel. I couldn't do this anymore.

****

Snowflakes and sleet pellets blew against the window behind me, and the smell of frying schnitzel filled my nostrils. I had isolated myself in a dimly lit side room of the same restaurant where we had our first meal. A fire roared in the fireplace, shadows flickering on the oak table. Most customers had disappeared after lunch, and I welcomed the quiet.

My downtime lasted less than an hour before my colleagues found me. Full of schnitzel and more than tipsy from two tall steins of Fohrenburger, I eyeballed the same waitress who had served us last time.

"Can we join you?" Eddie asked. He gave me a disapproving eye.

"Great, have a seat. Good liquor loosens lips." I wasn't in the mood for niceties. Besides, if I resigned, it didn't matter what they thought.

"Ike, I've talked to Angie, and it's time we all get on the same page."

"Fantastic. Are you going to let me talk or try to whip my ass?" I asked.

"Boys, boys. Don't get it started again. Everything's on the table."

"I can whip your ass any time you want, and you'll thank me when I'm done." A grin broke across his face.

"Ask me something. We can talk while we eat," Marconi said.

"But that's all we do."

"What do you mean?" she asked.

"Talk over coffee, talk over breakfast, talk over lunch, talk over cheesecake at my apartment. I'm ready to do something…today. Let's get this going or go home. And no more intrigue. I'll do anything for you two, but I need to understand what our plans are. This is a showstopper today, Angie. Those two men know of our reasons for being here—they knew of your late husband's, uh, history, and said you're obsessed until they question your sanity. Commissioner Bates may have been right about the Captain Ahab routine."

Marconi shrugged and wiped a cheek. "I could be as crazy as they come, but you must decide whether to stick with me, and I guess, Eddie too?"

He did nothing but take another swig of beer.

"Did you recognize a voice?"

"A deep voice. It didn't sound German."

"And with good reason. It's Rijad Kastrati, a/k/a Viktor Kruger."

"What?" Eddie sat up, splashing his beer in his lap. He soaked up what he could and then grabbed my napkin.

"Right. Rijad contacted me over three years ago, saying he had information about Jack that might interest me. He said someone set Jack up, then murdered him at the park."

"By?"

"Uncertain, but he claimed Manny had to be coordinating it all."

Eddie clenched his jaws. "Dammit, Angie, why did you keep this from me? You're one of my best friends, sister. I've been after the Kastrati gang for years. Another waste of my time?"

"No, it's not a waste of time. I think Rijad has had good intentions at home. Still, many ex-refugees and old family connections from Bosnia push him to keep a lid on things. Bekić Čazim is one example. If Čazim hadn't let revenge on Luka Jankovich get the better of him, none of this would have resurfaced."

"We already know that," I said. "My meeting at the doctor's office was with Kastrati? I should have recognized him under his big beard. But a partner joined him?"

"Right, and I guess so about the partner. Kastrati had set it up to take you back to a room and get all this in the open. He wanted to review your upcoming part of our activities in Prague, but you ran and blew that to hell. He's the one financing our trip and coordinating the Prague endeavor."

Eddie pitched our beer-soaked napkins into an empty chair. "But why? Why would Ike need to meet by himself with Rijad, and when would you tell me this? Something's not right."

"Rijad's contacts go deep, and the Austrian government and others are using him as a source for the goings-on in the refugee communities. You may have noticed Rijad is visible for a while in Alexandria, and then you won't see him for weeks."

I stifled a burp. "The other one, Bader, seemed the one in control—at least from my experience in the unlit room full of Roman heads." I watched our server approach again but declined another beer. I caught Eddie staring. "Need a refill, Eddie?"

"I may need several," he said before a deep sigh. "Angie, this will take time to process. It's hit me like a Mack truck—the second truck today."

"I know," she said.

Eddie persisted. "And how does Manny figure into all this? I never had a good feeling about him even though you kept saying otherwise."

"It's been so hard, guys. After listening to Rijad's suspicions about Manny's double-cross of Jack, it was all I could do to make myself go into his bar."

"Yeah? Why did you follow me?" I asked.

"It doesn't matter, but I can't be sure about Manny. It's still possible Rijad's comments are because Manny is a Croat. Remember, I told you Manny sold the bar? He's back over here, likely in Croatia, or who knows where. I guess he got spooked. They've lost track of him."

"Who's they?" I asked.

"Men in the Austrian security services, according

to Rijad. Much of this I've found out since your attack, Henry. Rijad noticed it on the news and came to me again a few weeks ago."

Eddie leaned back against the paneled wall, so hard it jiggled a picture out of place. He didn't seem to notice the chill coming through the frosty, patterned window. The server seated a couple near us, and our conversation turned into half whispering. "What might have been Manny's motivation? He and Jack were supposed to be best buddies."

"Money, I suppose. What else is there? And Rijad believes Miomir Kurić drives all this."

"That name keeps coming up," I mentioned. "I can't believe someone hasn't caught Kurić after twenty-something years."

"Right...different governments' protection, no doubt. And despite all of Jack's negative traits, he had to be on to something. Miomir Kurić had the blood of hundreds of people on his hands during the war, and since then may have been worse."

Eddie yawned and rubbed his forward. "How so?"

"I don't know all the machinations and details, but there appear to be multi-national activities involving currency manipulation, the European Union, and God knows what else. Bad actors are scattered everywhere, including in our own country. Kurić's organization is like an umbrella for all that...according to Rijad."

"What would it be about?" I asked.

"Come on, Ike. Money, money, money," Eddie said. "Look around us for the last seventy years and all these dictators and strongmen we either want to kill or keep propped up. They're nothing more than gangsters, wealthy gangsters. And in Alexandria's case, we could tie Stanich and his phony money to this, I would bet."

"What if Kastrati is the instigator?" I asked. "Maybe he's trying to divert attention onto Manny?"

Eddie scowled. "Look, my friends, I'm all in for finding Jack's killer, and I have been since he died, but we need to get this done and go home. I keep saying we're only small-time cops, and I mean it. Me hustling around the middle of Europe is way off my job description."

"I've got that," Marconi said. "Stick with me a little longer, fellas. Please. Henry, how much do you understand currency exchanges, and so on?"

"What?" The Austrian booze had me baked. "I exchanged my money for strong beer and schnitzel. That's all I can think of right now."

"Lord, you two need to get to bed," she said.

I glanced at my watch and stretched. "Eddie, I have first dibs on the bathroom, and then I'm out." I staggered out of the restaurant and somehow found the hotel lobby two buildings down. The clerk on duty guided me to my room, and I collapsed on the floor mattress, pulling a thread-bare comforter over me.

Chapter Fifteen

My mattress shuddered.

"Ike. Get up."

What fresh hell? I'd told them to leave me alone.

"Come on, you've been asleep over twelve hours," Eddie said.

"What? No, I got up once to pee. What do you want?"

He yanked my blanket away.

"Okay, okay, I'm moving. Get out of the way." I should sneak away with the barmaid and hide in the Alps.

"My head's not that great either, man. Jump in the shower and get your senses. It's too early for breakfast, but I'll get us coffee."

"Sounds good." I headed to the bathroom. "If you put Irish cream in it, I'll kiss your bald head."

I stood in the spray for at least ten minutes before stepping out and drying. I hadn't paid attention to the puddle left from Eddie's earlier shower. My clean clothes drenched, I snuck out to the bedroom and rummaged through my suitcase.

Eddie flung open the door. "Oh, come on, man, I don't want to see that bent-over ass." He threw a pillow at me.

"Sorry, but someone left water everywhere in the bathroom."

"Drink your coffee. Angie is sleeping…I guess."

I dressed right away, sipped the coffee, then gazed out our frosty-paned window seeing several inches of snow had fallen, but the efficient plows had cleared the streets. "I guess we dress warmly today. Now, what's on the agenda for two more days? Sitting and talking?"

"Ease up, Ike. We are tourists today, and Angie wants to visit a few old churches."

"I can't do it."

"Look, I don't enjoy being kept in the dark either, but Angie is Angie. She knows what she's doing."

"Really?"

"Faith, my friend. Ask yourself a question. Would you have told the world about a spouse's betrayals, especially after his or her death?"

"I'm not as worried about that, Eddie, as I am the whole Kastrati sidebar. Who is he for real? And Manny?" Light steps trudged down the hallway across its creaking wood-planked floors.

Eddie jumped to his feet and pulled a gun from his belt. "Be quiet." He opened the door a few inches and hid the old-style revolver behind him. Another door slammed, and Eddie returned the slam with ours. "Damn, I'm as jumpy as a kangaroo. The housekeeper was getting her stuff out of the closet."

"Uh, where did you get the long-barreled revolver? It looks like something from an old western."

"Yeah, it's cool, huh?" He blew the barrel as if he had shot something and chuckled. "Call me Sheriff Bart."

"Who?"

"Sheriff Bart. The sheriff in *Blazing Saddles*…oh, never mind. Angie gave me the gun."

"She carries around spare revolvers?"

"I'm sure it's from the proper sources. And you'll get what she gives you, so don't get all huffy again. I get it, man, you feel Angie's misled us, manipulated us, or whatever. But how do you think I feel? Angie and I have known each other for thirty years, and I keep getting these new pieces of info she's stashed away for who knows how long."

"Like I said yesterday, if we can stay on track to find enough information about Jack Marconi's murder, and even solve it, I'll be happy. All this noise about currency exchanges, money changing hands, international conspiracies. I don't want to go there and really don't give a damn. Crooks in government are everywhere. You and I are just some schmoes from Virginia trying to do our jobs. And now we're about to get neck-deep in this other junk? No, thanks."

Eddie shoved the revolver into his belt and picked up his coffee cup. "Let's see where it goes for a little longer. I'll try to keep Angie on the straight path here and not get distracted by this other hokey pokey. I don't want to get involved with that either."

"Hokey pokey?"

"Yeah, hokey pokey. It's an old detective term."

"Okay, okay, a fresh start today. Sleep and this coffee have made me feel better, even with a hangover."

"Let's take a cup to Angie. She wanted me to check in on her by eight o'clock sharp."

****

"This is the Kirche am Hof, also known as the Church of the Nine Choirs of Angels, which is now a Croatian Catholic Church." Our guide's voice echoed against the stone walls. "Completed in 1403, it was here in 1804 that Emperor Franz II dissolved the Holy Roman Empire at the behest of Napoleon."

Eddie's eyes heavy, his yawns flowed one after the other. He had no interest in this tour, but Marconi insisted we go. This was our third church or cathedral to explore, and lunchtime drew near. "Hey, Ike, what do you think? We come this far, and now we're in a Croatian church."

"We can't get away from it, huh?"

"Guess so. I'm hungry. Let's cut out of here and find something to eat. I noticed a market only two blocks from here," Eddie said.

"That sounds good. They had a bunch of fresh—"

"Not yet, guys." Marconi had found us again. "I've arranged a behind-the-scenes look at the church."

"You've arranged?" I asked. "I'm already suspicious, and don't give me your 'little ole me' look. You're always up to something."

"Have faith."

"And I wish these junk phones had a camera. These interiors are stunning."

"Come on, Angie, I'm worn slick with this cultural stuff and hungry as a bear," Eddie said. "Let's go eat."

"Hang tight, buddy."

A monk appeared through a side door, obscured by the massive brass organ pipes looming over the altar. His head covered by a cowl, he strolled to an exit behind the organ player's bench seat, pulled a key from his brown robe, and pushed it into the mouth of a gold lion's head, serving as the keyhole. He rotated the key, and the ancient door released from the wall. He gave a wave to Marconi, and she motioned us to follow.

I ducked under the doorway, low enough even

Eddie had to stoop. Echoes rebounded after Eddie let the door slam behind us.

The bright chapel transformed into a dark corridor dripping in moisture and gloom. It smelled of mold with a catacomb of rooms hidden behind ancient dark doors lining the passageway. Lightbulbs had replaced torches in the holders lining the passageway.

"This is the old monastery," Marconi whispered to me.

"I guessed that," I said. "Where are we going, and why are you whispering?"

"I can't help it."

"I'm hungry, Jesus," Eddie yelled, spawning more echoes. "And my feet hurt."

Marconi gave a pretend kick.

"Where are we going?" he asked.

She pointed at Eddie and then our guide. "I said, I don't know. He's leading the way."

The monk halted near the hallway's end and raised his right hand, his sleeve slipping down his hairy arm. Dim light flashed against a gold pinky ring. Reaching to his right, he struggled to pull the door open with one hand, then used both, and the door's hinges groaned from movement. The monk disappeared into a chamber.

"Well?" I tried to see through the cracks in the door's shiplap slats, held together with rusted iron straps. It opened again, a stubborn squeal echoing through the corridor.

A hand motioned to us. We stepped inside and stood against a cracked plaster wall. The tiny cell had a square window fitting snug against the ceiling—one hanging bulb provided the other light. A half-folded blanket covered a canvas cot shoved against a wall next to a blue porcelain washbasin sitting on top of a rickety square table. Above it, someone had taken down a Christian cross, its outline a bright white on the dingy wall. The monk pulled back his hood.

"Rijad?" Eddie asked. "What the hell?"

"Yes, Eddie. Good morning, Director Marconi…Sergeant Pierce. My official Vienna welcome, I suppose." He had shaved his beard, leaving only the thick black mustache.

"It beats dark rooms in museums," I said.

"Yes…it does. My supposed superior made a show of tracking you down at the museum. I must be careful as I'm not convinced of his alliance." He eased his rear onto a three-legged stool.

Marconi smoothed her bangs. "Thank you for meeting us, Rijad. None of this would be possible without your help." She smiled.

"Hey, Rijad," Eddie said, "I have a simple request."

"Yes, what?"

"I want to know what the hell is going on, that's what."

Marconi frowned. "Eddie, come on."

Eddie shrugged. "Two-thirds of my career has been about Jack and his murder, blah, blah, etcetera. Sorry, Angie, but it's time to fish or cut bait, as my daddy would say."

"Let's see what he has to say."

"Please listen to Angela," Kastrati said. "I'm here to help."

Eddie nodded, then winked at me.

"Let me catch everyone up. Please sit, maybe on the cot."

Eddie and I squatted onto the cot that looked as if from the Napoleonic Wars, a heavy smell of mold and body odor wafting upward when we sat. "Okay. Go on," Eddie said. The canvas bed sagged in the middle, causing us to lean toward one another.

"Eddie, I've abused the trappings of this church to hide my business, and I apologize."

"A rationalization," I said.

He shot me a glare much as he did the first time we met in his coffee shop. "Let me finish, young man. It is a place few would think to search for me." He smoothed his mustache. "As Angela should have told you, I am not who I seem."

"Guessed that one," Eddie said.

"All you've known about me is correct. Much of my family died in Bosnia, and I came to Virginia to begin a new life. I brought my surviving sister with me. That part of our dream came true. She married and had several children, and since, more of our cousins have joined us in Alexandria. But her first husband grew homesick and returned to Bosnia in 2010, leaving her with my five nieces and nephews." His face grew red. "Even more unfortunate was her second marriage to stupid Bekić Čazim—a loser and an instigator. He wanted to get cozy with the Stanich orthodox family, but even *they* kicked him out. He married my sister but never got over the Stanich woman. Now he sits in jail, and I hope he rots there. Nothing is too horrible for him."

Eddie held up a hand. "But wait a minute, Rijad. There are more than a few Kastratis around. We've had our eyes on your operations for years."

Kastrati shook his head and sighed. "Yes, yes. You

have a job to do. Nine Kastratis live around the District, and their friends, and their friends' friends. Picture a pyramid. One person gets to America, and many more follow. But I have no control over most. I tell them not to throw away a chance for a new life. I remind the younger ones of old Bosnia and all the death, but they do not understand what they do not know."

Marconi pulled the blanket from behind us and used it as a pallet to sit cross-legged on the floor. "I'm glad you have come this far despite all the disadvantages."

"Now, wait a minute, Angie," Eddie said. "It wasn't too many weeks ago we were all up in his business about the Jankovich murder. Another act, Rijad?"

"No, no," Kastrati said. "We were all angry that day. My personal connections upset Angela, and I grew angry. I had guessed it involved stupid Čazim in Jankovich's murder but could say nothing without first talking to my sister. She knew nothing of his crime but refused to let him sit in jail. She offered to pay for an attorney, but …"

"But what?" I asked.

"That information is unavailable."

"Oh? You don't know or don't want to tell us?" I asked.

"It isn't relevant," Kastrati said. He studied the wall, scratching his chin.

"And what do you know about Archie Sullivan?"

Marconi smirked. "Let it go, Henry. Don't get distracted."

Eddie rubbed the back of his neck and squinted. "Rijad, how did you become an Austrian detective named Kruger? You might as well tell me you're a Martian."

"My friends, you all know of the influx of refugees from the Middle East. They are desperate to get away from wars and turmoil, much as I was over twenty-five years ago. Many are taking advantage of this situation, trying to find an easy escape north. This includes a few men with a violent agenda mixed within. An employee at the Austrian embassy contacted me a few years ago in Alexandria. That led to visits with other officials, and they reach out to me sometimes for help. I come back to Europe if they identify a problem."

"Problem?" I asked.

"I cannot tell you everything."

"You're an informer," Eddie said.

"A basic way to state it, but it is one of my functions."

"And what of Manfred Jurić?" I asked. "He acted as Jack and Angie Marconi's friend for all those years. But after we started pulling back a few layers of this rotten onion, he dumped his whole American life and disappeared."

Kastrati grimaced. "Jurić is a scoundrel wrapped in an enigma. Security forces here are familiar with his name. He can vanish like a Croatian ghost and reappear somewhere else."

"Manny's no ghost," Eddie said, "but the vanishing part is correct. He owned his bar for many years and lived the dream. Wasn't it suspicious that he bailed on his entire life in Alexandria when all this stirred up again?"

"You cannot trust that man, and I have told that to Angela."

"Do you think he's hooked into the Stanich operation?" I asked.

"Everything on the East Coast flows through Stanich," Kastrati said, red-faced. "I despise the weasel. If he gets control of you, he never lets you go. And his nephews…should be in jail or on death row for genocide. *Die Teufel's Engels* brought their hate with them to America. Those Bosnians killed years ago, your cold cases—all victims of the Stanich nephews' constant thirst for blood. Those were reprisal killings related to loans they did not repay…another Stanich side business that went bad. They did to them what they did to their victims in Bosnia and Croatia."

I glared at the phony monk. "Bosnians? Too bad you couldn't have come forward. They buried those men in unmarked graves a quarter-century ago. Angie and Eddie have made themselves crazy trying to figure this out. Sounds like obstruction of justice—"

"Bad loans? That's it?" Eddie asked. "Why weren't they reported missing?"

Kastrati ignored Eddie and returned my glare. "I kept to my business. It served me no purpose to go to the authorities. I had no proof of Stanich's nephews as the killers, but the methods they used were exact."

"We might have helped, Rijad," Marconi said.

"And why did a federal district court block a further investigation?" I asked. "Where's the link…this doesn't make sense."

Marconi rolled her eyes. "That's beside the point."

My face grew hot. "Beside the point? Those murders are why Jack eventually went to Europe and got himself killed."

Marconi pointed at me. "I know that, Henry. But

the federal interference came long after Jack died." She turned away. "It's the money, isn't it, Rijad? It's always about money."

"Even if it's fake?" Eddie asked.

"Counterfeit money is one piece, and we could list other crimes until sunset," Kastrati said.

"That's what the list of names is about, isn't it?" I asked. "The list I found at the warehouse at Stanich's strip mall. He buys people off."

Kastrati shrugged. "I do not know of this list, but it seems likely…or he blackmails them. Aleksandr Stanich presents himself as a doddering old man and has convinced many of his significance in the community. As far as the district court, I'm sure his money found its way to the suitable judges to help hide his nephews' activities."

"Weren't you in business with him for a brief time?" I asked.

Kastrati sighed. "My sister's voice. She convinced me to invest with Stanich to open a bakery, shortly after meeting stupid Čazim. She saw it as a way to get on his good side, and Čazim found a way to stay connected to the Stanich family after his divorce. But Stanich being Stanich, the problems became inevitable. I cut my losses as soon as possible. You all did the city a favor when his buildings burned."

"His doing, not ours," I said.

"Yes, which brings us to the next subject," Kastrati said. "Stanich's business operations."

"Pawnshops or fake money?" Eddie asked before shifting his rear end on the cot.

"I do not have a complete understanding of all this, but I'm confident to say Stanich has printed millions of counterfeit Euros over the years and shipped them to central Europe. Čazim confirmed a piece of this for me when he told me he saw the counterfeiting presses. His one bit of usefulness to everyone, I suppose. Those operations have ceased, at least temporarily, with the destruction of those buildings."

"To what end is the counterfeiting?" Marconi asked.

"I do not know. I know he ships it straight to Prague, right under the Treasury Department and other American agencies' noses. You will see."

Eddie made a fist with his right hand and pounded his leg. "But why Prague?"

"I cannot say why Prague is the destination city, Eddie." Kastrati held a finger to his lips. He stood, then brushed by me, the scapula on his wool robe smacking me in the face. He grabbed the door handle and smashed an ear against the door.

"Rijad?" Eddie asked. He struggled out of the slope in the cot and stood behind him.

"A moment." Kastrati let the door float open a few inches, then he peered out into the hallway. "I heard something, but see nothing." He pushed the door closed and studied the three of us. "I have known Angela Marconi and Eddie Stone for many years and trust you two. You are fearless. My knowledge is limited, but this is bigger than Stanich."

Marconi held both hands toward the ceiling. "What is bigger than Stanich?"

"Stanich is only one of many others like him. Several cells are in...let's see, Eastern Europe, Hanoi, Pyongyang...maybe Havana."

"All these countries are communist-era relics," I

said.

Kastrati shook his head. "No, no, no…irrelevant. The coordination is from Miomir Kurić's organization and no other. I'm not sure what communists would have to do with this."

"The cities you mentioned, that makes it relevant," I said.

Kastrati fidgeted with his hood. The others kept silent.

"Are we sure he's alive?" Eddie asked. "Kurić seems more like a legend."

"Not a legend—a monster. A 1990s wannabe Hitler or Stalin. Thousands died," Kastrati said.

"I can't understand how Kurić went from mass murder, avoided a trial at the Hague, and is controlling an empire of counterfeiters," I said.

Kastrati turned toward Marconi. "Angela, think about this. If a currency is a third counterfeit, what happens to its value?"

I glanced at Marconi and said, "It's devalued."

He continued to look Marconi's way. "Yes, and other currencies?"

"They might increase in value," I said.

"Yes, and that, my friends, is where I turn it over to you all. Many officials in several countries enjoy the benefits of Kurić's arrangements, the depths I do not understand, much less can explain."

My colleagues seemed to have lost their voices.

"At the museum, you said Angie was a means to an end. Why is that?" I asked.

Kastrati shrugged. "Not my words."

"That wasn't your partner's voice, and what do you know about a mask…a balaclava?"

Kastrati bowed his head, but his eyes glared upward. "I know nothing of masks."

"Okay. So…what's next?" I asked.

Kastrati folded his arms. "Prague. But remember, keep your eyes open beyond your bubble of detective work in Alexandria. People with dual loyalties can be the most dangerous."

****

Ten p.m. and bus number twelve came into view, its dim headlights providing low light as the driver pulled into a line for boarding. Instead of waiting until morning, Marconi told me to spend an extra twelve Euros to get a ticket on the last bus. Earlier, I watched the green coach rumble away with my colleagues aboard. The bus company had canceled two other routes, our careful plans changed, and my bosses left me at five o'clock. I never got a simple answer to why we needed to go at different times or why we couldn't take the train. Marconi would only tell us to follow the plan. They would arrive in Prague before my bus departed.

I scanned the nearby passengers waiting in the terminal. None appeared suspicious, but I was wary of everyone these days. The prospect of traveling through the Czech countryside well after midnight didn't ease my fears.

An announcement came from a remote intercom. A German speaker and too muffled to understand. I hurried toward the source, waiting for a repeat in English. "We are now boarding for Prague and Berlin. Our apologies for the delay. The bus's departure from Budapest could not proceed on time because of flooding. Please have your tickets ready and begin boarding."

A young woman in a red uniform stood near the bottom step of a yellow bus. "*Guten Abend*."

"Good evening to you." I handed her my ticket, marched to the back, and dropped my bag on the seat next to me.

She shuffled down the aisle sideways, greeting each passenger until she stood next to me. "Are you going to Berlin tonight?" she asked. "I'm afraid it will be almost five a.m."

"I'm going as far as Prague," I answered. "One o'clock?"

"With our stop in Brno, closer to one-thirty. Would you like a glass of wine? Our company has allowed two free drinks tonight as an apology for the delay."

"Sure. What's your name?"

"Stefana. And yours?"

"Henry Pierce."

"Welcome, Henry Pierce. You sound from southern America? Texas?"

"Virginia, southwest Virginia."

"Ah, I am from Ostrava, near the Polish border."

"Good to meet you, Stefana." She continued to the back, where a seat had been removed and replaced with a small refrigerator.

We waited again. Fifteen minutes later, the bus backed away from the terminal as I emptied my second glass of wine. Prague would be a two a.m. arrival. Too bad for my colleagues. They left me on the late bus, so they would have to enjoy my appearance in the middle of the night. I stowed my glasses and nodded off, a cracked window acting as my pillow.

****

Squealing brakes and my head bumped hard against the glass. I fumbled for my glasses, then squinted through the frosty window to see a red traffic light on a dark street—a road sign with Cyrillic lettering wobbled in the wind.

Stefana stood near the front holding the microphone, first speaking Czech, then German. She glanced at me and smiled. "And to our traveler from America, we have arrived in Brno. The break is twenty minutes, or less, if everyone is back early. Limited services are offered, but toilets and snacks are available down the hill to the right of the terminal."

We bumped along into a shabby stall as the clock approached eleven-thirty—the cement pad our bus crunched onto had dissolved into smaller, misshaped chunks of gravel. The darkened shops across the street looked the part of Soviet-era buildings. Most appeared closed with windows boarded for years. Restrooms sat to our right in a cinderblock building, at least forty yards at the end of a poorly lit gravel path. The other passengers and I stood ready to exit.

We waited as the bus driver opened the door, rose to exit, then turned toward us. His black and gray beard merged into a mass of hair covered partly by a red driver's cap. This man…something was wrong. My ears grew hot. He reminded me of Charlie, Nika's chauffeur. A beard now, but he had the same build, and I couldn't forget those giant arms wrapped around me in the caverns. Surely, this had to be my tired imagination. How could the same man rebound from a chauffeur's job in D.C. to driving a Czech bus? But…it had to be him.

As far as the outside world knew, I sought medical

treatment in Vienna. Who would know to look for me here? I dug into my bag, grabbed my baseball cap, and found my glasses, hoping that and my scruffy face offered a disguise. He exited first. We followed, one-by-one, while I tried to remember one of my grandmother's prayers. I couldn't get beyond 'Dear God.'

Last off the bus, I glanced left, then right—the driver had disappeared. Even though the night air chilled me, I used my coat sleeve to mop the sweat sprinkled on my forehead. Light sleet peppered my face like icy needles while I watched the other passengers veer toward the toilets. If the driver had gone to the restroom, we would pass one another on the trail as he returned. I took a few steps and ducked behind the trunk of one of the ancient oak trees lining the road. I fumbled for my phone and dialed Eddie. No signal. A second call failed…then a third.

I trudged toward the toilets, wary of anyone approaching. It would be better to use a tree and go back to the bus, so I stepped off the trail to do that. The ground was rocky, so I leaned on the tree trunk to balance while zipping my pants.

"Feeling better, Detective Pierce?" That growling voice. It was him.

I tripped on rocky ground, steadying myself with a broken branch resting against the tree trunk. "Charlie, or is it Chasna? You changed professions?"

"My profession hasn't changed."

"A chauffeur, then a bus driver? You still hanging with Nika and Erik?"

"The little broad took off as usual after she did what we needed. She's with her mother now. Erik…has moved on. And you? Vienna doctors help you out?"

"How would you know?" My hold tightened on the dead branch. Its rough, cold bark fit nicely in my right hand.

"You're a fool, Pierce. You shouldn't have trusted anybody, least of all Rijad Kastrati. But I don't have time to discuss it. The passenger list is growing shorter." He smiled with yellow teeth through his ragged beard, then crept toward me.

The branch I held delivered a dreadful crack to his left temple, knocking him to the ground. He fell to his right, groaned, and rolled on his back. His right leg twitched, then he lay still. I grabbed his feet, pulled him nearer the trail, and leaned him against a pile of slick, lichen-covered rocks. Blood trickled from his nose into his mustache. Fitting, I thought, the way he had left me in the cave. His pockets near empty except for his phone, I found a half-empty flask of alcohol that I dumped on his face.

Hurrying back to the bus, I found Stefana sitting in the driver's seat playing with her phone. "Hey, Stefana. Do you have a standby?"

"What?"

"I noticed your driver stumbling toward town."

"Ah…damn. That's not the first time." Stefana formed a fist and beat it into her other hand. "*Je to zatracený blázen…* a fool." She plopped into the driver's seat, grabbed the set of keys thrown on the dash, and yelled for the remaining passengers to board. She ground the gears into place, and the bus plodded back onto the road, leaving poor Charlie sitting in the cold.

****

Snow had replaced sleet and grew heavy. As we

231

came into Prague, Stefana drove slower and slower, making it three o'clock when we arrived. I had a mile to walk to the hotel.

I pounded on Marconi's door. She opened it with the chain still attached. "Henry. What the hell? Get in here." She closed the door. I heard the chain pull back, then she reopened it. I pushed my way past her and slammed Charlie's phone on the table.

She crossed her arms and considered me with contempt. "You smell like alcohol."

"I had a six-hour bus drive instead of three. But guess who else likes a drink? Chasna Kovačić. Better known as Charlie."

"Who?"

"The guy that attacked me in the cave. And tonight, he was my bus driver."

"Henry, you need to slow down and tell me what happened."

"Director, I'm tired. If you're a part of this, it would be faster if you took a gun and killed us."

"I need to get Eddie over here."

"Please do," I said.

She left and returned with Eddie, rubbing his eyes. "What the hell are you doing? Half the city can hear you shouting like a fool."

"Did you forget about me? I walked for twenty-five minutes from the bus station in the middle of a blizzard."

"Why didn't you call?" Eddie clenched and unclenched his jaws.

"With what?" I pitched the phone in the trash can. "The damn thing doesn't work."

Eddie's hands slammed into my chest, knocking

me into the cloth chair next to the bed. "Son, you shut down your attitude and tell me what happened."

I stood. "Sure. Isn't it something that whenever I get isolated on our little adventures, our Serb friend Chasna shows up?"

"The guy that attacked you in the cave?" he asked.

"Yeah, he disappeared from the chauffeuring job and changed to driving a bus route to Prague. And who would have guessed…the same bus I rode tonight."

"Henry, I …" Marconi's chin quivered. She sat hard on the bed.

"He said he hadn't changed professes and worked for the same people," I said. "He told me that when he snuck up on me again during our rest stop."

Eddie stood straight. "Were you hurt?"

"Not this time. We were off to the side of a path. I grabbed a branch and knocked him out. I left him against a pile of rocks as he left me—another driver brought us the rest of the way."

Marconi bit her lip again. "Kastrati," she mumbled.

"You think?" I asked. "Kovačić said anyone who trusts him is stupid."

Eddie had bags under the bags under his eyes. His t-shirt couldn't hide his belly, and his blue pajama bottoms were so faded, his late wife must have bought them. "Angie, time's up," he said.

"What?" She messed with her hair, trying to make a ponytail.

"Your decisions will get us killed," Eddie said.

She offered nothing, fell back onto her mattress, and covered her face with a pillow.

"She's mixed up with it," I said. "There've been too many quirks."

"Stop. She's not in on it. But Angie, twenty-five years of this has beaten you down. You're desperate for answers, and your judgment has gone to crap. Jack Marconi isn't worth it, not from what you've told us about him. You hired this young man to help, and now he's almost lost his life…again. I promised his family I would bring him home safe, and that's what I'll do. Let me have your damn phone."

Marconi pushed up, then leaned back on her elbows. "My phone?"

"These burner phones are going in the trash, all three of them. Ike, grab yours from the trash can and throw them all in the chute that falls into the alley dumpster. We'll do it the old-fashioned way. And Chasna's phone there. Turn it on, and even if it's locked, leave it on. We'll use it for bait and see who bites. Angie, pack your stuff. For safety, I'll find a new place to stay."

She remained silent, playing with her hair.

"Sounds good. Can I go take a nap?" I asked.

"Yeah, but take a shower. You smell like a two-bit whiskey," Eddie said.

Marconi grabbed my sleeve. "Jack…God…I mean, Henry, I'm doing the best I can."

****

There wouldn't be much sleep, and I should've known. I had left a guy unconscious in the cold, and he would freeze before someone found him.

We left Marconi alone, and Eddie ventured out after sunrise to find us different lodgings. He was at his wit's end to understand what to do with her plans. I didn't care. We needed to make new ones. After he returned, I rummaged around in the closet.

"Pack everything," he said. "We're sharing a room one building east of here. Angie's room will be next to us. The folks tracking us will be here soon if they aren't already. I told the front desk we had a change of plans, and we were leaving early."

"What about Angie? She'll give us away if she hasn't already."

"I don't see it, Ike. She's fought to keep this investigation going all these years."

"All this planning, hiding, and stupid phone tricks. I'm keeping a close watch on her."

"Whatever, man. Help me get this stuff to our new place, and I'll come back and get Angie."

We yanked and jerked our bags through the half-foot of snow. Our new place, as Eddie called it, was on the third floor, fifty yards down the street. He told me to get everything unpacked, he would be back soon with Marconi, and we would get breakfast. I piddled for a while arranging and rearranging our things, and then fell asleep on the soft leather couch sitting near our windows.

A soft knock on the door, then another. My glasses fell from my head as I sat up, then stumbled toward the door. Eddie had not returned. Another knock. I couldn't see through the blurry peephole, so I took a chance and opened the door.

A short blonde maid stood at attention with a pot of coffee. "Mr. Purse?"

"What?"

"Coffee for you, Mr. Purse, from the hotel."

"Thank you. My name is Pierce. Come in, please."

"Yes, Mr. Purse. Cups are on your closet's shelving. I will clean for you?"

"Okay. What's your name?"

"Adina," she answered, then curtsied. "I'm only maid to speak English."

"And doing it well," I said. I backed away from the door, almost crushing my glasses under my feet. "Do you have any cream?"

She smiled. "No, but I can get. I am back soon, Mr. Purse."

"Thank you." I sat, leaned my head against the arm of the couch, and closed my eyes.

Another knock. I glanced at my watch—nine-thirty. Adina had returned with cream, toast, and a cup of yogurt. "Great. How did you know, Adina? This is what I eat every morning."

"You look healthy, Mr. Purse."

"Call me Henry, okay?"

"A-OK, Henry Purse. I must go to downstairs. Call if you need myself."

"I'll do so. Thank you."

They served excellent food, and I knocked back two cups of coffee—still nothing from Eddie. I wrote out a note and left it on the bed. Back at our abandoned rooms, no answer came behind her unlocked door. I found nothing except for an unmade bed to show someone had used it. Once again, my colleagues had vanished. I hurried back toward the elevator. The custodial closet door flew open in front of me.

"Get in here." Eddie yanked my arm and slammed the door behind us. "Have a seat—there's an extra bucket. We'll make this our meeting room." He sat in a folding chair, a mop hanging over his head.

"Uh, Eddie, why are we sitting in a closet? Your hair looks nice."

He swatted the dirty strings above his head. "Keep your voice down. Angie's gone."

"Gone? In what way?"

"What do you mean, in what way? She's gone. I came back to get her, and she had checked out. The person at the front desk told me she caught a taxi and left."

"I told you, Angie's a part of this. No wonder we kept getting compromised every time we planned something. She knew we went to Stanich Plaza that night, and it blew up. She knew about my trip to the cave, and Charlie shows up, and I get a bus ride in the middle of the night, and sure enough, Charlie confronts me again. What else would it be?"

"It might be a lot of things. But that's not Angie."

"I've had enough of this. Let's go home."

"I don't have the tickets."

"We'll buy more. Otherwise, we'll wind up dead and hacked to pieces," I said.

"Now, don't go off the deep end. Stay put for a few minutes. Look." He held up Charlie's phone, unlocked.

"How did you figure it out?"

"I'm not as dumb as I look, man. Guess what his password is?"

"One, two, three, four?"

"No, I tried that. It's nine, eight, seven, six." He giggled like a kid. "Ain't that the shits?"

I felt woozy, probably from the ammonia stench. "Have you found anything on it?"

"No, it's all a bunch of Serb or German names on his contact list. But I got a call earlier."

"And?"

"He jabbered something, and I said, 'what?' I

mean, right away, he switched to English and asked me who I was."

"You didn't tell him your name?"

"Do I look stupid? I told him Charlie couldn't come to the phone, and I guess it pissed him off. He shouted again in German or Czech or Russian, whatever the hell it was. I told him if he's smart enough, I bet he could find the phone."

"Smooth. How long will that take, though?"

"Not long. I looked up the number, and it even pulled up a map for me."

"Your tech skills are improving."

"Yes, they are. The caller's in a town called Roztoky. Only a few miles from here."

"I've got an idea," I offered.

"What?"

"Leave the phone here, and let's go back to our room. We can watch from there and not burn up our lungs from these chemicals."

"Yeah, sounds good. Leave it up on this shelf behind these trash bags. I hope our fish bites."

Chapter Sixteen

We waited and watched. Thirty minutes, then ninety. Several people strolled through the hallway, but no one appeared on a hunt. The housekeeping staff poured out of the elevator with their carts, two of them opening and closing the janitor's closet. Neither found the bait left on the shelf. Soon, though, they would clean our suites.

"We'll have to leave this room in a few minutes and check out," I said.

Eddie pulled a footstool over and sat. "I know that. We'll grab the phone and find another way."

"What about Angie? What if someone kidnapped her, and we're sitting here letting the minutes tick by?"

"Angie can take care of herself."

"I don't think that's a good bet. What if she's headed to the airport?"

"You're making me tired, man." He shifted back and forth on the stool like a hawk on its nest. "Angie has never wavered on finding Jack's killer or finding the perps who killed our unknown guys all those years ago."

"But we know who the murderers are, Eddie—Stanich's nephews. That's what we need to be doing, wrapping up those cold cases. You all hired me to figure it out, and now we know the killers. Now, we're going on a wild-ass chase using my head injury as an excuse to come to Europe? Jack Marconi had many

239

issues, but he must have made a good guess about Alexandria's murders. Unfortunately, he went down a rabbit hole here in Prague when he met a lady and started an affair. That got him killed, and we're on the same path he took."

"Ike, I get it, but all the mess back home ties back to the garbage here. It should be obvious after what we found at Stanich's place. I don't know how much of Kastrati's story to believe, but I think he offered bits of truth."

"Kastrati? All those years, he knew who those cold-case victims were. He should be in jail for obstructing justice. And his sister paid for Čazim's lawyer, no matter. I don't trust him any more than I do Manny, and I don't know why Angie believes him."

Eddie shook his head. "We need to talk to Commissioner Bates about all that. Any of this other stuff is circumstantial and feels like you're throwing shade on Angie. I promise we'll find out more in the next couple of days."

"If we find her."

"We will." Eddie's fidgeting got the better of him. He stood, stretched, and wandered over to take in the view through the window. "Look at this. They move the snow fast around here. Streets are mostly clear, and the sidewalks, too." He rubbed his neck and searched through his pockets.

"Lose something?"

"I've got these Czech coins and a few Euros. I would do anything for another cup of coffee."

"Okay. Let's grab that phone and get out of here. I'm starving," I said. A ding and the elevator doors crawled open.

Eddie pushed his way in front of me. "Hang tight."

A man emerged, concentrating on his phone's screen.

I leaned close to Eddie and whispered, "I think that's him."

"Who?"

"Bader. The guy at the doctor's office with Kastrati—the same one who tracked me to the museum in Vienna." It seemed Bader's phone acted as a locator.

"Are you sure?"

"Yeah…I'm sure. Skinny, overdressed guy."

Eddie hid the revolver behind him in his belt and adjusted his jacket. "Okay. You stay here. He hasn't seen me before and won't pay me any attention." He took a deep breath and paused. "Wait for it," he mumbled, "wait."

Bader eased toward the closet and grabbed the doorknob.

"I'm up, Ike. Don't move until you hear from me."

Our prey slipped inside the closet. Eddie dashed the forty feet, threw open the door, and disappeared. No gunshot. In half a minute, his head appeared around the door jamb. "Get down here."

I ran through the hall, tripped over my feet, and hit the wall.

Eddie peered out again. "What the hell?"

"Sorry."

Bader had sprawled face down across the floor, out cold.

"Make a new friend?"

"Be quiet and help me get him to our room."

"Uh, we'll carry a body through the hall? Won't the cameras see us?"

"No cameras. I already checked." He picked up Bader's arms. "Well? Grab his legs."

"What about the housekeepers?"

"We'll put up the privacy sign. Now help me, dammit." We carted him into our room and dropped him on the bed.

"Good thing he's small," I said, breathing hard. "Now, it's eleven o'clock, and checkout time is noon."

Eddie hung the privacy placard on the doorknob before slamming the door. "Yes, I know the time. Use those pillowcases and tie him up. Let's see what he's got."

While Eddie rummaged in Bader's pockets, I tore the pillowcase into pieces and tied his feet and hands to the bedposts.

"Well, well…a gun—a .357. It's yours, Ike. Yeah, here's Charlie's phone again, and another one that must belong to this guy, I guess. A wallet with an I.D. and a passport in this other pocket." Eddie flipped through the document. "What did you say his name is?"

"He said Bader in the museum. Didn't offer a first name."

"The passport says otherwise. Vitaly Kharkov. I can't read the rest. Czech, I guess."

"Let me see that." I jerked the document from him. "No, not Czech. It's Russian."

"It involves the Russians? Lord…careful what you drink."

"It's a smorgasbord of countries, isn't it?"

"Kastrati mentioned this was a multi-national deal."

"Hokey pokey, Eddie?"

"Yeah, hokey pokey …"

"What happened in the closet?"

"I came in behind him as he stuffed the phone in his pocket. I asked him what he was doing, and he stood there with his mouth open like a bullfrog. So…I sucker-punched him."

"Now what?"

"You point the gun at him, and I'll wake him up."

"We're taking a Russian national as a prisoner?"

"We're already in deep crap, Ike. They had to have found that Charlie guy by now, dead or alive, and this rat will disappear for a few hours. Let's get what we can out of him and stuff him in the closet. We'll find Angie, hole up in those extra rooms down the street, and figure out what to do next. We haven't even started surveilling our target yet."

"If you say so. I think we'll wind up in prison somewhere, and Angie Marconi will come by for a visit and smirk at us for doing her dirty work."

"You're not going to prison, buddy. We'll bust this thing open. Now make your pretty face look as mean as possible and point the gun at him like I said. Let's get his skinny ass awake." He patted Kharkov's cheeks a few times, and the gray eyes blinked open.

He stared down his own gun barrel, glared back, and mumbled something.

"Speak English and speak it well," Eddie said.

"My jaw." He struggled against the four bedposts, but the knots held.

"You're not going anywhere, Mr. Kharkov. And my colleague has your gun and an itchy finger. He's been a little pissed since your friend Chasna hit him on the head several weeks ago. It's time to tell us a few things."

"That man was not my friend, and why would I tell you anything?"

Eddie must have delivered more than one blow. Kharkov's left eye had swollen, and crusting blood covered his upper lip.

"The authorities will have none of this. I will scream out."

"You should evaluate your situation," Eddie advised, turning his hand upside down, then tapping his heavy college class ring on Kharkov's head. "You're held in a hotel room, and we both have guns and nasty tempers. And which authorities are you going to call?"

My turn. "Your bus driver friend from Vienna. Have you been looking for him?" I asked. I had a great urge to bust this guy in the kneecap with his gun handle.

"He is dead, and he is not my friend. He hit his head and froze."

I winked at Eddie. "Better him than me. Thanks for confirming you knew of him. It tells us something."

He glared. "I only tracked him…and then his phone. And you know nothing."

"Yeah, we do," Eddie said. "Your passport says you're from Kerch in Crimea. Odd how you pretended to be an Austrian agent. Who do you work for, and why are you up in our business?"

"Don't be stupid. You are two unimportant detectives from a minor American city with no idea what you are dabbling in. This is what I told Detective Pierce in the museum."

"Eddie, which embassy would be best for Mr. Kharkov? Would the Austrians want to know about this impersonator, or should we go to the Russians?"

"Hmm. The Austrians would be nicer about it, but I would say we visit the Russian embassy and hand over his passport with this hotel room number written on it. What say you, Vitaly?"

"If I tell you something, what do I get?"

"There you go…that's how we do this." Eddie rubbed his hands together and faked a big smile. "You tell us something, and we'll decide. Ike, you go first."

I pulled up a chair next to the bed and stroked my new gun. "You've kept it in good shape."

"Again, what do you want to know?"

"Here's my guess. You don't work for a government but an organization, although the organization's tentacles reach into several governments. You're a hired gun, so to speak, trying to protect the organization, and somehow have passed yourself off as Austrian security for your cover story. I haven't yet figured out how Rijad Kastrati fits into your organization."

"Interesting fantasy, but Kastrati? Bah. He pretends to do a noble service for immigrants," Kharkov said. "He likes to play a role. Did you like his monk outfit?"

Eddie rubbed his chin. "Ike, I don't think he's telling us enough, do you? Kharkov, I want you to tell me the whereabouts of Kastrati, and I'm getting very anxious about my boss's location."

"Your boss is a fool. She should leave this for others and go home. All of you go home. Keep to your own business. The answers you seek are—"

"We've tried keeping to our own business," Eddie said. His eyes narrowed. "And we've gotten multiple deaths at home, including two dead cops."

"Your boss and her dead husband are of no interest

to us."

"Where is Kastrati?" Eddie asked again.

Kharkov hesitated, then looked toward the window. "He disappeared earlier this morning."

Eddie thumped him on the head again. "No, son, you can do better. Think hard."

"Why should I? What are you going to do with me? Murder a man in a foreign country?"

Eddie leaned over the bed, supporting himself with one arm against the headboard, and drew within inches of Kharkov's face. He grabbed our captive's collar and twisted it tight around his neck. "Don't make me do that, young man. Tell me where Kastrati and my boss are, or I'll choke you with your own shirt."

Kharkov turned pink. I grabbed Eddie's arm. "Give him one more chance."

He gasped for a few seconds and choked. "Three stones. Three stones."

"What? Three stones? Is that what he said, Ike?"

"Sounded like it."

"The three stones," he mumbled again, falling back against his pillows. His bright pink complexion highlighted purplish lips. He gasped for air, his chest heaving. "Kastrati…meeting in the park…three stones. The Croatian ghost…find the Macedonian."

"He's having a seizure. Untie his arms, and let's set him up straight."

Kharkov passed out before we pulled him up.

"What the hell?" Eddie asked. "I wasn't choking him that hard."

"He hyperventilated. You almost scared him to death." I couldn't stop a grin.

He wiped his brow. "What's so funny? I almost

killed him."

"He fainted—I don't think death was close. But we got nothing out of him about Angie."

"If we find Kastrati, I bet we'll find Angie."

"What are we going to do with this guy?" I asked.

"Right. Let's put him in the closet and tie his hands again. Stuff something in his mouth. The maids will find him."

"And? It might give us an hour head start, but they'll have a hundred more goons after us."

"You're right." Eddie pulled a small metal container from his pocket. "Let's get these down his throat."

"What do you have in there?"

"Sleeping pills." Eddie shoved two pills in Kharkov's mouth. I handed him the room's bucket, half full of water from melted ice. He dribbled enough into his mouth but spilled even more.

"Now what?" I asked.

"Take all of his I.D., and we'll go back to our new place I booked. I'll call an ambulance if I can figure out how, make crap up, and give them this room number. He'll be out of it for a while."

"Okay, I've got nothing better." We gathered his documents and stuffed them in our coat pockets. Kharkov had not moved, so we headed toward the elevator passed the housekeepers pushing their carts. "We didn't keep Charlie's phone," I said as we stepped into the elevator.

"What would you do with it?" Eddie asked. The doors finally closed.

"I don't think we—" A jolt, the tarnished gold elevator doors opened, and we pushed our way into a packed lobby.

"His phone wouldn't have done us any good other than for someone to track us." We passed the front desk, and Eddie stopped. "I've got an idea." He hurried to the young woman standing behind the counter. "Ma'am, do you speak English?"

"Yes. Can I help you? Did you enjoy your stay?"

"Yeah, the greatest. Say, when we left our room, an odd man wandered around the hall, checking doors, looking for an open room."

"I will call security."

"You might call an ambulance. He walked funny and mumbled something, sounded like Russian. It may have been drugs."

"Thank you. We will take care of it. And have a wonderful day."

"We're working on it," Eddie called out as we hurried to the street.

"You're quite the storyteller," I said.

"Whatever, man. It's time to find those three stones."

Chapter Seventeen

Eddie and I hustled down a path, moving around a young couple holding hands. Their black terrier yipped at us. "My God, this place is beautiful in the winter…and peaceful, too," I said.

Eddie snorted. "Yeah, peaceful like a cemetery."

We had deposited Kharkov's possessions in our new rooms, then wandered our way to Stromovka Park. Marconi's suite next to ours remained empty, which gave me a bad feeling. Either she had double-crossed us and vanished into Prague, or she had struck out on her own to finish her pilgrimage to find Jack's killer. In either scenario, she had disappeared.

"Where are you going with a full head of steam?" I asked.

"We're supposed to be looking for three stones."

I stopped on the cobblestone path. "Three stones? Look around. I see stones everywhere. Eddie, listen to me. Stop and think about a clandestine meeting of whatever kind. Would you meet anyone out in the open like this? We need to find a more isolated area."

"But where? This park supposedly covers two hundred acres."

"Over there. It looks like a planetarium. Let's see if anyone can tell us something. A map would help," I said.

"Yeah…better than wandering around until we freeze to death." Eddie led the way and yanked hard on the glass door, almost pulling down an older woman using it for support. "Sorry, ma'am, only trying to get through the door." He leaned toward me. "Not a good idea to use a door for a crutch."

The visitor's center appeared near its capacity. We stood in line to talk to an information officer dressed in a maroon uniform with a gray beret, looking like a flight attendant from the 1970s.

Eddie rubbed his forehead. "Not one of them has said anything in English. Man, what a bunch of characters around here. It looks like that Star Wars cantina."

"I'm sure plenty of Americans and Brits come through here," I said. "There have to be at least one of these women who speak English."

"We're up next," he said. The rotund, short German man in front of us looked happy and strolled away.

"Hello…Ms. Koepka?" I asked.

"Hello." She smiled, then leaned toward me. "You said my name correctly." She smiled again. "We have our next show in thirty minutes. Cost is two hundred korun each."

"We didn't want to go to the exhibits. We need information, please—"

Eddie pounded his fist on the counter. "Three stones, we're looking for the three stones." Several other visitors mumbled in the line behind us. A grim, middle-aged man in a similar uniform came closer.

"Three stones, sir? I do not understand. Can you be more specific?" Ms. Koepka asked.

Eddie slapped the slate countertop again. "Aren't you the information person? There's something called the three stones. Can't you tell us where it is?"

Her chin quivered. "Sir, I'm not aware of these three stones. We have information about the planetarium only."

"Ike, you try."

"Sorry, Ms. Koepka. Is there a general information desk somewhere? We're lost and need a map if we could."

"Excuse, please." The man in the maroon uniform hovered behind us, leaning to his right on a black cane. "I am Milan Beneŝ. Follow me to the red couches near the far exit. Thank you, Ms. Koepka. Please help the next guest." He led us toward the rear exit, where fewer people lingered. "Now, gentlemen, please tell me what you are looking for."

Eddie pounded a fist against the wall. "Three stones. Where—"

"Excuse me, Eddie. Mr. Beneŝ, my name is Henry Pierce. This is Eddie Stone. We are meeting a colleague near a place called Three Stones. Are you aware of this area?"

Beneŝ gave us a full review, then said, "How would you know that term, and why would you be meeting someone there?"

I answered first, trying to keep Eddie quiet. "It concerns a relative of our colleague. She sent us a message about a family matter. I'm not sure why they chose that area."

"Interesting tale. Gentlemen, the park's oldest section, near the Plavební Canal and the Vltava River, adjoins an area of old government ruins from the late nineteenth century. According to the stories, their original purpose served as office space and overnight housing for the park's administrators. They abandoned the buildings and ignored them for many years…then the Nazis came. The SS used it for their murders and the Russians, also, for the same purpose…interrogation, as they both called it…but essentially an execution area. There has been no interest since the fall of the communist government thirty years ago. I am not sure why anyone would want to meet there. It is a dark, ugly, foreboding place I wish not associated with Stromovka Park. Some say you can hear the screams of the hundreds of souls killed there."

Eddie straightened his back and placed his hands on his hips. "We're not interested in ghosts. Do you have a map?"

"They do not publish it on our maps—it is not part of the park, as I told you."

Eddie puffed up again, then frowned. "Sir, we have to meet our colleague soon. She has a sick relative, and we need to have her call home."

Beneš returned Eddie's frown. "I do not believe your story, but I cannot stop you from going there. We have no official restrictions, but please keep its history in mind once you find this place. Do not dishonor those who died."

"We will be respectful, Mr. Beneš," I said. "Do you mind if I write this down?"

"Nothing to write. Go due north of here almost a kilometer. Before you reach the river, you will see a large copse of trees. Walk off the path to the right side of this timber and keep going north through the growth. It offers no established paths. You will see old stonework and remnants of brick buildings—most have collapsed."

Eddie rubbed the back of his neck. "So, what are the Three Stones? That's my question. That's all we're after."

"You will find out, Mr. Stone. Good day, Mr. Pierce." He marched to the exit and opened the door for us into an icy drizzle. A cold draft blew into the building. "If you wish to explore our exhibits and visit the planetarium, you are welcome to do so. Otherwise, good day."

We scurried outside and headed due north. "He dismissed us, Eddie. Are you ready to hunt spirits?"

"I don't care about his damn ghost story."

****

The sky had turned dark gray again, as it had been most of the time since leaving Virginia. A ten-minute walk brought us to a grove of leafless birches and oaks—nothing unusual along the park's well-groomed path next to the small forest.

Eddie exhaled, then mumbled. "I hope you loaded your gun?"

"Yep."

"As soon as we get into the brush and out of view, take it out and be ready." Sleet ricocheted off Eddie's stocking hat as we left the path and trudged a few steps through dead grass and mud.

"Weird, Eddie."

"What?"

"My shoes are getting muddy."

"You're walking in mud, farm boy."

"These are the same shoes I wore the day we found Luka Jankovich's body. My first few days on the job…barfed all over them."

"The beginning for you—now we can end it." He

stopped, staring at the ground. "What's this? Rail tracks? What would they need—"

"Rails to haul people. Unused for decades," I said.

"Jesus. Let's get into a clearing." We pushed aside the brush like pulling a curtain. Our world transformed.

"What the hell?"

We crossed over from well-kept grounds to a world of twisted tree branches covered with dormant strands of ivy. The last season's leaves scattered into dead piles of rotting vegetation, emitting a heavy smell of mold. This was a place of dead silence, with a landscape of grays and browns, disturbed only by intermittent piles of dirty red bricks.

My breath spewed small circles of vapor. "This must have been what Alice felt when she stepped through the looking glass," I said. The stillness even seemed muffled—the wet forest floor masked the noise of our steps like walking on a soft carpet.

"Damn, Ike, your grandma may be right about bad juju."

"I can hear myself breathing.

"What happened to the traffic noise?" he asked.

"Growth is too thick, I guess."

"I wonder how many people died here?" Eddie held a finger to his lips. He pointed to his left at a depression running down the hill underneath the canopy of gangly birch limbs. A finger of fog floated through the sunken trail down to the river. Eddie squatted and considered his discovery. "Come here."

I leaned over and followed his pointing finger. "A path?"

"Seems so. See? More bricks twenty yards down." We worked our way to what had been a trail to somewhere. A massive natural stone wall came into view. Eddie walked next to it and gazed at its top. "Hmm...look at this. They carved a wall right out of this granite hill. Thirty feet tall, I bet...forty yards wide." Eddie eyed the rock, then rubbed his fingers on the gray monolith. "Yeah. That's what I thought."

"What?"

"See these indentations and chipped spots?" he asked.

"Yeah, they're everywhere."

"Bullets...or where bullets struck. Some holes are deeper than others."

I rubbed my hand across the rough stone. "God. They lined up people here for executions, and who knows what else."

"Yeah, I'm almost certain. You see these darker areas going from the ground to a few feet up?"

"Yeah."

"Old blood. They would get shot, and the bodies slid to the ground...Ike, this is an awful place. We need to take care of business and get out of here."

"Agreed." I kicked at a nearby brick. "These look like part of a collapsed wall."

"They bombed the entire place, artillery hit it, or something like that?"

"Yeah, Prague was one of the last places liberated," I said.

"Well, a good history lesson, but let's get back on higher ground. I see a mound back where we were—we can see better from there."

We climbed the incline and topped a knoll of dead grass, mud, and scattered broken bricks.

Eddie swung an arm from right to left. "I'll be

damned," he said.

We both had realized the same thing. "Left, center, and right?" I asked. "The Three Stones are three walls. Execution walls."

"That's what I'm thinking, buddy."

"Where is a meeting place? One of these three?" I asked.

"Maybe right here? You can see everything from this spot. Let's look around and keep your eyes sharp—Angie may be here."

"How might she have known about this location? Wait."

"What?" he asked.

"What's this mound we're standing on?"

Eddie's eyes widened. Without looking down, he took in a deep breath. "Let's pretend it's not dead people, okay? And keep your damn gun out. I don't want either of us to get surprised."

We separated, and I marched back to the wooded area, pointing my gun in front of me. Eddie scurried off the mound and disappeared toward the last of the three stone walls. A wisp of air blew up my neck. Two crows flew from their limb, silent but with their talons opened wide. The dense undergrowth showed foot-sized indentations. I kicked forward with my feet, startling a rat, then tripped over a log, falling face down into the mud.

Pushing up, I found my gun on a pile of Euro banknotes, wet and scattered in the weeds. Regrettably, what I thought a tree log wore a nice leather jacket. "Eddie," I screamed, sounding like a kid wanting his dad. "Eddie, come here." No response while I stood, then leaned against a slippery tree trunk.

A male body, and not long dead judging by the clean clothes. One thing missing, though: his head. I dry-heaved twice but pulled myself together, determined not to vomit. This body had its limbs— good for him, but maybe not for us. Eddie and I may have interrupted the killer before he finished. I stuck my fingers into the jacket's unzipped breast pocket and found a soggy mush of something, another pastry product, it seemed. The dead man's right hand clenched more Euro currency, with another wad stashed in his left jacket pocket.

A drenching rain had replaced the sleet. I jogged back along Eddie's path by the far stone wall, pushing through even thicker undergrowth. Another derelict brick structure appeared, this one intact but covered by vines. The sunken trail led to a doorless entrance with no light seeping to the outside. Leaves stirred to my left, and I retreated into thick briars. A dark hand inside a navy-blue sleeve motioned me to come over to the bushes near the entrance.

I trotted over and squatted next to Eddie. "What are you doing? Are you lost?"

"Me? I don't get lost. I heard voices coming from in there. I think one is female."

"Angie?"

"Not sure. We need to get closer. Did you see anything?"

"Yeah. I found a dead body with no head, wearing a leather jacket with crumbs in his front pocket. Sound familiar? And Euros scattered around the body."

"That's where he is—"

"Who is?"

"I found a head, Ike. Down the hill over near the

second wall."

"Who?"

"Uh…I couldn't tell—a bashed-in face…vicious. I know it was male, though."

"How?"

"Big black mustache. It might be Kastrati. Hell, maybe it's Manny. They both have those thick, hairy things on their lips."

"Recent, right?"

"Yep, it hasn't been long," he said.

"His body still had its limbs."

"The killer may know we're here." Eddie rubbed his forehead with a muddy glove. "And something else …"

"What?" I asked.

"Something white stuck out of the mud over there—I found a piece of skull next to the wall. I pushed around in the mud for a minute and discovered a bottom jawbone. Those may be the Prague killings that Jack Marconi investigated. Hell, it may even be Jack."

"Unless it's from the war?"

"Nah, didn't look old enough and wasn't that deep."

"What now?"

"Let's move around behind and climb the hut. Get on top near the entrance."

"The roof looks like mud and vines. It might collapse."

"We have to try."

Not as easy as we thought. The ground on the structure's back side had eroded, leaving about eight feet of mud, vines, and a jumble of uneven bricks to climb. Eddie slid back into me on his first try, knocking me back to the bottom with him on top.

"Thanks."

"Then you try it this time," he said. "You're two-thirds my weight and should be able to shimmy right up there."

"Watch this." My confidence didn't match my skills, but I clawed my way to the top. A mixture of mud and blood covered my hands, and my feet were blocks of brown mush.

Eddie looked no better when he joined me, his stocking hat missing. "Okay, you're filthy now, so let's hunker down and crawl over to the other side."

I proceeded with more of a squatting walk than a crawl. Piling fallen branches, we had our seats.

My shivering fingers probed into a crack in the roof. "Look at this. I'm telling you, Eddie, this whole thing will collapse."

"Keep it down. I can't hear much other than the river and my teeth chattering, but I'm sure I heard voices. One is higher pitched. Hell, they could be homeless people in there."

"The Macedonian," I whispered.

"Excuse me?"

"The Russian guy said something about a Macedonian. Could it be him?"

"I don't remember that, and why do we care about a Macedonian?"

"He said it. I don't know. God, what must it be like?" I asked. "As ugly as it is out here, it must be a mud pit. What now?"

"Can you jump?"

"Jump? Where?"

He pointed to the entrance. "Down there. Looks

around six feet."

"I suppose. What're you thinking?"

"I'll get my ass back out in the field and make a commotion. See if I can get someone to come out of there. If they follow me, you go inside."

"Got it."

"You'll have to improvise and decide when to go." Eddie squirmed to the backside of our hideout. A muffled grunt and a curse signaled when he hit the ground. His bald head dashed by to my right as he made his way back to the top of the incline. From there, Eddie waved once to me and yelled. "Hey. Anybody here? Show me the way out, and I'll give you money." He stepped to his left and stood behind a tree. "Hello? I'm lost."

Movement below me and a figure appeared. It looked to be a tall male with his face covered under a black jacket's hood, his hands hidden in his pockets. He didn't speak, but he ambled up the incline away from the door.

"I need help," Eddie called again, his voice now farther to my left.

The hooded man picked up his pace and stopped at the top of the hill, looking one way and then another. He chose correctly and hurried toward Eddie's last call.

I hurled myself off my hiding place and rolled to a stop outside the entrance. I crept through the dark opening with no flashlight and no phone as if entering an animal's den. Icy water dripped into my hair onto my shoulders. Lights flickered in front of me to the left, and bits of daylight shone through the cracked ceiling supports. To my right, a rotted door with no window opened to another compact room, this one with an overturned chair and stacks of rotting paper. There must have been other chambers to my left, but that section had filled with debris. Glass crunched under my feet as I eased next to a door jamb.

I peered around the corner, my hands white-knuckling my gun, and I saw a woman—her head drooped toward her lap, showing dirty blonde hair with streaks of gray. Someone had tied her trembling hands behind her back with a rope lashed through the slats of a splintering wooden chair.

"Angie?" I called out, approaching with my gun pointed.

She was conscious and turned toward me, her eyes and cheeks bruised, her body shaking from the cold. "Henry? My God," she sobbed and dropped her head again. "I'm sorry I got you and Eddie into this. It should have all died with Jack, but I hoped—"

"I'm sorry, too, but no time for that. Let's get you loose." I shoved the gun in my belt, struggled with one rope until it came free, and she squirmed out of the other.

"Where's Eddie?" She wiped crusted blood from her bottom lip.

"He's acting as bait. He went up the hill and made noise to get that guy to follow."

She wobbled to a stand and gave me a tight muddy hug.

I pushed her bangs away from her eyes. "How did you get here?"

"After spending a few hours at the train station, I found a locker for my luggage. I wasn't sure what to do, but I couldn't keep putting you guys in danger. I had returned to leave a note when I saw Kastrati come out of one of the mushroom-shaped buildings across the street from our rooms, the same building we should be watching. I followed him to the park, and he pushed through the grove of trees. I shivered in the sleet for a few minutes before I followed. I heard shouting, men cursing in some other language—I should have known better than to go in blind."

She noticed my gun. "Where'd you get that?"

"Long story."

"Anyway, I found a man hunched in the weeds. I called out...he threw something down, then came toward me. My God, he had blood spatter all over his clothes. I tried to run, but he caught me in a few steps, slapped me around and knocked me out, and then I woke up in here."

"Who?"

"I don't know. The guy covered his face with a black balaclava...leather...just like the old stories. And he had a mechanism at the mouth that disguised his voice—an odd modulation. Henry...I've been so blind. We've got to get out of here."

"Fine with me," I said.

A distant gunshot echoed, followed right away by two more.

"It has to be Eddie," she said.

"I hope you can run."

We headed toward daylight, then took a hard left turn out the entrance.

"Stay here in the underbrush," I said. "I'll make my way to where Eddie should be."

"I'm not sitting here defenseless while waiting on that animal to find me again while you have the gun. That's an order."

"So be it." I pointed toward the execution walls. "Last I saw, Eddie went this way. Toward the Three Stones."

"Three stones?"

"You'll see."

"These briars are slowing us down," Marconi said. We pushed our way through the thorny brush back into the open and hurried by the first wall—no sign of Eddie or the hooded man.

We passed the second wall. "Nothing there," she said.

"There's the third one."

Marconi stopped. "Look, bottom toward our right. Near the left side. That's a blue sleeve in the mud."

"He's down," I said.

"Oh, my God, please let him be alive." She took off, running down the incline in her muddy sneakers, then squatted next to him. "He's breathing," she called to me. A thick layer of mud covered most of Eddie's face. She rolled him to his side and tugged on his jacket sleeve, showing the left side of his rain-drenched, light-blue shirt had darkened with blood.

Eddie rolled back over on his back and mumbled through chattering teeth. "Angie? I thought we'd lost you."

"No such luck. And I thought you were toast too, but we're a team, and it'll stay that way. Arm only?" she asked while ripping his jacket sleeve. She took the revolver out of his hand, tore his shirt sleeve, and wrapped his bicep with it.

"Careful. Maybe arm only, but it stings above my ribs, too. He's a sneaky one, Angie. Slipped up on me and grabbed me around the neck. I bit his arm and got loose for a second, then we traded shots. I got off two rounds. He must've heard you and moved off into the brush."

"Did he say anything to you?" I asked.

"He mumbled something…I couldn't tell what. He had this weird ski mask. And Angie?"

"Yeah?"

"If I'm worse than it seems, let Edward know. I've got my estate ready whenever he gets out of prison."

"You'll be fine. Henry, keep guard."

"No need." The words sounded artificial, tinny. A man leaned hard against a tree trunk, his tan pants bloodstained from his left thigh down to his ankle. I'd let my guard down worrying about Eddie. I turned, and there he was. He pulled back his hood and yanked off the balaclava. "It's over."

"Rijad." Marconi shook her head. "You son of a bitch. I thought you were a friend."

Kastrati winced and shifted his weight to his good leg. "You thought so, but I have few friends." The corners of his mouth upturned into a slight grin. "All three of you together. How convenient." He waved his pistol at me. "Throw your piece over, detective." I hesitated, then pitched my gun toward his feet. "You all are so naïve. This is much larger than you can imagine."

Marconi sat into the mud and leaned back, supporting herself with her arms behind. "You had those great bakeries…but it was all a front, wasn't it? You've been a part of the old murders and the coverup the whole time. A murderer in plain sight."

"Those men in the local cemeteries? I told you, not my doing…but I am not alone," he said.

"Not alone?" she asked.

"I am part of the Protection Force. Many ex-warriors in several countries protect Miomir Kurić, her family, and her organization."

"Kurić?" I asked. "I thought you hated the Serbs."

Marconi glanced at me. "It's money…as always."

"I've wondered about people like you," I said. "How much money does it take?"

"Ah, the smart mouth detective. You know nothing about my family."

Eddie slurred between heavy breaths. "Ike, keep your cool."

"Stanich," Marconi mumbled. "The money came from Stanich."

Kastrati snickered. "Where else would I get enough money to open two businesses?"

"Manny was right about you," Marconi said.

"He could never mind his own business. And don't assume Manfred Jurić's innocence. I finally held him accountable today."

Marconi wiped her face with a trembling hand. "What do you mean?"

"It wasn't me that killed your husband."

"But the mask …"

Kastrati grinned. "Jurić's idea, I assume, to copy me. Should I be flattered? But no matter…Jurić's crimes were many, including your husband's death."

Marconi glanced toward me, then looked back to Kastrati. "I'll never understand."

Kastrati shifted his weight again. "It has been thrilling all these years watching you and Eddie Stone wasting time in your grand adventure…then they pulled you in, too, Henry Ike Pierce. And where did it get you?

You could have been policing tourists at George Washington's home for years and years to come, but instead, you'll die a young man in a mud pit in the middle of Europe."

I stood to face him.

He pointed his gun. "You should be dead already. Put your hands over your head. You and your smart mouth will die first against the wall like hundreds of others. Walk backward."

I raised my hands and took two steps back. A gunshot exploded…I felt nothing.

Kastrati appeared bewildered, his mouth hanging open. He dropped his gun and grasped for his throat, blood pouring over his hands as he fell to his knees.

"When you see Manny, tell him that's from his old friend, Angie Doll," Marconi said. She dropped Eddie's revolver at her feet. "Enjoy hell."

Kastrati faceplanted into the mud, his blood pumping onto the muck at the base of the third stone wall.

Chapter Eighteen

A man in sky-blue scrubs handed his clipboard to the nearest nurse and then approached me. "Detective Sergeant Henry Pierce?"

Another man in a uniform emerged from the hall, stopping at the nurses' station to watch and listen. Cyrillic lettering surrounded a police-style emblem stitched into his light-blue jacket sleeve.

"Yes, I'm Pierce."

"Your colleague is fine," the doctor said with a hint of a British accent. "The bullet sliced through his bicep with a superficial nick to the left side of his chest. He will make a full recovery but will be sore for several days. Where is the woman named Marconi?"

Marconi dashed back from the hospital's vending area, her mouth full of crackers. "I'm here," she mumbled. The on-duty nurses had brought us towels to clean ourselves along with fresh scrubs to wear. "I heard. Splendid news."

"For him, yes. Unfortunately, while Mr. Stone is in recovery, you must both proceed to the Police Presidium."

The uniformed man stepped away from the nurses' station. "Good afternoon. I am Commander Stepan Hrubý of the *Policie Ceské Republiky*. My English may not be as well as the doctor's, but I assume you do not speak Czech?"

"I'm Director Angela Marconi of the Alexandria,

Virginia Police Department's homicide division. This is my colleague, Detective Sergeant Henry Pierce. And no, we don't speak Czech."

"Director Marconi, you appear to have bruising around your face. Should I retain the physician?"

"A hot bath would be great."

Old frown lines flared around his mouth. "First, you will need to follow me to the Presidium. The doctor assured me Detective Lieutenant Stone is out of harm's way."

"Can we see him first?" I asked.

"He is not out of recovery. Please come without delay. The Presidium is nearby."

Marconi sighed and motioned me to follow. The elevator reacted slowly, but we made it to the first floor, then exited the hospital into a blizzard.

Hrubý offered no overcoats before we crossed the street into the police station, a building on the corner facing the medical facilities. The stone building had iron bars on many outside windows, giving the impression of a remodeled mid-century prison.

"I told you we were close. Please keep behind me." Slowing at the entrance's security desk, the man at the desk nodded.

We marched through the hall, passing several busy bureaucrats' offices, our hair and shoulders dripping again from melted snow. "Where are we going?" Marconi asked.

The commander ignored her and kept walking. We matched his rapid strides, snaked into another corridor, and then took a twist to our right into a u-shaped auditorium. A handful of uniformed officers sat behind elevated desks surrounding a rectangular table next to the podium. The small theater reminded me of a college lecture room, except everything was white: walls, ceiling, desks, floor tiles.

Marconi shivered in her damp scrubs in the cold room.

"Please take a seat," Hrubý said.

I leaned near my boss and whispered. "I don't think it's a welcome party."

Hrubý removed his long gray overcoat, threw it across his chair, then sat next to Marconi. He signaled for silence from our observers. "Director Marconi and Detective Sergeant Pierce, I have brought you here for questioning. We will attempt to make this as short as possible. I have asked our subcommanders here to listen to your statements." He nodded toward the men and women in the room. "We will treat you with proper respect as officers of another jurisdiction."

She returned a blank stare. "Thank you, Commander Hrubý, I appreciate your courtesies. What is this related to?"

Hrubý sighed. "Let us not start this way, Director Marconi. A man shot your colleague, and you contacted emergency services to take him to our hospital. We found a dead man with three gunshot wounds at the Three Stones area next to the park, and another body, beheaded, was at the crest of the same area. The head was ten meters from where your colleague lay, and we found the skulls of six other people in the same area. We are autopsying two dead bodies as we speak, and we have taken the older skulls to our forensics lab."

Marconi rubbed her eyes. "You see—"

Hrubý held a hand up and frowned. "You had guns in our country, for which you have no license. We found our associate drugged in a closet at a hotel apartment you relinquished this morning, and he described exactly the appearances of your two colleagues. We are not appreciative of foreign agencies causing such mayhem in our country. Much less do we appreciate chaos caused by a city-level American police force."

"We can explain everything," I said.

Hrubý crossed his arms. "It is our habit to let the superior officer speak."

"Yes, sir, but I'll depend on Sergeant Pierce to offer information as needed," Marconi said.

"Very well. After receiving your earlier statement from one of our officers, I contacted your Police Commissioner Bates in Virginia. He stated the City of Alexandria suspended you and Detective Lieutenant Stone."

"Yes, a political move."

Hrubý held up a hand again for silence from his colleagues. "Commissioner Bates informed me of your status. He offered a similar explanation but claims no official City of Alexandria knowledge of, or response to, your presence here. The three of you are in grave circumstances. Our laws here are as important to us as yours are to you."

"Commander, we didn't intend to disrupt anyone in either country. May I continue with a summarized version of our story?" Marconi asked.

"Yes. It will fascinate us."

"Thank you. In 1995, five murders in Alexandria happened within a few days of one another, all occurred at two parks, and we now believe the five deceased men to be Bosnian immigrants. Rijad Kastrati, one of the dead men you found today, confirmed this, *if* his story is correct. My late husband, Jack Marconi, investigated those murders, but he resolved nothing after several months of inquiries. The bodies were beheaded, with hands and feet missing, which prevented us from identifying victims in those days. Subsequently, my husband joined an American intelligence service and pursued similar murders here in Prague, guessing something connected them to the Alexandria killings. Soon…I received word that he, too, was a victim."

The commander nodded. "We also suffered here from those types of killings. I lived in Brno, and much was in the news." His comment stimulated whispers in the audience. "*Prosím, přestaň*," Hrubý called out, quieting the room again. "I am sorry your husband lost his life in our city. Please continue."

Marconi nodded, and the room grew quiet again. "Over the years, as technology improved, we asked several times to exhume the bodies in Alexandria. The courts always denied us. In fact, a federal court intervened to stop us." A younger man sitting at the front row had eyebrows remindful of black caterpillars. Marconi's comment about the courts caused both to arch into his forehead. "I tried over the years to keep my department interested, and I received permission last summer to hire two more detectives. Detective Sergeant Pierce was one of those hires. I had hoped to reopen those cases, then a similar murder occurred last November."

"Excuse me. May I say something, Commander?" I asked.

"If your superior concurs."

"Of course. The floor is yours, Henry."

Now wasn't the time to be nervous. I had to stare above the caterpillar-like eyebrows to concentrate. "My first week on the job last November, I investigated a murder similar to the ones from 1995." Murmurs grew in the audience. "We believed the killer wanted to reproduce the methods of twenty-five years earlier. This time, though, we could identify the body with DNA analysis, and we determined the victim to be from the local Serbian community. Other 'characteristics' gave us hope of tying this together."

"In what way?"

"The recent victim wore a leather jacket, and a breast pocket contained a pastry."

The room erupted, bringing the commander to his feet.

"Like our victims," a voice shouted from the second row.

Hrubý grabbed the club from his belt and pounded on the table for order.

"*Teufel's Engels.*" The young man with the eyebrows stood and shouted. "*Teufel's Engels.* They are in America."

Hrubý pointed a finger. "Sit, lieutenant. Director Marconi, the breakup of Yugoslavia opened the gates for those animals to feast in central Europe. We have identified over thirty Prague victims whose deaths had the same characteristics, fifty or so across our republic. Most were Bosnian refugees, but a few Czechs became victims. A task force tracked down these so-called Devil's Angels, and many are dead or in prisons across our country."

"But the latest in our country was not such a victim," I said. "We believe the killing a fit of jealousy between local Bosnian and Serb families that led to the murder. As I mentioned, the standard method of dismemberment did not match exactly. We also determined one of our undercover narcotics police officers aided in the murder. A local Serb patriarch paid him to track our activities, or that's our conjecture."

Marconi interjected. "The perpetrator of the newest murder in Alexandria is a brother-in-law of the man named Kastrati you found shot yesterday. Apparently, Kastrati had been a member of Miomir Kurić's organization. A 'Protection Force,' as he called it."

"Stop," Hrubý ordered his noisy audience again, annoyed with them and agitated by her last statement. "Director Marconi, your information is of great assistance. I would like to discuss this with you in a smaller group setting."

"Very well. I would like to involve Detective Lieutenant Stone when possible. He could add his view to this."

"Fine. All dismissed except for Lieutenant Talích."

"Sir?" The younger man with the bushy eyebrows remained seated. His uniform was a dark shade of gray instead of light blue, and he held a black beret instead of the traditional dark-blue police hat. Hrubý waited a few moments for the others to disperse before continuing.

"Lieutenant Talích, please accompany our guests to their hotel and let them freshen themselves. Director Marconi, we already determined where you are staying, and we will join you for dinner. I will have to insist you consider yourselves under detainment until we have had more discussions. Lieutenant Talích is assigned to us from our Section One criminal division and has been indispensable. Mr. Žăk, a member of our Unit for Peculiar Activities, will join him later."

"Peculiar Activities?" I asked.

"Yes, an extremely proficient unit of ours."

****

They escorted us back to the hospital. A quick visit with Eddie found him awake, hungry, and ready to get out of bed. The doctor assured us he was fine but refused to tell us a day for his release.

Eddie had chosen well the suites he booked for us that morning. We gained more space, and Marconi's third-floor suite had a direct line of sight into the building we needed to surveil. Mr. Žăk accompanied me to my door and stood outside while I showered and changed. I dressed in jeans, sneakers, and a maroon college hoodie. Žăk faced the hall when I opened the door.

"Please come in, Mr. Žăk. I'm ready." I guessed him near my age when he turned and faced me. A buzz haircut highlighted his round face under a red beret, and his all-black uniform was a tight fit on his muscled frame.

"Thank you, Detective Sergeant Pierce. I have yet to hear from Lieutenant Talích. Director Marconi is slower than you, it seems."

I smiled. "Nothing new there. Please come in and have a seat. How do all of you speak such good English?"

"I appreciate your offer. However, please understand the Commander has assigned me as part of your detention team, temporary, I hope. I am to guard your safety. English was the favored language at school—our parents and guardians learned Russian."

"What is the Unit for Peculiar Activities?"

"That name is an odd translation, but we can think of no other for *Jednotka pro Zvláštní Činnosti*. We are a specialty unit within the police criminal division serving as an elite security organization for the Czech Republic."

I offered to shake hands. "You can call me Henry if you like."

He reciprocated. "I will continue as Mr. Žăk. We may not use our common names while on duty."

"Interesting." I offered a package of cheese crackers, and, to my surprise, he shoved two into his mouth.

"Thank you, Henry Pierce. We have not eaten since last night. Commander Hrubý's assignments gave us a hectic afternoon. I am not always attached to his division, but he requested I join this investigation."

"I'm uncertain what you do?"

"I cannot offer details, but Lieutenant Talích from Section One, for instance, is a more traditional investigator, albeit with a military aspect to his job. Consider my job as a combination of one of your FBI agents and perhaps…a special forces officer."

"Even more interesting."

Mr. Žăk placed his hand against his left ear and listened. "They are ready. We are to meet everyone in Suite 499. They will deliver dinner, and we will talk again."

"But this complex only has three floors."

"No, we use the lift for three floors. You must walk up to the fourth. Please come."

We marched to the end of the hall and stopped at Suite 399, three doors down from Marconi's room. Mr.

Žăk brought forth a brass door key and a security card, both needed to enter. We walked through the doorway into a chamber full of equipment. Several LCD screens covered the wall to our left, showing maps from around the city. Two men with old-style headphones covering their ears sat in rolling chairs near five narrow vertical windows overlooking the street. A man in a uniform matching Mr. Žăk's stood near the door watching over the activities.

Marconi and Hrubý joined us, then we continued to a side door leading to a circular metal stairway. We twisted up the stairs and had to duck under a roaring metal air duct producing tremendous heat as it transferred warm air through the building. A few more steps and, at last, Mr. Žăk opened a gleaming steel door. We stepped into a rectangular room full of what appeared to be junk equipment of various kinds.

Marconi wheezed. "Are we there yet?"

Mr. Žăk cracked half a smile. "We are now." He pulled back what appeared to be a brown shower curtain and revealed yet more space. This zone housed a conference table and assorted modern equipment, encompassing an area the size of at least three of the suites on the lower floors.

A massive screen hung over the conference table, displaying our own Commissioner Bates sipping coffee from his desk in Alexandria. "Hello, Angie…Pierce. Seems you've had quite a trip."

"Commissioner?" Marconi approached the screen and craned her neck upward.

"Angie, the commander contacted me early this morning, my time, about the three of you. Good afternoon, Commander Hrubý."

"It is eight o'clock in the evening, Commissioner Bates. As you can see, your staff is safe with us."

"How is Lieutenant Stone?"

"We saw him at the hospital, commissioner," Marconi answered. "It could have been a close call, but the bullet didn't enter his chest. His arm will be sore, and he may be out of the hospital in a day or so," Marconi said.

"Good to know. Give him my best. Commander, I appreciate your flexibility in dealing with the Alexandria police department. I want to reaffirm that this foray into Europe is not an official undertaking blessed by our city. It would violate several U.S. laws for us to strike out on our own—"

"Your colleagues' adventurers came close to causing a much bigger incident," Hrubý said. "As I noted, all of you are far out of your element here. You have blundered around for days and, luckily, have survived. Commissioner, I am glad we had our talk earlier, or our interrogation would have been much harsher. I trust you have contacted us in the method I requested?"

"Yes, our I.T. department proceeded with the encryption processes. I believe our staff—"

"Good. Again, I must state unequivocally that we must remain covert on both ends if we are to continue these discussions. My superiors would be suspicious of these methods."

"Understood, and I know my three colleagues will be more than willing to follow your lead."

"Thank you. Please, Director Marconi and Sergeant Pierce, take your seats to my right. We will touch on your exploits again. Lieutenant Talích will also ask questions."

"Where should I begin again?" Marconi asked. "We discussed earlier the old murders—"

"You don't have to explain those again—all related to the Stanich family in Alexandria. We know of his connections to Serbia, and we have known of the scoundrels Manfred Jurić and Rijad Kastrati, and their actions here in Prague and elsewhere."

"Scoundrels?" I asked.

"What American synonym would you prefer, Sergeant Pierce?" Hrubý sat hard into a larger cushioned chair.

"Murderers, killers, among others."

"Whatever your pleasure, sir. Now, Director Marconi, why were you following these men, and why did they want to kill you?"

"We weren't following Jurić," she answered. "I didn't know he was here. He, I thought, was an old friend of my husband's. They worked together many years ago. And you may not know, shortly before Jack died in Stromovka Park in 1996, Manny quit his government job, whatever it was. He opened a bar and restaurant in Alexandria several years ago but sold it within the last month…then he disappeared. The man named Kastrati paid our way over here."

"I found a file in our records regarding Mr. Marconi's death," Hrubý said. "His was not an ethnic killing, obviously. I am not sure if you are aware, but the authorities were lucky to identify him, unlike so many others. The killer missed the identification in his left back pants pocket."

"Jack was left-handed. They identified him…but I never thought of how."

"NSA, correct?"

"Yes. How did you know?"

"We winnowed out hard-core communists in the 1990s and sent them to prison, sparing only a few if they cooperated with us. Their data collection methods helped us find foreign nationals in Prague, including Americans who *visited* us."

Talích's eyebrows arched again, and he squirmed in his seat.

Hrubý sighed. "You have a question?"

"Not a question, Commander Hrubý. Several statements."

"Do not pontificate, lieutenant."

"Yes, sir. Director Marconi and Detective Sergeant Pierce, I will make a few statements, and you are free to comment if you like. It is my way of asking questions, you see."

Hrubý rubbed his temples. "Proceed, Lieutenant Talích, please proceed." He snapped his head toward Marconi. "And my American guests, remember your utmost secrecy remains a requirement. We cannot be successful unless we are discrete."

Talích steepled his fingers under his chin. "As we said, Manfred Jurić was most familiar to us. In fact, our agencies had suspicions about him going back to 1992." He waited a moment to watch our reactions. "His methods as a member of the so-called 'Protection Force' copied those of the Devil's Angels. During his autopsy, we discovered a tattoo: '*Uradi sve što je Potrebno*,' or 'Do Whatever is Necessary.'"

"Same as we found on a body at home," Marconi said. "The Protection Force again? Kastrati admitted to being a member, too, but isn't that unusual? The

Devil's Angels were Serbs preying on other ethnic groups—Manny was Croatian, and Kastrati was Bosnian."

"Those groups were fluid and intermixed. They had different command structures but the same results. Unfortunately, with the end of the Yugoslav wars, Miomir Kurić's organization blossomed rather than meet justice. Drugs, smuggling, human trafficking, and, most notably, counterfeiting, are the organization's new weapons. That's where our investigation has hit many barriers, much like yours has in Virginia, it appears. We have cleared many avenues, but the terminus remains uncertain."

"Different paths to the same destination," Marconi said. She popped a Nicorette in her mouth and recrossed her arms.

"I presume, as educated people, you are familiar with the Big Bang Theory of universal creation?" Talích asked.

"Sure, we are," I said.

He continued. "One minor event created an explosion that is expanding our universe, or in this case, our universe of knowledge. Likewise, the foolishness of a Bekić Čazim—"

"I sent them the files, Angie," Commissioner Bates said. "I wanted them to have context—"

"Thank you, Commissioner," Talích said.

Hrubý frowned. "Be respectful, lieutenant."

"My apologies. As I mentioned, Bekić Čazim's jealousy and the murder of Mr. Jankovich served as the minor event. Your police officers' deaths, the explosion and fire at the shopping center, the attack on Detective Sergeant Pierce in the cave, and your subsequent

European visit began with that one incident. Otherwise, this intrigue would have stayed buried for how long?"

"Yes, we've thought of that, lieutenant," Marconi said. "The killings in 1995 were near-forgotten—Lieutenant Stone and I would have retired, never having solved them."

"They would have remained a part of a cold-case tale for many more years, or maybe forever," I said. "But, Lieutenant Talích, Rijad Kastrati said unpaid loans caused those murders."

Talích considered my statement. "I see. We had assumed a different reason, which leads to our next item, Rijad Kastrati, who reverted to his old ways, weaving an intricate web of intrigue all his own."

"Rijad encouraged us to come here, and he paid for it," Marconi said. "Then, he tried to kill us."

Talích shook his head. "Everyone massively underrated him…in most ways. In your case, he used you and quite effectively so. Much of what he told you, his help with immigration issues, and so on, were true, but he did not tell you everything."

Marconi glanced at me, seemingly confused. "I'm not following. Commissioner? How do they know?"

Bates wiped his nose with a tissue. "Angie, please just listen."

The steel door opened. Air hissed from the heating ducts, then silence after the door's slam. The curtain pulled back, and in strolled Vitaly Kharkov, the Russian we had tied up and drugged that morning. "Mr. Kharkov, I'm sure you remember Detective Sergeant Pierce?"

Kharkov glared at me. "I want my gun back."

"What? I thought…we thought …"

Talích held up his hand. "Relax, Sergeant Pierce, Mr. Kharkov understands it was business, right, Mr. Kharkov?"

Kharkov glared again. "Sure."

Hrubý interrupted. "He *is* a Russian national, but he works for us. You see, Mr. Kharkov, Lieutenant Talích, Mr. Žăk, and another man all had Serbian parents who were also victims of the Devil's Angels at a massacre in northeast Kosovo. The gang accused their parents of collaboration, and their executions followed. We found foster homes for these young men, and years later, I recruited them back to Prague to work in our agencies. So, back to the subject. Mr. Kharkov, could you enlighten our guests about Rijad Kastrati and the driver, Chasna Kovačić. I believe you are well acquainted, Sergeant Pierce?"

"Yes, I have a soft spot in my head for him."

Kharkov sat to my left. "Rijad Kastrati had his own secrets. A Bosnian, but at one time, an acquaintance of Jurić *before* they emigrated to America."

"How so?" Marconi asked.

"In late 1992, Mr. Kastrati gathered a force to protect his home city of Bihać. They failed. The Serbs killed or captured many men—the survivors broke into several secondary groups. Those individuals retaliated by adopting the methods of the Serbian Devil's Angels. No outcry occurred against Kastrati's Bosnian gangs since many people supported their revenge. Kastrati and a sister eventually made their way to Vienna, followed by the Croat, Manfred Jurić. Manny, as you called him, was a member of one gang under Kastrati's umbrella."

"My God," Marconi said.

Kharkov sighed. "Killing was their work. Kastrati

had as much blood on his hands as anyone, but since they considered him on the so-called good side, his past behavior never became an issue. He begged U.N. representatives in Mostar for a position, and they found him a sinecure as an advisor in Vienna. This caused his rupture with Jurić. They both received asylum in your country the next year, despite their histories. Jurić took a path like Kastrati's, somehow talked his way into an adjunct position with your National Security Agency, and he became an acquaintance of your husband's. Is this true?"

"Yes, I suppose so," Marconi said while rubbing her swollen eyes. "Protecting Miomir Kurić's ass was Manny's actual business. I'll never understand." She became teary again, wiping the last bit of mascara from her eyes. "He killed Jack. It must have been only a business transaction for him."

"That's not all," Kharkov said.

Marconi jerked her head. "What do you mean?"

"It wasn't transactional, Director Marconi. He killed your husband in a rage, a covetous rage."

"Jealousy? What the hell are you talking about?"

Kharkov's face reddened. Turning to me, he said, "It's what I warned you about in the Vienna museum, Sergeant Pierce. Answers will hurt more than not knowing."

Marconi's neck and ears blotched pink. "Never mind. Who was Manny jealous of?"

Talích interrupted. "Your husband."

"Jack and me?"

Talích closed his eyes and lowered his head. "It wasn't you, Director…Mr. Marconi's love interest caused the rupture. Were you aware of these things?"

Marconi sighed. "Yes, yes, I figured it out. He found a girlfriend in Prague."

"This wasn't just any girlfriend."

"Who?"

"Miomir Kurić is a woman." Silence, except for Commissioner Bates blowing on his coffee.

"Kurić is a woman?" she asked.

"Yes."

"Wait a minute," Marconi said. "Are you telling me the person Jack tracked here was Miomir Kurić, and somehow, they hooked up? What utter crap is this?" Marconi stood and grabbed my shoulder. "Come on, Henry, this is an elaborate hoax, psychological ops, or something to blame this on us."

I remained seated.

Kharkov continued. "Director, from what we know, the legal authorities had, at first, conjectured during the Hague trials that the Kurić name is not of a particular individual, but the name of a syndicate. They never identified a face or a composite of Kurić. Rumors also circulated that the actual person named Kurić is a woman, but it didn't fit other narratives at the time."

Marconi covered her face.

Hrubý stood and placed his hands on her shoulders. "I'm sorry, director, but please have a seat. I am afraid it is true…all that, and a child was involved." Marconi leaned in a heap against Hrubý's chest. He waited a moment, steadied her, then led her back into a chair.

A man appeared with a cart clattering across the floor, bringing several food trays and drinks from behind the curtain. Hrubý leaned toward her. "Please have something to eat, Angela."

Marconi grabbed a bottle of vodka from the cart

and poured a fourth of a glass. She searched for something to mix, found nothing of interest, then gulped it straight away before pouring another.

Silence except for machinery noise.

"I'm sorry, Angie," Bates said. "They told me a few minutes before you got here."

"Not your fault, commissioner. A finale of sorts, I guess." She took a sandwich and suddenly changed the subject. "These sandwiches look delicious. I'm starving."

Hrubý scratched his chin. "These are Chlebicek…an open-faced sandwich. Trdelnik is coming in a moment as the dessert. It's a spiral-shaped pastry covered in sugar and cinnamon around a stick called a trdlo."

"Very hospitable, Commander," she said before taking another deep breath. "I'm sorry for making such a spectacle."

"Do not apologize. You have been through a terrible physical trauma today."

"Let's not stop," Marconi said. She took a deep breath and asked no more about her late husband. "Kharkov, I need more information concerning your association with Kastrati. Why did you follow Sergeant Pierce to the Vienna museum and corner him in the dark? And the biggest question is why you came to the hotel for Chasna Kovačić's phone? How is it connected?"

Kharkov glanced at Hrubý, who nodded for him to continue. "You are correct. It is all connected. Kastrati often left his family to run his businesses in America."

"A gang of villainy," I mumbled.

"Whatever your pleasure, sir. Over the years,

Kastrati pushed and pushed to be more 'official' because of the so-called help he gave us, and the Austrian authorities relented. He took the name of Viktor Kruger in 2017, an alias he made for himself, and they assigned him to EURODAC, the immigrant identification agency. Around the same time, Commander Hrubý appointed me as liaison to our Austrian counterparts. They partnered me with Kastrati, or Viktor Kruger, chiefly for me to keep a watch on his activities." Kharkov shifted in his seat and glanced toward his commander.

"Please continue, Mr. Kharkov," Hrubý said.

"Very well. Although Mr. Kastrati offered an occasional tidbit of information about our recent immigrant residents, my job as Vienna Detektiv Bader was to scrutinize his other activities. I learned of his initiative to bring you to Vienna and provide your way to Prague. At first, I did not understand why he would want you here and thought it peculiar three Americans from a local police department wanted to come to Europe on a law enforcement mission. His efforts helped get you here, though, hoping you would flush out his old enemy, Manfred Jurić."

"They weren't exactly hiding at home. Manny had a trendy bar, and Rijad was in the public eye with his two bakeries."

Hrubý removed his reading glasses, giving her a darting glance. "But they both had hidden pasts. Jurić killed your husband, and Kastrati's history as the 'hooded one' stayed buried until his demise, did it not? Kastrati's killing of Jurić would have been easier to cover up here, and he could have disappeared back to Alexandria."

"The last gasp plan to find Jack's killer." Marconi rubbed her ring finger.

"That's how he used you," Hrubý offered. "His bait was the death of your husband and your quest to find his killer."

Commissioner Bates glanced away from his screen and tapped his pen on his desk. "Angie…after this expedition, well…I'd taken too much heat on this fixation of yours for years, it got you and Eddie suspended, and they've attacked Pierce how many times?"

"I know," Marconi replied, "but I—"

"Excuse us." Hrubý faced Bates and held up his right hand. "Please, let us finish."

Bates' face reddened, but he said nothing more.

"That is why I accompanied Kastrati to the neurologist's office," Kharkov said. "He had kinder things to say about his American acquaintances, Eddie Stone and Angela Marconi, but he was not a fan of yours, Detective Pierce. I believe he would have given you a story at the doctor's office to isolate you from your friends."

"He didn't like me?" I asked. "But wait a second. I became isolated a few days later on the bus. Was he working with Chasna Kovačić?"

"Kovačić worked for many people—a mercenary of sorts," Kharkov said. "He stayed in contact with a young woman at the U.S. State Department, and he followed you to the cave with her guidance. We are not sure if he had a relationship established with Kastrati at that point. Later, though, they joined forces. Kastrati booked the three of you on individual busses as insurance, if he needed, how do I say, take care of unexpected problems. Those plans went askew when a bus broke down, and Director Marconi and Detective Lieutenant Stone traveled together to Prague. This provided the opportunity for Mr. Kovačić to act as a substitute bus driver."

Marconi bowed her head and sputtered. "So…blind."

"Director, we believe Detective Sergeant Pierce was to die that evening," Talích said.

I leaned forward on my elbows. "That's where my anger came from, Angie. You got to the point you believed anything to move this forward."

Bates yelled. "Be quiet, Pierce, and listen."

Kharkov ignored us while looking at his notes. "We believe Kastrati paid Bekić Čazim's legal fees, including his attorney, a Mr. Milosh Sahiti. Commissioner Bates asked about this today."

My face flushed hot. "Commissioner, if you'll recall, I asked to have Kastrati's business records subpoenaed, but you refused my request. Do you remember why?"

Marconi waved a hand at me. "Never mind. Mr. Kharkov, I had been in contact with Kastrati since late 2017 outside any regular police business. God…it gives me chills…he came to me and declared Manny was someone to distrust. His statements were vague…practiced, I thought, and I assumed it only gossip. He came to talk a few other times as the months went by and then presented this plan for our trip to Europe."

"He sought only revenge," Kharkov said. "Now, they are both dead."

"Why did Manny have wads of Euros in his

pockets?" I asked.

"Yes, there may have been a financial piece to this we have not discovered," Hrubý said. "We also found an interesting gold coin, but we cannot be sure if it plays a role. Perhaps a payment to Kastrati for an undetermined reason? If a payment, Jurić might have, unknowingly, offered counterfeit money. Kastrati would not have appreciated the gesture."

"Not much of a loss," I said.

"But it is a loss, a huge one," Talích said.

"How so?" Bates asked.

"The building to surveil? Kastrati identified it as a key distribution point for shipping counterfeit Euros."

"How did you know?" Marconi asked. "The location, I mean."

"Kastrati told me about the counterfeiting before we left Vienna," Kharkov replied. "Then he told me he prepared apartments for you near the building where the distribution takes place. He knew everything…but hid it well."

"I sent them the picture Pierce took at the Stanich building that showed a return address on one box," Bates said.

"We had our suspicions, but the picture confirmed them," Hrubý said.

"Kastrati came out of that building this morning," Marconi said. "He left there and headed to the forest."

Hrubý's face reddened. "I did not know this. Lieutenant?"

Talích glared at us. "No one had informed me."

"Would he have a connection there?" I asked.

"We don't know the details, do we?" Hrubý asked. "Lieutenant Talích, I would encourage you to excuse yourself and see if this alters our plans." Talích stormed out, pulling down the brown curtain as he left.

Marconi suppressed a grin. "How did you get everything set up here so fast? It's only been a few hours."

Hrubý swung around in his chair, his back to the enormous screen. "There wasn't much to do. This is my...satellite office. You see, my background is much like yours. We have our everyday duties, but other things happen that I cannot explain. As you have noticed, associations between people in authority are sometimes stronger bonds than our laws. Your federal court has stopped you occasionally, no? Multiple levels have halted us, too."

"Eddie Stone says it's about money and power," I said.

"Yes, an astute observation by Lieutenant Stone," Hrubý said. "This area where we sit is the headquarters of the Unit of Peculiar Activities. We staff it, officially, with only two people: Mr. Žák, and his associate standing near the now-damaged room divider, Mr. Žicăn. We tie other positions here to the national police body. Our surveillance of this building across the street is not new, and today's information allows us to move forward."

"You organized this in such a brief time," I said.

"The equipment has been here, but, yes, Mr. Žák is always resourceful."

"Is it that serious, commander?" Bates asked. "I know we've had our interesting moments with Mr. Stanich and came across a multitude of payments to various people."

Hrubý pushed back in his chair. "Mr. Žák? We

have talked ourselves into your area of expertise. Would you like to take over from here?"

"Yes, sir." Mr. Žăk approached us and stood at attention, facing Hrubý in his chair and Bates on the screen. He pulled off his beret and glanced at Marconi. "I am sorry the information today has been upsetting, and for your horrible kidnapping and the shooting of Detective Lieutenant Stone. However, it looks as if these events have helped us join our plans together. Commander Hrubý, Lieutenant Talích, and Mr. Žičăn agree your participation is welcome if Commissioner Bates concurs?"

"Certainly," Bates answered. "Commander, may I please interrupt?"

"Yes."

"A one o'clock appointment is waiting. My colleagues will be interested, though, to know we are negotiating pleas with two of the Stanich nephews concerning the 1995 murders."

Marconi sat forward, resting her elbows on her knees. "What?"

"I guessed you all could use a little good news. Sylvia Johnson-O'Brien came through, Angie. A deal for her, too. We pressured her, and she's spilled her guts in exchange for receiving a reduced sentence with probation. She admitted to receiving money from Stanich for destroying various parts of Sam Wulz's records and evidence. That was her connection."

"So, Sammy's car wreck wasn't an accident?" Marconi asked.

"That's logical, but she denies everything. We turned the screws hard on her. She offered nothing else about Sammy."

"How did you produce evidence to charge the nephews?" I asked.

"It seems Sylvia got around. She had a brief affair with Mr. Stanich," Bates said.

"Good God." Marconi snorted, then smoothed her bangs.

"Stanich was more than forthcoming during their pillow talks," Bates said, "and he admitted to Sylvia those murders in the parks implicated his nephews. When we hit them with that, the coverup collapsed, and they admitted their parts in all this. We're leaning on them for more."

"You said two nephews," I said. "What about the third one?"

"The youngest nephew is dead—we found him in the creek. Stanich claimed the cliff collapsed. Coincidentally, that nephew had been the most cooperative and willing to talk to us. We're keeping Stanich under surveillance." Bates leaned toward his screen.

"Did he murder his own nephew?" Marconi asked.

"Don't know, but the attorney, Sahiti, disappeared, and his wife with him. We don't want Stanich to vanish. Commander Hrubý, please use the representatives of the City of Alexandria to whatever ends you need. The city's official position remains that the three of them are on disciplinary or medical leave, and these activities in Europe are their own choices. I'm sure they'll be accommodating. Please have Director Marconi update me as practical."

"We will be in contact," Hrubý said.

"Good afternoon…I mean, evening. Give Eddie my best, Angie." Bates' arm shifted in front of the camera, and our screen went black.

"So, then, my new colleagues, I would suggest a good night's sleep and an early start tomorrow. We have arranged with management to clear other rooms on the third floor where you are staying. My men here will use those suites, so you should be safe. Breakfast will be at seven, then Mr. Žăk will present his plans to us at seven-thirty sharp in the morning. Good evening."

Chapter Nineteen

A timid male voice seeped through my door after a light knock came a half-hour earlier than expected. "Detective Sergeant Pierce?"

I hurried to the door and opened it to a familiar face. "Yes?"

The young man straightened his stance and forced a slight smile. "Good morning. I am Georg Valenta. Commander Hrubý requested I fill you with information since he delayed the meeting until one o'clock. They cannot avoid it, and they offer their sincere apologies. I trust you received your breakfast, and it gratified you?"

"Excellent. I wondered why it came early."

"We will clean the dishes. Lunch will be available once my superiors are accessible."

"You look familiar, but I don't believe we've met?"

"No," he said and then shook my hand. "I sat near the windows last night. An associate and I had headphones listening to our assignments."

"Those headphones look like something from the seventies."

Valenta grinned and leaned closer. "I have requested an update. They do their job, though."

"Good to meet you."

"And you. They also instructed me to inform you that Mr. Žăk will take you to the hospital at eight-thirty to visit Detective Lieutenant Stone. He has been asking for his colleagues."

"Thank you for telling me. Did you talk to Director Marconi?"

"Yes, sir, and she is eating breakfast."

"She's up early."

"Oh?"

"Never mind. I'll talk to her in a minute."

"Use caution, Sergeant Pierce. Commander Hrubý insists on your continued safety."

****

Another knock, just past eight-thirty. "Sorry to be late, Detective Sergeant Pierce." Mr. Žăk stood at attention with Mr. Žicăn close by his side. Their uniforms made them like twins, except for a shock of curly blond hair falling from under Žicăn's beret. He had a thin scar running from his left earlobe to the bottom of his jawline, and his ear had a small piece missing right above the lobe. Curious wound.

"Would you two care to come in? I talked to Director Marconi already, and she should be ready soon."

"Yes, thank you." Žăk pushed by me and sat on my unmade bed. Žicăn followed but stood near the open door. "Mr. Žicăn will watch the hall for us."

"Pleasant time for morning, Detective Sergeant Pierce." Žicăn offered his hand. "I am pleased we work together."

I glanced at Žăk. "Uh, good morning to you."

"He is working on his English."

"It's excellent, Mr. Žicăn. I'm sorry I don't understand Czech or Serb. Are we going to the hospital to visit with my colleague?"

"Even better," Žăk said. "The doctor has agreed to discharge him into our care later this morning to keep him safe. We are setting up the room across the hall for him. The doctor insisted we allow a nurse to attend him for another forty-eight hours."

"Great news. Lieutenant Stone can be a little stubborn. I hope his nurse can tolerate him."

"*Mezek*?" Žicăn grinned.

"What?"

"A mule. Stubborn like a mule?" Žăk asked.

"Yes, yes, that's true. Can we call each other by our given names in private?" The two men right away showed their discomfort. "You can call me Henry."

"You can call us Žicăn and Žăk in private, Henry. No mister. Remember, these names we present to you are, as you say, work names. We have our reasons, and Commander Hrubý requires it."

"Okay, no problem."

"I am glad you have no problem," Žicăn said.

Marconi peered into the room. "You have guests?"

"Boss, you look like a movie star. A good night's sleep?"

"Thank you. Sleep helped, and I woke up feeling a hundred tons of worry has vanished. It will take me a while to cope with Kastrati's and Manny's betrayals, much less Jack's, but all of it can be closed now. I've spun my wheels for over a quarter-century, but no more."

"Please know we've had only informal discussions this morning with the sergeant, Director Marconi," Žăk said.

"That's fine, but can we be less proper?" she asked.

I shook my head. "I tried that, Angie. Their current

assignment requires them to use their work names."

"Thank you, Sergeant Pierce," Žăk said. "Director, I have already mentioned that your colleague, Lieutenant Stone, has been released early and should be here in a few minutes. He will continue to receive care."

"What? Oh, my God," she said. "Is he doing so well?"

"They'll bring a nurse for him," I said.

"The poor thing. I hope he's nice to her."

"We will do our best to accommodate him," Žăk said. He held his right ear—a voice chattered through the earpiece. "They are coming." The elevator groaned to a halt as Marconi, and I hurried from my room. Eddie talked away as it opened.

"My mother and father were both excellent cooks, Mariana. Later, my wife kept me fat and happy." He waved and showed a grin. "Good morning, my friends. How do you like my outfit?" They had dressed Eddie in well-worn, blue scrub pants, brown hospital footies, a white t-shirt, and a green overcoat a size too small.

"I like the shoes," I said. "They match your eyes."

"How are you doing, buddy?" Marconi asked. She bent over and tried to hug him.

Eddie frowned. "Watch the left side. It hasn't even been twenty-four hours yet."

"Sorry. Let's get you settled."

He rose from the wheelchair, hobbled through his room's doorway, and then parked himself into the faux-leather recliner near the window. The nurse scurried around getting his breakfast ready, while Žicăn trudged in carrying a hefty medical bag.

"Detective Lieutenant Stone, I am Mr. Žăk, and my

colleague is Mr. Žicăn. We are associates of the *Policie Ceské Republiky*, the Czech police. We will work together over the next few days following up on your mission."

"What?" Eddie fumbled with his plate and dropped his fork.

Žăk nodded to Žicăn, who pulled the nurse into the hall away from her flurry of duties. "We will work together on the next phase related to your mission here."

"I know nothing of that," Eddie said. "We did our jobs here, and our 'mission' is over. Don't you think, Angie?"

"It's complicated, buddy." Marconi patted his shoulder.

"Lieutenant, I will leave you alone for a few minutes with your colleagues. They will explain. Director, I would suggest a brief conversation then rest, as the doctor ordered. When you leave, please tell the nurse, and she will attend to him. Commander Hrubý would like you to attend our one o'clock meeting. It will enlighten."

"Commander who?" Eddie asked.

"Never mind, Eddie. We'll catch you up," Marconi said. "You finish your breakfast while Henry and I talk."

Mr. Žăk pulled on his beret and left us.

Eddie munched on a piece of toast with orange marmalade. "Well? Talk away. I can't go anywhere."

Marconi sat on the bed next to his recliner, and I leaned against the skinny window.

The view from this room faced the north. I shuddered to see Stromovka Park in the distance, showing the line of trees near the Three Stones.

"You okay, Henry?"

"Got a chill, I guess."

Marconi pulled his blanket and covered Eddie's feet. "So, sure shot, you got him twice. Did you know that?"

"What?"

"You shot Kastrati twice and hit him both times, one in the leg and the other a superficial to his ankle, according to our hosts."

"What would you expect? Those little trophies on my desk aren't cooking awards."

"True."

"And who nailed him in the throat?" I asked.

"Yeah, Angie, a helluva shot. Kastrati was so distracted with Ike that he never noticed you pick up my gun."

"Thankfully," Marconi said. "They told me you nicked Kastrati's femoral artery—a goner, either way. As soon as our hosts discovered our circumstances, they contacted Commissioner Bates. He got them all the information they needed. An intense discussion for a time, but it all came together last night with dinner. Bates' face stared over us on a giant screen, and—"

"Can you pour me a coffee?" Eddie slurred his words—we needed to cut this short.

"How about a two-minute version of everything?" I asked. "Even I can do that."

Marconi snorted. "You? Two minutes?"

"Sure. Bates ignored all the noise and, with Sylvia Johnson-O'Brien's help, put the screws to the Staniches. Two nephews are in custody, and Bates is working on final negotiations. The police found the other nephew dead in the creek behind Stanich's old strip mall. A terrible accident, according to Stanich. Through our hosts, we found out Miomir Kurić is a woman and was the woman Jack Marconi had an affair with and…and he may have fathered a child."

Marconi shot me a glare. "I could have mentioned it."

"What?" Eddie asked. "I must be under anesthesia."

"Nope. You're here, Eddie," she said. "Go on, Henry, finish the story."

"Our hosts are running an operation, offline, if you will, because of similar interference as we've gotten."

"What do you mean by offline?" he asked.

"The fourth and now the third floors of this building are headquarters to a select group of law enforcement individuals who are examining the criminality I mentioned," I said. "Prague hosts a cell of the Kurić organization in Europe."

"Stanich is the contact in Alexandria," Marconi said. "Commander Hrubý has his regular duties, and it seems he's running this other operation because his public efforts have stalled."

"The multi-national thing?" he asked.

"It's your hokey pokey, Eddie, like you said."

Marconi held up both hands. "Okay, you keep using that term. What are you two talking about?"

Eddie rubbed his eyes again. "I mean, it's a bunch of crap we shouldn't be involved in. We need to dip out of this and go home."

"It's too late for that," she said. "We've closed most if not all of this mess in Alexandria. Hrubý is making plans and counting on us to help here. Frankly,

I'm not sure they would let us skate so easily if we didn't play along. I think our only choice is to help."

"Yeah, we've left a trail of dead bodies from Vienna to Prague," I said.

Eddie yawned again. "They deserved it, but I won't be much use for a few days …" He dropped his fork again. "Throw me the pillow, Ike."

"Here you go," I said. "We'll meet a variety of people after lunch, including the guy we drugged in the hotel yesterday."

"What? That Russian guy? Lord Jesus," he mumbled. "I hope he knows—"

"Let him be, Henry. Send the nurse back in, and let's find Mr. Žák."

A quick search of the third floor found only Mr. Žicǎn. We did not have access to the operations room at the end of the hall, and Žicǎn had planted himself by the elevators and stairs.

"What do you think? Protection or detention?" Marconi asked me while we lingered in the hallway.

"Both," I said. "Let's go to my room. I've put together a few thoughts I want to review."

"Good. Yesterday was a blur." She stopped me at her suite and grabbed the hotel's pad and pencil. "Five small pages I can write on." She smirked again, something usually irritating, but this morning more than welcome. "Maybe we should take notes on this size paper at home. It would keep your presentations faster."

"Rude. I want to tell you what I know."

"You know I appreciate it, and so does Eddie."

"It will be nice to get back home and take on a case that has nothing to do with this." I struggled to push the brass key in my door.

"Isn't that the truth? It doesn't matter what happens from now on. We discovered Jack's killer, and I can be at peace with it now. My thirty years in the department are coming up next year. I bet I can hang in there until then, and…what's wrong with the damn door?"

"I don't know. This key is jacked up." I jerked the knob to the left, and the key fell to the floor. "These old-style keys are a nuisance." I pushed it back in the hole, but before I turned it, the door creaked open to a dark room. "I'm sure I locked it before we left…and I know I left a light on."

"Forgetful, are we?"

"Where's the light—"

"Good morning, my American colleagues," a voice said from the corner. The lamp came alive. Talích had stretched out on the brown sofa pushed flush below the window.

"Good God. You scared me to death," Marconi said.

I wasn't so pleasant. "I should be more careful locking my door. You never can tell who might wander in."

"Detective, these are not normal hotel suites. Section One of the Czech police has occupied them." Marconi pitched her ratty black purse on the bed and sat on the wicker chair near the bathroom. I opened both nightstand drawers, stuffed my notes into my pocket, and picked my coffee cup off the floor.

"You left in a hurry last night," I said.

"Yes. I did not sleep until early this morning. I wanted to nap while you finished with Lieutenant Stone."

"You know it's odd—I left my notes in the top

drawer of the nightstand, but I took them out of the bottom drawer. I wonder how that happened?"

"We have no secrets between us, okay? Commander Hrubý requested I visit with you and Director Marconi before we have our meeting. I need to know your thoughts before we offer an addendum to our plan this afternoon."

"You could have waited," Marconi said. She crossed her arms and gave him one of her scorching stares. "Sergeant Pierce wanted to review a few ideas with me before anyone else. And what is that smell? Peanut butter?"

"Crackers. Director Marconi, I did not rummage through the detective's things."

"The notes did not move by themselves," I said. "How did my cup end up on the floor?"

"This is concerning." Talích sprang from the couch and adjusted his earpiece. "One moment, please." He rushed out, leaving us alone again.

"Lots of drama," I said.

"How can we trust anyone? Either Talích is lying or—"

A woman's scream ricocheted down the hall. We scrambled to the door and saw Eddie's nurse held against the wall by Talích and Žicăn.

Žicăn pointed a finger at us. "Return to your room."

We hesitated and then hurried inside my suite. Marconi slammed the door behind us and groaned. "Good God. What now? Eddie's by himself …"

"Hang tight."

Talích burst through the door. "Everything is fine." He beamed a smile.

"Excuse me? A woman screamed, and you and Mr. Žičăn held the nurse. I insist we check on Eddie," I said.

"I'm fine," Eddie called out, leaning on Georg Valenta. "Help me to your couch, Ike."

"Okay, Talích, what's going on?" Marconi asked.

"I will need to discuss details with the commander, but we believe they have infiltrated us. Mr. Žičăn is taking care of it as I have requested."

"They? Are you talking about the nurse?"

Eddie answered. "Her name is Mariana, and an unfamiliar face from the hospital they sent with me this morning. She made enough noise in my room that I woke up with her holding a syringe over me. I kicked at her, and she ran out the door."

"We will investigate," Talích said. "Detective Lieutenant Stone, I will have to ask your colleagues to take care of you until we find a replacement medical representative."

"Sounds good. Hey, Ike, help me stretch out my legs. Puff up those pillows, too."

I grinned and pitched a pillow into his face.

"Come on, guys, focus. Listen to Lieutenant Talích."

"Please return to your duties, Mr. Valenta." Talích pushed the door closed behind him. "Mr. Žičăn noticed the nurse go into Sergeant Pierce's room and back to Lieutenant Stone's suite. A few minutes later, she dashed through the hallway. He stopped and questioned her—she assured him she was helping her patient."

"And how did she get in? I remember locking this door," I said.

"I am uncertain."

"And you came in and waited on us in the dark," Marconi reminded him.

"Lieutenant?" Eddie asked. "Is this area as secure as you believe?"

Talích scanned all three of us. "Apparently not. I will have a word with Commander Hrubý." His phone vibrated. "Excuse me," he said and left us again.

Marconi let loose a sigh. "He's tiring me out. Eddie, are you doing okay?"

"As far as I know. Ike, check the medical bag. Is my personal stuff in there?"

The tattered plastic bag had a hole, but his clothes had acted as a dam to keep everything inside. "A few coins, your passport, and two watches? Why two?"

"So what?" Eddie mumbled after yawning again. "I like to change watches sometimes. I guess the nurse wanted none of the good stuff."

"Henry, the so-called nurse must have seen your notes. What's on there?" Marconi asked.

I pulled them from my back pocket and handed them to her.

"Interesting." She sat hard on the wicker stool.

"Come on, guys. Catch me up, catch me up." Eddie sounded like a toddler.

"They're a review. I've mapped out the sites for the counterfeit money Kastrati told us about. The cities are nothing special as far as I can tell other than former or current American adversaries. But what's the fake money for? Eddie, remember when I opened the backpack at Stanich's place, and the Euros scattered everywhere?"

"Yeah…you're clumsy."

Talích burst through the door once again, followed

by two more men in uniforms matching his. His associates carried worn but menacing machine guns.

"God, Lieutenant, can't you ever knock?" Marconi asked.

"Apologies. We are to go at once to the fourth floor and wait for Commander Hrubý."

"What about Eddie?"

"My associates will carry him if needed."

"Holy…look at those guns, Ike," Eddie said while trying to sit upright. "Are those UK59s? I haven't seen one of those since my training days forty years ago." The two men stared.

"They do not speak English," Talích said. "And, yes, those are UK59s. Those are the best Czech guns ever made."

"I know. Serious firepower," Eddie said.

"What's going on, Lieutenant?" I asked.

Talích removed his beret and wiped his forehead. "It has incensed the commander. We continue fighting this issue. He has added men to guard the third floor and insists it's time to move forward. He has accelerated our mission by two days."

"Our mission?" Marconi gathered up Eddie's plastic bag and her purse.

"Please follow me. It is time for the next phase."

Chapter Twenty

Hrubý's men had joined us, and we waited around the conference table.

Eddie grabbed a thirty-minute nap. His journey up the spiral staircase had turned into an adventure. Talích's men tried to be careful of his wound, but he yelped more than once while they maneuvered up the stairs, Marconi complaining the whole way.

Slapping aside the room divider, Hrubý marched in, cleared his throat, and began. "My apologies for my lateness and the earlier dramatics. With our security breach, we need to quicken our pace."

"Commander, I appreciate all you have done for us, and your continued hospitality has made us feel at home," Marconi said. "While we're getting Lieutenant Stone settled, would you mind telling us what's going on?"

Hrubý stepped toward Eddie and offered his hand. "Detective Lieutenant Stone, I am Commander Stepan Hrubý, head of the criminal division in Prague plus three specialty units reporting to our division."

Eddie nodded. "And the same as Director Marconi — thank you for your hospitality, especially my care in the hospital." They had carried a beige vinyl-covered loveseat with chrome armrests up the stairs to give Eddie a place to stretch.

Marconi brought pillows from Eddie's room to set behind him, and he leaned back gingerly onto the improvised sofa. "Everyone I've met has been outstanding, except for the nurse with the syringe. I take it she wasn't a nurse?"

Hrubý straightened himself. "She *was* a nurse. We have detained and are questioning her."

"Why would the nurse be looking through my room?" I asked.

Hrubý frowned. "That is why we are questioning her, Sergeant Pierce. Lieutenant Stone, I apologize for the awkwardness of your ascent. Are you comfortable?"

"Enough. But I want to let you know ahead of time that I'm not bored with this. The drugs they've given me cause me to nap. No offense intended."

"None taken. I am sure your colleagues can fill in any blanks."

Marconi didn't hide her annoyance. "Commander, I don't understand why we had to haul him up here. Eddie, do you need to check your bandage?"

"I did it earlier," he said. "Everything's good."

She wagged a finger at him. "You checked before the stairs. Feel around and see if you notice any wetness or leakage."

He did and sighed. "I'm good, Angie."

She blew out her cheeks and slumped into her chair.

Hrubý sat and motioned us to do the same. "I will bring you up to date."

I sat next to Kharkov with Eddie behind us. Had it been only twenty-four hours since we tied the Russian to the bed? His eyes had swollen, and he ignored Eddie.

Marconi's temper still bubbled when she asked, "What's going on? Security breach? Someone broke into Henry's suite, and Eddie had a nurse up to God knows what. And I don't mind telling you I don't care for Lieutenant Talích coming and going in our rooms without our knowledge."

"I understand," Hrubý responded without looking at Talích. "Lieutenant Talích means no harm. While correct that we have appropriated a portion of this hotel for our use, it is only temporarily our property. However, you need your privacy, and I offer my apologies."

"Thank you."

Another frown from Hrubý. "But it's become a moot point."

"In what way?"

"The deaths of Jurić, Kastrati, and Kovačić drew attention from many inquiring minds."

"How so?"

"Same as you have experienced. As you have seen, the wheels are already in motion, with the untrustworthy nurse as an example. We took her to another one of our locations, and she is undergoing interrogation by our Section One officers. Correct, Lieutenant Talích?"

"Yes. My two best people have that responsibility—they will succeed."

"Thank you. Sergeant Pierce, what caused your notes to be of such interest to this woman? Can you share it with us?"

Eddie snorted, and I had to speak louder. "I have them here. A few general points I needed to review with Director Marconi."

"Please tell us. I do not mean to pry, but it may be of value."

"It involved the names of the cities, we thought—"

"May I see instead of you reading?" Kharkov asked. He snatched them, scanned the pages, and shook his head. "These are incorrect. Did this information come from Bader...I mean, Kastrati?"

"The list of cities? Yes, he identified those as distribution points for counterfeit Euros."

"Incorrect. He guessed or made those up. Kastrati always presumed he knew more than he did. Other than Virginia, everything else we are discussing is Eurocentric." He glanced toward my noisy, sleeping colleague, then moved to the front, pulling down one of several maps rolled into the ceiling. "These pockets of corruption, or cells as we call them, are here: Brussels, Paris, Berlin, London, Oslo, Madrid, Vienna, and Prague. And not coincidentally, these cities are home to settled Yugoslav refugees, including elements of Kurić's organization scattered among them. Your points here about the reasons for counterfeiting are correct in one sense, but counterfeiting is only one piece of criminality."

Hrubý stifled a yawn. "More detail, Mr. Kharkov."

"Yes, sir. There continues to be an attempt to place fake Euros into circulation. If so, a devaluation effect can occur, but the volume of Euros needed for the greatest impact has not occurred. They have dribbled into circulation...so far."

No one else spoke, so I asked, "But why? Is it currency manipulation? Didn't the Nazis try that during World War Two?"

"Yes, Operation Bernhard. Attempts to forge British notes were successful, but the plan never emerged as expected because the volume of currency never met expectations," Talích said. "We do not know if the goal is a devaluation of the Euro or inflating the value of other currencies...perhaps both."

Kharkov ignored our side discussion. "And what is this one point on your sheet?"

"Which one?" I asked.

He pointed farther down the list. "The last one."

"A brief summation of how to proceed," I said.

"Where did you get this?"

"I wrote it, as I said."

"Commander, this looks purloined from our discussions. We addressed this in our meeting only this morning."

Marconi scowled. "Purloined? Henry, repeat out loud what you wrote."

I shrugged. "I noted that the capture of the individuals is more important than the counterfeit money at this point. I guess that's obvious, but where else to start? We won't get additional information about this until we can interrogate the participants. But that's no different from any other crime we would investigate."

"That is central to our plan," Kharkov mentioned. "Why did you have to write these down—"

"So...do it. Execute the plan," Eddie said. I hadn't noticed his snoring had stopped. "You remember me, Mr. Kharkov? We had the tussle in the closet."

"What is your point?" Hrubý asked.

"Get moving—no more meetings. Let's get this done. Do something."

"We are," Talích answered. "They have forced our hands."

Hrubý didn't respond to Eddie but focused on me. "Yes, your notes are fine, Sergeant Pierce, but we should move on. Director, the elements in these cells opposing us are scurrying to outmaneuver us. I am concerned for your safety, and you will need to comply with my requests."

"Really?" Marconi smoothed her bangs again and cradled her head in her left hand. "How are we at risk? Are you detaining us?"

Hrubý stepped to a window and looked down to the street. "Please listen. I have much to say, and we will begin if that is an answer to your demand, Lieutenant Stone?"

Eddie smiled. "Fine. Talk away, Commander. You talk, and we listen. That's a plan, at least."

"Very well. I believe you are in immediate danger of assassination. Through your machinations at home, you have kicked a leg out, as you say, from under the North American operations of the Kurić organization. Aleksandr Stanich is the last remaining piece."

"That's the good news, right?" Marconi asked.

"Yes, but the political and business elements linked to him remain in place," Hrubý said.

"I'm not following." Marconi offered a look showing ignorance. I knew better. We had discussed this corruption many times, trying to guess all the players burrowed into the district.

"Director, the people to which Stanich has tied himself for years, continue in their sinecures. It is a symbiotic relationship in America, as it is here and in other places. As Mr. Kharkov mentioned, this is an international consortium of crime and graft spread throughout Europe. It is not a coincidence that the organization's cell coordinators live near these countries' capitals. The Kurić organization is the conveyor of benefits, and, in turn, those individuals protect the organization. Such a cell is in Alexandria, and Aleksandr Stanich is an example of a cell coordinator."

"I see," Marconi said, "but it will be hard to do more than superficial damage to the organization. Pulling it up by the roots—"

"Is difficult, like all weeds," Hrubý said. He dropped an empty water bottle into his chair and stroked his new close haircut. "Stanich has been shipping fake Euros to Prague for at least a decade. No one in the American government attempted to stop him, even though it is a certainty people knew."

"Big damn mess," Eddie muttered.

"Yes, Lieutenant Stone."

Eddie shuffled on his makeshift couch, wincing several times. "Okay, someone tell me how this works. Let's say I want in on this. Somehow, I've heard about my buddy making big money. I want to make money, too. What happens next?"

"Money is the lure," Kharkov answered.

"As always," Marconi said.

"Yes, the organization has money to give. You want money, and the organization can make you rich. You take the bait, and it begins," Hrubý said.

"What begins?" Marconi asked.

"You provide something in return, no?"

"I would think so," Eddie said.

Hrubý removed his uniform jacket and stepped out of the warm sunshine flowing through the skinny window. "Sergeant Pierce, do you have proficiency in presentations?"

"I know complete suites of software," I said as if

answering an interview question.

"I'm sure you have built representations of life cycles of various plans, procedures, etcetera."

"Sure, I've organized financial and other cycles. It helps to view—"

"Yes, yes, excellent. Consider this cycle: power, influence, money, protection."

I drew a circle and scribbled down the points. "And once someone takes the lure, they have power, influence, the money—but what is the protection piece?"

"We all know the American saying, 'I scratch your back, you scratch mine.'"

"You need to protect your investment?" I finally realized the scope of this hokey-pokey.

"Correct. You protect the organization, and the organization protects you."

"Hell," Eddie said. "It's just a damn protection racket."

"In a rough sense, but we are talking about billions of dollars and influence over national policies rather than changing local crime statistics."

"Angie, think," Eddie said. "Power, influence, money, protection. What's the abbreviation?"

Marconi stared for a few seconds and then broke into the biggest smile I'd seen from her in weeks. "P-I-M-P."

"Pimps, JoJos," Eddie said.

She snickered. "No better way to describe it."

Hrubý and his men seemed dumbfounded.

"Why is it entertaining?" Talích asked.

Eddie sighed. "Oh, that hurt."

Kharkov rolled his eyes. "Commander, P-I-M-P, or

'pimp' is a word used for sex hustlers in America. They are bosses of many prostitutes and recruit tricks or sex for them. Whatever money the prostitute receives, the pimp gets a portion. True?"

"Yes," Eddie said.

"And what are jojos?" Hrubý asked.

Eddie grinned again. "*Jojo* is an old song about a pimp. It's appropriate, though, am I right?"

Hrubý didn't share in the humor but said, "We call them mules, but a decent analogy. Someone can use sex as a lure, too…correct, Sergeant Pierce?"

"What?" Did he know about Nika?

Marconi waved her hand. "Commander, there's an element you haven't mentioned."

"And what is that?"

"Blackmail."

"Yes, definitely."

"Once an individual takes the money and provides a return service, the relationship becomes mutually beneficial," she said. "The PIMP, if you will, continues the relationship to preserve not only the money flow but his or her freedom from a jail cell."

"Yes. In your own case, you have said federal judges shut down your investigations," Hrubý said. "And recently, your city's mayor slowed an investigation and likely assisted in your and Lieutenant Stone's suspensions. Now, we all understand what we are up against."

"It's daunting," Marconi said.

The room's air had grown stifling. Trying to stretch and tired of sitting, I stood to speak and shuffled next to Eddie. "If the whole of the organization is too large to strike all at once, we should damage it in pieces. My guess is our adversaries are reeling in Alexandria right now. We have cut off the payroll, and Aleksandr Stanich will soon be behind bars with his nephews. The 'M' or money part has disappeared from our acronym…followed by what? Protection? If no protection, then power and influence are lost."

"True again, Sergeant Pierce," Hrubý answered. "And Prague is our next step. But our resources are small. Our gathering here includes the only people I trust."

"Back to the threat you told us about," Marconi said. "Why us?"

"I have heard through contacts that the organization has given a kill order for all of you," Hrubý said. "The breakdown of Stanich's operations was met with…disquiet."

"Not a surprise," Marconi said. "I'm sure revenge is their next step, followed by attempts to regain footing back in the D.C. area."

"We feel the same way," Kharkov said.

"Director," Hrubý said. "I would like to move forward with the demolishing of the Prague operations first thing in the morning."

"What can we do?" she asked.

"For safety reasons, we will make this fourth floor your quarters for now, and we will find more comfort for Lieutenant Stone," Hrubý said.

Eddie clasped his hands as if to pray. "Yes, please."

"We also request Sergeant Pierce's participation tomorrow, if he is willing and you concur."

She fidgeted with her collar. "Okay, but I want to help—"

"My preference is for you to stay here with me to direct our actions. Detective Lieutenant Stone can take part here as he pleases, depending on his fitness."

"Okay," Eddie said. "Sorry, Ike, I'll sit this one out."

"You need to heal, Eddie. Who will I partner with on this operation?" I asked.

"Me," Kharkov answered.

Nice. I hoped my new partner didn't keep a grudge.

"Mr. Kharkov will be a participant along with Lieutenant Talích," Hrubý said. "Mr. Žăk will coordinate this effort with Mr. Žicăn's help. You are to follow their orders exactly. Understood?"

****

Our Czech hosts disappeared again, and our lair seemed a prison. Marconi and I wandered down twice to the operations area. Most faces looked unfamiliar except for Georg Valenta, and he only offered a nod. Eddie was cranky when awake, and even when asleep, he shouted in his dreams. We had no phones and nothing to read. Marconi said she welcomed the quiet time to recover from yesterday. In between naps, she broke down a few times when talking about the years she had spent chasing Jack Marconi's killer.

My shoulder spasmed, and my head ached like someone had driven nails into both temples. The clock said six-thirty p.m. A three-hour nap. My arm twitched again. "Detective Sergeant."

I sat up straight. "What? Oh…Mr. Žicăn. What's going on? What happened to my friends?"

"Lieutenant Stone demanded to walk the stairs on his own and visited with our operations personnel for an extended period. Director Marconi followed him.

She is worried about the lieutenant's health. We gave them access back to their rooms for a brief time to refresh and change clothes. They are dining with Commander Hrubý."

"Should I join them?"

"Unnecessary. I have brought your possessions with me, and we will store them in our lockers. You will find a shower behind the red door over there." He pulled folded clothes from a bag, all black, with a red beret sitting on top. He placed a dusty, zipped plastic bag on the table. "Your communication device. Later, I will show you how to use it."

"I'm to wear your uniform?"

"The opportunity will come when needed, but not tomorrow. You are a part of us now. Make yourself comfortable in the reclining chair. I will cut your hair and give a close shave."

"You are multi-talented, Mr. Žicăn."

"My adopted father was a barber by trade. I cleaned floors and learned his occupation." I sat in the recliner, leaned back, and he got to work. The shave felt great, and he grabbed the clippers to use on my hair.

"Easy there, Mr. Žicăn, I pay good money to a lady to get my hair—" The shears buzzed, and most of my hair fell to the floor. I rubbed my hand over my burry head. "Now we have the same style. Do the ladies like it?"

He grinned. "Yes, they do."

"I thought only two of you wore the black uniforms. Are you sure you don't mind me wearing one with no training?"

"Mr. Žăk and I understand the circumstances. We have no problems with it, but tomorrow isn't an issue, anyway. Please go shower and dress."

I dug through the clothes. "Can I wear my own underwear—t-shirt, skivvies?"

"We provide your underclothes. They are black, too. We are to meet our team at the presidium at eight." He glanced at his watch. "We will have dinner and review our plans. Please take less than ten minutes."

"Got anything for a headache?"

"We can provide that. Food will help. You can have these." He pulled a package of cheese crackers from his left jacket pocket. "I went to the supply store."

Starving, I didn't hesitate. "I don't want to take them all. Let's split the package. Thank you, and I'll see you in a moment."

The shower's warm water was perfect, and my headache disappeared. I struggled in the compact room, fighting with my new attire, much tighter than my old Mount Vernon police uniform. I fell against the door twice, almost bumping the scar on top of my head. After stashing my civilian clothes in the same bag, I waited for Žicăn in the conference area. Several heavy footsteps stomped up the metallic circular stairs.

Žăk pushed back the repaired room divider, followed by Žicăn. "Good evening."

"Mr. Žăk, good to see you again. What do you think?" I asked while stroking my head.

"Mr. Žicăn offers good haircuts, no? And clean-shaven faces."

"Thank you, and again, I hope my wearing this uniform offends neither of you. You have earned yours as I earned my police uniform at home."

"Please stop," Žicăn said. "It is a part of our efforts. I brought your boots, your protective gear, and your jacket."

"Thank you."

Žăk crossed his arms and gave me the once-over. "Detective Sergeant Pierce, whenever you wear this uniform, you must follow our other traditions."

"An initiation?"

"No. You must use your Unit Name when on a mission. We talked about this before."

"Right."

"And for security reasons, we will keep it that way. We will call you, Mr. Žích."

"Žích? Any special reason?"

"It starts with a Z."

"That's it?"

"Yes."

"Okay. I'll practice my resting Žích face."

Žăk squinted, then glanced at his watch. "You confuse me. Commander Hrubý requires us to be at the Presidium in…twelve minutes for a quick dinner with Lieutenant Talích and Mr. Kharkov. Our planning session will follow. Firearms training at eleven, lights out at midnight, and we will awaken at five o'clock for breakfast. Then it begins."

Chapter Twenty-One

After a short early morning meeting of good luck wishes and breakfast without coffee, Kharkov and I strolled across the street in the bright sunshine to our long-scrutinized building's west entrance. He had dressed as a student and carried a denim backpack holding a laptop and a thick physics textbook inside.

"*Pěkná Hranatá Houba*," Kharkov said.

"Excuse me?"

"The name of this complex. *Pěkná Hranatá Houba Apartmány*."

"I saw the sign. What does it mean?"

"These structures. What do they remind you of?"

"Um…mushrooms?"

The complex of ten prefabricated buildings each housed four dwellings with the quad of apartments all on the second floor built around a central staircase. The smaller first floor, surrounded by glass, provided entry and exit into the building. Its unique architecture suggested construction after the communist government fell, but the past thirty years had not been kind to the dingy white dwellings.

"Correct, Mr. Žích. *Pěkná Hranatá Houba* means Pretty Square Mushroom. Unfortunately, half of this complex has been abandoned."

"I wouldn't call them pretty. By the way, should you be calling me Mr. Žích since I'm out of my formal uniform? I had hoped to wear my all-black, Johnny

Cash look today."

"Who? Our mission is always more important than any uniform. Besides, you blend in well with the hoodie and Prague University cap. But where did you get the hideous corduroy overcoat?"

I covered my lips with an index finger and pointed at my pocket. We had to stay aware of our conversations. We had stuffed the communication links in our pockets, but I presumed they could still hear us. "Mr. Žicǎn acted proudly to let me borrow it."

Kharkov nodded. "Stop here." He approached the mushroom building's glass, metal-framed door covered with a thick film of grime. He cupped his hands around his eyes and stared through the glass. "The on-duty clerk is not here, as expected. Commander Hrubý took care of it."

"Don't you think the residents will notice a fresh face? Won't our persons of interest get spooked from a change of any kind?"

"Spook? A ghost?"

"Never mind."

"Very well. The desk clerks are student workers, mostly from the Prague School of Economics across the river. Faces change all the time. Here, let's see what we have." He pulled the door once, then again with no success.

"You said this unit stayed unlocked for mail delivery. Why is it locked?"

"It stays open twelve hours, beginning at seven a.m. Let me try again." He yanked with both hands, and the stubborn jamb freed the captive door, bashing against Kharkov's forehead and nose. "*Prokleti.*"

"Excuse me?"

"It's…a Serb curse. My apologies. It hurt."

"There's a mark on your face but no blood." We took a few steps inside the hazy lobby. "God, look at this place. It smells like a wet gym towel in here. Dust is an inch deep."

"Dusty and musty are not our worries. Lieutenant Talích told me a similar structure on the city's north side collapsed on itself last year."

"Nice. You said earlier that the residents all leave around the same time?"

"Correct. Three of the apartments each have one resident. As I mentioned this morning, they are not a problem, and they will leave by eight o'clock for either their workplaces or other appointments. Apartment D is unused and our chief concern."

"Commander Hrubý said an old man leases it."

"Yes, an old man is the official lessor," he said.

"So, who is this guy?"

"We will both find out."

The stairs looked like stained cement with scattered patches of a red carpet. Dusty artificial plants sat on each side of the bottom steps, matching the other three pots lining the picture window, exposing sidewalks and street traffic. Another glass door opening to the east exit revealed an overgrown, littered courtyard with more mushroom-shaped structures surrounding us. A quick glimpse upward from the road, and I noticed the skinny windows in our building from which Georg Valenta and his colleague used for observing. The only sign of Hrubý's fourth-floor conference room was the building's bulging roof to our far left.

Kharkov unloaded his backpack.

"Hey, Vitaly, all the residents' mail slots are

behind the desk, and the storage room is where larger packages go. Is this what you expected?"

"It's time to go online with our communication headsets, and, yes, the layout is as expected. Remember, I am the point of contact since I know several languages. Are you comfortable with your role? If not, we need to make other arrangements."

"I'm more than comfortable. And Vitaly?"

"Yes?"

"It's unfortunate our first meeting turned…volatile. We were doing our jobs. Eddie Stone is a good guy and an outstanding detective. I wish you all had time to work with one another."

"I am sure Eddie Stone is a fine colleague." A creaking sound and a door slam. "Busy yourself. Our first resident is leaving."

The tip-tap of women's heels grew louder on the stairs. She rounded the corner, didn't glance up from her phone, then struggled to push the door open. After waiting in traffic, she rushed over the crosswalk to a crowded bus stop.

"That is Liliana in Apartment B. She works five blocks away at a bank. No car, but a boyfriend drives her around and stays overnight…almost every night."

"She's cute, and you sound jealous."

"Stop. Keep your mind on the mission, and it doesn't matter—she doesn't know me. Did you notice how she never looked up from her phone? Many residents come and go for mail here as well. We will be unremarkable to them."

"Can I have the key to the storeroom? I want to see what's in there."

He pulled a chain from around his neck, a key

dangling from the middle. The key fit tightly, but it opened the door with no trouble. The light switch was not on the wall, and I fumbled around until I found a string to the mailroom's light hanging from the fixture above. I yanked it, and a bare fluorescent bulb blinked awake, revealing two card-table-sized cardboard boxes in the middle of the room—nothing else. Wooden shelves on three walls were empty except for dusty cobwebs. Someone had scribbled a variety of names on a few of the cubbies.

Kharkov peered around the storeroom door. "Resident leaving." I opened the door and pretended to work on the lock. A young man carrying a laundry bag nodded, pushed through the exit, and stood on the sidewalk waiting for the trolley. "He's in Apartment C. One more resident to go."

I went back inside the storeroom and called out, "Hey, Vitaly, both these boxes have the Apartment D address. Odd, the postmark date on one is nine days ago. I thought you confirmed—"

"Georg Valenta confirmed it. He told us the last one delivered was three days ago."

"Okay, it matches one of these, and it has a return address here in Prague. *Pokojná*?"

"Interesting. Yes, it is a road near the main Catholic Church and much closer to us than I thought. We suspected a spot on the city's far south side as an origination site."

"This older one—it looks like it's been opened and re-taped. Wait a minute. Someone has marked through the name, but the return address…E1215 Elisabethstraβe, Vien, Österreich. Vitaly?"

"Yes?"

I escaped to the lobby again. "The return address on this box is right across the street from our hotel in Vienna."

"Bader…rather, Kastrati—it's his address."

"I never saw him there." I leaned against the desk. "Did you catch the conversation when Director Marconi mentioned Kastrati entered this building before heading to the park?"

"I remember, but no one asked questions after Lieutenant Talích stormed out of the room. It seems we should have studied that variable," he said.

"So, Kastrati mailed a package to Prague and checked it after he got here? Should I open it?"

"Not yet."

"Apartment D is the locus of everything," I said.

"Yes, as I said earlier." Kharkov pointed upwards. "Quiet."

Running shoes appeared at the top of the stairs, and their wearer hesitated on each step. An older man, sweating and panting, stopped at the bottom, then stared at the floor. I hurried back to the storeroom, letting Kharkov handle this.

The resident chattered away, Kharkov responding now and then. I tried to use my phone's translator, but the voices were too muffled for the app to work. At last, the stubborn glass door squeaked open and closed.

Like a turtle, I stuck my head out of my hiding place. "What did he say?"

"He introduced himself as Mr. Chměla, which is a name not reported to us. Our investigation named him as Mr. Doubêk."

"Someone is wrong, aren't they? Who gave you the information?"

"I do not know the original source. This man leaves every morning to visit his wife in a home for the elderly. His routine is to return after lunch. He asked about the kid that normally sat at this desk and wanted to know who I was, what I studied, and my intentions after graduation. My physics book and laptop satisfied him, then he asked about the person in the storeroom. I told him you were here to investigate a water leak, but he seemed skeptical. We should be wary."

"It wouldn't surprise me if someone pays one of the permanent residents to act as a watchdog."

He glanced at his watch. "True again, Mr. Žích. We have twenty minutes until our first PIMP arrives."

"You like that term, don't you?"

"Not especially. I thought you did."

****

Kharkov called to me. "It's a black Škoda Citigo,"

I pulled the Czech pistol given to me by Mr. Žicăn and readjusted the leather holster hidden under my turquoise hoodie. The CSA Vz.15 was like Marconi's and Eddie's Berettas, but with an eighteen-round clip. I had three clips…surely, more than enough.

"Is it the right car? I've seen other black Citigos pass."

"It's the one. 009-HP55. It is stopping, and the back door is opening…the man has a red backpack. Please take your place in the storeroom."

"Done."

The sticky entrance squealed, and a deep voice chattered away with Kharkov. My pistol ready, I pushed myself against the wall next to the door. It opened, and Kharkov yanked on the light. He pulled the box out with the Prague return address, jerked the light

327

chain again, and slammed the door. The deep voice grew quiet—I assumed Kharkov was alone. The door flew open again. "Clear, Mr. Žích."

"Good, I've got to pee. Tell me what happened after I find the toilet. Where is it?"

"Outside. Your bladder must be tiny."

"I have to pee outside?"

"No. Out the courtyard door and to the left."

"I have no coins."

"Mr. Žích, one day, you will learn. Here, take these. And hurry." Hurry, I did, kicking cigarette butts off the sidewalk all the way there and back.

I let the door slam behind me. "I feel better."

A man leaned against the desk.

Kharkov gave me a nod. "Good morning, Henry. What is better? Your flu? You almost became a hospital patient, from what I heard."

The blood drained from my face like water down a sink. "Uh, yes, thank you, I'm much better. My friend may have received mail from home. Do you mind looking?"

The little man raised an eyebrow. "American?" he asked in his deep voice.

I extended my hand. "Yes, sir, Henry Pierce."

He shuffled a few steps over and offered an arthritic hand. His balding scalp had a few hairs strewn across the top, his gray sideburns extending well below his ear lobes. "I am Nemec. I once traveled to New York to see a dear friend."

"I'm from Virginia."

"Why are you here?"

"I'm visiting a friend at school."

"Maybe I know him. What's his name?"

"Erik. Erik …"

Kharkov rescued me and continued the conversation in English. "You are looking for a second package, Mr. Nemec?"

"Yes, there should have been two this time. You see, Henry Pierce, my mother lives in Apartment D, and I come to check on her. She's expecting two packages instead of only the one I took upstairs."

"How nice."

Kharkov called from the mailroom, "Could you identify the package, Mr. Nemec? Where did it originate?" He must have been moving the box around, making it sound like several parcels filled the room.

"It originated in Vienna. I have a brother in Austria too, Henry Pierce." He appeared nervous. "Should I come and help?"

"No," Kharkov shouted. "I found it." He pushed the box out as he had the first one and shut the mailroom door.

Nemec struggled up the stairs, pulling the box a few steps, then resting before starting again. The door slammed on Apartment D, so hard the bells jingled on the courtyard door handle.

Kharkov whispered. "Come back with me to the storeroom."

I pulled the door closed except for a sliver of space for Kharkov to see into the lobby. "Is that Kastrati's brother?" I asked. "Rijad told us his brother had died in the Bosnian war."

"No, this Nemec fellow had no Bosnian accent. But he knew of the two packages."

"I shouldn't be seen again," I said.

"No, you should not. I pulled the sickness idea

from my butt. You are as white as a ghost...or is it spook? A clumsy reaction, Mr. Žích."

"Yeah, I'll do better. Did you learn anything else?"

"One moment." He opened the door wide, walked to the stairs, checked the top, and then returned. "No, I learned nothing. He said his mother lived in Apartment D...an obvious lie."

"Red backpack, right?"

"Yes, as I said, but it was flat, and he did not struggle with it, meaning it had to be empty. I will shut you in this room and do not come out. Our second visitor will be here in exactly five minutes. Pee in the corner next time if you must." The door slammed, and he left me in the dark.

I scanned my watch every few seconds. 9:46 a.m., and the front entrance squealed again. Several footsteps, muffled voices became louder, then all quiet—nothing from Vitaly. Five minutes passed. Our final of three guests would arrive in ten—more silence. I gripped the storeroom door handle and gave myself an opening enough to view the desk...with an empty chair. Where was he? Maybe the restroom. I hurried outside and noticed the bathroom entrance propped open—no one in there. Back to the desk to see Vitaly's laptop in screen saver mode, his backpack spread across his book, and his communication headset in the trash.

Back into the storeroom to call Mr. Žák.

"Mr. Žích? Why are you calling me? Your third man should arrive in six minutes, and he is our key."

"I know that, but my earpiece is giving me static. Listen, the second man showed up at the scheduled time. I heard a few voices, and then nothing. I waited five minutes to check the lobby—Kharkov is missing.

He's not outside either."

"Kharkov missing? And was the second bag yellow?"

"I never saw it. Did you see Kharkov?"

"No. There has been no one except you going to the toilet."

"Now what? Have they abducted him?"

"What? Speak up, Mr. Žích."

"I'm in the storeroom and trying to keep my voice down. Should I investigate upstairs?"

"No. You must wait for the third man to arrive and the second man to leave. Lieutenant Talích has followed the first man as planned, and Mr. Žicǎn will follow the second."

"But what about Kharkov?"

"Stick to the script. Sit at the desk. Contact me when the third man goes upstairs. We will continue the mission, now with the added element of finding Mr. Kharkov."

A door slammed upstairs, and soon our second man, much younger, stood at the front entrance staring at the street and wearing the near-bursting red backpack. I pretended to be busy on my phone while he glanced toward me several times. "You are the American?"

"Yes, how did you know?"

"Lucky guess."

"And you are?" I asked.

"No concern of yours. My ride will be here at ten o'clock."

I exaggerated a glance at my watch. "Any time now, then."

He stared outside and mumbled something.

Squealing brakes and the squeaky door announced our last guest's arrival and the younger man's departure.

Our third visitor tripped over the entrance, then stood still, gasping for air. He carried two backpacks, one red and one yellow, and both appeared empty. They said this man is the key, but to what?

"*Koj si ti?*" Much older than the other two men, he reminded me of a walking corpse. He had an eyelid sewn shut, and a greasy fringe of gray hair hung below his fedora.

"Sorry, I don't speak Czech."

"Czech? It's Macedonian, fool. I am Karonos Tasev…since I doubt you know. Where is the regular front desk man?"

"I'm waiting for him to come back."

He glared at me. "American." He struggled up the stairs, reeking of alcohol and cigarette smoke.

The apartment door slammed, and I tapped a speed dial number. "Our third man is upstairs, Mr. Žák. Time to move."

"Those decisions are mine, Mr. Žích. Lock both exits and hold him if he comes out of the apartment. Use your gun if you must. I will be there, momentarily."

I locked the exits from the inside, grabbed Kharkov's things, and stashed them in the storeroom. I heard nothing else from the upstairs apartment. The courtyard door rattled with a heavy knock—it was Žicǎn.

"Mr. Žích. Step outside with me."

"Here," Žák called out, standing near the restroom. "Follow Mr. Žicǎn's lead." He disappeared around the far corner of the building.

"Unlock the west entry, and we will hide in the storeroom," Žicăn said. I followed him back inside. We stood with the light on and closed the door tight. "We have communicated with Lieutenant Talích, and he will soon be in position at the Ministry of the Interior. Mr. Žăk wants the mission to keep going. I will go to the Ministry of Justice."

"What do you think has happened?"

"We will soon know. But why can't you communicate with your device? Doesn't your earpiece work?"

"No. It's been static the entire time."

Žăk mumbled something on the other end.

"I can hear a voice, but I can't understand what he's saying."

Žicăn flicked the device and my ear with his middle finger. "You should have said something."

I rubbed my ear. "Okay, better."

"Mr. Žicăn, please proceed with haste to car eleven," Žăk said. "Your man has a two-minute lead on you. Report to me when you arrive at the Ministry of Justice."

"Yes, sir." He scurried out the courtyard entrance and headed for a navy-blue Renault, sitting in a reserved spot across the street.

I turned back toward the desk as a waft of air passed me, bringing with it a smell of alcohol and cigarettes. The old man stood near the bottom step, peering at me with his unpatched eye. "*Šta se dešava?* Oh, of course, you cannot understand. What is the commotion here?"

"I'm looking for a friend," I muttered, rushing him, then grabbing him in a headlock. "The actual question is, who are you, and where is my associate?" I tightened my grip around his neck, knocking the fedora from his head—his weak arms struggled to push me away.

The old man drooled. "Choking me…you are a Hrubý man …"

Žăk's voice in my ear. "Mr. Žích, who are you talking to?"

"Come in here. I've had to detain the last man."

"Coming."

The old man pulled against my arm. He wheezed and then collapsed to his knees as Žăk entered from the courtyard.

"Ah, Mr. Žích. I see you have things under control. I believe we should go to his apartment and let him host us for a few minutes until his car arrives—" He bent closer to the man's face. "Unfortunately, he seems unconscious, and I will have to carry him."

"Sorry, I must have squeezed too hard." I readied to grab his feet.

Instead, Žăk grabbed the man's arms and pulled him over his shoulder. "I have him. Bring yours and Kharkov's possessions upstairs. The real desk attendant will return in thirty minutes. We will claim the apartment for ourselves." Žăk struggled a bit getting up the stairs, a breeze of cigarettes and body odor trailing behind them. A silky orange scarf fell from the man's back pants pocket. I followed with his hat and our belongings. "How nice…he left the door open for us." He kicked the door wider and dumped the man on the couch. "Go check the bedroom."

The bedroom door looked as if a fist had punched a hole above the doorknob. I peered through the hole and saw Kharkov crumpled on the floor, his eyes closed but breathing evenly. "He's here." I drove the door hard against the wall and kneeled next to him. "Vitaly, wake up."

He groaned and raised his head. "God…this keeps happening. I hyperventilate under stress."

"Sorry, Vitaly, I couldn't hear anything from the storeroom. What happened?"

"Nemec grabbed me before he left, and the younger man hit me over the head with something…then a blur."

"Mr. Žicăn?" I tapped on my earpiece again. Static, but I heard a voice.

"Yes, Mr. Žích, I'm trying to drive. What do you need?"

"They abducted Kharkov and held him in the apartment. He's okay, but they're aware something is up."

"We go no matter," Žăk shouted from the living room and into his headpiece. "Mr. Žicăn, you know what to do." He stuck his head through the bedroom door. "Mr. Žích…Vitaly…this would be an excellent time to join me, okay?" I helped Kharkov off the filthy, red shag carpet. He stumbled into the dining area, sitting hard onto an orange, molded plastic chair. The old man was face-up on the red-and-blue plaid couch, his open eyes staring from his pale, gray face.

"Dear God, this place stinks," I said. Empty food boxes lay around the kitchen, with older trash piled in the corners.

"The smell is about to get worse," Žăk said. "The Macedonian is dead. Take him to the bedroom."

"He's dead? I didn't realize—"

"Do not worry, Mr. Žích. This man you

extinguished, Karonos Tasev, is…was…a killer working for the Kurić organization. We will not miss him. It is problematic, though, for our Foreign Affairs appointment at eleven-thirty."

"*That* was the Macedonian?"

"I told you this involved him," Kharkov said.

"He was the one to be afraid of? I would have guessed a younger man."

"As a younger man, Tasev was an assassin, a strangler, Mr. Žích."

"He mentioned Hrubý's name."

Žăk squinted at me. "He knows the commander? Interesting." He studied Kharkov. "Vitaly, your luck continues, but what are those specks on your face?"

"What?" He rubbed his hand across his cheek, and the specks moved. I studied his face, then scraped off a creature.

"You're infested with bed bugs. Now we may be, too. They're probably all over the bedroom."

Kharkov grabbed his hair with his fists. "*Můj život je prokletý. Zatraceně.*"

"What?"

"He said someone has cursed him. Get the body into the bedroom and shut the door—I don't want to see that scum. I will intercept the driver of the last car coming to pick up the Macedonian. Commander Hrubý has ordered the driver's retention at the Presidium, and we will take his car for our piece of the mission. The two boxes from the storeroom are behind the couch. Please open them by the time I get back." He slammed the door.

"Come here, Vitaly," I said. "Oh, dang, he stinks."

"My head is like a cushion with a hundred pins

stabbing me." He took a deep breath. "I can do this." We pulled and pushed the old man's corpse into the bedroom. I dropped the fedora on his face, then we slammed the door. "I feel itchy all over."

"Me too." We slung the backpacks on the coffee table. "Let's get these boxes open first, and I want to know what they've stuffed in those bags."

Vitaly ignored me and picked up both bags. "The yellow one is much heavier than the other." I took it back and yanked the zipper. Ten rectangular containers, around six by three inches, fell back to the particleboard table, denting it in several places. Vitaly did likewise with the red one and dumped Euros held together with bank straps.

"Our first two men today took red backpacks with them. This Macedonian had yellow and red." Kharkov stopped and gave me a look. "The second one…red, right?"

"I never saw it…this color-coded stuff is crap."

"We told you red is real, and yellow is fake money."

"Whatever. What about these?"

"One moment." He sifted through the pile and rearranged the bills into neat stacks. "Forty bundles here. Each bundle contains one hundred notes, so this would amount to four hundred thousand Euros in total." He held one up to the glare of a dingy bulb hanging above the table. "And they are real."

"That's quite a payoff."

"I do not think it is for one person, but yes, significant money."

"Let's see what's in these little vessels." The rectangular containers looked to be pewter, a blue-gray color, with a sliding cover and the shape of a double-headed eagle carved in the middle. I slid back the top, exposing gold, half-dollar-sized coins.

"What's this? 1931. A man and a woman on the front, and a coat of arms on the back." I handed a coin to Kharkov.

Kharkov scratched his head. "The royal dukats? The people are Alexander I and Queen Maria. The back shows the double-headed eagle and shield—symbols of the Kingdom of Yugoslavia. From what I remember, others may have a four-legged dragon copied from the family's crest. They minted these dukats in the 1930s, and they should be twenty-carat gold, not meant for circulation—exceedingly rare. I would guess each is worth at least five thousand American dollars, which is only the gold's melt value."

"Let's do a count."

All became quiet except for Vitaly counting in Russian. "Ninety-nine coins on each side," he said.

"Odd amount, but if the containers all have the same number, then we are looking at—"

"A fortune." Vitaly placed his coins into stacks to load back into their holder. "And judging by the pewter container, these are part of the royals' collection, making them even more valuable. After the royal family's exile, the future President Tito hid the coins during World War II, and then they disappeared during the Bosnian War. Apparently, someone has found them."

"I think I heard through the static that Mr. Žǎk is coming back. Let's look through these bigger boxes." I pulled each around the couch, and Kharkov dug through the open one.

"Yes, only wadded newspapers in this box—it likely held the real Euros and coins. It would be consistent with what we thought would be in the backpacks."

"Right. Let's see what's in the other." I took my five-inch, thin-bladed knife from its leather sheath and split the clear tape. "It's been opened and re-taped." We found more wadded pieces of newspapers, this one the *Alexandria Banner*.

Kharkov flipped out the papers like a dog digging in the dirt—more money appeared. "Look." He waved a bundle of banknotes. "The straps are different."

"Let me see." I fanned through a stack. "Good chance this is all counterfeit. Old dates and bills. None have the holographic icon the new bills have. These are like the bills Eddie Stone and I found in Alexandria." I scraped at the box's return address label and peeled it. "I can't read it all, but I'm certain the older label says Duke Street. Vitaly…this box originated at Stanich's business. Look at the date—January twentieth. This container could have been one of the last ones shipped before the place burned."

"Stanich?"

"Yes, the one and only," I answered.

"Good, we have found a direct tie. More evidence for your Commissioner Bates." The doorknob on the apartment door jiggled. I pulled my gun, pushed Vitaly toward the kitchen, and ducked behind the couch before a voice came through my earpiece.

"Mr. Žích, please let me in. I have brought gifts for both of you."

"We're good, Vitaly. It's Mr. Žăk." I opened the door, and he stepped in carrying a small paper sack and a grin, then reached into the bag. "Two gifts. This is for you, Kharkov. Your bottle of anti-anxiety medication. Did you take it as scheduled this morning?"

"No, I remain too reactive to them. I feel like I am floating all day."

"Better floating than hyperventilating. You must be consistent with this, or it will threaten your status with our projects. And this is for you, Mr. Žích." He handed me a sandwich bag.

"Two white donuts?"

"Yes, from Lieutenant Stone. He said you and I should share them, and you would understand."

A lump formed in my throat. "I do. Where did he get them?"

"Mr. Žicăn prefers American food. He bought them last night for the lieutenant, and they together devoured half the bag this morning."

"My first day of work with Eddie, I noticed he always carried a baggy of these, and…oh, never mind. Eat one, and let's get on with it." We chewed and wiped our fingers while Vitaly watched. "Sorry, Vitaly, Eddie didn't think about you being here."

"I get pills. You get donuts."

"You are valuable to us, Mr. Kharkov," Žăk said. "Now, emergency services will be here soon to remove the body. We will have our man embalmed and give his body to the Macedonian authorities…and his family, I suppose. Commander Hrubý would like for you to return to the fourth floor for the removal of your infestation. And he means right away."

"He is always thinking of me. When will I rejoin the mission?"

"That is up to Commander Hrubý." Žăk nodded

toward the pewter containers. "What are these?"

I pulled back the sliding lid and showed the coins, sparkling even in the apartment's dim light.

"Are those the Royal Yugoslav Dukats? There have been rumors of these coins floating around on the antiquities black market. I had assumed rumors only."

"I counted one hundred ninety-eight coins," Vitaly said. "There should be two thousand coins in these ten containers, around ten million American dollars."

Žăk flipped a coin over and over in his hands. "I am not so sure. Black market buyers might pay twice that for their rarity."

"Mr. Žăk, somewhere in our conversations over the last day, Commander Hrubý mentioned they found a gold coin on Jurić's body. Have you seen it, and was it like these?" I asked.

"I remember his words, and I have not seen the coin. But the commander told me two coins."

"What?" I asked. "What about the other one?"

"Manfred Jurić's coin was stashed in a canvas bag in his jacket pocket, along with a picture of a woman. The commander said the picture was damp, but the face easy to see. No one recognized her. Commander Hrubý ordered an Interpol search. Also, inside the brick and mud hut where Rijad Kastrati hid—a purple velvet bag contained a gold coin."

"Interesting. And no idea on the woman's picture?" I asked.

"No, it might be anybody," Kharkov said. "Did not Jurić have a wife many years ago?"

"True, it could be his dead wife," I said.

"Another mystery for now," Žăk said, seeming to lose interest, "and much more to the story it would seem." Hrubý barked something to Žăk through the earpiece. I kept forgetting the command center heard our conversations—we had gone too far off-topic. "Mr. Žích, we need to move along. We are to take one coin container when we have our luncheon with the ministers, plus the counterfeit cash of two million Euros and the half-million in real Euros. The commander believes all are a part of the conversation."

"Possibly. Are we sure—"

"That it is what they are expecting? We will soon know." Žăk holstered his gun and rebuttoned his coat. "Mr. Kharkov, Georg Valenta is coming immediately to take your place. Please proceed to your disinfection and take these other coin containers with you. Put them in one of those trash bags from the kitchen to stay inconspicuous when you cross the street. Commander Hrubý is updating your part of the mission. Are you well enough to carry that, your laptop, and other belongings?"

Vitaly nodded. "Certainly."

Žăk adjusted his beret, then tilted his head. "It is our turn."

Chapter Twenty-Two

We pushed onto crowded Horákově Road, our confiscated Škoda trudging along like a dutiful horse. Car horns blew at one another like geese in a flock, but the noise did nothing to hurry us along. They scheduled our eleven-thirty appointment at a French restaurant near Prague Castle, two miles from the mushroom-shaped apartments. Our colleagues' meetings would coincide—Žicăn's farther south at the Smíchov train station, and Talích near the Old Town Square.

"Twenty blocks," Žăk said. He removed his beret and scratched the crown of his head. Constant background communications from Hrubý's command center hummed in my earbud—nothing in English.

"Fifteen minutes. Can we make it in time?"

"We will make it," he said. We eased ahead two blocks before stopping again. He motioned a throat slash with his thumb, followed by a finger to his lips. He yanked off his headset and did the same to me, scratching my old head wound with the mic. "As we've said, Commander Hrubý does not like to hear conversations about anything other than the mission. Going dark in…eight more minutes. After that, you can say anything. Put on your device and make no unnecessary comments."

"Got it."

"Twelve more blocks." The chatter increased in our ears. "The delay of our guests requires us to adjust our schedule," Žăk said. "At the next light, we will make a circular turn near Prague Castle. I will drop you off in the Hradčany neighborhood. You are to proceed to the American Café while I park. You should take the yellow backpack and wear it for visibility, and I will bring the red one. I will explain after parking."

"Not French? What's the name of the café?"

"The American Café. I said that. Near the cathedral."

"American Café? That's it?"

"It is the only one," Hrubý called to me through my earbud. "Mr. Žăk? Lieutenant Talích and Mr. Žicăn are on schedule. Time to go dark. We expect your communication with us at twelve-fifteen p.m. *Hodně zdaru, Pane Žăk*. Best wishes, Mr. Žích."

"Thank you, Commander—" The static ceased. I pitched the device on the back seat, and Žăk did likewise. "I thought we were doing this together."

"Something delayed the deputy ministers. Do you remember their pictures? Please repeat."

"Yes, both a bit under six feet tall. Stranksy is forty years old, heavyset, and balding. Vojacek is near fifty, thinner, with curly gray hair. The latter sometimes has a mustache, sometimes not. But why deputy ministers as targets? Isn't the head minister for each department a bigger fish?"

He scowled. "Why are you interested in fish? You should understand the deputy positions have less turnover. They survive one administration to the next and can give more long-term benefits back to Kurić's organization."

"The deep state?" I asked.

Žăk smiled. "A political term, but your choice. I

would call them corrupted individuals with government jobs."

"I think that makes it worse."

He shrugged. "Here we are—time to get out."

I slipped my cap on, grabbed the bulky backpack, and strained to stand.

"I will find you in five minutes," he said. "Speak to no one." He raced away on the cobblestone circle, leaving me in the middle of a score of Japanese tourists.

Through the bright sunshine, I walked in the best weather since our arrival in Prague. I headed toward St. Vitus Cathedral's darkened spires, pointing to the sky next to Prague Castle, a ninth-century edifice with an assortment of architectural styles.

I attracted attention. Even though many tourists displayed great imaginations when dressing, a tall man in a turquoise hoodie, dark pants, red cap, and yellow backpack caught some notice. I trudged up the cement drive making a corkscrew turn around the castle feeding into a sizeable parking lot. It provided an overlook of Prague, a beautiful scene of red-tiled buildings and church spires against a bright blue sky.

"Can you take our picture?" a teenage girl demanded while shoving her phone into my hands. I ignored her American accent and nodded my head to show I understood what they wanted. I took several pictures of the five friends posing in various positions, giggling the entire time.

"Thank you," one shouted.

"He's cute," said another.

"Yeah, he's a bit old, though. And look at those clothes. My little nephew looks like that when he dresses himself."

Twits. "American Café?" I called out. "Where is the American Café?" The girls realized I spoke English and hurried away.

"Mr. Žích, are you so lonely you must make friends with American teenagers? Female, of course."

"What?"

"I rounded the first corner and noticed a man in a red cap with a yellow backpack taking pictures of girls. You must stay on the mission."

"They asked me to take a picture. I tried to find the café but didn't see it here."

"No. It's not St. Vitus—it's near St. Nicholas."

"You told me, Prague Castle, near the cathedral," I said.

"Never mind. We are off schedule. We must walk two blocks in four minutes. Our guests will be there soon." The café was much closer than he thought—we stood at the entrance just after eleven-thirty. Žák stuffed his beret in a pocket and checked the inside tables. He ambled here and there between the Elvis and Marilyn Monroe pictures pasted against the windows, and he returned with a smell of fried onions wafting around him. "The deputy ministers are not inside. The café's onion burgers seem to be popular."

"I noticed, but I want breakfast, and I don't see those guys out here either. I suggest a table in the far corner over yonder in the sun."

"Excellent choice. Yonder? What does that mean?"

"Over there. The table over there." We strolled over the flagstone path snaking its way through the many tables scattered in a pattern between the restaurant and the main sidewalk, busy with tourists. We sat at the glass-covered, aluminum table farthest from the entrance, near a broad alley leading to Na Kâmpe Street. I dropped the loaded yellow backpack on the glass top.

"Careful, Mr. Žích, or you will buy yourself a table. Here, take the red one, too, and slide them under."

The server handed us our menus and poured us cups of coffee.

"Thank you. This is my first cup today." I pushed the yellow backpack away from my feet. She nodded and walked away. "Why are they late? And you said you had something to tell me."

"Yes. The head minister's business delayed the deputies' plans. One man wanted to reschedule, but Commander Hrubý's contact in the ministry insisted they must both be present today or no deal would happen."

"For the money?" I asked.

"Yes, but let us stay guarded about the coins. They may not realize we have them."

"That gives me a reason to talk even less."

"Yes. As we told you, we think they only understand Czech and English—from you, I need English in a fake German accent."

"I know, I know. Right now, I'm hangry."

"What is hangry?" he asked.

"Hangry is like when you're so hungry, it makes you angry."

"You need to be angry more often, Mr. Žích. You should place fear in your opponents instead of keeping the feeling within yourself."

The server interrupted. "Excuse me, gentlemen," she said with a midwestern American accent. She placed a plate of toast on the table with peach, plum, and grape jam packets. "Compliments of the café. We are serving lunch now, but we have breakfast all day. Also, sir, the two men have arrived matching the descriptions you told me." Žǎk saw them and raised his hand toward the distant figures.

They strolled to our table, talking loudly, and scattering several pigeons and starlings bobbing and darting in front of their paths. Both fit Žǎk's description perfectly. The one I assumed to be Vojacek looked familiar. A man wearing sunglasses had lingered near the castle by the teenage girls, and, without a doubt, this had to be the same man. The other man I did not remember seeing. We stood, and Žǎk offered his hand first. "I am Mr. Žǎk, and this is my colleague, Heinrich Zích."

"I am Mr. Stranksy. This is Mr. Vojacek. Do you not understand Czech? Slovak?"

"We do not. Serbian, German, and English for me. I apologize," Žǎk said.

Vojacek sighed, removed his sunglasses, then replaced them with half-sized reading spectacles. "May we sit, or should we compare our academic credentials also, Mr. Stranksy?"

"Yes, please sit," Žǎk said. "We are in the sunshine, for now, so we should make the best of the time."

"Mr. Zích, are you a student?" Stranksy scooted closer to the table. "You dress like one. And it seems Mr. Žǎk is a fan of black?"

"Are you now a fashion show judge, Mr. Stranksy?" Vojacek held a hand under his jaw to prop his head, making it difficult to understand his jaw-clenched mumbling.

The server appeared from the shadows. "Are you gentlemen ready to order?" Despite the sun and nearby heaters, she had bundled herself in a massive, red-and-black plaid coat with matching mittens.

I ordered first in my phony German-English accent. "Scrambled eggs, bacon, a biscuit with more strawberry preserves, and orange juice." She struggled to write with her mitten-covered hands.

"Mr. Žích, it seems you have a liking of American brunches." Vojacek unclasped his hands and flicked leftover toast crumbs off the table, then pushed his readers higher on his nose. He picked up an empty plate, flipped it over, and frowned at the American flag design in the middle. "Made…in…China." He flipped the plate over again and sat it to his right. "Have you traveled before, Mr. Žích?"

"I have been to America, several trips for school. I've been to Washington—"

Žák raised a hand off the table. "Gentlemen, we have business to complete and other appointments today. Perhaps our server would appreciate finishing our requests." They ordered, and she withdrew back to the restaurant.

"Why did you pick an American restaurant?" Vojacek asked. He pulled his readers off his face and tried to clean them, dropping his napkin. "The Macedonian knew I detest anything American, as did he."

"Oh?" I asked.

Žák spat a jittery cough. "The French restaurant does not open until three o'clock today. Too late for our meeting."

"I see. Unfortunate," Stranksy said. "Our meeting always includes a mid-day treat—a treat of consequence. We work hard for this."

Žăk's face revealed nothing other than his pressed lips. "Do we not have business to complete, or would we rather discuss fashion, food, and French treats?"

"Get on with it," Vojacek said. He grabbed his napkin off the ground, stealing it away from two pecking sparrows. The sun peeked through the bare limbs of a beech tree, the dappled light flickering on their faces.

Our server and her helper returned and placed our plates in front of us. In no mood to talk, I stuffed a third of a biscuit in my mouth, drawing the others' attention. I swallowed hard. "*Ich bin sehr hungrig*," I said in my best German.

"Obviously." Vojacek glared at me, then picked through his scrambled eggs as if looking for a prize.

"*Sprechen sie Deutsch*?" I asked.

"*Nein*. Only a few words…but who cares about you? Mr. Žăk, you have replaced, for now, the old Macedonian as our liaison with the organization. How did he die? We talked to him only two weeks ago."

Žăk frowned. "They didn't give me a diagnosis, Mr. Vojacek. I met the man once, and he did not offer a pleasant conversation. Not a surprise, considering everything. Would you like to proceed?"

Vojacek sipped his coffee and sniffed the air. "A pleasant day, at least. Go ahead, Stranksy, Mr. Žăk doesn't care to engage in niceties."

Stranksy seemed eager to explain. "The Ministry of Foreign Affairs is sputtering along as always, Mr. Žăk," he said after swallowing a piece of toast. He pulled a strand of hair back across his head. "As you may have been told, our program is an outreach for Czech culture across Europe and to other points in the world. It's for the children. The government has been unsuccessful in promoting these...cultural aspects...and we want to highlight our division. We cannot do this with the usual resources provided. Thus, we must be innovative, and part of this innovation is to capture other funds to help us meet our goals. Our program requires the help of foundations supportive of our efforts, but this requires us to go under the ground, as they might say in America, in collecting those resources."

"And that's why we're here, it seems," Žăk said. Given his scowl, I feared Žăk would reach across the table and grab their necks. "We have brought your resources to you today, but with the Macedonian's unexpected death, we need further instructions affecting the amount of resources you are expecting. It remains a mystery to us."

Vojacek mashed his coffee cup into his picked-over food. "I'm aware of many mysteries in life, Mr. Žăk, but this should not be one. The Kurić organization is precise with its instructions. Mr. Žích will give the yellow and red backpacks to Mr. Stranksy—he will check them and then return to our table. Mr. Stranksy? Please proceed."

Stranksy leaned toward me, pulled the packs off the ground before I reacted, and disappeared into the restaurant.

"Where is he going?" I asked.

Vojacek frowned again and then turned his attention back to Žăk. He snapped his glasses off his nose, then leaned so far forward his face hung over the umbrella hole in the table's middle. "Listen to me...both of you. I am not stupid nor a fool. The Macedonian proved himself dependable and kept his mouth shut. He took care of many things for us...always. He understood that errors are not tolerated and are dealt with in a way that becomes very uncomfortable to mistake-prone individuals."

Žăk's face grew crimson, a lighter pink creeping up through his near-shaved scalp. He remained quiet, gathering his words. "Your warnings are unneeded, Mr. Vojacek. We will continue the Macedonian's standards."

Vojacek nodded toward the restaurant and leaned back against the metal mesh of the chair's back. "Ah, Stranksy is returning." Stranksy wore the red backpack and carried the yellow one. "Well?"

"The currency count is as expected, Mr. Vojacek," Stranksy answered. He dropped the bags and sat hard in his chair.

"Are we done?" Žăk asked.

A new line crinkled in Vojacek's forehead. The corners of his mouth drew upward as if to smile, then stopped. "Done? Mr. Žăk, you are an odd one. Your obtuseness seems forced."

"Is there more?" I asked. Vojacek and Stranksy offered smirks to rival Marconi's best.

"Yes, Mr. Žăk, is there more?" Stranksy asked.

Žăk remained unruffled. "Isn't there always more?"

Vojacek smiled at his partner. "Ah, Mr. Stranksy, it seems we are to now have our conversations with Mr. Žăk in the form of riddles." He shifted in his chair, leaned his elbows onto the table, and interlocked his fingers. "Mr. Žăk, you have crossed into a dismal space with me. We received yellow and red backpacks today, as intended. These other inquiries...I am not sure whether you are dishonest or simply incompetent."

Žăk remained stoic, observing Vojacek like a cat does a mouse.

"Gentlemen, are you expecting these?" I pulled a pewter container of coins from my hoodie's front-connecting pocket and placed it on the table.

Stranksy grabbed it, pulled a magnifying square of clear plastic from his pocket, and examined the double-headed eagle carved into the pewter. "The box is real," he told Vojacek.

"Not so hard, Mr. Žăk? Open it, Stranksy."

Stranksy pulled back the lid, exposing the two rows of gold dukats. He snatched two coins, gave one to Vojacek, and kept the other for himself. They brought the coins close to their faces and rubbed them like Aladdin rubbing his lamp. "Extraordinary," Stranksy mumbled.

"They really exist," Vojacek said. He seemed to have lost awareness we sat in a public venue.

Stranksy's face glowed. "I am sure the House of Karađorđević would like to have their treasure back."

Vojacek grinned. "Then let the crown prince raise an army in Belgrade, and he can come get them. Gentlemen. A toast." He raised his water glass, and Stranksy tipped his in return. Žăk lifted his drink off the table but offered nothing else. "What? No celebration, gentlemen? Our market contacts will pay six million Euros for a box of these treasures."

"That is seven million American," Žăk mumbled. "More for your *cultural* items, as you say?"

Stranksy ignored him. "Multiplied by the ten boxes the organization has reportedly gathered here in Prague." This confirmed the number of coins we had found in Apartment D. "Our sources tell us the organization controls another two hundred fifty containers. True, Mr. Žăk?"

Žăk shot a glance toward me, then glanced at the center of the table. Our lunch mates tried to bait us. He stared back at Stranksy. "I am not aware of the number, which would be close to a billion and a half Euros."

Vojacek sneered again. "Quick math. One billion Euros is the organization's cost."

"I would guess," I said, almost forgetting my accent, "the release of counterfeit Euros increases the value of the dollar even more. If you have an American coin buyer—"

"Quite observant, Mr. Žích," Stranksy said, "but wrong. This has nothing to do with American money. We have hoarded enough counterfeit Euros to cause more than a ripple when we release it. Once the Euro devalues, it will take many more of them to buy the organization's dukats. After that, as they destroy the counterfeit notes, the Euro will increase again in value, increasing the organization's investment. We needed years to get to this point."

Vojacek's face grew red. "Thank you, Mr. Stranksy. I did not know you claimed leadership of this project and are willing to share such information with any miscellaneous imbecile listening to you...present company excepted, of course."

"Of course," Žăk answered, his lips barely moving.

Stranksy placed the coins back into their container and thumbed both rows, listening to the gentle clank as they fell back against each other. "Interesting, Mr. Vojacek, as there appears to be a bit of space in each row."

"Please count the coins for us." Stranksy placed the container into his lap and began counting. The motionless bare tree limbs above us no longer blocked the sun after it had disappeared behind the spires of St. Nicholas. The shadows grew chilly while we listened to the clanking coins.

Our server hid in a corner at the bottom of the stairs, talking on her phone. Two black Volvos with darkened windows had pulled into disability parking, both bumping the curb, engines running off to my right, and unseen to our guests. I glanced at my watch—12:10 p.m.—five minutes before our update for Commander Hrubý.

Stranksy placed the coins back in the container, slid the lid closed and stuffed it into the red backpack. "Mr. Vojacek, is it your understanding that each container holds two hundred coins?"

"Yes."

"Unfortunate. This container has one hundred ninety-eight. I counted twice."

"Two missing, it seems?"

"Yes, two."

"So, Mr. Stranksy, two coins have run away from their little pewter home. What say you, Mr. Žák? Did each of you want a souvenir?"

"Ah, you assume right away we took something for ourselves?"

"Why wouldn't I?"

Now Žák leaned over the table. "Gentlemen, this container appeared to have two coins missing when it came into our possession. Perhaps the Macedonian wasn't as trustworthy as you pretend?"

Vojacek squawked. "Preposterous." He crossed his arms and scowled.

"Or someone intercepted the delivery—"

"Stop your idiocy. You stole from the organization and are trying to short us," Stranksy said.

Žăk nodded his head toward me. "Mr. Žích, would you like to mention to our guests who possessed the other two coins?"

I noticed our server snaking along a crooked path toward the black Volvos.

"Have you heard the name Manfred Jurić?" I asked. Both men stiffened in their chairs.

"Yes." Stranksy adjusted his collar. "A Croat…a member of the Protection Force."

"He's dead. A Royal Dukat was found among his possessions," I said.

Vojacek blew a sigh. "Yes…rumors of his death came to us already. But so what? Men of his background never die of old age. Stealing from the organization—"

"And another." I returned his sneer. "Rijad Kastrati? He killed Jurić, and law enforcement killed him. He, too, possessed a dukat."

"That name is also familiar—the hooded one," Vojacek said. Stranksy had grown mute, his eyebrows raised into his forehead.

Žăk followed my lead. "The organization believes it will have to deal negatively with anyone circumventing its plans for these coins. You mentioned it would not be pleasant? We hope it is not something you or your colleagues—"

"Outrageous." Vojacek snatched the vibrating phone from his jacket pocket. He glanced at the screen, hesitated, then answered. "Yes. Yes. I see. We will do so."

"What?" Stranksy asked.

"Our time is up. Gentlemen, you will excuse us. We must return to our offices." He stood, turned his back, and hurried away toward the street without another word, bumping into the server as she approached.

Stranksy nodded and scurried away.

The server smiled. "Who's paying the tab, Mr. Žăk?"

"Commander Hrubý." He reached behind his back and pulled out a wire. "You heard everything?"

"Yes, leave your car and take the Volvo. They are waiting."

"Wait a minute. You know the waitress?" I asked.

"She works for us, Mr. Žích. This is Lydia."

"Hi, Mr. Žích. I'm from St. Louis."

"The phone call, Lydia?" Žăk asked.

"Another leak. Someone in Foreign Affairs got word of the arrests in Justice and Interior. Lieutenant Talích was successful as planned. Mr. Žicăn's efforts also resulted in arrests, but …"

"But what?" I asked.

Žăk frowned, pulled on his beret, and closed his eyes.

Lydia's eyes grew watery. "Someone shot him, Mr. Žăk. Lower abdomen. That's all they've told me."

"I see. Thank you, Lydia. Arrange for the tab, and we will reimburse you later." Žăk froze and then took a deep breath. "Mr. Žích, we now pursue our lunch friends who are transporting counterfeit money and stolen gold coins. You and I will end this."

Chapter Twenty-Three

We sprinted to our ride. The passenger side window opened on the closest car, and Angela Marconi thrust her head through the opening. "How was lunch?"

Another voice from the back called out, "Hey, Ike. Guess who?" Commander Hrubý sat behind the wheel, talking into his headset.

"Angie? Eddie? What are you doing here?" I asked.

Žăk trotted to the other car and took over the driver's seat from Kharkov, who slid over to the passenger side.

"Commander Hrubý let us come with him...after I insisted. Eddie has several pillows back there," Marconi said.

"No time for talk," Hrubý said. "Mr. Žích, please take your place in the other car, and do it quickly. Those men are escaping while we exchange greetings. Mr. Žăk's car will take the lead, and I will follow as a backup." He pointed to the other car and called out, "Ready, Mr. Žăk?"

"Yes," he said.

I threw myself into the back seat of the other car and searched for the seatbelt.

"Mr. Kharkov, I will rely on you to guide me through the streets. Are we tracking?" Žăk asked.

"A clear signal." Kharkov buckled his seatbelt, then twisted toward me. "Hang on."

359

Žăk stomped the accelerator. My head bounced against the rear headrest, then knocked against the window. We swung in a semi-circle onto the street, slinking between and around vehicles on either side of the road.

"They have crossed the Charles Bridge and are running south on Smetanovo waterfront."

We bottomed out when crossing the metal joint attaching the bridge to the road, then a hard right onto Smetanovo. I glanced back and noticed Hrubý's Volvo in the distance. "Mr. Kharkov," Žăk shouted. "Give me constant feedback."

"Yes, sir. They are going south. We are gaining. Wait. Right turn. Across Legions Bridge and Shooters Island."

"Shooters Island?" I asked. "How nice." We swung hard right again and clipped the sign showing the bridge's name. "Oops."

"Quiet, Mr. Žích. Kharkov?"

"Back south on Janáčkova waterfront."

"Do they know we are following?" I asked. "What are they driving?"

"A light blue Škoda Superb," Kharkov answered. "We saw them leave in it."

Žăk slapped the dash. "Mr. Kharkov."

"Sorry. We are a half a block behind, left onto Jirásek Bridge…slowing now. They've stopped on Ressalova. No…they are moving again. Three hundred meters. Speeding up."

"I assume they will turn onto Zitná," Žăk said.

"Correct. Left on Spálená, now right on Zitná."

"Good guess?" I asked.

"A satellite office of the Foreign Ministry sits near

Žižkov. I would speculate it is their destination," Žăk said.

"Žižkov Television Tower? I've seen it in the distance," I said. "Isn't it like seven hundred feet tall?"

"Yes," Kharkov answered. "It's one of the tallest towers in the world…and one of the ugliest."

"Thank you," I said as if it mattered. Flashing lights reflected off the inside of my glasses.

"Mr. Žăk? Orders?" Kharkov asked.

"Please message Commander Hrubý to take the service entrance to the tower and come in behind the Foreign Affairs building. I want our PIMPs sandwiched. Is that a correct term, Mr. Žích?"

"PIMP sandwiches," I said. "Perfect."

The two-story, gray-brick office building sat a hundred yards from the tower's base, trees lining a dirt and gravel path between the two. Dust still settled around the light blue Škoda, straddling two spots near the front entrance between four other cars of the same color and make, all with Czech government plates. Hrubý ran to the far-right corner and waved to us as we drove into the grass. "I believe we are to guard the rear entrance," Žăk said. "Mr. Kharkov, please take a position in the trees along the path."

"Yes, sir."

We skidded to a stop on the gravel. "Mr. Žích, follow me."

We dashed to the bushes lining each side of the rear exit, ducking under windows running the length of this side of the building. It faced toward the park surrounding the tower's base.

"Now what?" I asked.

"Since we no longer have our communications, I

cannot know except for what I am trained. I believe Commander Hrubý will try to 'smoke them out' as you say. Pull your gun and be ready." Several minutes passed while we squatted in the bushes.

"Do you think they're in there?" I whispered. "The car is here but—" The air crackled with the sound of a voice over a bullhorn. "What did he say?"

"He told them to come out. What else?" A noise erupted like someone beating a sheet of tin. Screams came from inside the building. "Now, Mr. Žích." He scrambled out of the bushes, up the three steps to the building's steel doors, and peered through the rectangular window. "Nothing in this hallway. Let me try," he said.

He pulled his knife from its sheath, then used the four-inch blade to pry through to the slot clamping the doors together. A window exploded to our left, followed by an office chair landing on the dead grass. A head poked through the broken glass, withdrew, followed by a hand with a gun shooting blindly toward us.

"Go," Žăk signaled, jumping from the steps, then dashing around the corner.

I jumped off the steps as the doors opened, Hrubý holding one while returning fire with his other hand.

"Well? I am covering for you, Mr. Žích. Come in now."

I crawled up the steps, keeping my head down, and sat on the tan carpet covering the hall floor.

"Where is Mr. Žăk?" Hrubý asked.

"He went around front." Several more shots echoed outside the door.

"Looking for me?" Žăk slammed himself against

the wall of the corridor.

"A speedy trip."

"Odd coincidence, Mr. Žích. Bullets make me run faster. Commander?"

"Stranksy is our shooter. We've had no contact with Vojacek. Three other occupants in the building escaped when I entered."

"What do they think they're doing?" I asked. "Shooting at police? Their stupidity—"

"Is unlimited," Hrubý said. He scratched his chin with the barrel of his gun.

"Where is everyone?" Marconi appeared, strolling around the corner. "Oh."

Hrubý frowned at first but broke into a smile. "Director, I asked you to stay in the car. You are unarmed."

"If I could interrupt your meeting, the one fellow has slipped away."

"What?" I asked.

"He carried the yellow bag and headed up the dirt trail. I heard a door slam down below—it sounded like steel. Is there a basement?" Marconi asked.

"*Hovno.*"

She looked to Žǎk. "What did he say?"

"He said…shit."

"Never mind. Mr. Žǎk, you and Mr. Žích take the path and track down Stranksy. Kharkov should help. Director Marconi and I will search the building again for Vojacek." Another gunshot echoed near the trees lining the path. "Go now."

A meandering path connected the office building and the tower through the woods. Žǎk halted, and I ran into his back. "What?"

"A noise." He held a finger to his lips.

"I can't see anything."

"Neither can I, but I heard it. Look." A hand appeared from the brush, followed by the arm and Kharkov's upper half, pulling himself back onto the path. Žăk helped him lean against a tree trunk.

"Deputy Minister Stranksy ran with the backpack. I ordered him to stop. He fired back blindly, and it grazed my knee."

"Do your best and return to the office building. They are searching for Vojacek. Give Mr. Žích your tracking device, and we will follow Stranksy."

Another gunshot.

"Go now, Mr. Kharkov. They may need you."

He limped away.

"Mr. Žích, give me updates on the tracker as often as possible."

Kharkov had locked the settings—a blue dot flashed on the screen.

"This tracker is a nice invention of his," I said.

"Yes, Vitaly is our most creative. Where is Stranksy?"

"Inside the tower. Why would he go there?"

"I cannot say, but he has escaped into his own trap." We jogged around dormant gardens and stood at the tower's base. Tourists milled about, most gazing upward to the top of the seven-hundred-foot edifice. Three matching white steel tubes thrust into the sky supporting the tower. Several unusual, brown fiberglass figures of crawling babies were attached to the infrastructure—ugly but serving as art, I supposed.

"Mr. Žăk, we have two choices of access. Which elevator would you suggest?"

"You have the tracker, Mr. Žích. You tell me."

"Does 'up' help? What good does the tracker do when he's hovering over us?"

He frowned and took a deep breath. "So, my American friend, I believe it is time for you to make this decision. You have been a follower during today's mission. It is time for you to lead."

"Fine. If I had access, I would take the service elevator. But to where? The observation deck? How high is that?"

"A hundred twenty meters."

"Then what? He's trapped here with gold coins, fake money, and a gun. The observation deck may be full of people—"

"And what can he do in a crowd of people, Mr. Žích?"

I hesitated, then shouted, "Hostages." I drew a stare from a woman who pushed her children away from us.

"Must you? The service lift will take you to the deck, but first, stop at the restaurant. If you do not see Stranksy, proceed to the observation area."

"And you?"

"Meet me here."

"What?"

"I cannot do heights, Mr. Žích. You are on your own. I will make sure he does not escape down here."

"And the security guards? I look like a student. Should I go busting up there dressed in a hoodie and waving a gun around?"

"I will take care of the guards. Now go, Mr. Žích. You will bring this man to justice and help us cripple another piece of the Kurić organization."

My face flushed hot—I turned away. A security

guard nodded at me, I slipped into the service elevator, and he pushed the button for the first stop at the restaurant. Žăk had a point—time for me to lead. Four months since Eddie took me to Ivy Hill Cemetery to see those graves, and now I rode to this place in the sky, in a city in the middle of Europe facing a desperate man.

A ding—the elevator bounced to a stop, and the doors opened.

A voice shouted at me. "*Haló, pane? Haló.*" Another security guard stared at me while I stood with my mouth open, eyeing him over my dirty glasses.

"What? Sorry. Is this the restaurant? Do you speak English?" I stepped out and to my left saw a glass door with an etching of the tower and the word *Vidĕt*. Whiffs of garlic floated through the foyer.

"They call you Mr. Žích?" he asked.

"Yes."

"You a-ok, Mr. Žích? You are white, like a cloud. Should I bring the medical team?"

"What? No, no. I'm getting my bearings," I answered.

"Berries? You are hungry?"

"No. Is this the restaurant?"

"Yes, *Vidĕt*. I can save you time, though. I have appraised the guests, and no one matches Mr. Žăk's depiction."

"Depiction?"

"No one has face."

"You mean description?"

"Yes, yes, that is it. Come back to the lift. Three of my people escaped from observing deck. The man with a yellow backpack remains. He is alone."

"He's by himself? No hostages…thank goodness.

Thank you, Officer…?"

"Brezni. My name is Henrí Brezni."

"Thank you, Henrí."

I stepped back, he pushed the orange button, and to the top I went. Kharkov's tracker showed no movement from Stranksy.

The elevator lurched, and the door opened to three guards waiting for me. An older guard nodded, his potbelly partly hidden under a heavy flak jacket. "Mr. Žích, this man shot twice at the exit door. He has 9mm CZ75, semi-automatic with a sixteen-round magazine. He has fired three shots."

"And several before he got here. Okay, good to know." I pulled my pistol.

"No, take this." The rotund guard smiled, handed me his rifle, and took my gun. "CZ Scorpion. Fifty rounds."

"Awesome. Which way to the top?" I followed the three men to the opposite end of the darkened hall, smelling fresh paint but with shades of graffiti still showing through. The stairs snaked around twice up to the exit door, its tiny window watching us like a cyclops eyeing its prey. I eased to the window and peeked through.

"We cannot see him. Maybe on other side?" the guard mentioned.

After pushing my way in front of them, I said, "I'll crack the door and see if I can get his attention."

"I do not think door will crack, sir."

"No, no…stay back," I said while turning the knob. Two inches, then three. A sudden squeal of metal grinding on the hinges. "I don't have to worry about surprising him now, do I?"

"Sir?"

I crept forward two steps onto the deck. "Stranksy? This is Zích. Give yourself up. You have no place to go."

Stranksy screamed over the howling wind. "Zích? You are law enforcement? This is entrapment. Foreign Affairs will not be happy—"

"With a deputy minister hauling counterfeit Euros and stolen gold coins, and shooting at law enforcement? Come on, Stranksy. Time's up. Surrender before you get hurt."

Silence.

"Stranksy, help us. We need information on the organization. You can help end this."

I crept forward, gusts of wind whipping so hard I struggled to hold my rifle straight. Stranksy appeared to my left, having climbed near the top of the eight-foot-tall, chrome balustrade surrounding the deck.

His voice sounded childlike. "It's empty." He pitched his pistol over the side of the tower. "My wife…my children—I cannot surrender. My grandfather fought the Nazis…my father acted underground against the Russians. I am nothing but a traitor. Do you not understand? They will kill my family if I'm captured."

I eased closer and lowered the rifle. "I'm sure the authorities can keep your family safe."

Saliva oozed from both sides of his mouth. "How naïve. The authorities are the devil, too. Do you not understand?"

"No."

"Many of the authorities are also the organization. They are the same. I had no way out."

"We all have to make choices—"

"No, Mr. Žích…only the powerful have choices—I have none. When I joined the Foreign Ministry, I joined the organization. I am part of both."

"Okay, okay. Just come down and talk to us. I know people here—"

"You don't know the right people." He grabbed at his back, zipped open the backpack, and shook it. Fake Euros blew up and back, floating around the deck and over the side. He climbed higher, wobbling with the wind gusts, then leaned back and stared at me with lifeless eyes.

"Stranksy …"

He released his grip. I ran to the rail and looked down. A strap of the backpack had hung on a cement strut. The other shoulder strap closed tight around Stranksy's crooked neck. Another burst of wind broke him free. His body slammed twice against the tower's superstructure, causing a head-to-toe spin while his body hurtled to the ground.

The steel door behind me creaked again. "Mr. Žích?"

"He jumped…afraid not to."

****

Žăk and I said nothing while retracing our steps near the barren gardens. Marconi emerged through the woods as the black Volvo slid to a stop, rearranging the stones lining the end of the path. Hrubý got out, slammed his door, and opened the back.

Eddie's head appeared. "Hey, Ike. He didn't bounce, did he?"

Kharkov scrambled from the passenger seat, then leaned against the car's hood.

369

Waiting for a coroner, we stood over the broken body, partially buried in the soft earth. Three of the tower guards blocked nosy tourists—another picked up dukats strewn about the dead grass. Counterfeit bills floated and fluttered around us in the light breeze.

A dark-blue Renault approached, its flashing blue lights extinguished as soon as the engine stopped. Lieutenant Talích bounded from the vehicle, removed his beret, and wiped his brow. "Sir, Mr. Žicăn's wound is severe, and he remains in surgery."

Hrubý's expression didn't change. "I see. Thank you for your successful efforts today, Lieutenant. Report please, Mr. Žăk."

Žăk wiped his brow and a wet cheek. "Commander, we heard a gunshot from your location."

"Vojacek. We cornered him in the basement. He killed himself, and his body fell back into a heap of yellow backpacks piled to the ceiling. They've stashed hundreds of millions of phony Euros down there."

"Stanich, I bet, and they've hoarded it," Marconi said.

"How did they hide it without others knowing?" I asked. "Are more people part of this?"

Žăk stared at the ground, half paying attention. "Likely."

Hrubý removed his cap and stroked the back of his head. "Today is done."

One of the tower's security guards shouted, held up something, and jogged toward Hrubý.

"Sir?"

"What do you need?"

"Look. This dukat. It is not gold."

"Excuse me?" Hrubý snatched the coin and handed

it to Žăk, who brought it close to his eye and then flipped it over to Talích.

"He is correct. A fake," Talích mumbled, scratching at the coin's surface. The guard handed him shattered pieces of cedar. "And this splintered container is definitely not pewter."

Žăk glared. "Someone switched them. Mr. Žích, the container of coins—I never saw it exchanged from one bag to another. Did you?"

"No, but remember, Stranksy shoved the coin container into the red backpack with the real Euros, not the yellow bag."

"I noticed two cars drive away from the ministry's office when we arrived," Žăk said. "I assumed other employees were escaping the gunfire."

Hrubý's head bowed while he listened. He leaned back against his car and crossed his arms. "Everyone in this branch of the ministry could be connected to Kurić. Can you track the red bag?"

Kharkov's face melted into a frown. "We had only one tracker…in the yellow bag."

Hrubý pitched his cap onto the hood of his car. He rubbed his eyes, then whispered. "Karanos Tasev is finally dead." He looked up, then offered his hand. "Thank you, Detective Pierce. You took significant risks today." Glancing around at our group, he said, "It seems they have tricked us, and we have lost valuable coins worth millions of Euros along with the real Euro banknotes in the red pack. Is that correct?"

"Yes. These are slugs painted gold," Talích said, drawing a massive sigh from Hrubý.

"Someone, somewhere, has more coins, many more," Hrubý said. "We will find them all."

"It seems you have your own MacGuffin to chase," I said.

Hrubý shot me a sideways glance. "The dukats will lead us to Kurić…eventually. She is our 'MacGuffin,' as you say, not the coins."

Marconi ran a hand through her hair. "Commander, I don't want to change the subject, but I need to ask. The woman's picture found in Manfred Jurić's possessions…did your search find a name?"

"Nothing."

"I would like a copy before we leave," Marconi said.

"Agreed."

"You've got a start, Commander. Can you fix the rest?" I asked. "In Prague, at least?"

Hrubý shrugged. "Unknown. The powerful will continue to protect themselves. That is what they do best." He stared up and past the tower, watching an airplane move into the clouds. "What is the old saying…hope can deceive more men than cunning?"

"Hope isn't a plan," I said.

"So, what would you have me fix…greed, lust for power…human traits that are thousands of years old? We can only change ourselves, Henry Pierce, not humanity."

Chapter Twenty-Four

Warm, sunny weather greeted us our first day back to work. With luck, my family would visit later in the month to see the cherry blossoms lining the mall. I drove onto the pitch black, newly resurfaced parking lot, aiming for my usual spot near the end of the last row. David Wulz stood at the entrance, waving me down.

"Hey, Pierce. Welcome back," he called out as I rolled down my window.

"Thanks, coroner. What's going on?"

"Over there." He pointed to the first row of spots in the parking lot near the building's entrance. Marconi stood next to a young woman, both looking as if waiting for a bus. "Angie has something to show you. Drive over there."

I let my Toyota idle and glide to where Marconi stood with her arms crossed. "Hey, Detective Sergeant, about time you got here. How do you like this sweet spot?" She pointed at the cement curbs set in front of each parking spot. Three had a layer of fresh, dark-blue paint with white lettering. She had parked her car in the first one, and the name Stone had been stenciled on the next. The last one said HIP.

"HIP? Is that my spot?"

"Seems so. Someone got cute and decided they liked your initials," Marconi said.

Wulz sauntered up, snickering the entire way. "You? Hip? That's the funniest thing ever."

"I'll take it. We're much closer to our wing of the building."

"Hey, Ike, remember me?"

It was the woman I had sent the photograph for analysis. "Linda? Linda Alvarez?"

"Yep, it's me. I like your short hair."

"Yeah? It's my…European cut. How did you get here?"

"I drove from my apartment. Monday was my first day with the City of Alexandria."

"You work here?" My mouth froze in a smile.

"I told you sometime back that Linda would be an impressive addition to our department," Marconi said. "She's our new imaging expert in the forensics lab. So, I guess you're sticking with us?" She hugged me, and my face flushed.

"Here comes Eddie." Wulz pointed the Ford toward us. "He doesn't know about this either."

I stepped aside. The old Ford lumbered in, parked, and the driver's window came halfway down before sticking—a Commodores song, "Lady," blared from the speakers. Marconi and I bent forward to see a woman sitting in the driver's seat and Eddie in the passenger seat. A familiar face, but I couldn't remember her name. "Hi, ma'am. Eddie? We have new parking spots."

"Good deal," he said.

The woman slid the window back up, got out, then shoved trash into the overflowing bin sitting next to the building's front door.

Eddie struggled with his arm in the sling but soon

freed himself from his seatbelt. "You all know Doris Chen, don't you?" He propped himself against the car's trunk.

Marconi offered her hand. "Doris, good to see you. Are you driving Eddie around while his arm is in a sling?" Chen worked in the lab—the woman Eddie had claimed for months wasn't his girlfriend.

I interrupted. "Ma'am, I'm Henry Pierce. We've met in the hallway several times."

"Sure, Henry," Chen said. "Everyone knows you. Most of the girls in the lab talk about you."

Linda giggled, and another blush scorched my cheeks.

"I saw the curb on your parking spot when I threw away the trash. HIP, huh?"

"I guess so. Doris, this is Linda Alvarez. She's new."

Linda gave me a slight eye roll. "I work for Doris, Ike. We already know each other."

"Oh…right."

Marconi asked again, "Hey, Doris, you're driving Eddie today?"

"Yes, we'll come together from now on whether he's riding or driving." She grinned and offered her left hand to Marconi.

"A ring? Eddie Stone. You said you didn't have a girlfriend."

"I don't. I have a fiancée."

Marconi smirked and hugged him. "I knew something was up, buddy."

"Angie, after our adventures and my getting shot, almost blown up, and everything else, I thought it time. Life is too short, as everyone always told me.

Commander Hrubý would agree." He winked.

"Don't start."

Wulz offered his hand. "Congratulations, Eddie, and you too, Doris."

"Thank you, David. That's truly kind," she said.

"When is the big day?" I asked.

"First of June. Maui. Be there," Eddie said.

"Maui? I've never been," Marconi said.

"Me either," I said. "But why Maui?"

Eddie radiated a brilliant smile. "You'll see." He grabbed Chen's hand, and they strolled away.

Slipping away from the crowd, I stopped at our building's entrance, then turned back to my chattering colleagues. A few days in Hawaii—what could be better?

A word about the author…

Mark Edward Jones is retired from the world of higher education finance after thirty-three years.

Peculiar Activities is his first novel published with The Wild Rose Press. A portion of this manuscript won first place in the Mystery and Suspense category of the 2019 Oklahoma Writers Federation annual contest. The manuscript was selected as a finalist in the 2020 Page Turner Awards contest.

Mark's flash fiction piece called 'Alone in Warsaw' was published in the Autumn edition of the U.K. Publication, Printed Words.

Mark has served as an editor and consultant for two other publications: The First Hundred Years by Carolyn B. Leonard, and Real Musings by Dr. Ed Cunliff.

Mark has three grown children, all married. He and his wife, Jackie, will celebrate their fortieth anniversary in November 2021.

http://mejbooksllc.com

Thank you for purchasing
this publication of The Wild Rose Press, Inc.

For questions or more information
contact us at
info@thewildrosepress.com.

The Wild Rose Press, Inc.
www.thewildrosepress.com